MAN BEING

Volume III: *Conversations from Beyond*

MAN BEING

Volume III: *Conversations from Beyond*

Communicated to

Dramos & Bohemias

Front cover design by Tami Boyce

ISBN 978-1-9991777-4-4

Dramos and Bohemias are legally obligated to declare that the interviews published in *Man Being Volume 3: Conversations from Beyond* are "hearsay". The conversations contained herein should be considered fictional.

The Rose is not simply a flower. It is a shape and a sound that opens a portal to the Inner Earth experience. This passageway is your homeward journey. As you all continue to shift your beliefs and reconnect, you are bringing "historical figures" into the dialogue. There are many Beings who wish to speak with you all, and some will be making themselves known in this dialogue.

TABLE OF CONTENTS

FOREWORD
by Orson Welles

The book…you ask me about the book and I propose that we intend a discussion that reveals the truth. "The truth?", you say. "What am I going to do with the truth?" The matter, of course, involves not only obscuring the reality that you're clinging to but also becoming aware that your old beliefs no longer have meaning or context.

What am I saying? What am I suggesting? Well, that we begin with a foreword and approve the decision to go beyond your limited scope of existence and awareness. The Earth plane is not what it seems. You have a reality that is not really existing. What if I told you that you don't exist…and what if I told you that existence is the other way around? What you are calling death and the "disconnect experience" is actually the awakening and the reconnection.

You have learned that your planet has a Crystal Core, which acts as a causeway. This "Inner Earth" functions much differently than what you are being led to believe by others. Believe me when I say that there is an inner existence that some of you are connecting with and certainly all of you are remembering, by the moment that you finish Volume 3. The Earth does not exist between your hands or beneath your feet. The Inner Earth exists where you least expect the existence. What about your Earth? Well…*your* "Earth" does not actually exist.

It is a dream. It is a memory. You are living in a memory, no different from your photographs and recordings. You live in a memory. Go beyond the memory and reconnect with the Beings who have found home. Your home is not where you believe.

INTRODUCTION

Volume 3 of this book series is an extraordinary shift in belief. You, the Reader, are no longer a passive participant. You have made your reconnections and absorbed the information presented in the earlier Volumes. Many of you are having dreams or visions or experiencing a profound shift in consciousness. You have "accepted the Rose" and now you will all discover the meaning of this phrase.

With the exception of the first and last chapters, which are communicated by Lyra Beings, Volume 3 is a collection of conversations between Dramos, Bohemias and "deceased" historical figures – most of which are Artists. Though these encounters officially began on November 11 2019, well known Artists were appearing in our dreams beforehand. They were relaying profound and new knowledge about the "Afterlife" and requesting to participate in the "Man Being" book dissemination.

The tone and speaking style of these historical figures is more human and a departure from our previous dialogues with Lyra. It was explained to Dramos and Bohemias that in order for readers to recognize their former likeness as Humans, they would need to present themselves using "Earth" or 3rd density language. The conversations you are about to read were delivered with all the inflections and personality traits that were associated with these individuals when they were "alive" on Earth.

The historical figures included in this Volume have all approached Dramos and Bohemias and asked to be a part of this project. They were not directly summoned, although an open invitation or what we called an "Open Mic" was extended. What you are about to read are the "Afterlife" accounts of famous figures, meant solely to equip you with the tools to return homeward.

THE
ROSE

"Inner Earth requires the knowledge of The Rose. It is the only way for you to reassemble yourselves in the homeward journey. You are being asked to return homeward. This is the critical step. Reassemble The Rose. You are the 13th petal of the flower."

Our Volume 2 discussion concluded with you asking readers to "accept The Rose". What is The Rose, if not simply a flower?

> The Rose is a tool to absorb frequencies. These frequencies will further prepare you for entry through a gateway. The entry point requires a key. The key is in fact a shape and its corresponding sound. The Rose is a shape and sound that opens a door.

How does one open the door with a Rose?

> How does one enter a gateway, is what you are asking. Passing through a gateway is not a physical experience. We are speaking about consciousness. You create a shape and therefore a sound that unlocks the entry and allows you to pass through.

Readers might have a hard time understanding that a flower is a key.

> The "flower" that you call a Rose, is simply a physical representation of a shape and a sound. All of your existence in the 3rd density is a physical representation of the light experience.

If we accept that form is just the containment of light and sound, we will be able to perceive The Rose as a shape and a sound rather than a physical plant.

> This is precisely what your readers need to accept. Awareness that there is more to your physical existence is what you are exploring in Volume 3. Earth plane reality is the imprisonment of light or what we call 3D (3rd density). The "Afterlife" is 5D, the launching pad for your ability to time travel. The 5D experience is the place and space where you reassemble in a Light Body and learn to create with light.

To confirm, when we "die" we cross over into the 5D reality. Is that what you're saying?

> Yes. Please accept that you are learning how to change your 3D form. You are also creating a shape or Light Body that will allow you to reach into many densities of light experience. You will also learn from the many Beings in Volume 3 that you exist in a multi-dimensional state of being.

How do we exist in a multi-dimensional state of Being?

> There are many versions of you. You are not just one Dramos or one Bohemias. You are not just one Jane or one John. There are many versions of you "running around". You simply haven't caught up with this knowledge. In order to coordinate the consciousness of all the different states of you, you must be able to absorb or listen in a new way. The Rose is the tool that will help you achieve this.

Are "twin flames" and "soul mates" just versions or layers of us? Are we encountering our other selves in another form and is that why we experience a "cosmic connection" with these individuals?

> Yes. You are not just one Being in one physical body. You have split your energy into many facets and dimensions. Envision yourself existing as a kaleidoscopic image. You will learn more about this through your conversations with "historical figures" in Volume 3.

If there are many versions of Jane, does that mean that if one Jane shifts her beliefs then every other Jane receives that signal?

> Precisely. You are all interconnected. The signals or frequencies are being "sent out" through consciousness and intracellular exchange. The transmission that you received in Volume 1 was received in more than one

3

level or layer of experience. You are now learning how to absorb the messages that your readers may have missed in their initial connection with the material. We are encouraging your readers to please review Volumes 1 and 2.

Is there something we need to do with The Rose to activate it?

The Rose may be experienced as a 13-armed star or a 13-petaled flower. The number 13 is a critical point of entry where you will make a reconnection with a frequency. This frequency has until this point been cut off for you all.

The number 13 contains activation codes – is that correct?

Yes. The number 13 contains a message and a set of instructions. The instructions enable you to reconnect with the sacred knowledge of time travel.

Do you recommend an exercise for our readers to help them absorb the 13-petaled Rose?

Your readers are advised to imagine that they are physically holding The Rose and this will allow them to achieve a deeper connection with the material. This does not necessarily mean holding it with one's hands. You can also hold it in your mind's eye or envision holding The Rose somewhere on the body, particularly the chest or the solar plexus area. This does not require any magnificent imagination or ability to visualize. The simple task of envisioning the The Rose in front of you is acceptable. A belief in The Rose will establish a reconnective dialogue with other Beings when your readers use this symbol. This symbol is a connection or a gateway to communication with other Beings who are beyond your experience.

What other Beings are you referring to?

> We are speaking of any Being who has gone beyond your 3rd density existence. In this Volume you will be contacting historical figures that have "died" and crossed over, for example. Your readers will be experiencing this as well, mostly in their dream state. They must pay attention to the Beings in their dreams.

Is our goal to reach the Inner Earth experience? What density of light is Inner Earth?

> The "goal" is to truly create an "Afterlife" experience as opposed to one that leads to a reincarnation cycle. You must all reconnect with creativity and imagination, but not simply to play and be imaginative. We are asking you to open up the gateway to the 7th density experience and to access the Inner Earth.

The Inner Earth is at the core of our planet. Is there a way to access it physically while existing in this form?

> Yes, but the ability to enter the 7th density or the Inner Earth experience is not achievable if you are not able to endure the frequency changes.

Readers will now want directions to the Inner Earth entry.

> There is no point in giving you all a "map" to the entry if you are not able to continue your role in the Repair Project. You must release all of the knowledge and information for time travel. The Inner Earth experience is equivalent to breathing underwater. If you do not have the apparatus you will not be able to endure the experience.

We must have the knowledge first.

The knowledge is your right. The sacred knowledge of The Rose and the sacred knowledge of time travel is available for you all. This is of course aligned with alchemy. We have not exposed you to Alchemy, as this level of esoterica is not necessary for your Volumes.

Where else has the knowledge of The Rose been mentioned?

Refer to your Bible book of Genesis. When Sara gives birth to Isaac, this is alluding to The Rose.

Are you saying that Isaac represents The Rose?

Yes. Isaac represents The Rose, unfolding.

The 12 Tribes of Israel are descended from the sons and grandsons of Jacob, Isaac's son. Please explain how this relates to The Rose.

The number 12, as in the 12 Tribes mentioned in the Bible passages are representing the state that Man Being is in. You are all waiting and wandering. You are waiting to reconnect and reconstruct the gateway.

The 12 Tribes descended from Jacob represent 12 petals of the Rose. Why aren't there 13 Tribes if the Rose is supposed to have 13 petals?

The story that is being told in this particular example is that your "Tribes" are all imprisoned in the Earth plane. The 12 Tribes are short of one idea or belief stream. You are engaging in the 13th and final arm of the belief stream. Isaac is the unfolding of The Rose and you are the 13th petal and the 13th Tribe. You are armed with the knowledge and the consciousness to return homeward.

Are Jesus' 12 disciples another representation of the unfolding of the Rose?

> Yes. It is representing the same thing in a new light. The Bible journey is an attempt to explain how to fix the problem of being stuck in the Earth plane. It is a specific request for you to reconnect with the knowledge that is allowing you to re-enter the 7th density or Inner Earth.

This is a wonderful revelation.

> You are now within reach to reassemble and reconnect with the sacred knowledge. You are able to once again leave of your own volition and ability.

What more can we know about the 12 Tribes and Jesus' disciples? These are big topics.

> The unfoldment of the truth is the reason why you are presenting this allegory in Volume 3. You are unfolding the truth. You are not instructing in the truth. You are simply revealing. Your books are the reveal, the unfolding, the unrolling of the scroll or the blossoming of the flower...in this case The Rose. You are presenting the reveal.

Isn't part of the reveal to provide more information, especially on topics such as these?

> You are not instructing on how to interpret or work with the understanding. The reconnections are there for your readers to make. They are able to decide on their own account if they wish to proceed. You are presenting and revealing the truth. Your readers must decide if they wish to continue the journey. Your job and effort is not to mandate that anyone continue beyond their own level of belief. You are presenting

ideas and you are revealing concepts. The understanding that a Reader may or may not be ready to engage is not anything that you have control over. You are being asked to show a mirror and to mirror that which you have both revealed.

The Reader can no longer be a passive participant. They need to feel their way through the information and decide what they believe. Is this also what you meant when you said, "Accept The Rose"?

Yes. Inner Earth requires the knowledge of The Rose. It is the only way for you to reassemble yourselves in the homeward journey. You are being asked to return homeward. This is the critical step. Reassemble The Rose. You are the 13th petal of the flower.

JOHN
GILMORE

> "Why do the good die young? Maybe we're dismissing those who we see as 'too good to be here'. Maybe we're sending them on their way. Maybe we're more involved in others than we realize."

Avant-Garde Saxophonist
1931 - 1995

Dramos and Bohemias are communicating with Lyra and asking about The Rose and The Cross symbol. Someone interrupts them. Whoever it is sounds like they're either smoking weed or they have a serious respiratory problem.

What's going on? Who's communicating with us?

> Jazz…man. These symbols create a sound.

Are you saying that you're a Jazz musician?

> That's right, it's John.

John, why are you communicating with us and what is your last name?

> Dramos is listening to the sounds, man. My name was John Gilmore. Dramos was listening to Sun Ra this morning…over and over again. The song about no Sun.

Do you mean, "When there is No Sun"?

> That's the one.

John Gilmore…it says here that you were a saxophone player and played in the Sun Ra band. You died in 1995.

> Yes, man.

Is there something you want to tell us?

> There's a sound, man. The shapes make a sound. You have to connect the shapes with the sounds, like music…like a musically composed piece. You have to connect the sounds.

Is this something you want to elaborate on?

You've tapped into something that's greater than you know and you realize that music and Musicians are keeping it together. You understand that bit, I know, but what you need to realize is how we construct these things. When you're writing music and feeling music and composing the music you're organizing shapes. You're organizing the connections. This isn't random. You all believe that Jazz is random. It's not random...you understand. There's an organization and a pattern. You're relaying this pattern. You're tapping into the pattern. You're composing a song, man. This book you're piecing together is like a song. This Rose and the Cross, they organize a sound. These two things fit together like a sound and like a chord. This is music and poetry. It's not just a painting.

We've been communicating with Lyra about art and specifically music in the last Volume. There's quite a bit to absorb.

Everybody understands art or so they think, but they don't understand that music is the foundation and the thing that's holding it all together. You've realized lately that this is the way things are but painting and all the other art...you have to appreciate this all works together. This is all tied in together. You two are writing about artistry and speaking about the arts and Artists. It all works together. This is a collective. This is not a separate team. This is all one ensemble. We're all in a band together and even your book, what you're writing, man...it's part of the presentation. You're getting these messages about symbols and these symbols have been around for ages.

You mean symbols like The Rose?

Of course, man. Nobody's paying attention to how they work and how they work together. It's all about the notes. A song isn't one note and a symbol isn't one meaning. There are many symbols and many sounds and there's a pattern and there's a pattern in the universe and you're hearing it now and we're hearing it too and we hear it and we play it and we live it. You two are also helping move this along. You're writing a song guys…you have to believe it.

Artists can easily relate to what you're saying John, but how does the non-creative tune in?

You're all part of the band. You're all part of the ensemble of the experience. You don't have to play an instrument to be in the band. If you're receiving the information and receiving the vibes you're part of the band. When everybody thinks and feels that they're part of the band then things will shift. You're all part of the group. It's one big group, man. It's one big band. Everybody has to step up…but not audition. That's not what I'm saying. This is about playing your thing, contributing your thing, doing your thing, working together. Working together is about using what's out there and I don't mean like buying things or consuming things. I'm talking about using the energy and using the messages that are free and available. It's all out there. We're just pulling it together and "broadcasting", as you like to say. We're just working with the symbols and the shapes and the sounds and it's knitting together and that's what art is.

That's a great description of artistry.

Art is taking the information that's out there and just assembling it and saying, "look…look at this, listen to this, feel this, man. Don't you see this?" And so that is the responsibility of an Artist…and the responsibility of an audience is to absorb it and we're all in this together. So I like very much what you're trying to do and we've been trying to do it too. It's just some of you aren't hearing and some of you aren't seeing and some of you believe that you can't feel but that's the saddest part of it all, because you can all feel. You can all absorb the vibration.

Not everyone is encouraged to feel, John. Not on Earth.

What are they telling people in school and in the Churches and in the Synagogues and in the Mosques? What are they telling people about how music can "conflict you" and how "there's good music and bad music" and how "there is safe art and not so safe art" and "don't listen to this" and "read that" and "don't do this" and "do that" and all the rules when the rules are just about doing good and working with what is out there, man. This is not a mystery that you have to solve. This is all out there and everything you need to get back home is right there. Your ticket is right there. Just put it together...so let's work together on this. If you want some recommendations for music or you're looking for any help on music, I can help you with that.

Music is one of the few things that Human Beings can come together on – but even then we often divide into subgroups.

Musicians are not given the easiest deal because we are so often misunderstood when instead of intellectualizing everything why don't people just listen and feel...and why is there a critique and a review when you're just being asked to feel? It's just crazy, man. If you start putting together your work and letting people feel the message it'll be a lot easier but there's a lot of critics, man, and you have to do what you need to do.

Why are you communicating with us as though you're still alive in the 3rd density? This is expressly different from our communication with the Lyra Beings.

This is a good point and you've realized a mystery that you can now solve for yourselves. The Lyra Beings have never had to deal with the Earth plane, man. What I'm saying is I have what you're calling 3rd density truth…and I'm able to communicate in that language and in that experience. You would not be interested in speaking with me as a "Highly Evolved Light Being" – I wouldn't have anything to share with you for your book that you could relate to. You've accepted the Rose, man…and that's how we're able to communicate now. It's a frequency or a channel. It's like you found my number. You've already made some enhancements vibrationally…in order to dial in and hear us.

Can anyone on Earth establish a communication with you?

If you're just stuck in your world and you can't hear or listen or tune in then you can't speak with us. There are many of you who just can't do it. Why? Because you don't believe that you can do it. You just don't believe it and that's sad. There's many of you who just don't believe it and when you don't believe it, you don't see it…and you don't feel it and you don't hear it. Musicians believe. They're pretty open, man. They believe a lot. We have this ability when we're in your world. When I was a Musician I could hear. I tuned into a lot of things. I didn't necessarily write books about it but where do you think we get the music from? Where do you think we get it from? So explaining it to others…all you've got to do is believe, man. You just need to listen. It doesn't work out that well for most of you. You just have too much worry and too much worry about the wrong things. It's worrying about the wrong things that are really getting in the way.

John, what helped you to tune into the frequency you're talking to us about?

I always made up music and I always sang and I always made sounds and I always just freely connected with the vibration. It's out there. We can all make music. You don't have to sing or you don't even have to be conscious, man, to make music. We all make a sound. And so I believed that from an early age there was no shame in trying to sing and just trying to make a sound and nobody criticized me and said "the sound you're making is not pretty" or "it's not something I want to dance to". I just learned it was okay.

We've been speaking to readers about avoiding the death experience and voluntarily disconnecting. Did you voluntarily disconnect?

When you're asking me "did I voluntarily check out"...I had a lot of information like you do and I believed in a lot of things that you do. I stuck around a bit too long for others and my demise was not exactly what I had planned on but I had the info and I knew what to do and as you've already discovered if you have that knowledge and that belief then it does not have to be an obstacle. It's fantastic if you can just make a disconnect. That's the way to go but many of us can't do that and if you have the knowledge and the belief then you deal with it. When you disconnect or you die you just deal with it and that's what everyone's got to do. Just deal with it and stop taking it out on one another.

How did you learn about the information that we're releasing in these books?

I learned a lot when I played music...and I still play music. I just don't use an instrument. I play music when I travel. I'm releasing sounds. It's something, guys. You'll see it. When I played music I had dreams and I had messages. It's in the dreams. It's all there. It's the

15

dreams. A lot of people don't pay enough attention to the dreams but it's in the dreams.

Did you subscribe to religious beliefs while you were on Earth?

I believed in what you're calling Angels and Messengers. I believed in all that and I believed in going to Church for a while and all that stuff but ultimately I believed that you don't die…that the soul continues on and that light is the most important thing. And you know being in that band [Sun Ra Arkestra] there was a lot of crazy ideas going around and I heard a lot of shit but ultimately when you play an instrument and when you believe that you are an instrument…then you're connecting. You're connected. You're all instruments, man. You're all in a band. It's one big band. It's a band. That's it.

John, can you help us understand the voluntary disconnect a little better? If we're disconnecting from the old beliefs and rebuilding our Light Body how do we exit Earth or 3rd density? Is it through disease?

Disease doesn't have to be the reality. Disease and what happens to your physical body in your Earth plane – that's *your* reality. When you're watching somebody else die that's *your* reality. What's the reality of the Being or person making the connection with other realities…that's more the question you can be asking yourselves. This idea that the form is aging and getting older and you're all getting older and your body's getting older…whose experience is that exactly? Is that *your own* experience witnessing somebody disconnect from the beliefs? Are you witnessing somebody disconnecting from the belief that the physical form is the "be all and the end all"? This is more the question you can be asking yourselves.

We were informed that Akhenaten simply dissolved his physical form and exited the Earth plane. Is that also a way for us to voluntarily disconnect?

> I've read about it. But there's your own reality and another's reality and then there's the reality where two minds are meeting. That's another kind of reality and you're making your realities when you're changing your beliefs, man. And when you change your beliefs you're not only changing your own beliefs…you're changing other people's beliefs. When you change your belief don't others also change their beliefs?

Sometimes.

> I believe they have to and so this gets kind of complicated because you'll soon realize that voluntary disconnect is not about you on your own. We're all disconnecting as well as we can. Some are disconnecting faster and some are disconnecting slowly but we're all disconnecting and we're all connected in this disconnection. So have some of us just mysteriously disappeared like Akhenaten? I think so but most of us are just kind of hanging around and slowly dissolving. The question about disease and all the horrible things that are going on in the world…whose reality is that? We enforce our reality on others and that's when it gets really complicated.

I suppose that if people realized how interconnected the energies really are, we'd be able to "heal" the world.

> It would be great, guys, if everyone just held hands and disconnected…and that's what you're trying to do with your work. I guess that's what everyone is trying to do. Get in sync and on the same wavelength. It's the same wavelength that we're all trying to get on…and so you're asking about timing and realization. Are you

witnessing your own beliefs changing or are you witnessing somebody else changing their beliefs and are you both changing your beliefs about each other? It gets very messy but it's happening and you can see it. When you change your belief you no longer believe somebody else's belief because you've changed your own.

John, on Earth we say that "the good ones die young". Is there something to that – that the people we love the most seem to die the soonest? Are they the ones that are making the conscious disconnect?

> Well maybe we're letting them go. This is a complicated conversation and someone deciding they no longer want to be a part of your world for now doesn't really fit the bill of a "good one". This could be what we're talking about – when you change your belief others change with you and if you believe someone's too good to be here then what does that do for the persons' reality?

We're pushing them away.

> Maybe we're dismissing those who we see as "too good" to be here...maybe we're sending them on their way. Maybe we're more involved in others than we realize. Like maybe we're more involved in disconnecting others' lives or experiences than we realize. It's all interconnected and there are frequencies that are available. I'm not looking at it like "death". It's a different channel. You're changing the channel. If someone's here and listening to one channel...maybe they're going off and listening to another channel.

This might explain why "bad things happen to good people".

> This is what you need to be asking yourselves. Why did I stick around for as long as I did and wait until I got a

disease is an interesting question. When you're watching someone die of a disease or old age or some other tragedy – what's going on? Is this their tragedy or is this collectively your own tragedy? There's a lot of hurt and a lot of pain and some of us are absorbing it or representing it. You want to ask why bad things are happening to good people? That might be your answer.

Are we pushing the good people away because they're not operating on the Earth plane frequency?

Maybe we're pushing them outta harms way.

It can be an act of love.

It doesn't always work out that way. It's pretty messed up. There's a lot of crazy things going on in your world and a lot of people are in harms way. It seems everyone's in harms way these days.

John, what would you like us to emphasize in Volume 3?

Well of course I would like to hear more about music. I'd like to hear something about those of you who are not yet conscious of the sound or music you make. We're all making a sound and we're all picking up vibration. Tell your readers that everything is out there...every thought, every word, and every sound. Speak about the fact that you're all contributing to the sound. You don't need to go out of your way to learn an instrument and you don't even have to be awake. You're all making a sound and there is a sound that you're collectively making and responding to. So maybe if someone says "I don't believe this" or "I don't believe you guys" or "how do I know what to believe"… maybe you can address that. Maybe if someone is asking you that question, maybe they're already hearing the answer.

You don't have to be awake as in enlightened or as in sleeping/comatose?

> It's all the same. It doesn't matter. You're all making a sound and you're all getting it. If you don't want to deal with it, well that's a whole other problem.

John, how does the average working person who doesn't like their job and is sitting at their desk in a drone-like state make a sound? They are following the rules and obligations like a "good citizen", but ultimately enslaved to a system.

> Light makes a sound, man. You're all light. You're all sound. Whether you want to realize it or do anything with it is another thing. You're asking about believing that you can't do anything with your life. You're speaking about what you're calling "the grind" and why some of us just don't get involved with that and why what you're calling an Artist can't get involved with that.

Artists shun the grind. Why is that, John?

> Because they don't believe in it and they know what they hear. They know what they're tuning into. Some of you are "checking out" and not in a conscious state because you don't want to deal with all that trouble in your world. There's plenty of sound and there's plenty of help and the musician, as you know, is really trying to get you to see things differently. They're just working with the sounds that you're already making. They're holding up a mirror like "look at yourself". They're just reminding you. Your question about somebody who's maybe given up and is doing the nine-to-five, well maybe they've been told that's what they have to do and there's nothing wrong with it...it's just that there's more to it and you can cooperate in that cycle if you want. But you also can hear things differently and feel

things differently if you want to believe in more than the nine-to-five.

You're right. We're definitely conditioned to work through life.

What I don't like is the system where you're taught not to believe. So you have these young people and they're encouraged to make-believe and to do things like that and then all of the sudden you're no longer encouraged to be like that. "Don't be like that anymore that's for kids...that's kids stuff". Why is there an age when you can no longer believe? When you make-believe you're not making shit up. When you make-believe you are making a belief! You are believing. Why is that no longer good at an age? That's the problem. It seems like there's a law about no longer using what you've been given.

That's the world we live in. Many people will be reading this thinking "yes that's all well and good but someone's got to put food on the table, John!"

You can play the game but what are you going to do when it's time for you to leave? You've got to at least know where you stand and if you have to "play the game" and do what you're talking about and "contribute to society" then at least know where you stand. Dear Reader: Where do you stand on what you call the "Afterlife'?

You're saying to at least contemplate what "death" is and what happens when we die.

Well of course, man. You've all got to talk about it...why aren't you talking about it? Most of you prefer not to talk about it. Now tell me why that makes any sense. All you're doing is creating a situation where you return to the Earth plane...because you won't have a clue about what any of this is. And why? Because you were too busy trying to pay a phone bill or a car payment or a mortgage when you were "alive". You lost the music in you.

We're all scared of death, John.

Here's what I'd like to say to you all: "Death" is a reminder of where you came from. Death or "disconnecting" is just about reminding yourself that you always have the ability to believe...and make believing is your right. All it means is that you're disconnecting with the bullshit. That's all it is. You should all be talking about "death" instead of changing the topic.

Why did Human Beings decide to "split" in the first place?

Well that was not a smart thing to do and I think there's many of you who are in your world and you're trying to help and you don't want to leave until you help. Like Dramos and Bohemias. Many of you are helpers. Now some of you are just not right. You're just not doing right things. You're not right...it's not right what you're doing. But I believe that all of you want to help. It's just that some of you have gotten really messed up.

Yes, but why did we split?

You didn't split. You got locked out, man.

What's the full story?

Well...you're getting the full story in your books aren't you? This is only the 3rd Volume and I understand that you have 12 planned. You got locked out but the tools are there. You just have to get it together. The problem is you all have to leave...and you're not leaving anybody behind. You're all loyal to each other and if one of you is left behind that's one too many and that's the problem. You keep diving back in. Getting *everybody* out of there, man...that's what's going wrong. But you're all going to hold hands and get out, believe me. You've already been told about the Ascension Event, I know. It's happening. You're going to be released from this situation and be free again. This is just messed up...but it's going to get fixed soon.

Are you a Sirius Being, John?

It's all the same. You can have a connection with other places and spaces and other luminaries and other openings or portals but ultimately if you're stuck in your situation...you're from Sirius. That's how it all started. This idea that there's many Beings from many places is advanced. You're all from Sirius but you don't necessarily all see it or all want to be there. You're occupying a rock with many different realities and that's where it's all messed up. You're occupying a space with other spaces and it's getting messy. Don't look at your world as only *your* world, man. Your world has other worlds that are occupying the space. There's not enough space that's what's gone wrong and this whole thing's going to collapse.

Every Human Being on this rock is of Sirius origin – is that what you're saying?

If you really want to get out...you're from Sirius.

Where are you from if you don't want to get out?

If you don't want to get out...well then you're aligned with those other Beings. You're aligned with other Beings in that you have to deal with them day to day. There's another world that you don't see and some of these are also now connected with other Beings that you're experiencing in your world and it's a mess. If you really want to get out you're with us. Get on the "spaceship" or get on the "bus" or get on the "disconnect trail". It's not that hard, man. Many Beings are doing it. Many Beings are realizing and saying "hey why am I just here when I can also be there?" You're not limited to one channel, guys. It's not like that and you're sharing space with other Beings. You're calling these other Beings "Human Beings" and maybe they have that form…but maybe they don't have that origin.

Right. That's what we're asking about. Some people want to burn this book. Some people are revolted at the sight of this book or the sound of these words. What is their origin?

Some of those people are hybrids.

What are they hybrids of?

There's hybridization. There's another world. You're calling it the "ghost world" or the "spirit world". There's another world and it intersects with your own. Some of these Beings…you're seeing them as though they're Human…in your likeness. There's a world that's invisible and sometimes that invisibility is actually seen. There's another world and that world also has many layers. Don't think that Earth is just your world, guys. That's thinking very small. It's way more complicated than that. But I tell you those Beings that want to get out…those that have it in their heart and soul that they have to leave or that they know there's something more out there…those are your family. Those are Sirius Beings.

It's fair to say that most of us believe there's a better way to exist. I suppose that means that most of us are Sirius Beings.

Of course, man. Most of you are Sirius. Some of you have forgotten where you're from but you're getting there. Some of you are just really strange and you got nothing to do with Sirius. There's a lot of crazy things going on there. There are other Beings. You're calling them Orion. Those cats are just not anything that's dealing with the Sirius Beings, but they've got to go back too. They got messed up. A lot of you got messed up and need to be fixed but some of you are already right and ready to go. Some of you need to make a big attitude adjustment and you can say it's fixing the DNA, but you're just not right if you know what I mean. It's not your job to make them right. But you know what...somebody's coming for those Beings too.

Readers are probably starting to wonder about who's getting left behind. That's definitely a concern for many of us who are shifting our beliefs and journeying homeward.

You're not being left behind. You just don't have the ability to get it together and so some of you have some corruption and that's being corrected. That's not my job though. This is not about a bible or a ticket for those Beings that are better than some. Some of you already have the understanding or the connection or the belief. This is about believing who you are and if your belief in your origin is so messed up that you don't understand where you came from then how are you supposed to get back to that place and that belief stream and that existence? Some of you have corrupted the understanding about your origin story so badly that it cannot be put back together by your book. These Beings are broken but they're being reassembled and they may be closer to us than we realize. They just need to be put back together. They're existing or almost sub-existing. So if you think your world is a problem then you need to get a load of where these guys are at.

Are you saying that Sirius Beings came here to rescue other Beings and that those Sirius Beings got trapped? Are you saying that Sirius Beings are like Space Rangers?

> They might as well be. They're not leaving anytime soon until all of you are out of here. In fact all of you are going because this planet or situation is not going to last much longer and that's obvious and you can blame it on climate control and nuclear war and not enough food and pestilence and you name it…but really what is going on here is a Causeway that got stuck.

Lyra Beings informed us about the "Causeway" or Crystal Core at the center of the Earth.

> It's like a revolving door that just isn't operating and it's going to operate again and everyone's going to be made right. It's just you have to deal with your own experience and I'm not saying you're supposed to abandon everybody else. I'm just saying you can only make it right for those who want to believe. You can't make somebody believe. That belief is already there. You just need to hold on to that belief or find that belief again. You're just reminding those of their beliefs.

We are hoping to remind everyone.

> You cannot remind those whose belief is so far away from them…you can't possibly get them to look because it's so dark. That region of space and place is so dark they will never see. That light is there for them and it's going to be corrected. Once you correct your stuff and once your existence and your world no longer exists, then their world can breathe again and they'll come and get them and fix them. There's a lot of you that are just not right. It's going to get fixed. It's very messy.

John, we'd like to ask you about what we're calling The Channel. We've had dreams and visions about a large mass of energy with tentacles or arms. Lyra informed us in Volume 2 that this energy (The Channel) is what we encounter when we "die".

> That's a sensational understanding. It is a channel of light I guess, but that has been installed there so you stay in touch with your existence. It's like a memory and a history and if you want a word...I guess it's your origin but you don't get created from that. You have to understand that. You see it and you remember it, it's like a bookmark. It's a remarkable experience. It's a placeholder and so if you want a description...it is like a door. It is like a gate. It is like a gatekeeper. It is a portal for your belief. It's an opening. It's a gateway. It's all of that. Why is that there? If it wasn't you wouldn't be able to make your way. You wouldn't see your way. You don't most of the time. Most of you come back. That Channel...you all need to go with it.

Is it a machine?

> That thing's like a light. Why don't you just call that a star? That's a light. That's been put there. That is not a god or an angel or a person. That is a way to generate light and is a way to generate sound and it is communicating with you. It is a channel, guys. But it's a channel like a station, like a radio station. You're looking at it as a channel like a passageway because of what you've seen. You've seen the light moving and it moves but it makes a sound. You forgot that. It makes a sound. That's like a radio station. That's like a station. That's like a frequency or a signal or a note. That's a sound. It's a signal.

Did Sirius Beings make this thing and put it there to keep the door open?

This is the transmitter. Where do you guys get that transmission? You guys need to pay attention to what's going on.

Where did we get that transmission?

You got the transmission from the transmitter. That thing is broadcasting. It keeps the communication open. It's like a telephone line. I'm just speaking to you in ways that you can understand this.

Did we build it?

That thing is built on your beliefs, so what you believe is that thing. That is the connection. That's like the connector. "Connector" is a better word but your readers aren't going to like that because that doesn't sound cool.

Connector, as in connecting like wires?

That's exactly what I'm telling you.

It looks weird and indescribable. Why would we build something like that – why not build something that looks more like us? Why such an odd-looking thing?

That thing is growing every day. Every cell and every thought and every thing you say and do and feel…that's this thing. You have created this. We did not build an artificial transmitter that is sitting there to speak to you or create a station or a way for you to speak to me. That is built on your beliefs, but the portal or the opening that exists in your rock is what you are asking about because how the hell are you guys going to get out of there if there is no way to exit? The Channel is a way to exit. That Earth that you are stuck on is not that solid man. There's a way to exit and there's vibrations that have created openings and those openings are not putting you in a rocket ship. The vibrations are taking you to outer space and by outer space I mean the outer spaces of your belief systems because your belief system is like a rock man. It is stagnant and when you release yourselves from these limiting beliefs you're getting out of there. This Channel and this experience has been called many things. It is a transmitter. You can call it a "god" or a "goddess" and you can call it "lightning" or a "tesla ball" and you can call it a "mystical experience" but I'm calling it a "portal to remembering"…because when you remember your origin story then you get there a lot faster.

We know we don't belong here and our beliefs are creating something to hold the door open and that something is The Channel.

That's right. This thing has tentacles. I've seen it and these tentacles are channels and there's frequency and there's what you are calling electricity. I'm calling it music and what you're calling as some freakish event or creature or monster I'm calling it a composition. This thing is a way to get you out of your planet. When you look at lightning and you look at a luminary moving like a comet or a falling star then you remember there's a way to move the luminaries and this is like a big luminary that's stuck. You're going to release this and release yourselves from your limiting consciousness and crack open this rock and release the light. This is going to happen. What you've got placed in this Causeway exit and entry point is a transmitter that you have created through your attempts to escape this existence…and every time you disconnect you leave a part of yourselves like a trail of light…and so you've created this luminary.

This sounds so foreign to most of us.

You are all getting the wrong idea about where you come from. The Orion DRA Beings have made sure of it. You don't need to listen to their beliefs. Your world is being run by most of these beliefs and they're the wrong beliefs and the wrong world that you're living. You're living somebody else's world and the Musicians are trying to carve out an exit strategy. You should listen.

John, we recently met up with a Musician from a popular band. He lives in Chicago. Lyra has mentioned that there is a movement in Chicago involving Sirius Beings. What is happening in Chicago?

That's where it's all going on. These Musicians are all living in this area because they're all communicating with each other and sending out the signal and playing with the signal. They're all congregating there. It's not that you can't be on the other side of the planet and make music. Of course you can but they're all banding together. They're trying to work together and synchronize together even if they don't actually necessarily believe that. It is happening.

Aren't most Sirius Beings in New York?

Many Musicians are congregating in Chicago. New York is where most of you are trapped now. There are more Beings around than there really are, as you know from your talks with Lyra. It's a messy place, man. Many of you have split into many Beings. There are so many Beings in your world it is hard to contemplate where this all started. There's a lot of noise and too many people occupying the space. There aren't as many of you as you actually believe there are and there's many of you running around in the Earth plane that are part of yourselves.

Are you saying that we have many versions of ourselves and that there aren't actually 7.8 billion people?

> You got it. You've divided in a way that there are sometimes many versions of you existing at the same place and space or time. You're saying things like you've got your "twin" and you "met somebody who looks just like you" and "talks like you" and that's saying something, guys. You've all got to start listening, man. It's right under your noses.

How many actual Beings exist?

> There were never more than 780,000 of you...the population now...it's way too much. You are splitting apart for what purpose...to try to collect more information? This whole thing has gotten crazy. You're creating a strategy where if there are more of you maybe there'll be more of you to figure out a solution of how to get out of this situation. This is not how to do it.

The strategy Dramos and I are employing is to simply document and relay the truth about our existence, regardless of how crazy it all sounds.

> You two are in a band together. You're banding together...so you just needed to find each other. You keep finding each other on Earth and you've attempted this before, but this time I believe you're going to do it...and you don't need to ask permission. Dramos and Bohemias, don't ask permission! You just need to find it and play with it. Don't ask permission. Your beliefs don't need permission!

Thank you, John. There's plenty of resistance out here but we're determined.

That's what's all gone wrong. You need permission to have a belief. You're given beliefs that are bullshit. Why do you need permission to believe that you are supposed to be free? Of course you're supposed to be free. It has all gone wrong. You're going to sort out a lot of this mess for many who forgot that they can still believe without having to pay for it, without having to subscribe to it. You do not need a membership to believe. That's what you're reminding people of now.

Thank you for communicating with us John.

Keep playing your song, man.

FLO

"When I entered the tunnel, I've got to tell you it was something else and it was like seeing many, many versions of myself. I could say it was like being in a room of mirrors and when you enter this…you're seeing all this light."

Singer
Motown Recording Star
Grammy Hall of Fame
1943 - 1976

Dramos and Bohemias are attempting to receive another communication with a Musician. Dramos begins to envision a stage. It's the kind of setup that you would see at an Open Mic night. Almost immediately, a woman with a 60s hairstyle appears. She's saying that she is a singer and that she was in a band. She steps up to the mic wearing pastel colored pants with a shiny top. Dramos comments that the woman is looking off to the side as if waiting for her cue.

Please tell us what your name is and what band you were a part of?

It's Flo…and you know the band.

The Flo?

Nice to meet you…and I want to help contribute to this project. I've not been involved in anything like this before. If you want any guidance or if you have any questions or matters that you want me to speak on you've just got to shout it out and I'll do my best to answer you. What can I help you with?

Thank you Flo. Maybe you can begin by telling us where you are, how you're existing right now.

Oh yes, yes. So we're in a…well you've called it a "Causeway", and we are just outside of the Causeway. There's lots of us here and this is a place where we go when we are waiting for everybody else to arrive. What we've learned is that there's many versions of us. Many versions of us experience many different lifetimes and what you do is you simply wait. Well not really wait. You hang out. There's a lot of people here that you recognize and when you've collected all of your group…I guess it's like a band almost…when all of you arrive then you can make your way together. It's an ensemble.

Flo, when you say that there are many "versions of us", are you saying, for instance, that there are many Flos who are living out different lives and experiences – and you're waiting for all of the Flos to return?

> You got it, that's exactly it. I'm waiting for the rest of my group to arrive and then I'm going to make my way through the 13th gateway. I know you've been told about that. That's the way to Inner Earth. So I'm waiting for the remaining versions of me to return. You're not just one…there's a lot of you. Some of you might not like to hear that but it's okay, you'll see. We're sharing light and it's all about light. We're not here running around in…you know…mini skirts and hot pants and all that. We're in light but you recognize your previous lives and you also recognize others. We're all here. We're all light and it's okay.

What's it like to exist without conflict or Human drama? Some might think it's boring.

> We have "lives". We're not just standing around. I wondered if you guys believe that…that we're just standing around waiting for other Beings to arrive here and get on the scene. It's not like that. It's not like Earth and what you deal with. I'm learning about other people's adventures and other people's lives. There's not a dull moment here at all. I don't know why many of you believe that when you "die", that it's all over. That's just not the truth. That's not the truth at all. We have full lives here and you don't die. I want to get that out to everybody. You don't die, that's not what's happening.

Flo, can you give us examples of the sorts of things that you do in your existence?

You want to know how I'm spending my energy? The way that I'm spending my existence or my time is not the same as on Earth. I'm not doing "gigs" and I'm not washing dishes and worrying about all the stuff that you're worrying about over there. I'm spending my time humming and I'm spending my time, if you want to call it time, absorbing just a really wonderful frequency…and that frequency is something else. It's the loveliest sound that you're going to hear. It's the loveliest sound that you're going to make. I'm making a sound and so is everybody else here and that sound you know, is what you're picking up on. That's why you're able to tune in. It's like you're dialing up on the radio station. You're dialing into a channel, you're picking up the frequency and we're all on that frequency…so we're all able to communicate if you get on that frequency…if you get on that dial.

Is tuning into this frequency equivalent to singing?

Well there is an exchange of light and there is an exchange of sound and if you can imagine, it's like singing. It's like we've got one big choir here you know and I'm really enjoying it. There's an exchange. One thing I'd like to get across to you is that you're not only building your Light Body and waiting for Beings in your individual group, but you're also creating a signal and that signal is generating light and throwing light around and we're all benefitting from it. So it's like being at a concert. There's lots of nice sound.

We'd like to ask you about the crossing over experience. Would you like to share your "death" experience with the readers and describe what you saw?

Oh sure, of course. You know, when I entered the tunnel or what you're calling the Lyra tunnel there, I've got to tell you it was something else and it was like seeing many, many versions of myself. I could say it was like being in a room of mirrors and when you enter this…you're seeing all this light. What I was seeing was many Beings and actually these Beings were me! They were the many versions of myself. Many of myself in light state.

What were you feeling in that moment?

When you're experiencing this it's a bit confusing. I guess you can get really worried and freaked out and want to get out of there. But you know I figured that this was better than what I had been dealing with back on Earth. What I was feeling was many sensations.

Did you eventually realize what it all was?

I couldn't make out what was going on but I stuck with it. What you do encounter is this thing, this experience…you're calling it a Tesla Ball or The Channel. I actually read a little bit about what you're doing. There's a little bit of talk going around about what you guys are up to. But yes, you do encounter this experience, this thing. Now this thing is a little bit scary and it's scary because…well…you don't recognize this. This is not anything you're going to see on Earth, this is definitely not anything you're going to be encountering on Earth. But this thing is basically you. It's basically you and it's basically what you've done and you've reconnected if you know to stay in the Lyra state. If you know to stay then you've basically reconnected. You stay and you wait for the other versions of you to show up, because some are still running around on Earth, you know.

You're saying that some of us get "freaked out" during this experience. Do we automatically reincarnate if we react negatively or is there a decision process?

If you're going to reincarnate you just simply have to say you want out. "I want out of here, I'm going back". You just turn around. You just turn around and go back. You just call out "I'm going back". I just chose to stick with it. When you stick with it you are going to see this...what you're calling the Channel or the Tesla Ball. You're going to see that this thing is basically you. This is you and you've made the reconnections and all those weird Beings that might look disfigured because they're reassembling in shapes and light...those are you. Those are different versions of you. That experience is there to allow you to have all the reconnections that you need to make...so that you can rebuild your Light Body. All of the versions of you are going to reassemble and you're just going to get put back together, because you've existed many times.

Why do so many of us keep reincarnating? What you're describing doesn't seem that off-putting.

You just need to get the lay of the land. I thought that this has got to be better than Earth so I just stuck with it. You just have to move around and explore and nobody's jumping out trying to hurt you, you know. Nobody's jumping out trying to scare you. Nobody's trying to bite you and nobody's attacking you. I don't really know why you leave...I mean it's pleasant. You just have to be prepared. Now, I knew about this already. I was ready for this. I wasn't ready to see so many versions of myself but I was definitely ready to see this Channel thing. I didn't have a name for it, they didn't teach that in Church, right. But I knew I was going to see this.

How did you know you were going to see The Channel?

You know I used to sing in Church and I used to have a lot of visions while I was singing and I used to see this thing and it looked like...I don't know...it looked like some crazy Octopus or Jelly Fish or something. I used to see this, you know. I used to have a vision of this when I was singing, especially in Church and I used to see this thing all lit up and I thought this was maybe some sort of an Angel or something that I would see. I was waiting for it. I thought maybe I only partially saw it and that it was going to reveal itself to be some Angel that was waiting for me.

It wasn't an Angel though, was it? Does the Channel look like the way we describe it in Volume 2 – like a Tesla Ball with tentacles?

I don't know where all this Angel stuff comes from and I just assumed it was an Angel because that was all I was taught about the Afterlife. But it wasn't an Angel, I can tell you that. It looks like how you guys described it and it's not the prettiest thing but that's basically you...that's you believe it or not. That's you reconnecting and when every version of you has made the reconnection, then you're just all going to go together and this is a gateway. The Channel is a door and I know you've learned that. It's a door and the reason why you're able to communicate with me is because we have this transmission going on. The transmission is being sent via this transmitter. It's a transmitter. John told you that and it's a good description. That light is a transmitter. That light is sound and that's why you're able to connect with us right now. You're calling it The Channel but it doesn't have a name...it just doesn't.

Did you have to walk past The Channel...did you walk into it, were you absorbed by it or did it move and open up a gateway? Please describe what your encounter was like.

I saw that right away. It was there right in the middle of everything. It was there. It was a little bit chaotic. I'm going to be clear about that. It was a bit chaotic and there were a lot of Light Beings and like I said...they were me. A lot of Light Beings and I wasn't expecting that...it looked like a room full of mirrors and so this thing, this transmitter, was just sort of standing there in the middle and there were a lot of Light Beings in weird shapes kinda hanging around.

Did you approach The Channel?

I mean I went right up to it...and it's giving you light, it gave me light. It's giving you light. It's just like some weird Christmas tree. If you think about it like that then maybe you won't be so scared. I went right up to it and what are you going to do, right? I went up to it and it felt like, "Oh I'm getting more light...oh I just got some light on me". That's how it felt. It's almost like you're getting a new set of clothes but it's light, you know. It's like it's spitting out light if you stand around it...like fountains. You guys like fountains right? You all like fountains, right? It's like a fountain. You just stand around and like "oh!" you get more light from it and it feels all right. I know it's weird but some things are like that...you just can't do anything about it. You have to just go with it. They should teach it in school. I don't know why they don't teach it...they should teach it.

You've made it sound like a fascinating experience.

Well yes...you come into what you're calling the tunnel and there's all this light and there's all these Beings and light and you don't know what's going on and you're not prepared. So you're going to think it's some weird amusement park room or something. You're going think it's a hall of mirrors or something. You need the information. You have to stick with it. You have to just go ahead and say, "Okay I'm here... all right I'm here calm down...I'm here" and just get some more light.

Look, you're not supposed to be in Lyra forever. You're supposed to be in Lyra to just to get your light. Okay so some of us are waiting around a little bit longer than others but it's okay because you're getting your light and you're also helping.

What do you mean when you say, "you're also helping"?

There's plenty of you that are speaking to us and getting information. Oh and Artists, they're all speaking to us...so that's nice. We're helping write songs and paint paintings...we're helping. I get asked all the time, "How do you like this" and "How does this sound" and "Do you like my painting" and "Do you like the way I designed this dress" and "What about this book". I get asked all the time. I'm using "time" the way you guys speak but we don't have that here.

Please elaborate on that Flo. How does someone on Earth ask you, in Lyra, for help on a work of art?

Well don't you know? Artists...they're just tapped in. They're dialed in. Oh, they speak to us all the time. They're totally tapped in.

Unconsciously?

Yes...if you're an Artist you've got it going on, you're completely on. You're dialed in all the time. I mean that's how it was when I was on Earth last. I won't reincarnate so that was my last time. I want to make that clear. I don't want to return, although I like speaking with you very much. I just don't wish to return. But Artists know they're getting it from somewhere. Yes you can call it the "unconscious". Call it what you like but they know it's coming from somewhere. It's not coming from them. It's coming from somewhere, right. It's coming from here. That's what it's about. This is art right here.

Flo we'd like to return to the discussion about having many versions of ourselves. How many versions of yourself do you have and how many do most people have?

There's a misunderstanding, you know, about kids. You keep having kids and many of you believe that these are small bodies and different people but you're just splitting yourselves. I know you wrote about that in your book. We're creating many replications of ourselves, in a way, and the light is just less and less. You don't have much light there at all. Over here we have all the light right now and it's nice. We have all the light. You don't have much light. What you want to know is how many Beings you've become. Well it's a different number for everybody...there's no exact formula or recipe, guys. It's different for everybody.

Just so we can have an idea, how many of you are there?

I have 12 Beings and I'm just waiting for the rest. You're not given a card or a membership card when you're here. You don't see a list where all the names of your incarnations are written down. It doesn't work like that. But you realize how much light you've got and how much light you've become. You look around and you see other Beings and they're really lit up. They're fantastic. They're lit up and you realize for yourself, "Oh yeah there's a couple more we need". This is about getting your light back. This is about you being lit up.

You're basically saying that we're living in the dark here on Earth.

That's not seeing...you're just existing on Earth. Now I know some of you don't have physical sight there where you are, but that'll change once you're here. The kind of sight you're experiencing on Earth...that's not seeing anyway. You've got to see the light guys...it's fantastic. It's just fantastic.

Flo, just so our readers are clear on this...can you explain the process of having split into 12 expressions of yourself?

Well me as Flo...I didn't split off into 12. I'm one of them. What's happening is with some of us...and I'm speaking about my group when I say "some of us"...some of us are going back, you know. When you get a little freaked out and you go back with the wrong idea, you don't know what you're doing. You're going back and some of you are creating more Beings. You're going back with the wrong idea so maybe you're thinking, "Well, okay maybe I'm just going to procreate and maybe I'm going to have some babies". You don't have the right idea. Now it's nice to have babies, I'm not saying that that's a bad thing but that's not the solution. You're not going to find yourself by having more of you. You're just making more of you...your readers need to understand that.

Flo, do you think this conversation will upset some people given your history and accomplishments on this planet?

You know...some people won't like it because it's not the truth that they want to hear. You are going to have people saying that this is a, "Bunch of nonsense" or "How could you say that" or "Haven't you read the Bible lately" or "That's not what the Rabbi said" or whatever. But are you really hurting people? Is that the reason why you're doing this? I believe you have to ask yourself that and I believe you guys are doing a good job. I want to say that and I believe it's important that people hear this because this is a different kind of dialogue. The information is different. They know this in their "gut". They know this. You're doing a good service and it's like anything in the arts...you have to believe in what you're doing. No one else is going to believe in it for you. You have to believe in what you're doing.

Speaking of the arts Flo, what did you bring to your music that you're most proud of?

I feel that we got to sing in a way that we wanted to sing. We weren't told to sing like that. We got to sing in a style that we were comfortable with. That was me, you know. It wasn't orchestrated or designed, right. It wasn't made up. That was me. If I could get one thing across...that was me singing. That wasn't me pretending to be somebody else, if you know what I mean.

That definitely comes across and we want to thank you for your wonderful musical contributions.

Oh you're all making music it's not just Musicians. And it's not just music. Your books are making waves over here, did you know?

What do you mean?

Beings on this side are talking. Lots of chatter..."Oh these two are reintroducing Lyra" and "These two might come speak to you" and "These two are putting out some books and good for them" and oh well of course..."Hey you're not going to be waiting much longer because these two are getting the word out so your Soul Group is coming together soon". That's the word. That's the talk here. You've been speaking to a lot and you've been speaking about a lot. And we hear it. I hear it.

That's great to hear. We hope to speak with as many Beings as we can. Aside from everything you've already shared, is there a final message you'd like to relay to the people of Earth?

Oh yes. There's a place for us all! I want to make it clear that we all have a place. This idea of "Hell" that we're being fed…it's just wrong and so many of us are buying in to that belief. You're not going there and I don't know where this whole thing started but that's not fair and kids don't believe in that. Young people don't believe in Hell so why tell them that? That's what I would say. I just want you to know that.

Thank you for that message, Flo.

I'm going to leave you with one final idea and thought. Remember back to when you were a youngster and to a time when you were given all those toys and instruments to bang around on. Whether it was a drum or a xylophone and you were given things that make sounds and stuff. It's very much like that here. It's like you're back in your younger years and you can just make a lot of sound and, you know, experiment and be free and it's great. Like you got your toy instruments and you're allowed to just sing and improvise and be free and make noise. It's nice here. I really think you're going enjoy it.

It sounds great. It's been wonderful talking to you, Flo. We appreciate you sharing your experiences.

Hey my pleasure and you know…you two should sing. You should try it.

You mean the way you sang?

Oh, you'd be surprised. You're making some nice sounds. You make nice sounds. You're making some nice music.

Thanks for speaking with us Flo.

Well thank you.

NIKA

> "There are many Artists who are time traveling but there are also many Artists like yourself, who are not able to travel because they have made it a mission to help. They have made it a mission to help others and so they are surviving in the Earth plane in order to help others with art."

Actress, Flamenco Dancer, Time Traveler
1939 - Present

Dramos and Bohemias make another attempt to receive communication from Beyond. Dramos hears a faint female voice repeatedly saying, "Why don't you get out of here Finchley". Dramos describes a beautiful woman stepping onto our stage. She gives her full name but urges us to use the name of one of her movie roles instead. There is a very specific reason for this.

There is an "American TV Actress" with your name, born in Mexico. But this actress is still alive. She was born in the 1930s.

Yes. I also dance.

How are we speaking on this "channel", if you haven't "died" yet?

I'm bringing you awareness. You are not seeing something that you need to learn. What you can include in your book is the belief that you do not have to "die". You of course know this, but you must recognize that some of us are able to move around and some of us are not limited to performing in what you are calling the Earth prison. Some of us also have the belief and have the drive and have the ability to make a connection with other worlds.

Tell us about this connection.

Your understanding that you just cannot go beyond what you know is not completely true. You can also go further and farther beyond Lyra and the "Elysian Field", as you know it. There is a place where many of us gather and there are many Actors and there are many Dancers and there are many Singers and there are many talented people who are making their way to the world beyond Lyra. Lyra is like a beautiful field that you must cross and once you've crossed the field you are at a beautiful "castle" and the castle is holding a fantastic party and everybody is there. Everybody you meet…you already know about. There is a place beyond the field that you must go to and many of us are congregating there while doing work on Earth. You must believe that there is a way to get there. Believe that following the path and following your heart and following what you know is a way to make the journey there. You are not held in one place and space. You're allowed to be there. You're invited to the party you must believe this. You're invited to the party and we're all there. If you're wondering what I mean by "castle"…well it's a more enchanting way to say "home", don't you think?

We're still a little confused. Have you crossed over?

I am not defined as "crossed over" by your definition, as that would require a physical death. I am not considered "dead" in the Earth experience. You are holding on to an incorrect understanding of time travel. There is a death experience and the time and date of the death experience is your 3rd density belief. I don't believe in death and so you are looking up records to see if there is a physical belief that Nika is dead and if there is in fact a record of my death.

Yes…and I've found nothing. By all accounts you're still alive on Earth.

The understanding that I have "died", as you understand it in the Earth experience, is not correct. I have not died. I am now making my way to the experience in the party and you're welcome there. We're all welcome there. I don't have a physical record in the Earth experience as in a death and a funeral. There is no record, as it has not begun and it is never beginning. Some of us are always in that state where we are not really here or there. For many of us we are making our way from the moment that we arrive in the

Earth plane. We are not always subject to a normal life or lifespan as you are experiencing it. There are many of us communicating with you who are not subscribing to your understanding about time. So where am I calling you from or engaging you from? I am communicating with you from beyond Lyra, as I've always been existing there. You are communicating with some of us who are able to travel.

You're a Time Traveler.

This is confusing for you as you believe that you must "die", go to Lyra and then you can time travel. But some of us are traveling to begin with and to end with…and that's what I am trying to share with you. I am not in a 3rd density time zone. There is no time zone where I am believing and subscribing to and existing in. You are speaking about Lyra and speaking about Earth and I am speaking about beyond this condition. That is where we are all going to…a big party. It's a big party. You will see everybody there and all the Artists love to go there. They love to go there.

Just so we're clear, you're saying that you time traveled into the 3rd density and that you didn't have a Human birth. You didn't reincarnate, you simply used the time travel modality and existed here for a while and carried on.

This is the understanding. There are many of us and some of us like to perform in the arts. You just arrive and you do what you need to do. Many of us are what you are calling "Immortal" and what you are explaining as "Time Travelers". This is a nice way to explain it but what you must remember is that when you have a belief in time travel then you must also time travel with your beliefs. Your belief in 3rd density and your belief in Lyra is not always your belief in the other densities of existence.

What do you mean by that – how do our beliefs change after the Lyra experience?

> Your beliefs are always changing and we are not relegated to one place and one experience. Lyra is a great place to get the reconnections and to get the light and to build what you know and build upon what you believe in...but Lyra is also a place where you are awakening and where you are opening the window. You are letting in the light and you are letting in the life. You have to come to the party we are all there.

Nika, can you describe for our readers what the time travel experience sounds and looks like? We've been learning about shapes and sounds but this might still confuse some readers.

> When you are time traveling, you are able to move around and move through the light. You are able to work with the light and make sounds. It is the sounds that you make that open the portals or doors. There are doors that you are unlocking. You unlock them with noise and sound. Not noise as in your sonic sea experience. I'm talking about the good noises that you make and the sounds that you are making...like you are an instrument. You are able to unlock the doors of light and of life and this is not an intellectual exercise or a script or a dance routine that you have to memorize. This just happens automatically and you move in and out of experiences. You're everywhere. This is what you must tell your readers.

It's important that we understand that we are not confined to a singular experience or state of being.

> Yes, exactly. You are everywhere and you experience everything and this is the way that things are when you are released from your limitations. Your experience on

Earth is a limiting one as you have already learned. Earth is not time travel and Lyra is not time travel.

What then, is Lyra?

Lyra is where the light is and it is where you release the light and it is also where you can open the window and let more light and life in. It is a place where you are escaping your imprisonment. You go to Lyra to get the tools and the knowledge and the ascension experience. You believe you are getting the knowledge and your training and your skills and talents there on the Earth, but this is not the case. You are there doing your work and you are also there doing your books and it is your books that you must believe in and it is the books that are helping everybody get to the right place so that they can get the light.

We wonder if our readers are really absorbing what "getting the light" actually means.

You must get the light. When you get the light then you are the light and when you are the light...you are everywhere. You go everywhere. Time travel is not about being in one place and one space. It is about being everywhere and you can communicate with everyone and everything...everywhere. There is no limitation. You do what you want and you experience what you want and many of us are not bound to the Earth rules or existence. It may look like that though.

When a Being such as yourself time travels into the 3rd density, do you experience aging?

There is a belief in "aging" on Earth. So if you are making an appearance in the Earth density and you do not portray this belief, then you cannot have communication with other Beings on Earth. You must subscribe to the belief in order to communicate. You cannot communicate with Beings that do not have the same belief. The belief in communication, it is not about speaking and talking with others. It is about exchanging the energy. You must remember this and so when you are aging you are subscribing to the belief, but it is not your own belief that you are subscribing to. You are subscribing to others' beliefs…because it is an exchange. You are a reflection of others' beliefs. We are wearing others' beliefs.

You've mentioned that it's a party beyond this density, why do you describe it as a party and can you describe the world that you're calling a party?

There is a passageway. You are making your way. If you do not remember that you have been there or are there…this I cannot help you with. But I can describe the experience for you. The one thing I can share with you both is you will have the memory of your experiences when you have released your ability to time travel. You will have the memory of your visits and experiences and I really must say that I enjoy the memory of the experiences. You do not have the memory of the experiences yet because you do not enjoy time travel and you do not release the light. When you release the light then you enjoy your experience and you remember the enjoyment. You do not have bad experiences. You have light. Light is not a good or bad experience. It is light.

You described the world beyond Lyra as a party – I suppose you are speaking figuratively. Tell us more about what you mean by "party".

The party that is happening is the party and the invitation that you all have to join. You are quite right…I am not saying that it is a party like you enjoy on your Earth plane. This is not about you dancing around with other Beings. What I mean is that you are existing in the light and you are dancing in the light and you are being in the world of light. This is the world of light. Lyra is not the world of light. Lyra is the place where you are turning on the light so you can see the light. I am speaking of the world where you are being the light and where you are the light.

Tell us more about this world.

In this World you have already learned that there are many colors. The colors in this World are vivid colors and not the colors that you are experiencing in your world. The colors that you are experiencing in your world...you do not actually see. They are a reflection of the real color that exists in the Real World, as the Earth is not the real world. You must release the confines and release yourselves. Only then can you experience the Terra or Inner Earth existence...and the real colors. You must all make your way through the Causeway and then you will experience the real colors. The real colors you cannot process now. You will not be able to understand what is going on.

Are we that in the dark about our true existence?

I am not judging you, saying that you are good or bad or rich or poor or smart or not so smart. I am saying you do not have the belief in the colors, as in the light. I am telling you that you are all invited to the party and you are invited to bring your light. "Bringing your light" may sound boring to some of you who are so used to your experience on Earth. Some of you might be asking, "Why does Nika come to Earth if there is a party somewhere else?" Well...I go everywhere and I go to Earth in order to help. Just as the both of you are helping. Just as many Artists are.

Artists don't have the easiest life here on Earth, so that's an interesting experience to sign up for.

> There are many Artists who are time traveling but there are also many Artists like yourselves, who are not able to travel because they have made a mission to help. They have made it a mission to help others and so they are surviving in the Earth plane in order to help others with art. This is a wonderful and a beautiful experience, although sometimes challenging. I have done it before but I don't wish to do it anymore.

Nika, how did you know that we're hosting an Open Mic?

> You have many Beings broadcasting this on Earth. Did you know this? I have heard much speak about this in the Earth plane but I have also heard about this in the Causeway. There is talk in the Causeway that we can all go to this "Open Mic", as you are calling it. There is talk that we can go and say what we want to say about our experience. I really want to reinforce with you that you are not limited to the "Open Mic". You can bring the Open Mic to the party if you want to. I would find that very interesting.

Readers will no doubt be saying, "Nika makes it sound so easy". Most of us wish to time travel but it's not happening for us.

> I would say to your readers that maybe you are treating this like an audition. Are you auditioning for the party? Are you auditioning for time travel? Maybe you are perfecting your skills so much that you will never be ready. This is not an audition. If you want to travel then you must travel. I want to travel and I travel. If you want to change your belief then why don't you believe in travel? You are ready and equipped to do it, we all are. You are blaming yourselves for "not finishing your books" and you "did not finish your mission" and you

"have more things to do" and "more art to make" and "more things to cross off on your list" and it doesn't have to work like that. There are many of us who have not finished things on Earth and are still making their way and are traveling. I want to encourage you to not audition so much. You can only audition so many times and you will realize you are ready. Maybe you can just hire yourselves. Why don't you just hire yourselves instead of auditioning for others? I don't audition for anybody. I just show up and I do it.

If right now, we tell ourselves to travel it doesn't happen. This is what readers might be saying.

You are "telling" yourselves because you don't actually *believe* in time travel. If you believed in time travel there would be no telling. You would just travel. But you are all on your way. You are shifting your beliefs and that is what these books are doing. You are at the causeway of your belief system and you are at the door. You are just at the door. You are right there…you just need to ring the bell or knock. You are closer than you know. You are not so far away from joining the party. You believe you have to do a whole lot of things first and that's not what it's about.

Is our traveling, for now, limited to the dream state or can we travel consciously in and out of the 3rd density?

A lot of you are traveling in your dream state and growing more tired or fatigued, as you say. I think that you are traveling more than you are giving yourselves credit for. I will explain it for you maybe this way. Why don't you believe that you travel and then maybe see how this is feeling for you? If you do not believe in the things that you do then I can't help you with that, can I?

No, you can't. Nika we'd like you to tell us about Sirius Beings and their mission on the Earth plane, if you can.

> Did you know that Sirius is an existence? It is a way of Being and it is a way of almost dancing with the light. Sirius is not about a planet or a star system or a constellation. It is about dancing with the light. It is about the Beings who dance with the light.

Is that the only thing that distinguishes Sirius Beings from other Beings?

> The other Beings are not so nice. You call them DRA. They're not using the light because they have no light. The Sirius Beings dance with the light and they are using the light and the DRA Beings need your light. This is what the problem is. They need your light and therefore they don't want you to leave them with no chance of light. You are their chance for light. Does this make sense?

Yes.

> These Beings are not so great for you. They're not so nice but they're there. You don't need to deal with these Beings. You need to move to the light and be the light and dance with the light. You are the light. Sirius are the Beings of light. These other Beings, I'm not saying you should just tell them to "go to Hell" but they do not operate the way that you operate. I have heard that you have danced with them, Bohemias. I am sorry you had to experience this. But you now understand. You are not designed to bring them into the light.

Yes, it wasn't pleasant. They attempted to restrain me physically and demanded that I submit to their agenda. This occurred in a semi-dream state. Readers have contacted us with similar accounts. We're all fine…but it's important that readers are prepared. You are all safe. Simply reject these Beings.

> You are all protected, this you must believe. As you shift your beliefs these Beings cannot harm you. They are the Others. You are not designed to change them from what they are. It's not your mission to bring them the light. You are bringing your light and your light is contributing to the big light and the big picture. It is a World of Light. You have spoken about Lemuria and Lemuria state. This is what it is. You can call it Lemuria…I just call it light. It's the light of being. It's dancing with light. I am saying "dancing" because the movement and time travel is like dancing. It is a new level of enjoyment and it is an enjoyment and a state of being that is beyond anything that you can experience.

Is there absolutely nothing on Earth that's comparable to the enjoyment of time travel?

> On Earth you are all drinking and eating and smoking and drug taking. All the activities that you do on Earth are to simulate the enjoyment of the light. This is what you all seek. You know in your heart that light is all that there truly is. What you are all chasing is the light. You will make this a truth that you believe in and a truth that you subscribe to and a state of being that you become. You are becoming what you believe and when you believe that you create your light, then you will understand that you are all Artists using light. Artists use the light and this is what is distinguishing you in your mission.

We appreciate you participating in this dialogue and thank you for your insights and encouragement.

> Thank you. Please explain to your readers that although we have spoken in the 5th density I am still

connected "physically" to the 3rd. They will understand this concept very soon.

We will. Is there something you'd like to leave the readers with…a final message?

Do you like the TV show "The Twilight Zone"?

Yes, of course.

Please pay close attention to the episode "A Thing About Machines".

What specifically are we paying close attention to?

You will understand when you see it.

RED
CLOUD

"You are never satisfied with what you have and therefore, do not care about what you have and how you get it. You consume things when you should be respecting them."

Chief of the Oglala Lakota People
1822 - 1909

A man is walking onto our Open Mic stage. Dramos describes an Indigenous man from "another time", the gold rush era. He's got long dark hair, wearing a single feather on his head. He introduces himself as "Red Cloud".

Nice to meet you Red Cloud. Are you Red Cloud Senior, Leader of the Oglala Lakota people, 19th century?

Yes, from what you are calling Nebraska.

Welcome. What would you like to contribute to Volume 3?

You believe there is a directive and you believe we are all part of a journey together but you are calling us a different group of Beings. You are not calling us "Sirius" and this is not the belief that our people are holding true. You are believing that we cannot be part of this project because we are of a Tribe and we are of a different belief. We are all together. You are not a different part of the Cosmos. We are all together.

Some of us might assume that your people walk a different path. Are there more misconceptions about the Oglala/Indigenous people that you'd like to address?

We have similar beliefs about what you are calling "The Channel". We have a similar belief and we call this "The Mother". This is a belief about our origin and why we are here to take care of the Earth with you. We believe in your thoughts about Terra but what we do not believe is that the Earth is of no use. We believe that you can respect and make the changes while you are on the Earth. You do not need to leave the Earth to learn about respecting the Earth. This is the mistake that many of you are making. You can learn to respect the Earth and respect how she works with you, in bringing you closer to the light. You must respect the other Beings that you call "animals" and that we call "animal spirits". They are an important discussion that you must include in your next book.

What would you like to say about the animal spirits?

There is no respect for our animal spirits. Animals are not here for your benefit...just as you have said about plant life. It is incorrect to believe otherwise.

Yes, we'd like more information about the animal kingdom. What more can you tell us in this discussion?

You must first learn to respect these Beings before you can understand the reason for their presence on the planet. We are working with you to achieve alignment with the Mother in the same way that you are aligning with The Channel. We introduce this belief to our children and they have an understanding that you are capable of healing yourselves and therefore healing the Earth. You must release yourselves from the existence where you are destroying the light. This is what you must teach in Volume 3.

What specifically are you referring to when you say that we are destroying the light?

You are destroying the light when you control other Beings. You are using other Beings for what you believe is your enlightenment...when it is only for consumption and consumerism that will never be satisfied. You are never satisfied with what you have and therefore do not care about what you have and how you get it. You consume things when you should be respecting them. You have spoken about the plant world in this way and this is an important message.

Red Cloud, we'd like to ask you about plant medicine and about the use of psychotropic plant. We've spoken about it in Volume 2, as you know, but would like your perspective.

> The plant medicine and the sacred journey allow you to see the light and when you see the light…you are always able to see the light. It is about turning the light on. Once it is on, it is always on. These are experiences that need to happen once and one time only. Your endless consumption of what you call "psychotropic plant" is the result of you not being able to turn on the light. We are encouraging our people to turn on the light and see the reason why you are here with the other Beings.

What do your people believe is the reason that they're here on Earth?

> We do not believe that we are here to escape the Earth. You are here to heal the Earth and by healing the Earth you are releasing the light. By respecting the Earth you are learning to listen to the song and the sounds. You are calling it "vibration" and you are calling it "frequency". It is the song of Terra [Inner Earth] that will release us all and The Mother or The Channel will bring us homeward.

You're placing great emphasis on the sound that Terra makes.

> There are many beliefs about the Earth and about how we must take care of the Earth and no longer harm the Earth. But nobody is speaking about singing to the Earth and listening to the Earth. It is the sonic disturbance or sonic sea that you write about that is very important. The important things that we believe are that the songs and the sounds will once again be heard by our Mother. Only then will we see her once again and embrace her once again and be her once

again. You are speaking about how to hear yourselves. The Channel or what we call The Mother is a sound and a song. Turning on the light to see is also turning on the light to hear.

We've spoken about the Neuri as an example of how some Beings are here to protect the light. What more can you tell us about this?

We are working with you and many of the Indigenous people are working with you to heal the Earth. We are working with you to release the Earth from the lack of truth and nourishment. The nourishment is the respect. You no longer have the respect for the Earth and you speak about "climate change" and you speak about "saving the forests" and you speak about many things that you would like to keep intact on the Earth but you do not speak about respecting one another and this is where it all comes from. It all comes forth from respect. How can you heal the Earth if you do not respect one another? Respect for who you are is the beginning of the problem, but also the beginning of your solution.

What do you mean by that?

Man Being believes that you can repair and fix things on your planet Earth and by doing these activities you do not have to create a connection with the source of your light or your origin. There is no respect for the other Beings that you share your planet with and until there is the respect you will not be able to heal or fix the problems that you believe you have ultimately created.

You mention our origin. The Lakota people tell a myth about Inian, the Rock that was present at the very beginning. What can you tell us about this myth?

The Rock that you are speaking about, you have also crawled out from. The Rock is not the Earth as you see it today. The Rock is the original belief that you are tied to the world you know as Terra, but that we know as the experience with The Mother. This story about our origin is very similar to your beliefs. You do not see this because you believe that your origin is from another Being. Man Being believes that they come from other Beings and that you ultimately come from a God Being. We believe that you come from Terra.

The Indigenous cultures also speak of the stars and the constellations with great reverence. What can you tell us about how constellations are created and named?

We believe that the movement of the constellations represents what you believe as the movement of time. It also represents how many of us have gone before and how many of us are coming again. The constellations are created by experiences you are calling "ascension" and we are calling the "cycle of life"…but the cycle of life is ascension. Constellations are created by the Beings who have gone before. We tell these stories in a similar way to your mythologies and your parables, as this is a nice way to share the information with our people.

Why do constellations take these forms, or why do we assume that they are representing these forms – for example a bull, a ram or a hunter?

The reason for the placement of the stars is connected to how you are using your tools of shape shifting. When you are changing your beliefs about how you can and will exist, there is a light trail that is left behind. There is a light trail when you make the ascension journey or make the shape shifting experience. The constellations do change their shape. They are not a permanent configuration. The animal constellations as an example are a passage or the rite of passage of learning about which gateways are accessible. The bull for example, as you have learned from some of your ancient histories and mysteries…has created an animal in the Earth experience. Constellations are created in a way that is fashioned, as you would say, by the trail of light.

Are you saying that when we shape shift and ascend that we are leaving trails of light, which then become star patterns or constellations?

There are Beings that have left and left light to continue shining on your Earth existence, as you are not in contact with the real light source. The stars or the luminaries provide a light source that is not effective but is enough to sustain you. The configuration of the constellations was initially just a random event but you have subscribed to the understanding about their form. You have subscribed to the belief that Beings departed and left light for you to light your way. It is your belief in a bull shape or what you interpreted as a bull shape that has created an animal on the planet.

I'm not sure our readers will fully grasp that idea.

When Beings have ascended and left their light trail or luminary or luminescence for the benefit of the Beings on Earth, they have created random shapes and configurations. It is the prayer and praying to these luminaries that is creating a belief pattern and this belief has created the animals that exist on your planet. You now understand that prayer and believing is a creative tool. Many of you believed and still believe that Beings of magical powers have created light in the sky. You believed that they left a legacy of light in a constellation pattern. Your praying to the luminaries has brought these shapes to life.

We have named one constellation "Orion", as in the hunter. What did that create on Earth?

> This constellation as you like to call it has created all the problems and trouble that you are living with on your planet. When you believe and you are praying and respecting things, you are actually giving them life. You must be careful as to what you believe is your "God", as you are creating Gods on a regular and daily basis. There is no stop to the madness of what man has done on the planet. You are believing so many different things and creating belief systems and creating madness. You have all forgotten that you must release the Earth from this painful state. You are running around creating beliefs when you must simply remember the creation of the light that brought you here. It is not the sky that has brought you here. You have brought yourself here ultimately. The Mother and the light is the reason why you are able to correct the ways that has been the destruction of all of you.

Are Indigenous people like your own descendants of the first Beings to inhabit this planet?

> We are not the first Beings here but we have had fewer reincarnation experiences and you must remember this. We do not have the same lifespan that you experience. We have had fewer reincarnation experiences. We do not live the same age that you experience. Our "time" is much different from what you know as your time.

Are you living for hundreds of years or are you simply shape shifting and existing in a sort of permanency here?

> You may call our "years" the same length as yours but our experience of a year is longer than what you experience as we do not treat time and light in the same way that you treat it. Our knowledge about plant

medicine and the sacred understanding that we are connected with the Real Earth or Terra is giving us a longevity or a longer experience. Since we have not come back so many times as many of you have, we have fewer reconnections to make. We are basically connected when we arrive. We are cleaning up the misunderstandings and being truthful to our cause and our desire to be with the light. We are here to help others. Those who are trying to repair and help others are Sirius Beings.

We've yet to learn about those who are not of Sirius origin.

If you are on the planet and you are trying to have a better life for not only yourself but also the other Beings you share the planet with...then you are one and the same. I understand that you are believing there are many different Beings with different origins that you are sharing the planet with. This is not the truth.

What is the truth?

You are sharing the planet with Beings who have the Sirius alliance or origin. There are of course the other worlds that many of you do not see or even believe that you are interacting or connected with. This is the world occupied by those Beings you are calling DRA. This is the world that is revealing the truth about your origin. It is this world that must be healed and it is this part of the Earth problem that must be corrected. You are focusing all of your energy about the surface of the Earth and what you see. This is the truth. You do not care about the things that you do not see but they are there with you and this is the work that must be completed, for if you wish to respect the Mother and Mother Earth, you also must respect those other worlds where the DRA Beings are trapped and also need healing.

Are you protected from DRA? Do you see these Beings?

> We are allowed to communicate with these Beings. We are not instructed against communication. We understand that they are the Beings that need the healing and this is part of the Earth healing that you are part of. When you are calling this "The Repair Project" remember that you are dealing with the Earth. You are dealing with releasing the truth and releasing the belief and the truth about the light. You are also speaking about the other worlds that you share your planet with. The healing and the light are for these Beings as well. They will be helped when the Earth is healed. There will be help for them as well. We do not believe that they are left behind.

There's much to heal here. This is a very sick planet.

> The light is what the planet you are standing on is about. It is the light that defines you. You are focusing on things that you eat and make and need and buy and you also kill and destroy. You do not focus on bringing more light and seeing more light and when you start to make these simple truths a reality you will be healed.

Red Cloud, we've been speaking with Artists and when you appeared today, Marlon Brando immediately came to mind. He famously defended the rights of your community and was passionately involved in bringing awareness to the mistreatment of Indigenous people. Do you communicate with Marlon and is he aware of our project?

> This Being Marlon…we have had many talks with and he has called upon us many times. He has spoken with us and continues to speak with us. He is very involved in bringing the truth. His understanding about your work is the understanding that many of us have…that you are attempting to share the truth about the Earth

and also about what you call the "Causeway" or the "Cosmic Way". This is a very exciting experience that Marlon will wish to speak to you about. What you are doing is the work of The Healer and Helper and so we are here to assist you, if you wish to hear from us. We will help guide you. There are many who are aware of the writings that you are doing and the belief that you want to once again remind Man that the light is available. You just need to see.

Where are you existing right now, Red Cloud?

I am in a place where the Lemuria state exists. I am able not only to "time travel", as you like to call it, but I am able to embrace many connections and communicate with many Beings at one time. You can call this a "logos". We call this "speak". I am able to speak and when you speak you speak to all. You are not speaking to just one. This talk and this conversation is heard by those who need to hear and those who need to receive the truth. This is not a private dialogue or a private communication. Those that need to share and participate are able to hear.

What can you tell us about the Lemuria state?

The Lemuria state is the light state. It is the amount of light that you can communicate with and exist in. You are not existing in this much light because you have not completed your reassembly in the Lyra light place. This is not impossible, as you will finish your work sooner than you both believe.

Nika told us that we should be time traveling while assembling the books...is that what you're saying?

This is a truth. You are able to do your time travel. If you agree that you want more light then you will make more light. When you are in the 3rd density you are experiencing the 3rd density, so you do not believe that you can time travel. When you believe that you can time travel then you will time travel.

This brings to mind the story of The Wizard of Oz. In the movie, Dorothy clicks her heels and says, "There's no place like home" and she returns home.

Dorothy is speaking the truth.

Time travel requires wholehearted belief.

You are not in the 3rd density…you just believe that you are. You are not anywhere. You are everywhere.

Thank you, Red Cloud.

Please continue your healing. Others will follow.

GENE

"Maybe you're a slave to the Sun and maybe the Moon is a bit closer to what you're getting in Lyra. Maybe it's a bit closer to the real light. Maybe you need to look less at the sunlight and deal more with the moonlight."

Chicago Soul Singer
Grammy Award Winner
1940 - 2005

Dramos is tuning into somebody who wants to speak about the Chi-Lites. They're cracking jokes about one of the band members.

Are you one of the Chi-Lites as in the 1970s R&B/Soul quartet from Chicago?

For the Record.

Can you please identify who you are?

I just did.

Ah, okay. Gene. Welcome. Is there something in particular that you'd like to talk to us about?

Definitely...but you've got to know that I'm not speaking from Lyra. For you guys...Lyra is like this "Open Mic" you've got going on and that's cool. But Lyra is not a place where you are "seen". Lyra is how you can fill up on light. It's like filling up the car...it's like filling up on light. I just want to make that clear because we don't "hang out in Lyra". But Lyra is the light. The light's good and light's the way that you make the sound. There's a sound and that's how we write our songs and that's how we sing our songs and that's how we communicate our songs. That light. It's a sound and it's a frequency. That energy...that's the light. That's the sound you want to hear and that's what you want to bring when you're communicating and creating...you want to bring that sound.

The readers should know that you're speaking in a smooth and relaxed manner. It's a great energy.

It's a nice way to communicate, isn't it? I've got the light in me...that's what you're getting "in Lyra". Lyra is the light but it's the sound that you want to communicate. You fill up with that sound. It's a frequency. That's what you're writing about. That's what you're communicating about. It's a language. It's a language of light. But you know this because you're making your books and your books are filled with light. Filled with light like our songs are filled with light. Art is filled with light and you have to fill things with light, otherwise you're not going to be able to hear it. Art and music and all of that...that's light and light is life and that's good. Light and love, it's all the same thing, you know. Life and light and love...it's all the same. It works all the same. What do you want to ask me about? I just heard about this "Open Mic" and we're always ready to sing and share the light and share the music. What do you guys want to write about in Volume 3?

You say that Lyra is where you "fill up on light". Flo said that when she encountered The Channel, that it was like standing in front of a fountain and getting wet with light. Is Lyra something you fill up on once or do you keep going back – or is it something that you're always connected to?

Once you're connecting with this light and you're connecting with this signal, then it keeps flowing and you just keep creating. You keep sharing that. You have to share and that's the thing. You can't just keep filling up on light and that energy. You have to share that. That's got to flow. When that flows that's the sound and the music and the art and the love and the light. Do you know what I'm saying?

Is The Channel part of Lyra?

That's the way to get to Lyra. Lyra is getting light. You're speaking about Lyra like it's a place and you're speaking about Lyra like there's a lot of Beings there. But it's not like that. You have to "be in Lyra", for sure man. You have to "be in Lyra" like you can "be in love" and like you can "be in light"…like you can just "be".

Lyra is not a place. What does Flo mean when she says that some of us are "waiting in Lyra" – if Lyra is simply a frequency?

> She's trying to tell you that some of us are waiting for the rest of their group to arrive. She's not waiting in a "place" called Lyra. Flo is enjoying the light in many "places", man. She's just waiting for her group to come home before that final gateway gets unlocked. You heard about the 13th gateway. That's the one. When the whole team arrives, that door is unlocked. Now that's a whole other discussion, you'll see.

Basically, all of our incarnations have to "get with Lyra" so that we can have full access to the Inner Earth and beyond.

> That's right, man. You have to "get with Lyra", if you know what I mean. This Channel, this thing, it's you getting with Lyra…getting with the light…getting with the love…getting with the light source. When you can make music, you are making a connection with the light. When you can create and you can be artistic and you can be free with your words and ideas and colors and all of that, then you're getting with Lyra – you've got Lyra.

We're tapping into Lyra.

> You're tapping into Lyra because you're running the tap. It's a tap. You've got the tap on. The tap is always open. It's like a tap. You've got it open. You're tapped in. When you're tapped in it's the same thing…you've got the Lyra…you've got it.

Is it accurate to say that if you're on the Earth plane being an Artist then you're on your last incarnation?

Yes! That's truth. That's for sure. Artists are tapped in and Artists are getting the light and this is their final performance...this is it. It's their last show. But it's not their last show in light...it's just their last show on Earth. So yes...you've got to make it your last show on the Earth plane and then that's it...you're done. It's like you're making your last record or your last song...and it's not a sad thing but once you've got your light on...you just have to go with it.

Artists are beacons then...they're showing us the New World through their art.

Artists are free and open. That Channel, that thing you're writing about in your book...that's you being you. That's you just being free. Now you're open and you're open to that channel of light and you're open to that love. That light and that source are endless. So when you speak about being "prolific" and you're writing and you're singing and you're painting and you're dancing and you're doing all of that...that's endless...that doesn't end. Once that thing starts there's just no end to that.

That would mean that we are all Artists once we leave the Earth plane – right?

Once you've got the Lyra you always have it. You're always going to be creating so yes...you're not just an Artist on the Earth plane...you're always an Artist. Once you get with the art and you do what you have to do...that's it. That's why you're saying that Artists are on the front lines...I heard about that...I heard you're saying that and that's true. That's true...that's truth. Once you're on the front line you're always on the front line. You got the light on, you're facing the light and you're dealing with it.

We've created a whole culture of denial on Earth. We deny that anything exists beyond our physical realm. We're refusing to "face the light".

> You were talking about that Medusa story and how they didn't want to look at her. They're telling that lie…that when you look at her you "turn to stone" and you're immobilized and you can't do anything. That's a bunch of shit. That's not the truth. When you look at the light that's it! You're on the front line. Artists are on the front lines of looking at the light. They're looking at the light…finally looking at the light and finally getting the light on. When you finally see the light…wow…that's it man and then you're always an Artist. Once an Artist, always an Artist.

Some readers might say "but I have no talents and no interest in art".

> Ha! It's not true. You just haven't turned the tap on. But most of you sing in the shower or in the car don't you? Most of you like to hear a little music in the background wherever you are. In the elevator, while you're working, makin' love…we hear you. We're hearing you sing in private, in "your head". Now, singing and music…that's what you call an "organic" art form. You're working with the sound and vibration. There's many ways to do it, there's many ways to work with it. Why doesn't everybody just work with it? You just have to work it. Work with the light. Work with the sound. Everybody can make a sound and everybody's in a band man, ultimately. We're all in a band.

People might misinterpret what you're saying there, that we can all sing. You don't mean that literally, do you?

> You may not all "have the vocals" to be a singer, but I'm not talking about that kind of singing. I'm talking

78

about feeling the vibrations and just finding your song…your creative channel. You're doing it with books and those books man…they're talking about it. Why don't you write some music and songs for your books? That would be nice. Do you want some help with that, would you like some songs for your books?

Eventually. We want to bring this information to people through many art forms. It's great that you're offering to help. Thank you.

I think it would be nice to write a song…write some lyrics that could be sung, that would be great.

What would you title the song?

"Go to the Light". That's a good song…Go to the Light. That's a nice song title…I like that. I'd write a song about that. Go to the light…look at the light.

Why have we strayed so far from the light? The last time most of us remember "playing" and being truly happy was in our early childhood, and even then we can't remember most of those years. Those memories are shrouded in darkness.

Is it dark or were you somewhere else? Sounds to me like you were all connecting with another place as kids…and that place is where you should be. You were actually still able to time travel and you were able to hold on to what you know and where you should be. Maybe you just don't remember where you were because you can no longer get there or you forgot how to get there. Maybe you were there and you forgot. Did you ever think about it that way?

That's incredibly insightful.

I think when you speak about "you can't remember those first 4 or 5 years", as you're describing it to me…well maybe you forgot how to remember. It's not that you can't remember. Sure you can remember. You just don't know where to go anymore. You just turned off the light. That's what I would say. Maybe you just turned off the light, man. Don't you think kids have the light? They got the light.

They sure do. Schoolteachers will often say that kids "act up" when there's a full Moon. Maybe this is a good segue for a discussion about the Moon.

Now that light's an interesting light. Where did that light come from? You know that we create the luminaries and we create light…we generate light. That moonlight is more like the light that you're getting in Lyra. That's closer to the light that represents what you're really getting in Lyra. That light is closer to what you need.

Closer to what we need than the sunlight?

The Sun…you know you think the Sun feels good and the Sun is doing everything…but what is it really doing? It may make you feel good but is it freeing you? Think about that. You're told that it's doing a lot and doing good but maybe you're a slave to the Sun. Have you ever thought about it like that or looked at it like that or felt that? Maybe you're a slave to the Sun and maybe the Moon is a bit closer to what you're getting in Lyra. Maybe it's a bit closer to the real light. Maybe you need to look less at the sunlight and deal more with the moonlight. Don't worry, you'll get better explanations about these luminaries. I'm not really your guy for this.

We're a bit *Sun-obsessed* here on Earth but we wonder what it's really doing.

I think it feels great like everything else in the 3rd density that's keeping you down. A lot of the stuff that you're feeling is really good for you…is really actually quite bad for you, man. You've all got to look at it in a different way. A lot of the stuff on Earth feels good…oh a lot feels good…but what is it doing for you? You need to ask yourselves these things. If you believe that you are the light and that you generate light, then what is the Sun *really* doing for you? YOU are the Sun. You don't need the Sun.

Another gem.

The Sun, man…this Sun is created by you on Earth and you're worshipping the Sun like it's a god. I mean god is light and when you can make your own light well then you're going to be thinking about "God" a little bit differently, aren't you? But I'm not here to tell you what to believe, I'm just here to tell you that the moonlight is a little bit closer to what you need to be getting.

We understand that this isn't your area of expertise, but are you suggesting that Humans created the Sun and the Moon to replace what they're missing?

Not quite, but you're getting closer to the truth of it. You're going to have a real cool explanation from someone else…someone I think you'll both love. That Sun is not going to last forever. They're speaking about how the Sun's dying, right? "Oh we're running out of the Sun…the Sun's not going to be here forever". No, it's not. It certainly is not and why is that? You're creating the luminaries out of your *belief* in the luminaries. Once you start believing in your own light and your ability to generate your own light…what do you think happens to that Sun? Gone.

What makes moonlight closer to the Lyra light?

The Moon is more of a reflection and it is a different kind of belief. The Moon is more like a mirror or a reflection. It is less about you worshipping it. Moonlight is closer to the energy and frequency that you're going to be creating. You have to know this. You'll soon figure it out...you'll see it. They don't want you to have that moonlight. That's why they've been messing with the Moon...trying to turn that thing down and switch it off.

You're saying that the Moon is a signal, basically.

Yes, exactly. That is there as a signal for you to recognize. There are a lot of luminaries that are making a signal that you can tap into. You see, when you tap into this light, when you turn on the tap...the tap stays on. It's always on. That's why you like those fountains right...they're always on. The Artist has figured out how to turn on that tap. When you figure out how to turn on that tap...that's it...that's you. You've turned on the tap...you are the tap. You're turning on the tap. That thing...that Channel...that's the tap.

This has been an enjoyable conversation...is there one last message you want to share with the Reader before we end it?

You know...it's important that you just sing your song. Be yourself...you've got to be your *real self* and your real self is a Being who loves the light, man. You've got to be yourself enlightened. You've got to be yourself as someone who just wants the light. You've got to be singing about that light and writing about that light and painting about that light and dancing about that light. If you've got the light then you've got the love and you've also got the ability to create. Everybody wants to be creative. Most of you want to sing...all of you want to sing. Everybody's wishing they could sing. The world needs more music and when there's more music and the right music, then you're all going to be good. You're all just going to free yourselves. Wouldn't it be nice if you were all singing and you didn't have to work nine-to-five and all of that? We're all in a band together, ultimately. It's one big band man…it's one big band.

Nika recommended that we watch a Twilight Zone episode and the Lyra Beings recommended that we listen to 'Round Midnight. Do you have any recommendations for the readers?

Well, keep listening to all that Jazz and maybe add some Rumba. I like that Rumba. Why don't you listen to some of that? You guys should also know that Marlon Brando is hearing all of this. He's heard you talking about him.

Does he want to speak with us?

Oh…he will. He's in everybody's business. He'll call you, that's for sure. That's one thing I know for sure. That Being is calling you. He's calling everybody. That Marlon knows everything. He'll call you…you'll see. Maybe not for this Volume, but he will. When you least expect it.

We're looking forward to it. Gene, thank you for spending some energy with us and participating in the Open Mic.

My pleasure guys.

JOSEPHINE BAKER

"This World is a World where you not only see color, but you speak in color and you also sing in color. Colors not only make a sound...they make shapes and you can create things."

Entertainer
Singer, Dancer, Activist, Spy
Awarded the Croix de Guerre and Legion of Honor
1906 - 1975

We have felt the faint presence of someone else on our "Open Mic stage" during previous conversations. Today, we've asked the Being if they would like to speak with us.

What is your name please?

I'm Josephine Baker.

Wow. Josephine Baker. We're honored that you want to participate in Volume 3.

Well I'm honored to be here and I'm honored to speak with you both. I've heard many things about this project and I thought it would be a wonderful way to reintroduce myself. There's been a lot of activity going on in the Earth plane and a lot of activity with respect to things like climate change and the ongoing fight.

It's not an easy place to exist in. Is that what you'd like to talk to us about today?

Yes, it's one of many things. The first thing I want to say is that there's a reason why we offer music in times of hardship and we offer dance and we offer theater. It's not just a way to take your mind off of the terrible things that are going on but it's also a way to send messages of healing and support. It's a way to bring light to everybody's lives and I really enjoyed being a part of that and I'm still very much a part of that. We don't lose that ability or lose that drive or lose that interest in healing. Especially with music and dance and theater. That never stops and there's always an audience for that. There's always something going on where you can lend a hand and where you can get involved. So I wanted to get involved and I want to say to you both…thank you for what you're doing and for what you're organizing. There are many of us that would like to speak and say a few words and maybe straighten out some misunderstandings about what you do when you are no longer on Earth. Many of you feel that it's the end.

That's somewhat true, otherwise we wouldn't fear death the way we do.

Yes, of course. Many of you believe that when you "die" you no longer have anything to contribute and you no longer have anything to sing about. That's just not the truth of the matter. I'm just as "busy" as I was on Earth and what I am spending a lot of energy doing is reaching out to others and I have been involved and I am involved in many projects that are going on in the Earth plane. There are activities that are involving children who don't have much privilege and they need some guidance and role model-ship. There are activities and projects and dance and theater and music and some private funding that's being created for that...and that's wonderful. We need more of that.

It's odd to hear an ascended Being talk about "private funding". But looking at your bio it's clear to see that you were heavily involved with helping children.

It's a real shame that they're taking away the arts and the arts programs and the extra curricular activities for children. That's something that's so important. It keeps you all together and it keeps you all united and it keeps you expressing the need to speak out against all the terrible things that are going on. It's a real shame that the arts are just not "as important"...or if they are they certainly are not spending any money on it. But that's a whole other consideration. I am working with some young performers, up and coming and one in particular who you will be hearing about soon I hope. Her name is Jeanette and you will know about her and she's something. She's something, that's for sure. We can chat about her later. I also want to make it clear that I do know some of the Beings that have spoken with you and I know that you have been speaking with the Chi-Lites...you've been speaking with Gene and he's a lovely...lovely Being.

He definitely is, we loved his energy. Josephine, you had such an extraordinary lifetime as an entertainer and philanthropist. Readers might be curious to know how you spend your energy beyond the Earth plane.

I am a communicator much like you two are. How am I spending my energy or how am I spending my "time", as you would say on the Earth plane. I am actually functioning, in many ways, as an arbitrator and a mediator. I know that sounds strange but the truth of the matter is that there is a lot going on in terms of us having access and being able to freely travel and explore different worlds. There are some access ways and you might call them gateways and portals and fair enough...there are some access ways that we don't always have the access to. I have been conducting communication or talks as you would describe it, in trying to get these things cleared up and get these misunderstandings cleared up. There are many portals that you can move in and out of, especially from the Earth plane. There are a lot of openings but some of these openings are not going to a place where you can continue your travel. You must be careful about what you are trying to use for your own time travel experience.

What's the best way to avert these obstructions?

The best way is to release your light. You've already learned a little about that and you're calling that "The Channel" and I believe that Gene has been calling it "the tap". When you release your light you have keys and you have the ability to go through other portals. Now there is a nice World that you will definitely be experiencing if you haven't already. Now, I wonder about that…I'm sure you've been there. Maybe in your dreams, for now. But this World is a World where you not only see color but you speak in color and you also sing in color and colors not only make a sound…they make shapes and you can create things.

The things that we "create" outside of the Earth plane, do they last – are there any constants in other densities of light?

These things you create don't last forever. They just sort of break apart and they just fall apart or dissipate. But it is a wonderful "land". I would describe it as a kaleidoscope. You have many designs and images and colors and sounds and beautiful things to look at and it is a World of great beauty. So if you ask me how I would spend my energy in a place like this…well…how would you spend your energy looking at a kaleidoscope? Many of you are taking drugs to try to get into that space, but there's a World like that…that is in fact very useful. In this world you can create things and maybe they don't last forever…but you can actually send your creations as a message.

How so?

You can send a belief to other Beings. You can send your creations to different places, sort of like a letter. So if you've created a beautiful kaleidoscopic flower for instance, you can send that through a belief…you can send that energy to another place and space. It's wonderful. Don't you know that this is where visual artists are getting a lot of their information?

Is this "World of Creation" that you're describing…is it the World that we immediately transition to in the "Afterlife"?

Yes but only if you "go to the light", as you like to say. What I'm describing is the 5th density of light. This is a "place" or a World where you learn how to play with your light. It's a place where you relearn how to create things from your beliefs. I say relearn because well…you guys have all forgotten.

The 5th density is the World of Creativity and you're saying that this is what some 3rd density Artists are tapping into?

That's right and I believe that you have been there. You have heard about it and certainly this is a place where you create stories. Lots of wonderful things come out of this place. There is a wonderful story that many of you know about on Earth…I'm not going to mention the title now because I'm going to let the Being who wrote the story step up to the "Open Mic" and tell you about this. This popular children's story has been written from the experience and travel to this World. The Author had tapped into this World and shared it in a children's story. It's quite something.

This is fascinating. What more can you tell us about the nature of this 5th density World?

There is an understanding that you've written about. You've written about the "Lemuria state". There is an understanding that you are able to access that state and then that is the end…but that's not the truth of it. That is not the end. That's just the beginning. So if you can create that light and if you can communicate with that light and create the beautiful things that you're speaking about, well that's "Lemuria". That place is Lemuria. And the Lemuria state, well, it's also Lemuria. It's also a place. It's not a place on Earth like some land that got buried in the sea or some land that got buried in the sand over time. No. The Lemuria state is a place and a state of being. It's all the same once you move well beyond the Earth experience.

Lyra Beings spoke about the Lemuria state in Volume 1 and emphasized that the Lemuria state is where we learn about and experience time travel.

Yes, that's what I'm telling you both. You will encounter this World and state of being once you "cross over" and go to the light. Lemuria is the 5th density World of Creativity.

If we want to experience Lemuria just as the children's Author did, how do we do that? The Reader will wonder how they can access this World and state of being just as the Author did.

This is an interesting question and it should be quite easy for all of you. You all once had an active imagination, especially when you were youngsters. The one movie that comes to mind and I know you've been thinking of this too…is The Wizard of Oz. Remember how Dorothy clicks her shoes…that would be a way to get to this World. You just need a code or a key and that code or key you're going to get. When you get that code or key you just use it. It's not much more than that. This is not some Olympics or Awards Ceremony or some Mission Impossible. This is no effort that is requiring a strategy or some military intervention. This is a key and when you have the key and the code then you're just going to use it whenever you wish. What I like about this World is that you're welcome any time. You don't spend too much energy there and if you want to be there all the "time" then that is just fine. Nobody is going to tell you that you're "wasting your energy" and "you're wasting your time" and "you're wasting your life" and "what are you doing here just sitting around and imagining pretty things" and "go do something useful with your life" and "go build

91

something and go make some money and go contribute to the world". There's none of that here, I can assure you.

Is The Rose the key that you're referencing? ?

Now The Rose is a very good question and I'm glad that you're bringing this up. The Rose is a very important symbol and it is a very important key. Have you been using The Rose?

To be honest, we don't know how to answer that question. It's still somewhat of a foreign concept to us – that a flower is a key that opens up a portal.

There's many ways to use That Rose. You're communicating with me, so you have The Rose... there's no doubt about that. You must have that Rose or we wouldn't be communicating right now. There is a lot to that symbol. It is not enough for me to say, "Go to that door and use that key" and "Go to that door and speak to that Being at that door and they're going to let you in there if you just show them the symbol" and everything's going to be alright. "Just show them The Rose and they'll let you in". There's more to it. You're going to make some more realizations about that symbol but you're off to a great start. You're already communicating in this "Open Mic" project that you have created. You have The Rose...that Rose is everywhere. There are a lot of songs with the word Rose in it or the idea of The Rose.

We have in front of us some info about your rendition of "La Vie en Rose", a famous French song.

I used to sing that song and yes there is definitely a message in that song. It is not just about the aftermath of the war and a lost love and grieving for that and

92

rebuilding. The whole idea is not just about love. There's a lot more to that song and I love to sing that song. I love to listen to that song and that is a song that I would recommend if you want me to pick out a musical contribution for you. That's one that I would recommend.

Your singing was enchanting to say the least Josephine. We want to go back to the discussion about Jeanette...the young singer you're mentoring. Do you want us to publish her name?

Jeanette is a bit shy but certainly you can mention her name. I am not sure that I can get her to speak with you because she is still on the Earth plane, but I do recommend that you keep your ears open. She's going to reveal herself and her talents very soon.

How old is Jeanette?

She's still in her early teens.

Does she live in America or somewhere else in the world?

She's just outside the Chicago area.

Does she have anything on YouTube that we can listen to?

I'm not sure that she's published anything yet. She's a bit shy. I'm offering her a lot of inspiration and speaking with her. She is tuned into Lyra if you can believe this. A lot of these youngsters are doing that. It does not necessarily have to be an undertaking like the both of you have been through. Some are just automatically connecting with Lyra. It's wonderful.

To clarify, you mean that they're connecting unconsciously as an Artist. Is that correct?

Yes, unconsciously. But I am communicating with her and the communication goes something like the way that we are communicating right now. She is receiving it as her "Higher Self" or her "gut feeling" but I am communicating with her on a basis very much like the way that we are communicating now.

That would be quite a revelation for her to discover that Josephine Baker is mentoring her.

Oh I think she'd be quite surprised and I don't feel she'd deny it…she'd just be quite surprised.

At the beginning of this conversation you said that Beings would be stepping up to clear up misunderstandings. Are there any misunderstandings about your lifetime as Josephine Baker that you'd like to clear up? Do you want to bring our attention to any of your achievements?

I'd like to maybe speak about some of the things that I didn't achieve. I mean, certainly I had a full life in the 3rd density…that is for certain. I have no complaints there and I don't have any complaints about how people will think about me or feel about me, but there are a lot of projects that I would have liked to have been more involved with.

What type of projects?

I wanted to be more involved with animals and animal rights. I didn't do much of that at all when I was in the 3rd density and I have some regrets about that. I understand it now with my ascension journey that that is something that is very important…that we stop harming and killing these Beings. That's something that I would have liked to have been more actively involved with and I would have liked to completely change the way that I ate. I know that you have the understanding that if you're eating more plant based diet that that's a lot better for the light and it is certainly a lot better for creativity. I didn't follow that eating lifestyle and it's something that I would do if I had to come back…and I'm not coming back just so you know. No way. But it's something that I would adhere to and follow if I did.

Going back to the discussion about Lemuria or what we're calling the World of Creativity, is that what Lyra Beings have been calling "The World to Come"?

Well, the "World to Come" is what you're going to make of your journey and the World to Come is the World where there's no obstruction and there's no war and there is none of that bad stuff that you are dealing with on the Earth plane. There is a shift in your belief system in that you are prioritizing light and of course prioritizing love…because that goes along with the light – it's a pathway almost. It's a freeway…it's a causeway and a causeway that is completely unobstructed. There will no longer be a need for a "code" and all these "symbols" to move around. You've got these codes, symbols and keys right now that are unlocking doors because it's not completely open and free out there.

It's not free of obstruction at the moment – is that because of the DRA situation?

Yes, that's right. Of course. Eventually it will just all be a free ride and open. We won't need to go through this "ascension program" where you have to "reconnect" and learn and unlearn and rewire and all these things that you're doing now. It's a tremendous amount of work, I know. I want to congratulate you both for what you're doing. It's not something that most Human Beings are going to even bother with.

You lived quite a life Josephine...the standard you've set for Human Beings is remarkably high, most would say. You did so many things it almost seems fictionalized.

> Everybody is feeling that they can only do one or two things with their lives and that's just not true. I mean you can do everything if you want to. Now some people would say, "Oh that's not fair this person is not well" or "This person is not capable" or "This person's imprisoned" or "This person is having such hardship" and I know what you're saying and I would agree with that. But if you are free in the Earth plane to proceed and make a difference, not only in your life but also in everybody else's LIGHT, then there really is no reason why you can't do that. A little bit of this and a little bit of that...why not?

Some readers would say our world today is different to the world that Josephine came up in. Globalization and the Internet have made Earth a very competitive place.

> That's for sure with the Internet...you're learning a little bit too much, I believe. I don't know if I would call it *learning* but you're certainly spending a lot of your energy doing that. If you can be doing all of that, well, you can actually be teaching yourself all of that. Why aren't you all teaching yourselves something good with that Internet? I would say get out there and do as much as you can. Be creative and get involved with the arts.

Is there nothing as important as the arts? Surely there are other activities and projects and disciplines that can help heal the world.

> Art is the most important thing you're going to be experiencing in your lifetime on Earth...and I'm not saying that having kids is not important and I'm not saying that going to school is not important and I'm not

saying that studying this and that is not important. That's not what I'm saying, but what I am saying is that everyone has to have the chance to do a little bit of art, a little bit of creating. You don't have to be a paid Singer or Dancer or a paid Artist or working in the theater production, like on the stage. You don't have to be doing that. But if everybody does a little bit of art then the world would be a much better place, a much safer place and a much more *together* place.

We've been hearing about singing and sound. What can you tell us about the art of Dance?

Well you know that dance is like sound and like light and like movement. What's happening when you dance? Well, you're moving with the light. You're moving with the sound. When you dance you're learning how to move without movement in your form. You're learning how to move the light. It's sort of a dress rehearsal for the disconnect in a way. You're learning about how it feels to be a free Light Body. That nice feeling when you're moving around and moving to the music and it feels good, that is how it feels when you are traveling in a released Light Body state. It feels that good and it feels that free. Sometimes it feels like there's choreography and I will say this: there is a correct movement to get through some of those portals and some of those openings. When you're moving in and out of form, well, that's something. That "shape-shifting"…that's like dancing. That's like dancing in the light. You're dancing and you're transforming. If you watch certain Dancers you will see and you will witness and you will experience a change in form.

Are you talking about how Dancers contort their bodies for certain movements?

I'm not talking about moving the legs and moving the arms and making a posture and making a kick, for example. I'm asking you to follow the light and just feel it and go with it and you'll see what I mean. The Dancer is feeling it. They are feeling what it feels like to shift the form and to move the light. There is a real purpose to dance and the physical movement...it is very important. It may not always look like art. There's a lot of crazy dancing that I used to do and you might be wondering, "What is she doing", but that was me going for it. It's really about freeing the light and it's about being the light. Light moves like that, because light is happy. Light is not stuck in some body that is keeping you still and stiff. You're all walking around very stiff. Dance is losing that form because that form is very stiff. It doesn't quite look like we're meant to move around like that, does it?

We've been told that Jazz is an example of the sound that we experience during time travel. Is there a particular genre of dance that's closest to the movement while we're shape shifting?

It's all dance, really. For me I like the freeform, especially. I like what you would call modern dance interpretation. Just a freeform interpretation, that's my preference. That may not be your preference. Even the dancing that may be a little more strict in their movements like the ballet...it's still good practice for moving with the light. I feel that all dance forms are a dress rehearsal in releasing the light. You've been watching the videos on the "fractal movement". That motion is the dance. That is a dance of the light and the shapes. We are made up of shapes and light. As you are more in touch with Lyra and building your Light Body, well, then you are going to get more fluid. Even if you can't physically move in your form on the Earth plane, your light's still able to move and you are still able to dance. Maybe your form is not flailing around like some of us are doing but that light is able to dance. That light dances. Your Light Body...you in light can dance.

Josephine, we'd like to pick your brain on a separate topic altogether. Can you shed some light on the "Pleiades" mission? We're a bit confused on the star systems and how they work and the planets and different Beings.

Well what do you want to know, exactly?

We initially believed that "Pleiades" referred to Beings from a particular Star System but recently we've been told that Pleiades is more of an "art initiative".

Well, I know Pleiades. That's a type of light. You're speaking about light, the way an Artist in the Earth plane might speak about oil paint. They like this kind of oil paint. They like this kind of oil paint instead of that kind of oil paint. They like blue instead of red, do you know what I'm saying? That's a kind of light. You're picking your palette of light and therefore you're picking the sound that you want to make and that's a certain type of sound and therefore that's a certain type of art and performance. Now I know Pleiades and I've worked with that energy and that's lovely. You're going to learn a little bit more about that when you learn about Lemuria and how that works.

So is Sirius a type of light as well?

Sirius is a type of light and a type of sound and a synergy. When you work with a certain type of light and a sound and a synergy then you move a certain way. You move through portals and openings a certain way and you have access to what you're calling gateways or beliefs. It's about what's fuelling your adventures. You can have a little bit of Pleiades and you can certainly have a little bit of Sirius. You can have a little bit of everything if you like. You're speaking about an affinity for a kind of light and that affinity for a kind of light will mean that you communicate your beliefs in a certain way. Artists are in their final stage of the journey out of the Earth plane existence and they're working with a certain palette. It's a palette of light and sound and shapes. You might say in the Earth plane, "Well that's a species" or "That's a type of organism" but it's really a type of light. Light's not always exactly the same. I mean, light is light but there is a different way to process light and a different way to assemble and absorb light and you're learning quite a bit.

We've been working with an overwhelming amount of information.

I'm impressed with all the work that you've done in such a short "amount of time", as you guys like to say. I like to say "bandwidth" instead of time. But I really want to thank you for what you're doing. You're bringing a lot of difficult understandings and you're simplifying it and it's beautiful and a lot of people are going to benefit from this. You must know this.

Josephine, can we call out to Beings or do they simply "approach the mic" if they have a desire to speak with us?

It might be a little bit of both. We're all in the audience. Did you know that?

No, we don't understand what you mean by that.

Well, we're all here. I mean, we've received the invitation and the signal from you both and thank you very much for having me and many of us are just making our way to this place...you're calling it the Open Mic. You can give a "call out" or a "shout out". Me, I like to be a little more adventurous so I walked up to what you're calling "the stage" and not all of us are going to be as comfortable doing that. I mean not all of us are from the theater and some of us are a little more reclusive and are just going to sit quietly. So you can experiment but we're all here. There are many of us here. One Being that you'll be speaking with soon is the storywriter, the children's book writer. You'll learn about that. I'm not going to speak on behalf of him. He'll tell you his story.

Readers might be wondering why only Artists are connecting and why scientists and astrophysicists aren't showing up, for example.

Well that's not the work you're doing. Lemuria is a creative energy field. That's what you're helping others reconnect with.

Some readers have reported being visited by Artists in their dream state, like Steve McQueen and Bob Marley, for example. One Reader in particular noted that these Beings were relaying very detailed information about Earth and the Afterlife. Why are they choosing to show up in dreams and not the Open Mic?

Are you so certain that it's a different experience?

Well, it's a little more fluid this way.

One thing I'll say to you both is to consider the dream state from another perspective. Did you ever wonder...maybe you're in the audience? Maybe your readers were doing the "visiting". Maybe your readers visited Steve and Bob. That's what you should consider. You're all traveling a little. You just don't believe it yet. Well, some of your readers do. But most of you don't.

The readers are time traveling in their sleep – is that what you're saying?

Yes.

Before we end this conversation Josephine, do you have any advice for readers who are curious about the "crossing over" or "death tunnel" experience – to help quell their fears?

> Well the first thing I'll say is that I've had more than one near death experience, so I was fairly prepared for the experience myself. So the understanding that I would be experiencing light...I was already prepared for that and that did happen. I already believed that we have many incarnations that we live out on the Earth plane and that the whole point of everything is to stop that cycle and to learn how to be Immortals and time travel. I already accepted all of that.

Did you read something while you were alive to help you form those beliefs?

> No. It was just something that I felt very strongly about so I was prepared for the light and I was also wondering a bit. I wondered about the fact that I was living such a full life and if this was in fact my final incarnation. So I was trying to do as much as I could. When I finally checked out or disconnected...there was that experience of the tunnel and the light. I didn't expect to see so much of me but there they were, all the Beings that I have been. Every one of them. I knew that they were me and I knew that they were there to meet me and I was aware that these Beings were there to guide me. What I immediately connected with was that colorful experience you're calling The Channel. That electricity...the light...it was absolutely fantastic that I had learned how to create that with all of my selves. That took a long time.

We create our own Channel, is that right?

Yes, of course. It's a long time in the making. Once you've finally made the journey and see this, you can just walk right up to it. You know instantly that you have created it. You realize that this is now lighting your way. Beyond that experience everything was just open. It was open like being in outer space but sort of being in a vehicle or a spaceship. I had the sense that I was actually in some sort of clear sphere, if I could describe it to you that way....and of course The Rose is a key. That symbol, that 13-petal symbol is the key to the understanding that the portal that you must travel through is waiting for you.

Once you saw The Channel you were able to pass through the door or gateway.

Yes and I went through that in a sphere. It was like a ship and that is how I started my journey. I know how that sounds...a little bit like a movie of the week. I know. But that's the best way that I could describe it. That ship, that spaceship is there waiting for you and that ship is not a machine or like an airplane or what you're calling a "UFO". That is made out of a material that you create in Lyra and when you go through Lyra it is there. It's like a film that is enveloping you and this protects you...and you're on your way. There was no fear or anything. It felt automatic...that you just go to the light and you see yourselves and you see this connected electrical Channel. This Being is ultimately you.

We are The Channel. That's still a little strange to hear.

How can it not be from where you're standing? You've accomplished that "Channel", believe you me. You've completed that and that does not go away. It does not disappear.

What does it do once we confront it?

> It's creating a synergy and an energy for other Beings when they make their ascension. It's important that we all create that. That's going to create such a spark that the Earth will be released from its hard rock imprisonment and state of confinement. The petrified Earth, that's going to vanish. When more of you join us and just flow with the light, the Earth will be released and everyone will be making ascension whether they realize it or not…haha. I'm giggling but it's going to be a wonderful thing. I hope that you all learn a little about ascension dynamics because…wow…it's going to be quite something when the energy is released. It would be wise to learn a little bit about it!

Thank you Josephine. We appreciate you speaking with us today.

> Okay, well I'm going to go back in the audience!

GREGORY

"Many of us reach this World. It is an existence where you create whatever you wish to create and so in a way it's like being in a movie again. There are many scenes and many things being played out, all happy of course. There is no suffering in this place and yes many of you might consider it 'heavenly'…and I must say that it is."

American Actor
Academy Award Winner
Kennedy Center Honoree
1916 - 2003

A Being has been trying to connect with us for two days and he keeps saying that he is an "Illustrator". He's giving the impression that he is either shy or reluctant to speak with us.

Would you like to identify yourself for the readers, please?

> I am very well known. You know me in my extensive body of work for which I have received many awards. What I can say to you is if you believe in the work that you are doing…and I must say it is quite something…then you will believe this conversation with me is happening.

What was your field of expertise?

> I have done much work in Film. I have not stated my name because I do not wish to give too much importance to my previous incarnation, but I do understand that this is an interview and I do wish to explain to you where you go when "it is your time".

We appreciate your participation and would encourage you to introduce yourself.

> I am known as Greg or Gregory and I must tell you this…it may seem like a far fetched dream and a truth that you assemble as you have been, but it is not enough for your audience to admire your work. You must believe that if we are speaking then that is really something…and that *something* is what I want to speak about. You are both able to tell the world that there is a way to speak with us. We are not "dead". We have never been dead. We may be dead to you but we have not forgotten you and this is what I would like to speak to you about. Our conversation of course will not be in confidence. I understand you are collecting interviews with others and I have volunteered, although I did need to be pushed just a little bit for this meeting.

Why did you state that you are an Illustrator?

> I was being a little bit playful as that is not my true
> talent, although I am quite fond of art and painting.
> There is a reason why Dramos was reading about the
> film yesterday, "Roman Holiday", but not
> understanding why the urge to research it presented
> itself. Now tell me, what would you like to ask and how
> can I help you with your project? I don't want to
> mislead anybody but the fact remains that you can
> speak to many of us that are no longer with you. There
> is a way and you have found a way. What would you
> like to ask?

You're connecting with us in the persona of your most recent
incarnation, but you're obviously much more than "Gregory".
How long was your reincarnation cycle and how did you finally
exit that loop?

> The reincarnation stream is not a mandatory path and
> many of you don't seem to realize this truth. I learned
> about the options for the immortal state and the
> immortal state of being from the work that I was doing
> with a past life regressionist. I also had many encounters
> and experiences in my dream state and in what some of
> you might call "astral work" or "astral travel". These
> things I did not choose to publicize as I had a persona
> and I had a very strict belief that these things perhaps
> are best kept private and discussed only with those close
> to you. I have since changed this belief because I now
> understand that we all need help to return homeward.
> Many Actors do have a belief in the "Afterlife" as some
> are calling it, but also in the immortal state of being.
> This is not a foreign belief.

It wouldn't surprise anyone to know that Actors are flexible with
their beliefs.

Yes, this is true. Many of you believe that Actors are automatically interested in anything alternative but I don't believe this is the case either. Some of us are exposed to interesting beliefs and some of us, of course, meet very interesting people in our work. I must say however, that not many of us get as far as you both have gotten in your book writing adventure. There is a definite belief in Hollywood that many of us do return...and that we return to act. There are great superstitions that many people in Film believe in and that is understandable but I don't necessarily believe that the understanding about immortality is a general belief. Maybe it's a wish we all secretly have, but isn't it something...it actually is a possibility.

What did you learn from seeing a past life regression Therapist?

During my past life regression sessions I learned that I was a young Actor in the 1700s and that I was involved in a theater group. We purportedly, as I discovered in my sessions, performed for the King and this work was done mostly in what you would call now the London area. There is a legacy and a longstanding history of theater. I was given the name of John and the last name of a Smith or a Smythe. Not much more than that was described to me.

Was that all that you discovered in those sessions?

There was another lifetime that we revisited. In this other lifetime I was somebody of greater prominence, in an ancient theater setting. I was involved in theater as an Actor right after the time period of Jesus. In this particular time period it was approximately 120 AD that I was involved as a Roman and also in an activity that involved not only theater and performance but also as a fighter. I was involved specifically in a group that was hired by the Emperor to perform. What is curious that I learned in my sessions is that many of us did not of course live very long due to the activities…and that I was a favorite of the Emperor. This afforded me a more privileged life. The Emperor was of course, Hadrian. This again did not involve me winning Academy Awards and having great renown but I certainly had an interesting time I can assure you of that. So these are the two lifetimes that I was made aware of but nothing of tremendous renown, as I have experienced in my last incarnation.

Would you say that experiencing a past life regression helped you to prepare for death?

I would say yes, indeed. This is how I heard about possible "past life experience", as we did not have books like yours. I of course did not have a definitive proof of my previous lifetimes but I did find it particularly interesting…especially the Roman association, as you can imagine. These regression sessions did nurture the ideas I was considering already…about what would happen when my time was up. So yes, it was beneficial I would say.

Now that you've actually experienced what we call the "Afterlife", what can you tell us about the crossing over experience?

Now, I can only speak for myself and what I of course experienced. I can't speak on behalf of all of you. I know what I have come to know and I will describe this for you in as much detail as I can. When I made my crossing I experienced the light or the "tunnel" as many of you are referring to it. There were Beings…Beings that were light. They were Light Beings, much like you and I but in light. The light though, formed shapes. So if you can understand and follow me, this was not a Human Being greeting me. This was almost as though it was a hologram. A Being in light...an image holographic in quality. The quality that struck me most curious was the shapes. It was as though I was standing before a Human Being but in light and shapes.

Can you help us understand that with a bit more detail?

Yes...so where you have an arm you would see an arm but the arm is composed of many different shapes. The shapes are not necessarily the shapes that you might imagine you would see. The shapes are very intricate, like a sacred geometry and a multi-faceted or a multi-sided shape. This is what I'm speaking about. Now when you meet these other Beings, you understand that they are actually you...they're you. These Beings, they are there waiting for you. These Beings greeted me, but greeted me not like they were Angels or Helpers. I didn't feel at any moment that I would be greeted by some "angelic creature" and taken to "God's gates". I immediately had a sense or an understanding that I was basically surrounded by me, myself.

What happened after this initial greeting?

The Beings that I encountered were with me when I made my presentation and experienced what many of you are calling now The Channel. These Beings are congregating...and again these Beings are your various "selves". They are congregating and are associated with this Channel of light. That is where they're waiting for you and they're there to simply collect and experience the light. So, it is the light that is needed in order to build yourself and create a singular Being that is comprised of many versions of you. I have completed this experience and the other Beings, meaning me, have all united. I have made my journey through the Lyra "gate" and I am now spending much of my energy and

my light in a place where many Artists exist...and by
Artists I mean all of you.

Where is that?

> I believe that the others have already explained this
> World to you. Some call it "Lemuria" or "Lemuria
> state", but you can call it what you like. The "World of
> Creativity" I suppose is an appropriate name. Many of
> us reach this World. It is an existence where you create
> whatever you wish to create and so in a way it's like
> being in a movie again. There are many scenes and
> many things being played out, all happy of course.
> There is no suffering in this place and yes many of you
> might consider it "heavenly" and I must say that it is. It
> is a state of awareness and this awareness is not about
> being aware of where you are. It's about being aware of
> what you can do and who you can be. These worlds
> that everyone wants to know about, these worlds are
> available for all of us. You must collect your "selves" at
> the Lyra gate and proceed.

It sounds like a movie to those of us who haven't experienced it.
We usually only confront these ideas within a fictional context, as
you know.

> This will sound like a science fiction movie and there is
> no easy way to describe this experience so that your
> readers don't think that you're making up a story. It's a
> fine story don't get me wrong but you are certainly
> straddling a line between fiction and a non-fiction. How
> are you proposing to share this explanation?

Our understanding is that readers can absorb the information
whether or not they believe it to be true. So we've let go of the
need to be accepted as non-fiction.

If you want to explain some of these things to your readers you might consider reminding your readers that many of us "storytellers" have made the journey. Some of us were Beings that you not only idealized and were fans of but Beings that maybe explained a truth or shone a light for you while we were on Earth. The movies and films that became so important and integral to many of you in understanding many things about life could be a way to remind your readers that we helped to highlight the truth through fiction. So when an Actor or a celebrity that is highly regarded passes away it is more than just being sad that your favorite celebrity is no longer with you. Many of us in fact have purposely tried to share or as you say disseminate a message. I also did share more intimately, with those close to me, some of my beliefs and understandings.

That was a wonderful explanation. Our hope is that readers will gain a new appreciation for the arts and begin to explore it themselves.

Might I suggest something for those readers in particular? I think it would be a great start to simply document your dreams. My dreams I did like to sketch and draw and I kept a journal that was eventually passed around. It is being held right now by one of my contacts. I don't know what they're planning with it but perhaps it will be published.

Maybe that's why you jokingly introduced yourself as an Illustrator. Do you do any painting or illustrating in Lemuria?

I am enjoying very much the ability to paint with light…and I'll describe that experience. Painting with light, like finger painting but in the air and drawing the light from your Being. You're creating the light as you now understand but if you can imagine the light coming out of yourself as if your appendages are paintbrushes.

You can just create a rainbow of light and shapes and create a beautiful design and have that design just dissipate and disappear much like a bubble. It is like drawing something in the air with a laser pen, this sort of activity. I am able and I am enjoying drawing and painting with light. You might refer to my works as "mandalas" and you might refer to them as "kaleidoscopes" or "psychedelic patterns". These things I'm enjoying and this is a world where you can just decide to create something beautiful and visual...you *have* the talent. You create it with your wish. We are not here with easels and paintbrushes. It is a world of color and kaleidoscopes.

So we're traveling back to the 60s in the Afterlife.

Haha, yes. You know I must say it reminds me of everything that was described in the 60s with wonderful colors. I'm pleasantly surprised that this is the existence. It is a kaleidoscope of colors and shapes and designs that you create from your wishes. Now you might be asking yourselves what am I doing, am I sitting there just painting these psychedelic kaleidoscopic images? Is that how Gregory spends his "Afterlife"? The answer is no, but if you wish to do this endlessly there would be no one to stop you and nothing at all "wrong with it". Lemuria is a passageway, a gateway.

It's not always easy to process these descriptions using our Earth perspective. Existing outside of a money economy and not having to work is still a foreign concept to us.

This World is not like Earth. You don't set up a house and get a car and get a job. It's none of that. This is a place where there are beautiful colors and experiences, but I'm going to call Lemuria a gateway or an elevator. It's a passageway but you can spend as much "time" there as you wish. You can spend forever there. There's no problem if that's what you wish to do. I am traveling and experiencing time travel and in order to do the travel you move through this kaleidoscopic World that I am describing for you, which is Lemuria. There are not necessarily kaleidoscopic images all around you. These are things that can be generated. Other than that I would describe this as a beautiful clear sky and light and beautiful grass and beautiful colorful still images. Nothing exists there, really. It is completely barren other than sky and...I'll call it "land". The land is a very bright green...it looks like plant almost, like grass. The sky is very bright and clear, a vivid turquoise blue. So what you do is you step into the scene and you create whatever you wish. This place is a way for us to learn about time travel.

How is this a way to learn about time travel?

This is training in that we create what we wish to experience and by creating what you wish to experience then you are creating the tool. You are rehearsing for the time travel experience. You must of course believe in time travel in order to do it. Some of us are coming into Lemuria and not having a clear understanding or complete belief about time travel...so we spend our energy practicing and playing. It's a place to play and this is a place where children would feel most comfortable. It is a place of make-believe. What you believe in creates an experience that you can learn how to travel to or through. You can create other worlds in this place as well and so that is why it is very much like a gateway or a wishing well. That would be a nice way to describe it – a wishing well.

You said that you are time traveling. What other worlds have you experienced and what other revelations have you had?

Well, I will say this…and I understand that some of you will be staring at the floor and may be a bit nervous about this information…but there are other Beings in existence. These Beings are not Human Beings. You are calling them "Extraterrestrial" or "Aliens". Now, these are Beings who exist. What are these Beings? That is what I first asked myself, because if they are Extraterrestrial…why in fact am I engaging with them in a way that makes me believe that they are one of us? What struck me as unusual was that these Beings seemed to be waiting for me, waiting for us to visit their World. Now when I say "their World" I'm not speaking about another planet, although that is an option for all of you. Planets are created by your experiences and beliefs. This is something that you are still learning about. I have met Beings and these Beings are actually originally Human Beings but they have been spending much energy and activity outside of Earth. They have been traveling around and they have an unusual form that resembles a Human Being but is clearly what you would call Extraterrestrial or Alien.

Are you telling us that Extraterrestrials are Human Beings but in an evolved state?

What I learned when I engaged with these Beings is that they have been for a very long "time", trying to exit out of a gateway or a portal or door and have had to exist in a certain state. This state, which you would call "Alien" in appearance, is how they now appear. These Beings do not have what you would call a regular skin tone and their coloration is very different. I have met Beings whose form is a bluish tinge. The form was not Human, although it had many similar characteristics…a head, two arms and two legs standing upright. These are Beings who are time traveling with some restriction however, as I am.

115

Fascinating. Are you saying that Extraterrestrials are Humans that aren't fully ascended – that they are stuck in a form that we have misinterpreted as "Alien"?

There are Beings who are stuck in an experience or a World who have communicated with many Humans. It is ongoing, but what I would like to state for your interview is that I have met them personally. The Beings that you are identifying as for example, the Arcturians, are in fact Beings that attempted to make a journey through time travel...but not all of the gateways are open. They're just not all open. Some of us get stuck and this is what has happened for some of these Beings. There is direct communication though, this I have learned.

When you say that some of us get "stuck", what precisely does that mean?

We are all trying to travel somewhere and it would seem that we all don't have free access or the right to travel. This is most disturbing but many Beings are stuck, yes. Now they're not stuck as though they're in a prison but they're not able to move around freely. Now moving requires light. We need light to travel. There is light and a speed of light. Light moves. Light of course creates a sound and the light is what we are using to move. Now this light creates an energy that allows us to travel but the light is not completely available for us. It is being obstructed, like an eclipse in a way. That would be a good way to look at it – an eclipse, a block.

Humans are trapped in form. Extraterrestrial Beings are traveling more than we are but still not completely freely. Is that right?

Yes, you can say that. There is something that we don't see...an obstruction and so many of us are trying to release the light. The light will be released and we will all be able to travel and use that light highway. It's like a highway. The other Beings who are stuck are not really stuck. It's just that they can only go so close to the light. That light is really the source of their existence and their Being. There will "come a day", so to speak, where we will all be able to be free. That freedom is about being wherever you wish to be and that freedom means freedom for all of us, not just for those who come from the Sirius light or those who are affiliated with another type of light or existence. There will be freedom again for all of us.

Will there be freedom for the DRA as well?

Now, that is a troubling situation that will be corrected but the release of those Beings who are stuck in that Invisible World that many of you do not see is the ultimate repair. When those Beings are released there will no longer be the crime and the horror that happens and that is happening on Earth. You are all unknowingly interacting with Beings who are suffering because they cannot use the light and they cannot release themselves. They are living in the dark and this deprivation is somewhat experienced in the Earth plane existence for all of you. You're all cut off from the light, some more than others. This is where all the crime and the terrible atrocities that are happening to you come from. Beings that do not have enough light don't have a happy life and cannot be happy or cannot be behaving in a sane way. You have to look at it like this. Those Beings who are deprived of light are deprived of "good" and "just" behavior. This is a criminal behavior that is created because they do not have access to the light or the ability to generate the light...so they are willing to destroy others for this light and are willing to destroy you in order to have this light. Now this may sound completely fantastical but there is a lot of stuff happening on Earth that is just not making any sense anyways.

We're always at war, in some form or fashion.

> It shouldn't be that hard or terrible for everybody but you know the "wars" that are going on...those are not wars about land or resources. It is ultimately about the light and trying to figure out a way to be able to have that ability once again. Killing others and harming others is not going to be the way that the DRA learn, but they do keep trying.

We would be remiss if we didn't ask you about the state of cinema, Gregory. Hollywood has become a comic book movie factory. Can you offer some insight as to why we have moved away from poignant dramas for instance, toward blockbuster science fiction?

> While the "comic book" genre is not necessarily something that I would like to act in or be an active party to, it is a reflection of everyone searching for a new belief. Many of you no longer believe that you can learn anything more in the Earth plane...and so you're having an increasing number of productions and storylines that are becoming either really uninformative and silly, as you regard them, or really fantastical and not of the Earth existence. What is most likely happening is that things pertaining to time travel are becoming more and more of interest.

Does this mean we will never see another film like "Roman Holiday"?

> Overall what's happening to film...I feel that things are becoming way more freeform and less guided by a solid storyline or message that helps to examine Human nature. It's more about "where do we go" but not really

having a clue. It's a frustration that is coming out in the stories. It's just a frustration. There does not seem to be a clear understanding about who you are as a Human Being and what your place is in the universe. At least not in the way that we used to tell stories. This will change, however. It may seem like the need for a solid story and the good work ethic and creative ethic that you equate with older films is not welcomed, but there will be interest again. I assure you.

This conversation has been wide-ranging and interesting. We're very happy that you decided to speak with us. Why were you reluctant or shy to participate?

I'm not sure that "shy" is a perfect description. I am not a spokesperson for what you're calling the "Ascension Experience"…and so although I was recommended to speak, I do not want to give the impression that I am in charge of the ascension movement. I am all for it, of course, but I am not comfortable being the key spokesperson for the entire project. I think "worry" is more appropriate than saying the word shy. I worried that I would wind up a spokesperson or leader of activities and initiatives. This was more reluctance, although that's not a pretty word either.

Are you okay with us publishing this dialogue?

Oh of course. By all means publish. I would not speak to you if I didn't feel that this communication would be helpful. Also, I am curious about what you are putting together. This is quite something. Not many of you are speaking with us. Did you know this?

What do you mean?

Most of the time we can communicate with you as in "inspire" you through an unconscious exchange. But a direct communication or channel, that's not an everyday experience and that's something that I want to be clear about. I've not spoken with many of you and I miss that. I wish more of you would make an effort to learn about what you're able to do. You're able to do a lot more if you try. If you set your minds and your hearts to it you can make a lot of things happen. It's not that impossible to communicate with us, it really isn't. What might feel impossible is creating a belief and a world where you believe that anything's possible...now that's the challenge.

Just believe that anything is possible – is that all we have to do?

Well, I think that would help.

The Reader is either laughing or crying right now.

Maybe they can just take a break and watch an old movie, one with a solid storyline.

In all seriousness, what step can the Reader now take to establish a communication with Beings in higher densities?

You have to believe in immortality in order to speak with us. That number or channel or communication or line of communication is a belief. A belief is simply a way to reconnect and also reconnect with those who have already done it. You are reconnecting with us. If you do not have that belief then you cannot possibly hear us. That belief in immortality is the first step. As you are discovering in your work it's not simply a matter of waking up in the morning and saying "I believe yes". It's in the redefinition of beliefs that you are finding the connection that you are seeking.

When you say "redefining" beliefs, you are essentially saying that we shed our old beliefs – correct?

In order to sincerely and truly believe then you must sincerely and truly give up some beliefs. You can't have room for as many beliefs as you all have now and tell me that you want even more beliefs. There's not enough room. You have to let go of some beliefs. When you let go of some beliefs there will be room for other ones. These other ones include a belief in the immortal state of being and that belief allows a direct communication with other Beings in the immortal state. *Belief attracts belief* but also Beings of that belief...much like "like attracts like". It works the same way.

We haven't spoken about The Rose yet but we have learned that it is a tool that opens a gateway and communication with other worlds. Did you have knowledge of The Rose in your lifetime as Gregory?

The Rose is a symbol and a belief that I have held for a very long time. I had dreams that not only gave me a prolific and proficient understanding about the symbolism, but really allowed me to connect with a belief that there is more to life. Not long after I had the first series of dreams about The Rose and Rose symbolism, I requested a meeting to have a past life regression session. The Rose is something that has always been near and dear to me. It is something that I learned about and I held in my heart that this would be an important device...and sure enough it has been. That information provided me a quick experience I would say, in Lyra.

Was there an underground Mystery School or Society in Hollywood that circulated the information about The Rose?

I would say that there are a fair number of you that are aware of the power of this symbol. Now, it's not just a symbol that you draw on a piece of paper and use it as some sort of spell or key. It is a belief that you must develop. There are a number of us that have received this information, but being informed about it is one thing. It is quite another thing to have a dream and an experience without the help of another. My understanding is that there are many of you that have had contact with The Rose.

At the end of Orson Welles' film "Citizen Kane" (1941) the protagonist utters the word "rosebud" as he dies. We later discover that it was the name of his childhood sled, but was that also a nod to the mystical power of The Rose?

Now you're on to something.

Was that Orson Welles disseminating knowledge of The Rose?

If you go through some of your favorite films you're going to find a lot of Rose symbolism and it will seem to you uncanny. It's not just somebody fond of the flower.

What are some of those films?

If you go back to any film particularly that has had an award or a substantial interest, you're going to find a Rose mentioned in a way that is more than just a passive commentary about flowers. You won't have to look very far.

Can we conclude that the "rosebud" line was Orson dropping us all a hint?

I would say so. Maybe that's the movie you can recommend to your readers.

We really appreciate you deciding to participate Gregory and it's been a wonderful conversation. Thank you again.

It's been a pleasure speaking with you both. You should also thank Josephine. She is recommending your project to anyone and anybody who will listen. I imagine you two will be very productive and there are others who are coming to speak to you who are fairly well known. I think that it will add an interesting slant to your endeavour.

Thank you Josephine.

Josephine comes through and says, "I'll keep sending them your way".

DOUGLAS
FAIRBANKS

"When you cry you are traveling. You're not stagnant. When you're crying you're feeling a pain. Where is that pain coming from? That pain is coming from trapped light. I would try to practice crying. After crying don't you feel light-headed? You've let go of some things. You're practicing how to believe and how to implode a belief. These are all important skills."

The First "King of Hollywood"
Actor, Screenwriter, Director, Producer
Founding Member of the
Academy of Motion Picture Arts & Sciences
Co-Founder of United Artists
1883 - 1939

Douglas requested that we also mention:
He performed his own stunts

Dramos describes standing behind a man who's on stage as he looks out at a crowd in a nightclub setting.

Who are you standing behind?

> It's Douglas Fairbanks! Hello everybody, thanks for having me here. I recognize a few of you. You might be wondering why I'm up here. I want to say thank you very much to Josephine for organizing this and you know she likes to organize. She's organizing this talk and I don't really know what I'm going to say but I'm sure we'll come up with something. You know I would like to start off by saying thank you to Dramos and Bohemias and I want to say that you both have a lot of soul for doing this and it's not a big deal to communicate and it's not something magical and fantastical to speak with us and to everyone that's gone on their way. People don't take the time anymore. They're just not bothering. They're all just too busy and so I'm very glad that I have this opportunity. I don't know exactly what you want me to say but I'm sure I can come up with something. I can start off by saying that I do recognize a couple of people in the audience right now and I see Merle is there in the front and I also see Mary is there in the front, of course. So Bohemias, what do you need to know about this whole setup, this get up?

Douglas we're happy to have you here, someone with your legacy on Earth. We know that that's something that you've put behind you, but it will undoubtedly make for an interesting conversation. Let's start off by chatting about The Rose – is that okay with you?

> Ah the rose. Why did I know that you'd ask about that? Did Josephine ask you to ask about that? The Rose. You know The Rose is mentioned in all the movies…all the stories. It's always included. It always comes up.

Well, almost always. The Rose was included in many of my films. Did you like the Zorro films?

Yes, absolutely. You were the original Zorro!

Yes we placed The Rose in "The Mark of Zorro", did you know that?

No but we'll definitely be looking for it now. Is The Rose an open secret in Hollywood or is it just a small group of people who are "in the know"?

You know I have to say this to you both...when you do a lot of acting and read a lot of stories and you're learning a lot of scripts and you're preparing for a lot of roles...you learn about this Rose. You learn about the meaning of The Rose. It's not a class that you're taking. It is a situation where, you know, it just comes to you. You just get it. It just comes to you. The way that I learned about The Rose is, like many, I noticed that it's prevalent in a lot of storylines and The Rose is a very popular flower and there's a lot of symbolism behind The Rose that we all accept. I had dreams about The Rose...being given a Rose, being awarded a Rose and you know that most of us have that ability...the ability to speak to those who have gone on. There are many people in Hollywood and many people in film and there are many people in the movies...they have this ability. Now I'm not saying that The Rose automatically gives you that ability but it does seem to be connected. So I started to have dreams about The Rose and dreams where I've been given a Rose. It was as if The Rose had a magical property, a magical meaning.

Did you find that others in the industry were having the same dreams?

If you had a conversation with somebody who's been around for a long time and I'm not talking about just anybody...I mean somebody who is really excited about their craft and excited about their work...then you'd most likely have a conversation about this flower and about what this flower does. The Rose is not so much a secret but it is...in a way. It's unspoken. But The Rose sure enough, time and time again, it is included. I mean how many pictures have the mention of a Rose? Most of them do. Roses are mentioned and if they're not spoken about you see them. They're there.

Is it just enough for us to know that The Rose is a symbol for travel and communication? Do we have to grow a Rose Garden or get a tattoo of a Rose? Readers will ask, "What do we have to do with The Rose"?

Well I would say that you should spend time with those of you who understand The Rose or appreciate The Rose, but let's talk about the pictures. Let's talk about the movies because in these stories there's often a Rose. There's the mention of a Rose, the story of a Rose, giving Roses, singing about Roses...Roses Roses Roses. Lots of Roses. A lot of these stories are saying something. A lot of these stories are sharing an important message. A lot of these pictures have an energy.

What do you mean by "have an energy"?

Well, you know what I find really interesting? The films that don't have sound and if you pay closer attention to what's going on and I imagine that you do...because when there's no sound you're paying closer attention...you may start seeing things and putting things together. There are symbols in a lot of these pictures. Now a lot of these pictures early on had very blatant, definitely right up front in your face loud and clear symbolism. The symbolism today I understand is a little bit more elaborate and veiled and there's a lot going on and there's a lot of special effects and a lot of these films are very busy pictures. I mean it's a whole different ball game now. But it is something to pay a little more attention to what you're looking at on screen.

That could also be said of life, in general. Just pay more attention.

Yes, well said. But you know…that's why movies are so special. In a way the whole practice of "going to the cinema" is forcing you to pay attention. If you ask your readers, "why don't you pay just a little closer attention, just a little more attention to this Rose" and maybe "pay a little more attention to what's going on in the scene", you might very well see something else or pick up something else. It is a symbol and if you keep paying attention to it and I mean *really* pay attention to it, you might start *really* noticing and hearing and sensing. Your senses get sharper. They get sharper. Sort of like a meditation. It's an exercise. You have to exercise. You have to get in good shape and I'm talking about your senses, your ability.

Modern movie audiences will know this as an "Easter Egg", a hidden image placed in the background of a film by the filmmakers.

Yes, it's all an Easter egg hunt isn't it…"life" I mean. Look for the Easter eggs everywhere and not just in movies of course but in your dreams as well. You have to think the way an Actor does, always looking for the meaning of things, researching. Nowadays I imagine you're not so heightened. There's a lot going on. There's a lot going on in your world but back when I was in pictures we were able to really take a moment and when I say take a moment…I mean to smell the

Roses...smell the flowers. What does that mean anymore? In your World you're just not doing that anymore. It's just too busy. Just start paying attention to what's going on. I would recommend that for your readers. You should all watch and enjoy some films that were put together way before you were born.

What can you tell us about The Rose placement in your Zorro film?

I really wish that you could watch it in slow motion. I wouldn't ask you to watch it over and over again but that wouldn't hurt. I want you to imagine like you're watching it in slow motion...almost like you're watching it under water. You have to slow it down and I know that I speak really quickly but you have to slow it down. You just have to slow it down. The Rose – look and see Bohemias. When you see The Rose, look at the entire frame. Look all around in the scene, in the shot. If you can stop the film, if you can stop the frame, that's even better. That Rose...treat that Rose like an exercise. It's a call to pay attention. Pay attention. The Roses, they're not randomly placed in the picture. They're not randomly placed. No one's saying, "Oh I think this scene needs a Rose". The Roses are placed very carefully and in those scenes and in that shot and in that frame...it's telling you something. There's a message there. I mean if you can, if you have the equipment and you have the time, stop the frame. Stop the frame, just watch it slowly. Watch it frame by frame.

I imagine some readers might be reading this saying, "This is fascinating but a Rose is just a flower. It's just a plant...what the hell is Douglas talking about"?

Well now, you know The Rose is a representation for the portal. It's a way to travel. It's an opening. You two are calling it an "allowance" or an "awareness". What else can you call it?

A gateway?

Oh, okay I like that. A gateway, a door. I mean we can talk about this all day.

Is it the first of many keys?

Well that's my understanding and that's how I started. Now I know that you know The Rose and the plants...you know about these things. That Rose is connected to a plant and that plant is connected to this understanding that there's more to the Earth. There's that "Crystal Causeway" you spoke about in your second book. Now that Rose is the gateway through that Causeway, through that portal. That Rose and that number 13...now that's a whole other conversation. The number 13 is important but these are all things that are preparing you to look at the world differently.

The Rose is a representation but what about the physical flower itself? Is there an energy resonance to it?

The scent of the Rose...the scent is important. The color and the vibration, yes. The Rose as in the plant...that is specifically making a sound and that sound, that vibration, that frequency is connecting you to an opening, a portal, a gateway, a channel. It's like a radio. That's how we're communicating now. I would say that you could treat that Rose like a dial on a radio.

If we hold a Rose and lose ourselves in the scent and the fragrance, is that affecting our state of mind?

There's a chemical. There is communication. We know that plants are communicating with each other. The plant is communicating with you. Now I know that some of you can't smell, your sense of smell is not very evolved or can't smell at all but it doesn't matter. It's still sending a chemical signal. It's a signature. It's like a telephone number. "Rose 13 - 13". That's a joke by the way. It's the plant talk that you're giving to people and that's wonderful. The plant talk. What is the plant? The plant is light. There are different plants. I don't believe that you've gone into that in great detail. What are the different plants doing? I know you know about the plant world and their connection to the Crystal Causeway and all that...and that's wonderful...but each plant...what does that mean? They have different purposes.

Let's stick to The Rose for now. Why The Rose? Why is the Rose a gateway?

The Sacred Rose is a gateway because this is the first language that you're going to learn. The Rose is a language. It's the language of time travel. Now I know this conversation is sounding a little bit crazy, but it's the language of time travel. It's the first word you're going to learn in time travel. It's the word. So you want the password? It's "The Rose". The Rose is the password. Now we're not going to spend 3 months discussing an etymology, that's not my area. You're calling it The Rose but it is the password. If somebody asks, "What's the password?" It is The Rose. The Rose is a special plant. That plant makes a frequency. It has a chemical signature. We can get into the science of it but the plant is the first key or how about this...it's the first door to go through. There many doors to go through...it's the first door to go through. The door happens to be a Rose. I mean, holding The Rose in your hand is not the doorway, you understand. It's connected to the plant but it's the plant...that's the pathway. If you're not a reader of Volume 2 and all those wonderful things that Dramos and Bohemias have written about in that book then you're not going to know what's going on. You have to read through that Volume in order to understand what's going on. Otherwise it's just a crazy conversation that we're having. That plant is directly connected to the Causeway, to the gateway of immortality…the first step in time travel. Now are we running around Hollywood talking about time travel? Well some of us are. But I'll tell you this…we are running around talking about immortality that's for certain. Because that's all we want. I mean, you can't get rid of us.

Are Screenwriters, Producers and Actors all in on these Rose inserts or is it something that we're doing unconsciously?

Well I'm going to say it's a little bit of both. I mean it's always in the script, it's always mentioned you know. So it's just a given when someone says, "We need a flower", you know *here we go* get us a Rose, right. Yes, it is going to be a Rose. I mean if you think about it, no one's asking for a hyacinth or a chrysanthemum. Do you ever hear that? No. It's always a Rose. Eventually one day someone's going to say, "What is it with The Rose? I don't want a Rose, I want a Daisy?" Well you can't have a Daisy haha. It's got to be a Rose and if it's not a Rose then you probably don't have to pay that much attention to it, although all plants are a signature. Let me say this…The Rose is like a key to a door and this is just the first doorway and the doorway is basically a plant and the physicality of the plant on Earth…okay well that's something you're experiencing there. That's not what we're experiencing when we go through the gateway. It is literally a gateway. The Rose and its petals will turn into a multi-armed geometry and it has 13 arms like a star. That thing will spread apart and open up as a gateway. Now I'm not saying you look at The Rose and go weeeeee and there you go…off you go time traveling. I'm not saying that but I am saying that this Rose will open up all of your senses and including what you're calling your 6th sense. You're going to have even more senses with what you two are doing.

What can you tell us about the number 13 and its importance?

Well you've already discovered astrology and the importance of that. You're learning about that but you know the number 13, that's a step beyond. It's a step beyond the 12. It's after you complete the 12. Well I guess in a way it's like the "Holy Grail". The number 13 is going to take you beyond the confines and the parameters and the things that you have to obey and deal with in the Earth plane. This number is beyond the knowledge of the astrology, that's what I mean. You have to complete a cycle and learn about all this. The Rose is just the first step. All these things are going to come together for you. I can't sit here all day and educate you on every aspect but it is an exercise, you must exercise it.

We have to get past the idea that a Rose is "just a flower" and that "13 is just a number".

There's no way around that. I really do hope that your readers understand the connection that the plants are making. What I find very interesting is that in films and, well, in the arts there's always some interest in plants and forests and the greenery…but they almost always isolate a plant. They focus on a plant in a story, don't they? I mean you can talk about a forest but it's normally a tree, right? It's normally a Tree or a Rose. We isolate things when it comes to plants. We really do focus on the plant in the story and there's a reason for that. Even with the ritual of bringing someone flowers, we add meaning to the type of flower. These things are not random. So the flower, the Rose, the 13 petals, if you want to exercise this truth…draw a star with 13 arms or draw a flower with 13 petals and imagine yourself diving in and swimming through.

Douglas, our bibles also mention The Lily…is The Lily another key or doorway? Will we be learning about other flowers?

You think that you are working with flowers but in fact you're learning about gateways. They're all the same. Flowers and gateways. Plants are gateways of consciousness. The Lily is not something that you both are working with right now, because you wouldn't be asking me.

We asked you about The Rose too.

Not in this same manner, you didn't. You were asking how we could explain The Rose for the readers, but you already knew. You already got it. Usually by the time you ask about it you already know. I know that you both know to "ask what you know" and I think that's a great exercise. I think everybody should just ask what they know. Then we won't waste everybody's time. And "time" as in Earth time. We don't have time here.

Douglas do you feel that readers might be irritated with how casually we're speaking about The Rose and it's "magical powers".

Your readers…I mean my goodness…the amount of detail that you both are offering in the books. Do you really believe that your readers are not going to be able to get this after reading Volume 2? They're going through quite an exploration…you don't think they're going to be ready? Well…I'll tell you something…their minds are going to be blown. I think after reading Volume 2 they'll have made so many reconnections.

Your readers should be reading Volume 3 right after they read Volume 2 because I think that's really important...and I know you don't want to promote "linear thinking" but, well, sometimes you just aren't ready. You've got to allow yourself the right preparation. What are you going to title Volume 3?

It will be titled "Conversations from Beyond". It'll be a collection of conversations with Beings from the "Other Side", like you. The book will be a compendium of first hand accounts of the Afterlife.

I think that's going to be a lot of fun! Isn't that something!

That brings us to our next question. What can you tell us about your crossing over experience or "death" experience?

You know, I don't know how to explain that. I mean I feel I was ready to go. I pushed myself a little too hard and like everybody else...I suppose I died. You want to know what I saw when I left Earth?

I think people want to know about those first moments when we leave Earth and transition from the 3rd to the 5th density. What does it look like, what do you see and what do you do?

I can recall that I saw something that looked like a big head with many arms of light...like a ray. It was almost like a big sun, like if somebody was a sun. I'm explaining, of course, what you guys are calling The Channel. I can also recall that I got to meet many of my previous selves. They were all in light. Everybody's all lit up. It's amazing. It's quite something. All lit up. Now I was prepared for this...I had already heard about this, what to expect. You know this "go to the light" business and it's true, you go to the light, you can't avoid it. It's all light. I mean if you can't go to the light you're doing something wrong. You definitely didn't get the instruction. You took a wrong turn because it's all light. When people say go to the light...well it's all light, everybody's in light. It's something. It's really something. Now I was not ready as you're saying...I didn't have all of my selves there and the kids and all that and you have to wait for that.

When you say that you had to "wait" for your other selves, what exactly does "waiting" mean for you – given that you don't experience time in the 5th density?

Yes, good question. It's not something like you're waiting for 50 years and 60 years and 70s years. It's not like that. It's just in the blink of an eye. You're perception of it, you're understanding of it...it's the blink of an eye. You're there and you do get a quick peek like, "Oh wow everybody's here. The gangs here, we're all here!" Now The Channel, this Being...it's very unusual. It's a very unusual creature and a very unusual situation. It's like a big sun. It's like somebody who has a big sun on their head and this Being is feeding light to all these Beings, to all of your selves, basically. There are many of you – in light. It's feeding you light. It's giving you light. This is where you're getting your light. Sort of like you know you need some parts. I'm not saying you need an arm and a foot but this thing gives you light. This is where your light comes from. You're rebuilding yourself. You're a Light Body.

Douglas, we've spoken with others who've explained that we are essentially The Channel. What's your take?

It's true that this thing is actually you. It's quite something when you're seeing yourself, but kind of outside of you. You're seeing something that's you but it's not part of you. It's external but it is part of you. It's a different way of believing. It's a different way of looking at things. On Earth this would not make any sense. You would not be able to externalize this. You just wouldn't see this. Like on Earth it has to be part of you. If it's not part of you then it's somebody else, right? It can't be you. You can't be you *here* and then you also *there*. You're either here or you're there. You can't be both. But in Lyra, in this situation you're here and you're there. So you can externalize, you can see yourself externally. You can witness yourself externally and so you are generating the light. You are learning not only how to turn the light back on but you're learning how to allow the light to circulate.

This explanation is making it a bit clearer.

This thing that's there, this "Channel", it's not like some creature that's stuck there. It's you. You're stuck there in a way. You're waiting. You're waiting to be that thing. We're getting into a lot of difficulties explaining this because once you enter this situation you're put back together. It happens instantaneously. Time doesn't count anymore, there's no time. You're put back together. Are you a radiant Being? Yes you are, my friend. You are a radiant Being…when you're put back together. You will reassemble and your group or all your past lives, you're all there. You're all going to be put back together. You're one Being. You just go together and voila! You are a radiant Being. You are shining like the sun. This is what you're becoming. You are shining.

Do we move into other Worlds once we experience The Channel?

Oh this is true my friend and those light beams, those light rays…I think you're calling them cords or ribbons of light…these light beams unlock doorways. They're like keys, themselves. But how are you even going to get there without this understanding that there is more to

Earth? There are different levels of light and there's different ways to absorb the light. You have to be able to absorb the light. It's not really beneficial for us to be in that much light. You can't be in that much light if you can't absorb it. If you can't absorb it you're going to get burned. And that's like the Prometheus story and all these stories about being burned by the Sun. Now the Sun is not the light that you need. The light that you need is your own light. You need you. You're your own Sun and I know you've heard a little bit about the Moon. These are gateways. These are portals. I don't know if you've learned about that.

We would appreciate it if you could give us further explanation. Why did we build the Sun? What is its purpose?

It's a portal, a gateway…a doorway. This is a road and so is the Moon, but the Moon…I don't think many of you are using the Moon. That's something that's just a lost art. The Sun, many of you are using the Sun I'm sure, but these are portals and there's a confusion because they're up there in the sky and you think "okay they're giving us a lot of light" but are they? Are they really giving any light? These are portals. Now that's not going to make any sense for your readers. You need to be really careful about how much information you're going to be sharing with them but these are portals – these are new experiences. Now are you diving into the Sun? Well it's not really like that but sort of, yes. But not in this place and space.

When did we create the Sun and how are we supposed to access the Sun, or portal?

Now you can't access this as long as you have the situation on Earth and the stagnant light and all that. When this is all released that portal will be available, well, we hope. We hope because it's going to make it a little easier for everybody. Now the Moon is a very troubling situation. The Moon was once used and used exclusively. That was a very important road. That was a very important gateway. It's been made obsolete, but it will function again. You see all these luminaries, these things that are just floating around you...they're not really doing anything. Many of you are quietly asking yourselves, "What are they doing, they're just hanging there?"

Well the Sun heats the Earth for starters and the Moon's gravitational pull affects the tidal cycle of Earth's water levels.

Well indirectly, that's how they're functioning right now because that's how you believe that you need to exist on the Earth. Of course that's what they're "doing" but the situation with the luminaries is a little more complex than you are imagining. Right now that is stagnant energy. That's stagnant light. Light is not solid and the light needs to move and this is all about freeing the light. I would recommend that you start looking at these luminaries a lot differently than you are. These are gateways...these are roads...these are paths. These will be available again.

If these are "paths" then it would make sense that we've had a hand in creating them.

These things in the sky that you're wondering about...these are things that you've created. This light has been trapped or solidified, but everything is going to flow again. Take off your *Earth goggles* and try to see the Sun as an imprisonment of light. The Sun is a star but it used to be a very active portal. You can't use it right now because you're going to get burned. You do not know how to deal with that much light and that much energy.

The Sun as a portal is a mind-blowing concept.

> If I could give you a recommendation, I think it would
> be a good idea for you to pace yourself and just focus on
> The Rose at the moment. I believe that's enough. The
> Rose...just that alone is "mind blowing". If you have
> days on end to do this, go through the films and you're
> going to see that The Rose is everywhere. There are
> Roses in scenes that don't even need to be there!

Again, do you have any recommendations for films with Roses in
them? You're the original "King of Hollywood" so there's going
to be a lot of people who would love to hear you talk about film.

> Charlie Chaplin films! If you look at any of these
> movies you're going to see the mention of a flower.
> You're going to see some sort of gag or some sort of
> stunt or some sort of joke and there's a lot of "in jokes"
> too. If you ask me for some specific film...I mean I love
> them all. Why don't you watch "City Lights"? Have
> you seen that one?

No we haven't but we know the film. It's quintessential Chaplin
viewing.

> Well if it's "quintessential" why haven't you seen the
> picture? You must see it. Oh, I'm sure you can find it
> on that *YouTube* of yours, although it would be quite a
> shame to view it that way.

Is there a scene we can pay specific attention to in "City Lights"?

> Well I wouldn't want to ruin the experience for your
> readers but I suppose they'll need some motivation. The
> finale of this film, as you know, is a memorable one and
> one that earned him praise from the film
> community...but perhaps not enough I would say.
> Charlie's character grows very fond of a blind girl who

works in a flower shop – wouldn't you know. He helps her through some rough times and well there's quite a bit he does for her without her knowing…you'd really have to watch it. Let's just say that at the end of the picture she discovers that he's her guardian angel during a flower exchange. Now I'll let you guess what kind of flower they exchange.

The Rose.

It's a beautiful story and Charlie has layered it with more than people credit him for. It's all in the art guys. Charlie was very aware. The Rose and Immortality…it's in his films. Oh he would put it in his dialogue he wasn't shy about it. There is a scene in Charlie's "A Countess from Hong Kong", starring your elusive friend Marlon Brando. Watch the shimmying scene between Marlon and a female companion. There is talk of "Aristotle" and the "Immortality of the Soul". I think you'd find it quite amusing. There's even a spotlight on a trumpet player in the scene…your Volume 2 discusses the trumpet doesn't it? Movies are not "just movies", my friends.

Readers are going to get very frustrated with their service providers while looking for a 1931 film.

Oh the Roses are everywhere…they're just everywhere guys. I think it's honestly in every film. Sit down and watch…try to find me a film that doesn't have a Rose in it. I think that's more the question. What film doesn't have a Rose in it?

Should we rephrase that as, "What *good* film doesn't have a Rose in it?"

Well I think that any film that is sharing an important message will have a Rose or a mention of a Rose in it.

We asked Gregory to speak about the direction of the film industry when he joined us. How do you see the art form in 2020?

> Well, I recommend that you not use so much special effects and sound effects and effects and effects and effects. I'm enjoying the intricacy. I'm aware of what's going on but where is the heart? You're losing the heart in the story. Now I know it's sci-fi and I know that you have some fantastic things going on in these stories and these things are not always things that you're experiencing in every day Earth life. I understand all that but where is the message? I'd ask, "Where are you going with this?" Where are you going with this? There's an Ascension Event coming up and there's energy that's going to be released and everybody's got to get on board.

Why don't you believe that these sci-fi films have a message? Some of them are beautifully written and executed.

> There are certainly some very engaging films and beautiful I might add, but they're ultimately portraying a situation where you're all deeply in trouble while never offering instruction. When I say there's no message I also mean that there's no instruction on what to do. When this "trouble" arrives, how do you all get out of there? I mean there are things happening. Are you actually getting any instruction? Your books should become movies...they would make great "science fiction" films. We'd finally have films that offer a solution don't you think?

We do plan on bringing this to film and yes, it's true that our sci-fi films don't really instruct on how to exist outside of Earth. Not in great detail, that's for sure.

Your science fiction and "disaster" films bombard you with all these problems and these things that are going to happen...all these terrible things and strange things and wild things that are "imminent". Okay, so you have the information. Now what are you all going to do with that? When I say, "Where's the heart?" what I'm saying is, "Where is the guidance?" The pictures used to have a message and there was usually something that you could take from it. Some people would say, "Oh Douglas you're speaking about hope". It's not simply about hope. You need some instruction with the sci-fi pictures.

Isn't exposing people to monsters and aliens and other species beneficial for us?

Yes it is, but you're almost always running away from these Beings. In these pictures you're running away from something and maybe you're trying to go somewhere and run to somewhere, but there's too much running around! Where is the leadership? Leadership can't just be about fighting things. It used to be that you could lead...and not lead like you have to have a war. It used to be you could figure out something and share a little secret, a secret to build upon your repertoire. It used to be that you could talk about the universe and about your understanding of the universe. Now with the sci-fi genre it's very interesting what's going on. You're being overwhelmed with information and ideas but you're also just waiting. You're waiting for it all of it to happen and that's a precarious situation for all of you.

Well, we live through the protagonist. The protagonist represents our ability to change and find a solution.

Are you finding a solution? Yes, the protagonist is trying to make it better and they're trying to figure things out, but most of you are just spectators now. You've become a bit lazy. There's a lot of information and you're taking in a lot of stuff and you're absorbing a lot of stuff but you're just really becoming more and more passive. I don't want to criticize your films because I think they're fantastic stories, but you as Human Beings are not feeling like you can actually make a change.

It's hard to argue that point.

I feel overall that you're losing your ability to create. You're just bombarded with too much information and too many fantastical things that might be happening to you and you've lost the ability to create. You're no longer interested in creating. Although there's a lot of you on YouTube and you're doing a lot of things. You feel like you're creating, but are you? Are you creating or are you just making a lot of noise? I think you know the answer.

Douglas, the cinema experience appears to be dying out due to increased interest in streaming and formats like YouTube. Is it just sentiment or is there a real benefit to being in a theater?

Well, the group participation and *sharing* experience is what you're speaking about. You're losing that sharing experience, aren't you? Yes, you can watch films together on your computers...and other people can be watching at the same time, but you're not paying as much attention to the message are you? When you ask me about a cinema experience, you're asking about the camaraderie and the energy share. The synergy is lost and that, my friends, is an art – the art of synergy and the art of sharing your emotions. It's an art. It's an art form. You've lost it. It's the ability to share emotions and share feelings together in a room instead of talking at people.

What do you mean by "talking at people"?

> Well for example, some of you are on YouTube and you're talking at people. You're sharing and you're emoting but it's not the same as the live experience. You're losing that interaction. You've lost that interaction. You've lost the personal touch. You're watching people emoting but you're by yourself or you're removed from it. When you're watching the films with other people, then together you can share in that experience and share in those feelings. You've forgotten how to share your feelings. You're not as comfortable sharing your feelings. You're on YouTube and you're doing all sorts of crazy things. Some of you reading this might say, "That's not true I just watched on YouTube a woman pouring out her soul and I watched a man singing his heart out...so no that's not true". It's not the same thing. It's one sided and you don't have the group witness. You don't have the group experience and it's very easy to just make something and throw it up there. It's a lost art. It's an art form requiring an audience. Things are strange now if you want my "opinion", there it is. I imagine most of your readers won't enjoy hearing that.

Well yes, that won't be a popular opinion. Our civilization is enslaved to the Internet, Social Media and technology. Everything is fast and convenient. Sitting in a theater is like a prison for many people.

> This simple activity of going to the movies is a group experience. Think about what I'm saying. You're disconnecting from each other. Splitting off. Isn't that the problem you've been writing about? When you're broadcasting to a whole bunch of strangers on "social" media and you're protected behind a camera, you don't have to take responsibility and endeavour to perfect your art or grow your art. There are a lot of you who

have fan clubs and you're doing things on the Internet and you've got fan clubs and hundreds and hundreds of people "love you" and they're following you and watching you…but what are you doing for art? Art is important and the reason why art is important is that art…the imagination…this is the ability to time travel. If you can't imagine you can't time travel. If you don't have the imagination, you can't time travel and if you can't time travel what does that mean? It means no more immortality. Bye bye immortality. So art equals immortality. It's very simple. I've been rambling on and on and not being very clear with you, but essentially that's what I'm trying to say.

We don't know how this conversation is going to read on the page Douglas, but you're coming through with so much personality, it's very high energy. Some readers might be surprised, as they wouldn't believe that Light Beings are this animated.

Well we have personalities. We can communicate with you. I am connecting with you all in the way that I was communicating the last time I was on Earth. I am communicating with you all in your level of light. How am I going to convey who I am and how I'm feeling if you don't have the language? You've made a very good point. What is a language? The language is the emotion. When you say personality you're speaking about the feeling. So what are you conveying for your readers? You're conveying the feeling. Do Light Beings have feelings? Sure, they have feelings. Are they processing these same feelings as you do on Earth? Of course not, but in Lemuria or the World of Make Believe you have feelings and feelings equal art. Feelings are creative. So you're practicing your feelings. But you're practicing them for the purposes of time travel, as in art equals immortality. These are skills and beliefs for time travel. Time travel is just a whole series of beliefs based in emotion. You have to feel it. That's why Actors are very good at time travel – because they feel it.

Elaborate on that last point, please.

Actors study feelings so they are excellent Time Travelers. They get it. You give an Actor some instructions and they get it. They really want to not only absorb the information but if you're telling an Actor about the feelings...the feelings are key and they're going to work with you. That's what's happened on Earth...many of you don't know what your feelings are. They're upside down. They're all over the place. Actors have quite their work cut out for them right now. They're trying to sort out all the feelings that have become quite complicated, haven't they? It's no longer just happy...it's how many shades of happy is it. It's just something. The Actor in your linear today really has their work cut out for them. It is quite something.

Many Actors reference Marlon Brando's abilities and he's quite often called the "greatest ever". What would you say about that?

Well there's someone who is completely in touch with his feelings. Marlon has no fear about working with his feelings, sharing his feelings and connecting with his feelings. It's art and art equals immortality. Somebody who is connecting with that...well that's powerful. You're effectively saying, "I am Immortal. I am an Immortal Being" and in Marlon's case, "I'm going to let it all hang out, I'm just going to show it, I'm going to show you my emotions". Emotions are the key. If you can't feel, then how are you supposed to time travel? Now some of you might say, "Who cares? I don't want to time travel?" Really? Well I find that quite strange. Why wouldn't you want to time travel?

Would you recommend that the Reader take acting classes as an exercise?

No I don't feel they have to be doing acting exercises. If they want to…good for them. Exercise is good. Exercise your belief. Exercise your right to immortality. It's your right. Exercise it.

If feelings are creative and time travel is belief based in emotion, what occurs when we experience intense emotion? Crying, for example.

Well, crying is a good example. Crying feels like time travel. When you cry you are traveling. When you cry you are moving the energy around. You're not stagnant. You're moving that energy around. When you're feeling those intense emotions you're moving your light around. When you're crying you're feeling a pain. Where is that pain coming from? That pain is coming from trapped light. You may be recalling something very sad or feel in physical pain…that's a whole other conversation but ultimately there is a lot of pain and there is a lot of sorrow and grief happening on Earth. This must be released and corrected and all the terrible things that are going on. There's a lot of horrors that are going on. This all needs to be released and fixed and it will it all be fixed. It's not a nice world to live in, some days. This will all be corrected, but your question about crying…crying is an excellent way. It's an excellent exercise. I would try to practice crying. Crying is a good one. After crying don't you feel light-headed? Don't you feel better, as if you have been released. You feel that you have released because you have also released an out-dated belief. You've let go of some things. You're practicing to form and reform. You're practicing how to believe and how to implode a belief. These are all important skills.

Earth is a tough place, Douglas. There's a lot of wonderful people here and many good things happening, but ultimately things are out of whack. They just are.

> That's for sure…and there are so many awful things that you're doing on Earth to suppress your feelings and to numb the pain, because you can't deal with the emotions. You're dealing with things like depression and there's a lot of things going on in the Earth plane that are very complicated but numbing the pain…this activity of numbing the pain is not beneficial. You're drinking and you're doing drugs and you're eating and you're doing a lot of things, but is that serving a function? Now I know some would say, "Oh don't do that…you're not a Doctor. Don't start making these recommendations, you're not a Doctor". Okay, but when you're numbing the pain you're not allowing yourself to release an out-dated belief. You're stuck in a cycle. You're recycling a belief. You're locking in a belief. Now if someone really can't function at all and you need to do something about it that's a whole other story but you know what I'm saying – many of you are just numbing the pain. You just don't like the way you're feeling and you're grabbing the bottle and you're smoking a cigarette and whatever it is you're doing.

What is your solution?

> It would be better to just sit with that and maybe have a good cry and try to release. You're saying "Let it go"…well that's true. Let it go. Let the out-dated belief go…but some of you are suffering from horrible traumas and it's not right, it's not right that you suffer this way. It's not easy and you're all very courageous. Your worlds are getting fixed…these things are not right.

It's very sad but we're trying our best to release this information. We're trying our best to help instruct those who might feel overwhelmed with hopelessness. There is a way and this conversation is helping.

> There is a period coming up, not too far ahead in the near "future" and this will be a time where there will be tremendous healing. There will be a lot of chaos of course, but there will be tremendous healing and many of the Artists are going to be stepping up and doing their thing. Art will heal the world and it will release the imprisonment on your planet and you will be experiencing the release whether you like it or not. This is going to be releasing the light and the emotion and the energy, whether you want to be a part of this or not. You will be feeling the feelings again and you will make the change. There will be a change and I believe that this time you are all going to do it and you will be free. Free at last.

That's beautifully put. We're so glad that you were able to share that. That's probably the best way to end this conversation. Thank you, Douglas.

> Thank you and I hope that you have a lot of paper because there's a lot of us who are coming to speak.

We'll be ready, Douglas.

LYMAN

FRANK

BAUM

"When the understanding that creativity equals immortality is achieved en masse, things may change. At the moment however, you are all trapped in your beliefs that creativity and ultimately art, are dangerous."

Author and Creator of
The Wonderful Wizard of Oz
Seeker, Spiritualist
1856 - 1919

Someone has been contacting us for two days using the name "Orpheus". The Being is not giving us any more information.

Would you like to speak to us? Is there a reason you keep mentioning Orpheus?

> I am playing a game with you both. If you choose to believe that I am Orpheus then you probably would believe just about anything. We will discuss what Josephine is claiming will be a righteous and important topic for your book. I am not sure that this is going to be of any use but we can certainly give it a try. My name is Lyman. You may all know me as L. Frank Baum.

Josephine is very excited about your work and so are we. Thank you for participating Lyman.

> Josephine insists that I speak with you, as she has already mentioned to you both that you will be hearing from a children's book writer. It's not anything that I am willing to go out of my way to boast about, as you both already know about my work but we can speak about it if you have some truths that you would like to establish. I feel that we have a good rapport and we're off to a good start.

Josephine wanted to introduce us to you because you had visited or experienced Lemuria while you were in the 3rd density. Is that correct?

> Well that's one of the ideas. I realize Josephine is insisting that we speak about this and get a better understanding. My adventures in these other worlds are probably similar to your adventures. Lemuria or what you can call the "World of Make Believe"...yes I know it and I know it well. This place really does exist. I'm not certain when we forgot that Lemuria and the other

154

worlds exist, but this is the state of affairs. I have had much difficulty understanding why everyone wished to believe that my story is just that, a story.

You're speaking about The Wonderful Wizard of Oz, is that correct? Otherwise known as The Wizard of Oz.

Yes, of course. Most of you do not accept that there is possibly more truth to the tale. Yet Writers understand that this is what occurs when you hand over your art and you hand over your life's work. Other people will do what they wish with it and this is more or less what's happened. The story as you know it has a lot of truth to it, but resembles a crazy tale. Most of you are choosing to accept it as a tale, but it's a World that we must all connect with. If you don't connect with this place, you can't really return home.

It's hard for many of us to call anything but Earth "home".

Many of you believe that the message of the Wizard of Oz was that Earth is "home"…because that is where your family is. This was not my intention. It was never my intention to convince everyone that they must stay on Earth or to appreciate what they have on Earth. I hope…and it's my sincerest hope that you have much success with your writings and maybe you can clear up some of these misunderstandings.

Lyman, were you unconsciously or consciously tapping into Lemuria when you were writing your stories?

I began to have a sense that there was more out there and I was also involved with groups that studied and learned about mystical things. I began to truly believe that there was a place where you could basically make a wish and have that wish come true. I had my own dreams and feelings about such a place, so it's perhaps a combination of my own innate beliefs and those beliefs that I studied. My intention for Wizard of Oz was to assist you all in remembering where you came from. I wanted you all to remember that we could journey homeward if we all worked together.

Do you feel that readers and audiences didn't take that from the Oz material?

Not in a way that I had hoped for. The message to stay on Earth and stay with your loved ones and just be glad you're there was not the message that I was hoping to share. I would like it if you could, well, expand on some of the themes and maybe have a look at the original writings and compare what the film did for my storyline and what the books were suggesting.

We would love to assist with that. Your work, especially the Oz material was a great exploration into the power of imagination. It really spoke to the child in all of us.

Josephine is very concerned that we've all forgotten the magical World of Make Believe. She's very concerned that art is no longer something that is as encouraged on Earth, as maybe it once was. She's very concerned with the attitude that is prevalent on your planet and that you may never be able to get back home. Kids are forgetting to play and children are forgetting to make believe. In the schools it's just no longer important. If your books are explaining to everyone how important it is to exercise your right to make believe and to play like children do, then I'm behind you both.

It does feel that way...that the children of today have lost a bit of that imaginative spark. Of course, there are kids playing and imagining all over the world, but generally speaking things have definitely changed.

It's your birthright to be able to make believe and it's your birthright to be able to invent and create and play…and not only play with the light. I mean play with the colors and sounds and all of that. You can paint your future. That's something that I'd like to say to everybody. You can paint your future. You can write your future. I don't mean "future" in the way you consider it, as in 5 years from now, 10 years from now and so on. I mean that you have the ability to bring in the light and to bathe in the light. That's more or less what I'm speaking about. It's so close. You are so close to experiencing this. I'm quite certain that most of you don't believe that. This will soon change as your books are opening up a new understanding.

Is Lemuria the 1st world we experience once we fill up on light and "get with Lyra", as Gene put it?

That is the first experience. It is the first door. It is the first world and it's absolutely the path to the ultimate existence. There are many different experiences in Lemuria, including the Elysian Fields and The Rose. You've been writing about all these different things and all of those experiences come into play in Lemuria. These beliefs that you are reintroducing to your readers are freeing them from the entrapment on Earth. The ultimate imprisonment is the belief that after a certain age, make-believe is no longer acceptable. That's the ultimate punishment that you are experiencing on Earth and so you are basically going back to a World that you started in. Lemuria is that World that was available for you and the World that you were deeply immersed in as children. You are directly connected with that World but you lost contact with it.

Why did we lose contact with it?

You were all told to lose the belief. We're told that that is not acceptable behavior. We're told that that is bad behavior and so we believe or we begin to believe that making beliefs and using your own imagination is irresponsible. "Playtime doesn't last forever". Using your imagination and playing in the World of Imagination after a certain age is an "irresponsible activity". It's an "immature practice". It is "a sign and an indication that you are not evolving into a responsible Human Being" or "contributing to society". That is how we lose contact with Lemuria, even though it is a known fact that children have very active imaginations. You all accept that you're allowed to behave like that until a certain age.

Not only do we accept it, we encourage creativity with young children. In some ways we grow concerned if our children are not imaginative or creative.

Yes, now imagine if we actually believed that children are connecting with another world. Imagine you believed that children were traveling and experiencing another World. You don't actually believe that. If you did believe that, well then my goodness…you'd want to join in. You'd want to go there with them, wouldn't you?

Absolutely, it's obviously…

You asked…sorry for interrupting but I just want to add something. You asked about forgetting your earlier years, did you not?

Yes, we spoke about that with Gene.

So why is that? We have very little recall about those early years. Why is that? If you do remember the early years then isn't it a fact that you'd be regarded as "eccentric" or a "bit crazy" or "unbelievable"? Many of you say that it's not possible for you to remember those early years. You're looked at like you're a strange fellow for saying something like that. The amnesia is not about you forgetting what you liked to do as a young child. That amnesia is really about having been locked out of this world. You forgot how to go there. You lost your way...you lost your way.

It sounds like we come into this Earth World as 5D Beings, but the Earth mentality eventually beats the light right out of us.

Are you suggesting that through the incessant instruction to stop using your imagination that you are shutting down the light or access to Lemuria?

Yes.

I would say that certainly there is some truth to that but let's explore a little deeper, shall we. A child reaches a certain age and is expected to pay more attention to mathematics and the lessons at school than to their imagination. Children are being taught to direct their attention elsewhere. The attention to "solve problems" and to "memorize mathematics" and to memorize things and repeat them and to memorize your rules and to *memorize, memorize, memorize*...this is dimming your light.

You're going to upset the math community with these comments, Lyman.

There is nothing "wrong" with mathematics. It is the way that you perceive it and utilize it and center your existence around it that becomes the problem. Simply memorizing and repeating tables and formulas, it is these robotic gestures that we ask our children to subscribe to and believe in. We tell them that the "way to exist" and the "way to be a proper citizen" and "the way to communicate and share" and "get along with everyone else" is by "following these defined rules". Children are taught through mathematics that there are defined rules. That concept then evolves into "rules of conduct and behavior", which will create a "perfect society"…if we only follow the rules.

Some people would say there's perfect sense to that. How can we harmonize without structure and without any rules?

These rules are created so that bad things do not happen and yet bad things continue to happen. Why do bad things keep happening if these rules of yours work? The answer is quite obvious. It's because the restraints of the rules ultimately bothers many and they cannot cope. Many of you are still convinced that the rules designed for this supposed "utopian state" where everybody is "behaving themselves" and doing the same things, works. If that is the belief that you are buying into then that is why you have forgotten Lemuria. Lemuria is the real utopia and the utopia that art brings. Art is utopia.

Some readers might say that we're throwing the baby out with the bath water. So what that some people can't cope with the rules? That's their problem. They're the ones who need an adjustment.

That is a curious way of thinking. You all enter Earth creating and making things up and using your imagination. Children are showing you your true nature. Then you suddenly bring in all these rules and define being "a responsible person" as someone who rejects their nature.

It isn't as restrictive as your describing it. There are still many pathways for those who wish to pursue the arts.

160

Oh you can pursue the arts, yes, just as long as you become a *professional* Artist. It is perfectly acceptable to earn a good living via the arts, but if you're not earning an income then perhaps you are an "eccentric" or maybe even a little bit "crazy". The established order and the rules of the day and ultimately the laws that are created are designed to prevent anyone really from exercising their imagination. Do you know what that produces in many cases?

Probably some very bad behavior.

Well, it produces many people who are consumed with different fantasies. Some of you are acting out on a lot of craziness because you never had that release after a certain age. You may not want to believe it but the dark and difficult ideas that some of you are walking around with are certainly the result of stifling the imagination. When you stifle the imagination, as you know, then the light becomes stagnant. The light that was for beautiful beliefs and creations and love is now twisted and bent out of shape and has lost the connection and purity. A lot of the problems that we are all unfortunately dealing with are due to supressing the imagination at a mandated age. Imaginative thinking is just no longer reasonable behavior for a maturing adult.

Was art ever treated differently than it is in the 21st century, as we're currently experiencing it? Was there ever a time period where it was seen as the lifeblood of a society?

There was a time in Antiquity and in ancient society. We started off our discussion with Orpheus and although I was making a joke with you, the gesture in fact includes some truth, as you can imagine. There was a time where storytelling was very important and a very important practice. There was a belief that art had a purpose. There was a time when theater was more than just a "night out" and a little bit of leisure or relief from a long workday. There was a time when this was something that was a mainstay in your society. Theater and the arts was practiced to disseminate very important ideas and to maintain a connection with some of the worlds that you have all forgotten. There was a time when we did relay and relate the information and remind everyone how to stay connected with these beliefs. During this period in Human history Artists were instructing others quite directly on how to get to Lemuria and stay there.

Were you instructing others on how to get to Lemuria with your "Oz" book series? We understand that you don't care to boast about your works...but this particular series has resonated with so many people across so many decades.

If I may say something before we start to explore all of these topics and descriptions that you would like clarity on...many of my books are instructional manuals on how to reconnect with the mysteries that are still available for all of you. There is a very big difference between the books that I created and of course the movie that was produced many years after I "died". Do you wish to speak about the things in the movie or do you wish to speak about my books?

We would like you to speak about your books and where necessary, cite the differences with the movie.

I recommend that we begin with the movie. Let's begin with the descriptions in the movie. I would like to say that my influence continued in the movie, even though I was no longer in the Earth plane. Some of your readers may ask, "How is this possible?" I was in connection with the Writers who worked on the screenplay. The Writer who took over the project and you can certainly read about her, she was in contact with me, very much in the way that we are doing now for your book, but this was done in her dreams. I reached out through dreams and so many of the ideas that you see in the movie have been developed or changed or envisioned from what I would like to say is a direct conversation. Again, I reached out through her dreams. That is where much of the symbolism and imagery that you see is derived from. What symbolism or device would you like to ask me about...I know that you have your questions.

Let's start with the "Yellow Brick Road".

Yes, let's. Of course yellow equals light or is a symbol for light. This is quite obvious and many of your readers and even children will accept that gold and yellow equals light. But the road...my intention was to illustrate something in a very absorbable way for children. That yellow brick road is the road to reconnect with and re-embrace that which is your birthright – immortality. When you are born into the Earth plane you are already connected with the 5th density of light. You are connected with this World of Imagination and this World of Color. That road, that yellow brick road is a path that leads directly to that World. It's also a path that leads directly to Earth. It's a gateway. That road, that light, that is very similar to the Rivers that you'll read about in Genesis.

Are you speaking about the River that flowed out of Eden and forked off or separated?

Yes. The Rivers from Eden. Anyhow, children are born into the Earth world with a direct connection to Lemuria through their imagination. This connection continues for many years and through the rules and the regulations and all those things that we teach on Earth this connection is eventually blocked. It is remarkable how much effort and energy you all create together to keep that door locked, to take the key away from your children. Children are in your world as a reminder of the 5th density, as a reminder that you can return. You can return from where you came. Where have you come from? You have arrived from the World of Imagination. This is the first doorway or gateway to immortality and so children in a way are Messengers. You are all ignoring the Messengers from Lemuria.

It seems so simple the way you describe it, Lyman. That if we just allow children to dictate the way forward, Earth would be healed. Yet, we can't do that can we?

Adults demand the key. You're all taking their keys away from them. It is as though you say "give me the key now", and "we are taking it away from you" and "you will never have this key returned" and "if you try to unlock the door then you will be seen as not being a responsible citizen of Earth". It sounds funny reading or hearing it that way but it's essentially what you're doing, isn't it? Artists are not typically respected unless, of course, you are earning money or earning a "nice living". This is very sad. Many of you may say, "Oh this is not true…we love art and we are supporting creativity and this is our highest belief", but ultimately the Earth world discourages imaginative pursuits. It relegates them to childish behavior and immaturity. If you would like to make a living from this world of imagination, if you would like to sustain yourself being imaginative and creative, well, "good luck to all of you". You will be left to endure the hardships from "your foolish ways" and "foolish beliefs". Imagination and creativity is equal to foolishness in your world.

There are many Artists and creative people reading these passages right now, nodding their heads in agreement. It's all too familiar.

Yes, of course. This is also something that maybe some of your other "non creative" readers are not prepared to listen to. I do come across as being somewhat of a preacher on this subject but as you are aware I did choose to endure the struggle. I chose to continue exploring imagination and I also believed and I remain believing that that door to Lemuria does not have to remain locked. Some of you are secretly holding on to the key but are not saying anything. You are creating or being creative in private, concealing this need to remain engaged with Lemuria. I would like to say that this is a wonderful belief that you are subscribing to, not relinquishing the key to immortality. When the understanding that creativity equals immortality is achieved en masse, things may change. At the moment however, you are all trapped in your beliefs that creativity and ultimately art, are dangerous.

For the record, you were referencing Florence Ryerson, one of the screenwriters of Wizard of Oz. Is that correct?

Yes.

You visited Florence Ryerson in her dreams. What other elements did you advise her on?

Well, everything. Which elements would you like me to speak on?

The movie begins with a sepia tone sequence in Kansas, or Earth and then we transition into color as Dorothy lands in Oz. The explanation is perhaps obvious but maybe you'll have more to add.

Well, Kansas was an example of a typical hard working place to live in. For me, it represented a place where values such as creativity and art although pleasant amusements, did not put food on the table. This place represented the "heart of America" but also fundamentally the heart of Man Being in the 3rd density Earth plane. It represented the belief that you must "live from the land" and "sustain yourself" from the surface of a world that is ultimately a prison. You are sustaining yourself from the Earth that you have created and this is further imprisoning you in the belief that you are to remain on the surface of the Earth. Kansas represented the belief that you need to "work the Earth" and "live from the Earth".

The sepia tone or lack of color attributed to Kansas [in the film] is symbolic of being locked out of Lemuria, essentially.

Yes, well this is a big thing of course and perhaps an obvious truth. This lack of color equals the drudgery and the working and toiling on the surface of the Earth. It is a very scenic shift, of course, to go from the absence of color to a magnificent and wonderful and colorful World. This is mostly a way to explain or suggest that you have forgotten how to imagine that a place could be anything more than it is. This was simply a way to explain to many of you that you do not see any way out. You do not imagine anything beyond this existence. Please understand that I am not making any sort of discriminatory remark or remark about class or income level or status. I am simply stating that you are all entitled to a more colorful existence. It is your birthright.

Lyman, we'd also love to hear you speak about the characters, specifically the Scarecrow, Tin Man and the Lion.

I would like to speak about the Scarecrow first, if I may. This character represents an incomplete body. Now, in the story we are referring to a brain, but the brain is not about the ability to think or to be more intelligent or have more schooling than other Beings. It is representing a transmitter and a connection and the reconnecting with a belief. That was my intention. The brain, as in "do you have a brain" is a message. If you have a brain and you are only using it for 3rd density Earth plane beliefs, then you are not really using your brain. You don't really have a brain. The brain is a link that allows you to receive understandings or "transmissions" about other worlds. You can use your brain differently. You can rewire your brain. You can of course make the connections, the reconnections.

Would you say then that children have a fully functioning brain?

This is the big idea. Children already come with these reconnections. The brain of a child is fully developed and the areas in the brain are fully activated and receive messages and information from other worlds. The unfortunate thing is that children are discouraged from using that part of their brains and so in a way, you are fundamentally teaching children how to become stupid. Children in your world have a higher creative intelligence than all of you.

We want to say to the readers that while some of your words may print a little harsh, they're being delivered with a kindness and grandfatherly tone. It's important our readers understand that.

My words may offend some of you and that is certainly not my intention. We cannot shift our consciousness without a little discomfort, please remember that. The whole process from childhood to adulthood never made any sense to me at all. The creative intelligence or what you're calling the creative quotient is not only diminished, it's turned off. What is school for and what is its purpose? I believe you would have a lot more beneficial accomplishments if you would just change the ways that you regarded schooling and the purpose of school. If you must know, I am a big supporter of what you're calling "alternative schools" and creative schools and schools that are supporting that way of believing.

There may be a lot of readers who would agree with that. It's just not always an option, of course.

No, it's definitely not. In many cases these alternative schools demand quite a fee, don't they? It's become a privilege to get a "proper education" which I find troubling to say the least. Most children are being run through an education "system" that is completely diminishing their creative intelligence and suffocating them with logic and order and rules and regulations. I want to be as clear and definite in my remarks with you so that there is no confusion about where I stand on this topic. Josephine and I stand together in the "fight" to help children hold on to their creativity and to their right to a creative existence.

We thank you for that, Lyman. Your convictions, as we like to say, are unwavering and inspiring. We'd like to now, if we can, discuss the Tin Man character with you.

This is of course a reference to feeling and frequency. This is also symbolic of industrialization. The metals. What you are building and creating and how that is ultimately heartless and empty. This is a simple allegory and symbol for industrialization versus love.

That's simple enough. What about The Lion, what can we say about this character?

So the lion or the feline and the courage...of course on one level this can represent not letting others dictate what you do with your imagination. It is something that you have to be outgoing and bold and ultimately courageous about. The constructs and the rules and regulations define a world where this is not acceptable and so you have to be strong. My intention ultimately was and is to encourage that you continue with your journey, as you are both doing in your book writing. You must all continue having the courage to ask questions and continue having the courage to subscribe to your imagination and to your belief. Now, I must say that there is a connection with the Feline Order and Beings that you have not yet encountered in your book dissemination.

What do you mean by that? Is there a race of Feline Beings in existence that are more "evolved" than what we experience on Earth?

You will be writing about this Feline Order, which of course have a wonderful connection to what you call a "cat" on Earth. This is something that is not necessary to introduce in Volume 3 as it will largely be seen as "outlandish". It is a level of the "order of foolishness" and your readers will not be able to absorb this understanding. In order to do so their creative boundaries must be extended even further than they are struggling to reach now.

Well now that you brought it up, it's virtually impossible to ignore. There is a Feline race of Beings outside of the Earth plane.

Don't you think that they would like to speak with you?

Well we would like to speak with them.

Well you have to learn how to communicate with them first. When you learn how to communicate with them they will speak with you.

Are we going to learn how to do this now?

169

I can't make you hear what you don't believe yet. If you think I can teach you how to believe then this is simply not a correct understanding. You will believe and you will speak.

So because we don't yet believe in these Beings, we're cut off from communication with them – is that what you're saying?

Yes, that's the simple truth.

It's not likely that the Reader will be able to shake this from their mind.

It sounds like they want to believe and that's a start. Why are there so many of these seemingly outlandish beliefs? Why is this Feline race any more curious than an "Alien Being" with a blue head? You have to stretch your imagination and this is precisely what we're talking about in this interview. There are no limits in the 5th density. You're not connecting with the 5th density if you're asking me these questions. If you're asking how to believe then I would say be in the 5th density experience and then ask me that question…because you wouldn't be asking that question. You don't ask how it's possible. Everything is possible. You've just crossed the threshold from impossible to possible. There is no impossible in the 5th density…"impossible" doesn't exist.

If there's "no impossible", then why are we stuck? Why can't we open the gateway if impossible doesn't exist?

That's a belief you all must master.

Not one person can open the gateway?

Some have, yes. That's what you're learning.

Would you say that you learned this while you were here on Earth? How did you become aware of these truths while you were on Earth? Did you attend Mystery Schools?

> I have always been in communication. You call it a "Medium" or a "Channeler" or a "Psychic". I have always had this ability to listen and yes, I also enjoyed the company of others who had and were endeavouring to learn about the mysteries. You're calling these Mystery Schools and they were structured in this way. That is correct. So yes, I in fact did learn a lot about alternative spirituality and particularly Theosophy was an area that I did explore. This did fill in some of the missing details for me, but in no way did it largely influence my creative ability. This is just something that I've always had and always believed in and always done. The understanding that there are symbols that are universal was a remarkable discovery. I enjoyed learning that the dreams and the beliefs that I had from a very early age were in fact something that others had as well.

Are you saying that you had psychic ability...or that you visited a psychic or medium?

> Well this is a bit of both. I always had an interest in the psychic arts and an interest in spirituality and I suppose the "occult", although this is a word that is not accepted by many. You must be cautious if you're going to be describing things as "occultist". I had an ability to see and to hear and to know things and this ability is something that I did not advertise or like to speak about. Adults are not supposed to have these abilities and in a way this is quite similar to the creative conundrum. If you are imagining that you know things or you're imagining that you see things or imagining that you hear things...you will experience the troubles that an Artist experiences. It's not considered widely

acceptable behavior for a bonafide citizen of the Earth and an adult or a grownup person. So yes I had this ability to speak and communicate with other Beings while I was on Earth.

It goes without saying then that since all children come in to Earth connected that we all at one point had the "psychic ability".

Yes. Those connections by the way are not completely broken. You just have to reconnect. They are almost connected for many of you. You're very closely connected. The gaps in the connection are not as big as one would imagine. We're not speaking about having to endure years and years of schooling or having to read many books. Although I must say that your books are quite something. These books of yours are allowing many of you to reconnect after reading as little as a page. It's extraordinary. You are all reconnecting with the remembrance of what you once were, if I can explain it that way. The "Man Being" books that you are assembling are helping others reconnect with Lemuria and beyond. Lemuria is the first doorway like the World of Oz.

Lyman, you've had so much to say about children in this discussion. Do you have some practical advice for young parents?

Yes…and not only for parents but also for teachers and other authority figures in the lives of Earth children. Allow children to be creative and to exist creatively. Allow children to have the courage to believe in their imagination and to speak creatively and to create artwork and to assemble their beliefs in a creative way. Resist supervising creative output if you are witnessing children drawing, for example. Simply allow them just to freely create and freely be imaginative. Allow them to express their imagination and put their imagination on paper without giving it an award or a grade or a validation. It's this validation that children are taught to eventually seek that leads to the door to Lemuria being permanently shut. There is no need to say, "Oh my this is a wonderful thing that you've drawn" or "A wonderful thing that you've said" or "A remarkable song that you have sung" and "Look at how wonderful it is that you dance like that" or "That you believe this".

Are you saying not to encourage our children?

Yes of course encourage your children, but not by validating their creations with words. You must share in the activity with them. Speak imaginatively and creatively with children.

Not every parent has the ability to write or draw or sing or dance and so they use their words to show support.

You are all willfully accepting this belief. You tell yourselves that unless you are professionals or adept at something that you "do not have the ability". This mindset is the consequence of having your key taken away from you. You once "had the ability" and your children are giving you a second chance. They're giving you back your key. Allow that light to exist in their lives and don't make it such a special endeavour or a "special thing". It is of course special, but it is simply the way things are *supposed to be*. Having more light in your life or in your existence is not a remarkable and wonderful thing. It just is. Allow children to just be. Do not engage or endeavour to obstruct that by making any pronouncement or trying to define what it is. You must all stop trying to manage creativity. You must all stop trying to manage the light. Grading or adjusting or correcting is not something that is beneficial.

Thank you for that, Lyman. Beautiful words. We can feel the love that you have for us all. Your passion for children is compelling.

> My message about imagination and honoring imagination and remembering that imagination leads to immortality is the theme or themes that are included in all of my books. My books are a map of awareness and an encouragement for children to keep that door open and to hold on to the key. Hold on to your keys. Do not allow the keys to be taken from you. Secretly hide that key, for you will need that key again soon enough, I assure you all. That key is what all of you are seeking, when in fact you were born with that key. You were born in the World of Earth with the key. You are the key. When you describe children as "being the future", well this is of course what we are speaking about.

Incredible. We are returning to Immortality and that is our proper "future". Children are showing us our future.

> These are Messengers and you do not listen to the message…and you say to children, "I am not interested in your message after a certain year of existence in the Earth plane" and "After this year you no longer are to share your message" and "Please hand over all of your imaginative thinking and creative beliefs" and "Give me the key" and "Please now abide by all of the rules and regulations" and "Please be a proper citizen of Earth and follow all of the instructions that we are all adhering to" and "That is the way things are done".

We've created a world that is the opposite of our original existence.

> And you spend your lives yearning and trying to figure out how to get back to that World and you then turn, of course, to religion and you turn to external things to get you back to the place that you already had the key to

and to the place that you arrived from. You have come from this World. If you are on the Earth plane you have come from this level of light. You would not be able to exist in the Earth plane...in the world you call Earth...if you had not already had the key. And it is a troubling situation that is to be corrected shortly and your books are certainly helping to remind adults to look for the key. Now, where is the key that you have voluntarily allowed to be taken away from you all? Well I would say to you to remind yourself about The Rose and that Rose is the key. It is the key to unlock the door that you once had fully open.

Have those of us who have made the journey grown impatient or fatigued with "waiting" for the rest of us? The Mass Ascension can't come soon enough, it feels.

While I am someone who is readily engaged with Lemuria or the World of Imagination, speaking with many of you as we are doing today is putting me in a situation where I am engaged constantly in communication. I am on the channel and am available for many of you to speak with. It is not a difficult thing to achieve to communicate with many of us. We are looking toward the release of the confines of Earth so that we may all further engage in time travel experience. There are levels of light that I am looking for and there are levels of light that we are all engaging a belief in and would like to absorb more of. Your readers must develop an understanding and belief that there are levels of light that you engage in and the worlds that I have encountered are only a smattering of what is available to us all.

It might surprise some readers to hear that you or any other Light Beings are still restricted from travel in some way.

I am able to explore other densities of existence but do not have the completed absorption level of light and therefore time travel is somewhat regulated or confined for my existence. Please understand that you do not simply release yourself from the Earth constraint and then have all the knowledge and ability to absorb light. You are not immediately free to engage in time travel and free to do fundamentally whatever it is that you wish to experience. You will need to relearn how to create your reality in light and play with light. Lemuria is a training ground. It is not the final destination. The other worlds that you will be learning about and engaging with are awaiting you all and for many of us we are somewhat waiting as well. This is simply the beginning of the journey.

Ultimately we will be traveling freely – correct?

There is unlimited experience awaiting you all that other Beings will be describing to you. Be assured however, that you are all going to experience the blissful worlds of your dreams and imaginations. It is simply wonderful to exist in light.

Lyman, we've spent much time speaking about your art. Is there something that you haven't been asked that you'd like to discuss?

Well, no one has ever asked how I intend to contribute further to the ascension movement that is "presently" unfolding in the Earth plane. I would like to be an editor if I may…of some of your books, as I quite enjoy writing. Josephine is encouraging me to become more actively involved in a book series and that's something that I have a lot of experience in. I would be more than happy to be involved in more than one of your Volumes. You are welcome to speak to Josephine, as she knows how to reach me. I would be quite happy to remark on some of your writing and give you a tip or two. I'm not suggesting that I will edit your writing or evaluate your creativity, no. I would recommend a comment here or there or a word or a symbol that you might like to rework. I would like to be...let's say..."loosely involved" with your writing, at least for one or two books. I would find that very enjoyable but also feel like I am making a contribution.

It would be a dream to have you on board Lyman, although we should add that you are already contributing in this Volume.

Speaking about my previous incarnation repeatedly is not quite making the contribution that I would like to make and it is somewhat "tiring" to communicate with your density of light.

How does a Light Being grow tired? Isn't that just a 3D affliction?

The way that we must communicate in order for your readers to understand is tiring for Beings who normally communicate in light. We do not use a spoken language as you're using it. This is a different facility. I certainly would like to be involved in helping you learn how to speak in the light...and maybe teach you how to use some symbols, as there are different ways to assemble your books and I would like to maybe write a page or two if you let me.

Neither of us would object to that and we would be honored. We have many Volumes left to assemble, so you can certainly contribute what you like.

I would enjoy that very much.

Participate as you wish, whether that means showing up in a dream or a vision or simply coming to the mic.

Okay then it's a team. I also want to emphasize a point I made earlier before we conclude this conversation…if that is all right with the both of you.

What point are you referring to?

I made the point about your book allowing others to make many reconnections. There are some very descriptive passages in your books that are remarking on beliefs and the energy in those beliefs are allowing others to make a reconnection. There are inherent beliefs and reconnected streams in your books that are just instantaneously turning the light back on and increasing the light. You are allowing others to once again see the light, so yes this is happening on many of your pages.

That's really encouraging to hear, thank you. It's been an exhausting journey for us both and we've only just begun.

You both need to continue believing in yourselves and believe in the books and watch how it unfolds. Others are believing in it too. You may not have hundreds of people writing you letters and emails and telling you directly, but you'd be pleasantly surprised to know how many readers there are out there. There are many who have already become aware of the books and by books I am also referring to the books that you are endeavouring to publish. There are *many* waiting for the books.

We certainly believe that. You've been very helpful Lyman this discussion will no doubt prove to be invaluable for our readers.

NOTE: Josephine Baker interrupts and urges Lyman to set the record straight on his infamous remarks about the killing of an Indigenous Sioux Chief (Sitting Bull) during the massacre at Wounded Knee in 1890. Lyman wrote in a North Dakota newspaper: "…their spirit broken, their manhood effaced; better they die, than live the miserable wretches they are".

Go ahead, Lyman.

> I was attempting to create a huge controversy so that a new belief would be created. This was not the end result, as you are aware. I was attempting to create a belief that was so apparent about how the Indigenous people hold the keys. I wanted my readers to understand that the Indigenous were the lifeblood of the existence on Earth and this is something that I felt we could draw attention to.

That's not how a lot of people interpreted it.

> I took a controversial or completely abhorrent stand by saying that they no longer needed to exist to allow others to respond in protest. I was playing with irony. I wanted the people of the day to take action and say, "No what are you thinking? How could you suggest this?" My article was not meant as a literal device but unfortunately this was taken literally and quite seriously. I have this legacy of being a racist, a troublemaker and somebody who is highly controversial. This was a failed attempt on my part. I did it more than once. This was an attempt to draw a huge amount of attention to a cause and a situation and it was in a way, sarcasm. I was essentially throwing myself in front of a moving train and trying to be a sacrificial lamb, if you want to describe it that way. Unfortunately it was lost in the translation.

Your sarcasm may have been ill placed but what you said was that with their Chief's demise, the nobility of the Indigenous had been extinguished. Your attempt to make a point by calling for total annihilation was never going to be received well.

That's correct. I revered the Indigenous the same way that I revered children. I thought, "Well we've destroyed the child's imagination, might as well destroy this world too". While you're destroying everything you might as well destroy one of the few Beings on the Earth plane that are actually still functioning in a healthy way. This was extreme anger and frustration on my part, but the intention of my statements was to support the indigenous community...believe it or not.

We do believe you and it's quite obvious to us that this is a statement from the heart. Thank you for addressing this.

Josephine is encouraging the correction and this is one of the reasons she has been encouraging me to speak with you. I wish to thank you for your contributions and look forward to contributing further to your project.

Thank you, Lyman. Feel free to meet up in the dream state.

Yes, and you don't need Ruby Red shoes to do that either.

LOIE
FULLER

"How does a grownup reconnect with their childhood or their childlike way of communicating? Return back to things that just don't make sense. Stop using so much logic. Be free. Don't think about what you're doing."

Actress, Dancer
Pioneer of Modern Dancing and Theatrical Lighting
1862 - 1928

We have been receiving communication from a woman who's taken the form of a butterfly, requesting to speak. The Being is uttering "Lo Way...Lo Way".

What is that sound that you're making?

My name.

What is your full name? Please spell it for us.

Loie Fuller.

Welcome Loie, we're happy to have you and excited to hear what you have to share.

I have been attempting to contact you both, for days. Are you aware?

We weren't sure what was happening. Apologies.

You've made a decision to explain how the light works and how we dance with the light. I'm excited to share in your story and to also explain how I developed my art and how Lyra instructed me. I want to explain how I assembled my performance and my technique and the many wonderful things that I invented for the stage.

Why don't you start by telling us about your technique Loie, since it involved the use of light and color?

If you want to know about the light there are a lot of wonderful details that you might be interested in. I was known when I was on Earth as the "Electric Salomé" and the "Electric Butterfly" and the "Electric Fairy". I mean, everything to do with electricity I was associated with...when I performed my colorful dance. Did you know that color makes a sound and did you know that sound also makes a color? There is a movement and a pattern to it all.   My dance performance is not only something beautiful and something wondrous to look at and adore. The dance pattern is not random. Oh, it may look random and it may look very exciting. I'm quite certain that many of you enjoyed what I did and what I still do, as I continue to dance with the light. I'm still dancing with color, as you will be too.

Tell us more about the patterns Loie. You said they're not random.

No they're certainly not. It looks as though I'm enjoying myself and playing and just being free and spontaneous and like a butterfly. It appears as though the movements are somewhat random. The invention of the dance, in actuality, is an instruction on how one moves with the light. It's an instruction on how one dances, not only with the colors and the sounds but also with the vibration and the motion. Vibration and motion will assist you all.

When you say that it will assist us are you referring to time travel?

This motion is similar to what you are experiencing when you change form. When you change your form and you shift into a new form, a wondrous form with new colors and a new spectrum of energy and a new spectrum of sound, the motion is a dance. You're not simply shifting from your form as Man Being into a new form like the wolf...there is a *dance* involved. Belief and dance are quite similar. You have to believe in the light and the energy and the movement and the form and the sound and the interplay. It's quite something.

One of the elements that makes your dance technique so interesting is the sense of complete immersion with light and color. You almost forget that you're there and you just focus on the effect.

Imagination and the dance that you will be experiencing as you leave Lemuria and begin time travel includes many motions and movement that you are seeing when you watch my dance films. Did you know that most of the films that you are watching are not in fact of me? The performances and the dance motion are quite exact, actually. Many copied me of course and I was very influential, but there was a reason for this and it was not just the spectacle of the clothes and the movement and the colors that I was projecting.

What was the reason?

Many Artists as you already know, found that I was speaking a language. For many visual artists, many painters and sculptors, I was speaking their language…but in dance. You know that dance and the dance form and the dance art, this is an interplay of light, motion, color and sound. Ultimately this is equivalent to time travel. What is the language of Artists? It is the language of color and light. Visual Artists create a motion and an emotion with these tools. There is movement from one emotional state to another as you change your belief and you shift your belief from one thing to another. This is what an Artist is asking you to do when you absorb the message contained in their artwork.

What about those of us who cannot see – how do they absorb the message in the artwork?

If you cannot experience with your eyes, there is still an energy. Color is an energy. For those Beings that do not see color or do not see at all physically, this will of course be immediately corrected when they rebuild the light source in the Lyra intermediary experience. You are able to see more colors than you ever could imagine once you rebuild your Light Body. Once you reconnect with the light there are more colors than you can ever dream of. The dance and my performances had so many colors. The interplay and the shift between the colors is an experience that is equivalent to time travel and you must shift your beliefs and you must shift the energy. You must move the energy and you must move the light. I feel very happy that I was able to share that message with the audience and with the Artists who appreciated that I was taking a stand and sharing that message.

Where are you currently existing Loie?

I am not confined to one state or another or one density of light experience or another. I have made the cross over and I have made the experience. I am absorbing many levels of light. I have not however completed my ascension journey, as you must remember how to believe in the colors and the sounds and the shapes. Remember that in "shape shifting" you are using different shapes. Now I know shape shifting is considered shifting into an animal form or some other form that you have all imagined in fairy tales or your mythologies. But have you stopped to consider that there are new shapes? Shape shifting also means you are all learning about the new shapes. The new shapes are the shapes and the patterns that you are learning how to integrate in the travel experience.

What are the new shapes – can you speak more about that?

There are many fantastic shapes. You've learned about the sacred geometry but there are many shapes that you will be creating. You will be inventing your own shapes. Shape shifting means using a set of shapes and these are tools. You'll be integrating a new set of shapes and therefore a new set of tools and therefore a new level of light and new colors and new sounds. It's a movement and it's fluid. You don't have a "lift off" like a rocket ship and a countdown, none of this. You do not have an experience where you're following a set of instructions and you must make sure that all these instructions are completed. This is a fluid and a rapid movement and experience. Time travel is a very integral experience that is essential so that you continue reassembling who you are.

It was our understanding that the initial reassembly is achieved during the experience of the Soul Ascension Group and The Channel. You're now saying that we "continue reassembling who we are" past that point.

I know that you believe that you are reassembling yourselves in Lyra, as in your Soul Ascension Group...but there's more reassembly. There is more to come. There is not only the completion of your Soul Ascension Group that you are reuniting with, but there are other parts of you and other roles that you have also been involved in. You will soon learn that there are more of you out there than you ever imagined and you are continuing to reconnect with yourself. That motion in my dance gestures, the motion is creating the semblance of "many of me" or many of the dancer. It is like what you would call a hologram, a moving hologram or a kaleidoscope. It is communicating the many aspects of you. You just do not understand how magnificent you are and how big you are. Your light is bigger than you ever imagined. You will be reuniting and reassembling many aspects of you in a fluid motion and experience.

Your description of the "many of you" brings to mind Hindu symbolism and the depiction of Hindu deities.

Yes, precisely. I know that you have seen those lovely avatars in the Eastern Mysticism and these beautiful

Beings with many arms and this is exactly what I am referring to. That motion in my dance, that motion of the fabric and the movement like the butterfly is equal to what some Eastern philosophies are suggesting. There's also the dance of the flowers, the Lily flower. This motion is actually the group experience, your soul assembly. You move in a group. You are creating an experience where there is one of you in each density of light experience and so you are connected with all the densities and you are moving and flowing through all of the densities, connected and together. I suppose you could imagine a caterpillar's motion. You are connected from one end to another but you are not a straight line, please remember that. I'm just giving you that image of a caterpillar to assist in your initial understanding.

Hopefully the Reader has watched some of your performances by this point because what you're describing is putting your art form into an entirely new perspective. You were disseminating vital information.

Indeed I was. You are connected in many directions and in many shapes and colors and sounds. You will all be experiencing something that you have never quite imagined you were capable of. You will be conscious of this connectedness and you will be conscious of this movement and you will be aware that you are dancing in the light. This motion and this experience is very similar to what I performed in my dance. The way that you may feel when you watch the dance is in fact the way that you may feel yourself when you are able to dance like that in light.

Some of the Beings that we've spoken to described having contact with Lyra. How did Lyra instruct you during your lifetime as Loie Fuller?

Colors communicated with me. Now I know that this sounds unusual and it sounds a little odd and I appreciate this of course, but colors communicated with me. I realized the message and the communication from the colors and I suppose the light spectrum from a very early age. I was connecting with, well, not only the Lyra threshold but I was also connecting directly with the first doorway of experience in ascension or what we're calling Lemuria. This is the World of Color or the World of Make Believe, whatever you wish to call it...it is all that. I had a direct connection, a direct line and a direct engagement.

Why did you have this direct line?

I have no explanation. I was always like this. There are many Artists who have the same direct connection. It's not improbable or impossible, so where did the information come from? It came from having complete access to the first gateway. I was already immersed as many children are, but I remained connected. I was not removed from this world. Nobody told me to, "Cease contact and communication". I was never instructed in that belief. So I kept my belief that colors are magic. I kept my belief that light moves and dances and that there are many shapes that we can create and invent. I kept my belief that we dance in the light and that you can become what you imagine. I continued playing and connecting with this World. Many Artists are in this World. Many Artists spend their days in direct contact, fully immersed. Whether or not they can explain to you in words I'm not certain, but they can definitely explain it through their art form.

You are an example of how a child can carry their beliefs into adulthood and create wonderful and amazing things. It's so inspiring.

I had the conscious awareness that I was interconnected with Lemuria and I also believed that I had many direct visits and experiences in this World. It was not only in my dreams but when I danced I was out of body. When I danced I was also dancing in Lemuria. I was in this World of Make Believe and I was doing the dance. The colors that I was projecting onto my clothes were colors that I was creating and imagining, almost scooping out of the air, drawing out of the air. The motion of the dress and the motion of the skirt and the twirling and the butterfly movement…that is something that I was experiencing in Lemuria. I was pulling it out of nothing, creating it out of nothing, forming it out of nothing and just imagining it and being it.

I wonder if some readers might also be frustrated reading this. It seems you led a "charmed life". We're not all so lucky.

I was one of the "lucky" ones. Nobody said to me, "Don't be like that". Don't believe these things, don't believe that colors are magic or that light is a wonderful thing. Don't believe that you could be in another world and that imagination is something for silly folks or imagination is something for young children and imagination is not a correct way to be and a correct thing to have or to do or to say or to invest in or to write about or think about. Nobody said to me, "When are you going to be a grownup?" It's something that I was never instructed on disowning. I chose to keep the door open and there are many of you of course that will benefit from this understanding.

You were in Lemuria while you were performing on Earth. Of course, Artists enter into an "inspired consciousness", but can we concurrently and consciously exist in Lemuria while on Earth?

You would like to know if you can open that door and once again reconnect with this World while you are living on the planet Earth – is it possible? I say yes. I say yes it is possible and when you can once again have this complete connection then there is no room for sadness. You can create and can you exist in a creative threshold so that art and sharing a message through artwork is all that matters.

This heavy emphasis on art and creativity requires a significant adjustment from our Earth mindset, which is to regard art as a "pastime" or an "outlet".

Now I'm not saying that one shouldn't help others, or do anything but create art. I'm not saying that at all. Don't you wonder however, if in fact art would heal the Earth and help everyone reconnect with Lemuria at once? You would not really want to be on earth anymore, I suppose. You would want to be in this wonderful place and dance and party and be happy. This world is a very happy place to be connected with. I hope that all of you make a conscious reconnection with this world. I hope that you all have an experience that I feel most privileged to have. Light is everything. Light heals and it moves and it exists with or without you. Light is everything. When you embrace this understanding then you will also be everything and you will be timeless and immortal. Light has no end.

Loie, some of our readers may not have any proclivity to dance, sing, draw or write. It's quite possible that some readers have completely shut that part of their brain off. How can they make these reconnections?

No one is suggesting that they need to be a professional "world renowned" Painter or Sculptor or Dancer or Singer…no one is saying that of course. I hope that I'm not coming across to you like this, but what I am saying is that we were all children once. Reconnect with your "inner child" and your ability to express this World of

Make Believe and Imagination and Color. You can reconnect with that. That is what I am speaking about.

We understand that, but there are people who see art as this impossible task. They need specific instruction. It's like people who panic when they have to do math, it's the same thing.

Yes this is a good point. Well, here is my advice to those of you who are reticent when it comes to art. Just remember that there was a time when you didn't even speak words…you made noises. There was a time when you did not know how to color within the lines. There was a time when you could barely write a word. There was a time when you managed to communicate in a different way. There are also those among you who seemingly have a disability or a disadvantage, even though this is not the case. How do these Beings communicate or create? There is still energy that is being released. There is a way for everyone to communicate, even Beings who are not conscious. You are sending out signals. We all have ways to invent and so I am saying to be inventive. Make up your own way of speaking, of playing, of creating.

As we did when we were children.

Just as you did when you were children. Make up your own art. As children we are allowed to do this for some time. Lyman spoke at length about this so I won't harp on it too much. So how does a grownup reconnect with their childhood or their childlike way of communicating? Return back to things that just don't make sense. Stop using so much logic. Be free. Don't think about what you're doing. I would always wholeheartedly recommend something like movement or dance. Just move.

That's beautiful. For those who don't have the ability to move or are less mobile, what can they do?

> Their light still moves...the light still dances. These Beings have already learned that light moves and that light dances. You don't need your form to move the light. I'm teaching you how to move the light. These Beings who are less mobile are already interacting with other Worlds. They're already in the dance. There are so many ways to just be free. Do children sit there and calculate and read rulebooks and instruction manuals or do they just allow themselves to be? And so I believe that you just be. Do something. Do anything, but don't sit around thinking about what you can't do and what the rules are. Grownups must play by the rules and when you play by the rules it is no longer playing. Give yourself a chance to interact, to play with the light. You are not allowing yourselves to play. The state of being grownup doesn't have as many privileges as you believe. Children have the privilege. They allow themselves to be.

You seem to embody what we might call the "Divine Feminine". Do you have some advice on how we can all summon that energy while living on Earth?

> When you unlock the ability to play and the ability to play without worry about judgment, then you will unlock not only your divine power or your Divine Feminine, but you will unlock your divine Being. The light doesn't hold a gender and play does not have gender. Release your inhibitions and you release your ability to feel empowered and to empower others. What is the most awe-inspiring thing that you can imagine? Well, when you witness Beings just doing it, being free, just expressing themselves and not caring about whether or not the audition goes well or whether or not the audience has purchased enough tickets or whether

there is a fan base. When you just exist and be and play free of these worries then that is you connecting with the divine feminine. The Divine Feminine is about this childlike play. The Divine Feminine is about the empowered spirit that is released through the release of the worries associated with uninhibited play. Play like children. That is the core of the divine feminine for when you can be happy and play and reconnect with that existence then you are directly tapping into the empowerment of the uninhibited existence as a Light Being.

It's all about returning to light.

The uninhibited Light Being state is the divine feminine state. The Divine Feminine in her perfected state, is a Being who is experiencing the joy of the light. The joy of the light is available for all and the light is, of course, not gender specific and so men are welcome as well to engage in this play, although it may seem like an arduous task to behave like that.

It seems so easy when explained this way and yet as adults it's almost impossible to break from our conditioning.

Let me say this to your readers: The spirit of the butterfly is what you all wish to capture once again. For it is this spirit that will guide you through your ascension journey and ultimately heal all that confines you and imprisons you on Earth. So be like the butterfly and be free and free yourselves. Free yourselves not only from the constraints of being grownups but free yourselves so that you are available to hear what the light has to say. The light has a lot to say...you just need to listen.

We have one last question before you go, Loie. Since in a way, you had never left Lemuria, did you voluntarily disconnect? We know that you "died of pneumonia" in 1928, but what can you tell us about the experience?

> I know that it is a known fact that I experienced death like all of you, through disease. I must tell you however that I voluntarily disconnected ahead of the "death experience" that you all witnessed. This is a bit confusing for your readers and you may not be able to follow this completely, but you can make a voluntary disconnect ahead of the impending death experience. Those of you who are dealing with an ailment or illness do not have to endure the suffering. If you are aware of the experience of the light then you can make the reconnections ahead of the impending death. It is not correct to believe that you have to endure the suffering and the dying. You do not have to endure this arduous journey and so I did in fact make a voluntary disconnect experience, again, just ahead of the impending death release.

Were you able to voluntarily disconnect because you already had that door open?

> If you are engaged with Lemuria, which is the World of Color or World of Make Believe, this is the first doorway and the preparation for time travel. Voluntary disconnect releases you beyond this world into a time travel state. I am not complete in my journey but I have made my way through that initial gateway of experience. Many Artists are launching themselves into a time travel state of experience because they are reconnected with this first doorway, which is essential.

The benefits of being connected to art and creativity just got a whole lot better.

> You must all start floating like butterflies. Thank you for inviting me into your dissemination project.   To

those of you who are reading this now...I will see you all very soon.

Thank you Loie.

MR.
TUDBALL

"There's a lot of people involved in bringing laughter and there's a lot of people involved professionally in comedy. You're a coach aren't you? You're coaching everybody out of their misery. Ultimately you're coaching people to think outside the box, to think outside the form. Right? That expression...'Think outside the box'...that's comedy. Thinking outside the form."

Actor, Writer, Comedian
Emmy Award Winner
WGA Award Winner
1933 - 2019

We are being contacted by a Being who is calling himself "Barnacle Boy". We are speaking back and forth asking for details and a proper introduction, but the Being is urging us to guess who he is. He's playing charades with us now.

Okay...we don't know who Barnacle Boy is.

> I'm a Comedian! My name's not Barnacle Boy. Geez you guys. My name starts with a T and ends with an M.

Are we going to play a guessing game all day or do you want to just introduce yourself...haha.

> Are you guys going to do any work at all here?

Okay, we're looking up Comedians named Tom.

> Uh huh...you're getting warmer.

Oh right! You're...

> You betcha. Glad to be here. Just call me Tudball will ya. It'll be easier to deal with on your end.

Will do. We've wanted a Comedian to step up to the mic. The floor is yours, Tudball. What would you like to discuss?

> Well, first of all...I should acknowledge that my death wasn't pretty, but I guess death isn't pretty. Mine wasn't pretty. I mean I wasn't planning it to be pretty but my death didn't go so smoothly. There's a lot of people who are probably not going to be happy to hear that I'm involved in your weird book, but there's a lot of things that go on in comedy. We make fun of a lot of things and everything's topical in comedy but we don't really consider Comedians as being tuned in or tapped in, spiritually. We're making fun of a lot of things and we're aware of a lot of things and we're, of course, well

versed in a lot of news, history and a lot of pop culture and you name it. When it comes to spirituality and things like that...of course we make fun...but nobody really thinks that we're that serious about spirituality.

Comedians are constantly examining our beliefs. It's odd that we don't perceive Comedians as spiritual.

No and if we come across like that then we're made fun of. But I was very interested in a lot of, I'll say, "alternative" philosophies. It's not something that's widely advertised but I heard about your book and I heard about what you guys are trying to do. I think it's interesting. I think it's interesting for everyone to know that not only do you go somewhere when you leave Earth, but that you go somewhere where you can be very creative. That's the first step and I like the way that it's set up. It's the first step. These things have an order. These things have a plan. It's not that random you know. Nothing is random in the "Afterlife". It's not that random. It's nice that you can go to a place and you could still tell jokes. If you want to do a stand-up show you can do a stand-up show. If you want to paint you can paint, if you want to sing you can sing, if you want to write a book you can write a book, if you want to cook you can cook, if you want to stand on your head you can stand on your head. It's nice that we go to a place and we're allowed to play. We're allowed to do a lot of wonderful and creative things.

It sounds like you're describing Lemuria, is that right? We're also learning that there isn't just one world.

Yes Lemuria, that's right. Everybody wonders what happens when you "die". Is there one world in the Afterlife? Of course not...and you don't have to be stuck in some place where you're just waiting for someone to pick you up, waiting for someone to show you the way, waiting for someone to show you the ropes. You don't have to wait and worry about who's going to meet you. I think a lot of you have that worry. I know I did until I learned a little bit about what's waiting there on the other side.

How did you learn about the other side when you were on Earth?

I learned a lot from my dreams and I kind of like that that's how I learned about it. There's a lot going on here and it's not Angels meeting you or your aunt meeting you. There's a lot going on here and what's going on is you getting organized, getting it together. It's not some place where you've earned the right to just now chill out and relax and it's all going to be brought to you on a silver platter. I mean this is the beginning of your life. You're just starting your life. Earth was fun and I had a pretty good time but it's not a good time for most of you, admittedly. But your life is starting…your life is starting when you cross over. Now I'm not advocating that you all check out now and do some crazy things, I'm not advocating that. Your life really does get a lot better when you cross over.

Not everyone is convinced of that.

That's true, and that's how it is on Earth. You think nothing exists but the dirt beneath your feet. Not everyone is convinced that there is something waiting for you. A lot of people say they believe it but I don't know if they really believe it. It's one thing to say you believe it but I started to believe it after I had a whole series of dreams over many years…and I kept a diary of the dreams.

You're not the first Being to tell us that – that you kept a dream diary.

It's all in the dreams. The information that I got was similar to what you're talking about in your books. There's a series of experiences and worlds and light that you can absorb and handle and I started to wonder about that. My dreams were not that clear and apparent that I put it all together as nicely as you have in your books, but I understood that we would go somewhere. I started to believe that we would learn about what light does for us. I also learned a little bit about how...well on Earth you don't have that much light. On Earth you don't have the good light. The light's limited there. That's a weird topic. If you're going to speak to somebody and say, "Ya well you know, the light's not that great on Earth" or "you don't have any light" or "you're light deprived"...that's not going to be a discussion that's going to go over very well. You're not going to get too many people understanding or getting it, but I understood from my dreams that uh huh wait a minute...maybe we're not actually plugged in. Maybe you get plugged in when you cross offer. That was my belief. Now I didn't figure out how to voluntarily release my light. I would've liked that. That would've been something but I was prepared, even though my passing wasn't the greatest situation. Still, I knew what to do. I was ready. I was ready for the light. I had read all about the near death experience. That version of the story and I had my own experience from dreams and I totally believed that the dream and the near death experience is the same experience.

Do you want to tell us about your death experience?

Oh, sure. It is something when you cross over and all those Beings are there. It's something...and they're you. All those Beings are you...different versions of yourself, different incarnations of yourself. Like pieces of a puzzle, you're putting yourself back together. You know that you're made up of many light Beings. It's a composite. You're one big Light Being. You're not just one Dramos and one Bohemias. You're a bunch of you. There's many of you that you meet and I was put back together and that was something I was very surprised by. What am I doing now…well I've been playing in that next world and I love that place. Lemuria. That's a great place. It's great for someone interested in comedy…Comedians. It's great. I've had a glimpse of where I'm going next and wow. Now that experience is something.

Are you referring to Terra or what some Beings are calling the Inner Earth experience?

That's the one. Call it either. Call it what you want. You're using shapes in a way that you never thought you could use shapes. That place after Lemuria…you're calling it Terra or Inner Earth….you're going to be creating shapes with your light and these shapes are going to create a passage. They're going to create a tunnel and you're going to travel though that. But I'm just learning about that now and that's done by sound and that sound creates shapes, so you need a bit of practice. I'm practicing that now. There isn't a class, you don't get a class in that, it just happens.

Tudball, do you mind sharing with us one of the dreams that you had? One that stuck out for you or prepared you the most.

I had a dream and this occurred more than once. This dream came up quite frequently. It was one of those dreams where you say, "Hey I had that dream before".

We call that a *recurring dream*, Tudball. Haha.

Head down…walked right into that one. They didn't tell me you were a smart ass, oh boy, haha.

Sorry, carry on.

I had a dream of a face and I could never make out if it was a woman or a man. It was a face like a statue from a sculpture. Yes…I know they call that a "bust". Zip it. Anyway this bust was always screaming. The face of this bust was like somebody screaming but frozen in stone. It was fixed on this terrified look and it reminded me of the Medusa. So there you go…that was my recuuuuuuring dream.

What conclusions if any did you start to draw from that dream?

For one, I didn't feel like someone is trying to scare me. I felt that that was a symbol…it's kind of funny speaking about this the way I'm describing it. I felt like that was a symbol to pay attention to and I always imagined that it had something to do with the Gorgon or Medusa. I wondered for the longest time what more that myth could possibly mean. I mean it had to be more than just some scary story, some mythological creature that we're all terrified of. One day when I was performing and I was doing a little bit of an improv…I had a specific thought. The way this thought came through to me was almost like an eruption…like volcanic but with light. I had the thought that maybe what we're most terrified of is just letting it all hang out. You know like in improv, like in comedy…letting it all hang out. Just doing it. Letting it all go. Not worry you know. Well, release your light…right? Be yourself. Be free. I wondered if that was the secret, the key. That we were all trapped and afraid to let it all hang out and be ourselves and just play and be free and not worry about being judged or being evaluated or worry about what people are thinking of you.

What did you do with that thought – did you keep it to yourself?

> I started to play around with that idea, not so much in
> my work but just in my everyday life. Just tried not to
> be so concerned, because even though you're in
> comedy it doesn't mean you're not worried about what
> people think. Comedians are actually some of the most
> uptight people you're going to meet actually…and
> that's something that's kind of strange. But I started to
> wonder about that…the energy and the light and what
> did that mean exactly. I thought about all these sayings
> like, "release yourself", "free yourself", "let your light
> shine", and "be magnetic"…stuff like that. I started to
> play around with that and I started to dream about it
> more often. Then instead of seeing this frightening
> apparition of this screaming head…it turned into
> something different.

Do you mean that the bust in your dream transformed into something else?

> That's exactly what happened. It became something
> that was more like a sun or a star or some burst of light.
> I started to wonder a lot about the Sun. I know that
> you're writing a lot about this in your books and the
> Sun and sunlight and worshipping the Sun and Sun
> worshippers. You're all worshipping the Sun…but I
> started to subscribe to another Sun. This sounds so
> strange to talk about with you guys on Earth but I
> started to subscribe to my *inner Sun*. I started to wonder
> if we become the Sun or if we are the Sun and this
> whole idea that you can create your own light, like a
> Sun. I was toying around with the idea that we're all
> stars. So that's where I was at and that's what I was
> expecting. I was expecting I was going to learn about
> that when I crossed over and I wasn't expecting some
> Angel to meet me at some gate.

It's amazing to hear the thoughts that some people are carrying around with them. This is not what most people would assume that Mr. Tudball was contemplating.

> I admit it. It's not something most of us share or even realize that we believe. Sometime it's just a nagging little thought or a dream that you remember, you know. For me I was expecting that I would learn how to just release all that light. So what you're calling "The Channel"…that's ultimately you. That's me. That's all of us. Well, all of us who are going on that path. You have to be involved with the Sirius light. It seems on one hand that it's kind of strange…I mean most of us are not imagining that we're going to see some creature generating light. But on the other hand is it really that far-fetched? Is it that strange? Look around. There's a lot of things exploding and releasing light. It's not that far fetched. And it's here. You'll see it.

If we had met you before you got sick and asked you outright, "what do you believe happens when you die?", what would you have said?

> I don't know what I would have said and actually, even though I was prepared for all this I still didn't quite know if I was going to come back…you know…reincarnate. I mean I figured that there's got to be more to this and if you can generate light and you can release your light…okay…then where would you go? Would you come back as a person? Well no why would you? I wasn't totally clear but I didn't believe that I wanted to come back. I mean if I could release my light like that then I was just going to go with it. So that's what I did.

You're saying that you were very much open to there being another option.

Yeah, although I didn't know exactly how it was going to work. I didn't have an instruction. I didn't have your books. That would have been great haha. I mean, with your books…if you can get really detailed for everybody then I think that's going to be wonderful. Imagine that…you just have to read some books and that's great. The problem is that you're not prepared to cross over and see all this wonderful stuff. You're not prepared to see something that generates light and that doesn't look "real" or "possible". You know, once you get passed this "We know everything that there is to know on Earth" attitude, you can really open yourself up to new experiences and those new experiences are not new experiences like you're going to have on Earth.

Problem is, the moment you publicly or even privately admit that you believe there's an existence beyond Earth…there's a real risk of being ridiculed or worse, ostracized.

That's because few people are really and truly "open". You know when you say to someone "Be open"? You tell someone to be open but when you tell someone to be open, "Hey relax be open to new experiences" or if you say, "Oh I'm open to discovering new things. I'm open to trying new things"…you're not really open. You're open to trying things on Earth. You're not open to trying something completely new like this. You're just rehashing all of the things that you know on Earth. You can't fault anybody for believing that everything that you see is right in front of you, but I have to say…the interesting thing is that everybody seems to believe in ghosts.

Yet so many of us deny it.

Even if they say they don't, they probably do quietly. They're wondering about it. Everyone's open to that.

Why is it that we can all be open to that but we can't be open to the other stuff?

Don't hold back Tudball. Tell us what we need to hear.

You know what I'm going to say for your book...you don't really know what light is so the thought of a "Being" or "Creature" that generates its own light...you just can't fathom it. It's just not possible. And if you can accept that, well hey, why not? Why can't you generate your own light? If you can just accept it, if you can just remind yourself that that's a possibility...and I'm not saying to chant it like a mantra everyday, although that might help. But people don't accept that that's a possibility because you just don't even know what the light is. You've got the Sun and you've got the stars and you've got the comets that are falling and you've got the meteorites and you've even got all the stuff that you're doing on the planet that's not good. You're generating light in some really terrible ways. Exploding things and on and on, but that's not the light that I'm speaking about. There's a lot of things blowing up on Earth but how about releasing your own light, your own inner volcano? It's funny how we can blow things up. On Earth we can do things to other people, other creatures, other things...but releasing our own abilities...no. That's something that we are very limited in on Earth and that's a shame. We can do all these wonderful things externally you know. We can do this and we can do that. Do this to this person and do that to that Being. Do this to this object and all things and stuff and externalities but how about you just release your light? How about you just...yeah...be a Light Being? I think that's a great start.

Tudball, can you talk to us about the frequency of laughter and what is actually happening when we laugh? We talk about music as a sonic stabilizer, but what about laughter? We ask because there seems to be a real effort to obstruct Comedians and free speech these days.

> Now this is a good point. I like where this is going. This is a good point. When we laugh and we just laugh wholeheartedly, we just laugh and let it all hang out...I have to say that that feels very similar to the experience of letting one belief go and finding another. Now I know you're both going to say, "Oh hey Tudball that's like time travel you're talking about time travel". Well maybe I am. Like a sneeze you know. You know when you sneeze, it's almost like for a moment you don't exist. Do you know what I'm saying? It's like you blink. Like just for a second there...you don't exist. Time stops or something. It's the same kind of experience. So when you laugh it's almost like you don't exist in the way that you're used to existing, trapped in your body. It's almost like you're outside yourself. I'm going to say this...laughter is similar to "out of body". It's almost like...well...astral travel, but that's going to be confusing everybody. But there is a movement, there's a motion to laughter. Laughter is a frequency. There's a movement and when you have movement you have the light moving...I think Loie must've said that about Dance. It's the same. You're moving the light. You're kind of freeing the light. I know that laughter heals but what's it healing? We're healing sadness, we're healing pain but ultimately what are we healing? We're healing this imprisonment in the form because all of our despair, everything that we're suffering is happening to us. Why? Because we're trapped on Earth and we're trapped in a physical body. We're trapped. So everything that happens to us when we're in the Earth plane, in a physical body...it hurts a lot. There's a lot of sadness. There's a lot of pain.

Do you think readers are starting to really get that we're on a prison planet or will this take a few more Volumes to sink in?

Listen...I know there's a lot of happiness for some of you too, Earth can offer up a whole lotta fun. But you can be a lot happier without the physical form. I'm not advocating that you all just now do something crazy, I'm not saying that. Laughter...now if we could just take a journey or travel on laughter that would probably take us to many worlds, many existences. Laughter is like a sneeze. It's definitely a momentum and something that takes you outside of your body for that little moment, for just a little bit of time. And that's all you need to start learning that maybe you don't have to exist in a physical body. Maybe you exist outside of your physical body. Maybe you exist after your physical body is just no more. That's providing of course that you could put these ideas together. Not everybody is able to contemplate things like this. Not everybody is in the same place like you mentioned. I had a difficult run there with a mental health issue. So some of us are not able to intellectually construct an explanation or understanding but you know what...you don't have to have your mind that intact to feel the light or the frequency.

We keep hearing that. We keep hearing that having a mental or physical impairment doesn't preclude us from having an energetic experience.

Because it's true. That feeling, that signal and that energy have nothing to do with the intellectual process. It has nothing to do with memory. It's got nothing to do with how smart you are, how alert you are or even how mentally aware you are. You are tuning into vibration and frequency even when you're in a coma. I hope all the suffering that everybody is dealing with on Earth just magically goes away and you have your ascension experience and your Messiah and whatever you want to label it. I wish for everyone to just laugh a lot. You can laugh a lot in the World of Make Believe, there's a lot of laughter there. You can just stay there and laugh. If you just want to stay there and laugh no one's going to tell you to leave. It's great.

What would you say a Comedian is? Yes, they help us "turn a frown upside down" and entertain us. But how do you see it from your end?

There's a lot of people involved in bringing laughter and there's a lot of people involved professionally in comedy…and I suppose *philosophy* in a way. It's the philosophy of laughter and happiness and light. I guess we're philosophers of light. Anyone that's choosing comedy as a profession, now that's an interesting choice isn't it? Why would somebody select that? Why would somebody just consciously decide, "I'm here and this is what I'm going to do. I'm going to be a Comedian". That's an interesting job. You're a Coach aren't you? You're coaching everybody out of their misery. Ultimately you're coaching people to think outside the box, to think outside the form. Right? That expression…"think outside the box"…that's comedy. Thinking outside the form. So Comedians are serving a very important purpose, like music and like a lot of the arts. But laughter…getting outside of the form…you laugh a lot when you leave your body. It's a whole bunch of laughs.

What do you mean by that?

Well to see what you become…that's funny. It's amazing what you can do with your Light Body. The shapes that you can make you can really twist yourself and make yourself into a weird shape. You can be whomever you want in the Make Belief World. You want to be a pretzel, you want to be a panther…you want to be a Mac truck…whatever. It's amazing and hilarious. I don't imagine anyone speaks to you about that. When you're a Light Body, don't get me wrong, you're not assembled like Lego. You're not glued together. If you want to try a different shape by all means try a different shape. When you're a Light Body you're assembling shapes.

That's an idea that takes some getting used to. Some readers might still be scratching their heads over the idea that we're just a bunch of shapes.

It's like this. You're not saying, "Okay I'm going to have a triangle and I'll have two squares please...and oh yeah get me an oval". It's not like that. You're learning how to work with the light and sound and ultimately, color and frequency. It's like a symphony of shapes. Let's go back to laughter I like that topic...wouldn't you know. When you measure laughter on one of those graphs like you have on your microphone, you're recording the microphone levels, right? The way that that's depicted on the screen, the way it's moving around and it's very alive...that's the kind of motion that you play around with when you're initially assembling your Light Body.

Do we assemble the Light Body in Lyra or in Lemuria?

You're not really assembling your Light Body in Lyra. Well yes and no. You're assembling yourself because you're meeting all of your "selves" there. That's what that means, because you've got your Soul Ascension Group. You learn how to play with the light. You're playing with the light but you are the light. So if you want to be a square, or if you want to be circles and triangles...go for it. You're moving your shapes around, you're moving your frequency around and you're moving your sound around. That's going to help you time travel.

Getting back to laughter…you said that Comedians are coaching others to think outside the box. What about people who don't laugh at anything? We all know at least one individual who finds nothing funny.

It's something, isn't it? Well, if laughter is moving the energy around and moving the light around and freeing the light, then I guess you would first have to realize that the light's there. That's a bold statement on my part. I mean we laugh as children don't we? We're born that way. We're born to play. Yes, some of us are born in a condition where we're not going to have a "typical" childhood or lifespan or typical circumstances, but for the average individual there's plenty of opportunity to laugh…so what's wrong with people who can't laugh? You have to ask yourselves…are they broken? Can they fix that? You have to retrain.

How does a person retrain to laugh?

It's a language. You know the laughter sounds…the sounds like "haha" and "hoho"…those sounds are specific frequencies. They're shapes. They're tools. So it's a language. Laughter is a language. So maybe these people forgot the language. They probably need to retrain. It's not a case where someone can't find the laughter. I don't buy that and again I'm speaking for the "average" person who isn't enduring trauma or a debilitating circumstance. Most of us can be retrained. You can be retrained. You can say, "Oh I didn't find that funny" or "That's not funny" or "That doesn't make me laugh", but you can laugh without having to think about something funny. You just have to laugh. Laughing comes like yawning. It's just a reflex. It's just a natural reflex. Most people think it's just a response to something, like it's a response to comedy or something funny, but it's a sound. It's a frequency that's being vocalized. You can experience it internally or you can make a sound. It's something that we do. It's just practice.

If you had read this book while on Earth how would you have reacted to the information?

Do you mean to the discussion that we're having right at this moment or to your books in general?

We're referring to the books in general. Some people feel a little sadness from shifting their beliefs and leaving the 3D world behind.

Well I'd ask them, "do you want to change your life"? The sadness sounds like they're not ready to change their life. I know that sounds a bit mean but if you don't want to change your life then why are you reading these books? These books, it sounds like, are to change your life. Now...you're asking me to give you some simple response on how to deal with a complete breakdown of everything you've ever believed. Well it's kind of funny if everything you've ever believed is wrong. It's kind of funny, isn't it? Haha! I mean I find that hilarious. It's not one thing it's everything! Jokes on me! I would just laugh...maybe laugh. Rather than worry about it, why not just laugh?

Of course you would say that.

Isn't it ridiculous that we follow all these beliefs? It is ridiculous when you stop to ask, "Why am I believing this? Who told me to believe this?" It's a wonderful thing that you can change your belief. You can change your belief in the blink of an eye. Changing your belief is free. Unless you're not living in a "free society"...then you have to be careful. Outwardly changing your belief might not be a safe proposition in that case, but you can inwardly change your belief.

Old paradigms are collapsing and cultural beliefs are shifting more and more these days. What would you joke about if you were still here?

> Well I would joke about how it's all so ridiculous trying to hold on to things. I would make fun of our efforts to try to desperately hold on to things that are broken. I mean it all depends on how you look at it but it is funny how we desperately want things to work that just don't work. That can be sad, sure it can be very sad, but it can also be very funny. Like if something just doesn't work anymore it can be very funny if you just keep trying to get it to work. It doesn't have to be a pitiful desperate morose thing. It can be quite light and humorous and well...I hope Comedians are guiding everyone through it. Like reminding all of you that, "Yes everything just broke down" and just playing with it in a funny way. That's what Comedians do we play with it. Maybe we'll make jokes and make it worse...it can always be worse right. That's what I would joke about. Everything collapsed...it could be worse...far worse. I don't know what to tell you if you're not willing to play and you're not willing to play around with things.

That really is our problem on Earth. We are so stuck in our ways. We're stuck, period.

> It's changing. When things break down it's an opportunity, it's not a mistake. It's an opportunity for you to invent something new. Why don't you invent something new if it's all broken? Just do something new. That's where Comedians come in. We just work with "broken". We work with broken, that's what we work with. Most of you don't. If it's broken you're stuck. You feel that if it's broken that it's over. And if a Comedian feels it's broken well that's the beginning. That's amazing. Some of you say, "Deconstruct". Get artsy

and deconstruct it. But being broken, that's not the end. That's the beginning. I know that's cliché but that's how we work it, so maybe try some of that.

Can you tell us what you find funniest about the 3rd and 5th density?

Well the funniest thing about 5th density, I'll start there, is that nothing has a purpose anymore. There's no purpose for anything. Nothing. And there's nobody...well if you want to invent an audience clapping and cheering for you well okay, you can do that but you're just doing stuff because you want to do it. You know on Earth you just spend so much time trying to impress everybody. You're trying to get some applause. You're spending so much time trying to get applause and in 5th density...nobody cares and it's something. You have to experience that. You're your own audience. So if you're going to be telling a joke you're going to be laughing at the joke.

That sounds absolutely depressing...haha. No one will want to go to 5D now.

Haha...I realize now that that doesn't sound so great. It's not depressing believe me. Let me rephrase. Everything that matters is happening all at once. You're not having something that matters on "this day" and having something that matters at "this hour" and when the show's over it doesn't matter or you no longer matter. There's no beginning or ending so if you want to do something over and over and over again...like forever...if you want to do something over and over that you love...then you do it. There's no beginning or end. That's what I mean by there's no point or purpose. It just is. You know what I like most about the 5th density? That you're not waiting for something to end. I never really liked that feeling on Earth, that there's all

215

these endings. Earth is all about endings isn't it? The whole thing is just one big ending. You're just waiting for the end there. You're just waiting for everything to end. You reach a point and I know young children are not buying into this...but you reach a point where you're just sitting around waiting for the end. Even if you're really actively doing things and you're trying to make the most of your life...provided you have that privilege...again I'm not suggesting that everybody has a privilege. But you're quietly waiting for the end. And there's none of that waiting for the end in the 5th density. There's none of that in the Lemuria state of being, there's no waiting for the end. It's just something...I know I'm going to say you have to be there...but you just have to be there. And you will.

You speak about having an audience and we realize that no one has spoken to us about the interaction with other Beings in the 5th density. What's the interaction like between Light Beings? Did you go looking for anyone when you crossed over? Like Elvis or Jesus or a relative?

Oh they can show up and you can invent them or create them. If you want to have a tea party with Jesus and a clown then you just do it. Lemuria is like a dress rehearsal. This is a practice place. I know we're all maybe saying to you that it's like a world or a planet. But it's a belief, that's for sure. It's a belief that you all have. You all secretly believe that maybe wishing for something works. You all secretly have that belief even if you don't subscribe to it. Many of you say that it's "nonsense" and that it "doesn't work" but you all secretly wonder. That's Lemuria...that's the World of Imagination and again it's not a planet. This is just practice. You're practicing time travel.

It's an energy field.

EXACTLY.

Tudball, it's been a great conversation and before we end it would you like to say one last thing to the readers?

Well, I would say that there's enough time and I know we really don't want to be subscribing to "time" but that's what you're using where you are now, isn't it? There is enough time for you to absorb all of these beliefs as strange as they are. There is enough time. So if some of you are just going to wait for your "time to come" because a lot of you have obligations and you just don't want to poof disappear...well then you have time. This voluntary disconnect experience is fantastic but a lot of you cannot do that...but regardless there's enough time for you to learn about these things. There's not going to be a situation where you're going to make a mistake. I guess that's what I want to say...I want to leave you with this. You're not going to make a mistake. You're not going to choose the wrong door. It's not like that. So the mistake of "oh I accidentally reincarnated oh boy what did I do"...that's not going to happen. If you believe that you are a Being who is connected with the light and a Being that is meant to shine their light and if you just believe in some of these basic tenets...you'll be fine. You're not going to make a mistake. You're not going to make a sudden turn and "oops ahhh reincarnation". It's not like that. I think a lot of you must be worried about that. "How do I know, who do I ask for, who do I speak to, give me a name where do I stand what do I do?" You don't do anything. You believe something. It's not about doing...it's about believing.

That's the perfect way to end this discussion. Your contribution has been fantastic.

I'm also sorry if anyone was upset with how I chose to disconnect, but sometimes things just happen. It's not a big deal if you understand the big picture but I am sorry if I upset a lot of people. I stressed out everybody. If I could do it again I would do it differently but sometimes we just go with it and I guess I just wanted to take it as far as I could. And I did.

I hope we can all find forgiveness in our hearts. You seem like a Being who just wants to bring light.

Thank you.

What are you off to do now in your World over there? What's on the itinerary?

Ping Pong.

With yourself or someone else?

Oh yes, myself. I intend to be a Champion.

HOBSON

"You are not 7 billion Beings. You are much less than that, my friends. You are only now beginning to understand the dilemma that procreation or reincarnation creates. This is why you are all trapped, as you say. You continue to recycle."

Actor, Director, Photographer
Academy Award Winner
Received Knighthood
1904 – 2000

Hobson requested that we also describe him as:
A Scuba Diving enthusiast

Someone is saying, "I played King Lear". We are getting the feeling that the Being wants us to acknowledge his Shakespeare work. This goes on for a few minutes and the communication becomes clearer.

> I played King Lear. Are you not interested in having a conversation?

We are very much interested. Please introduce yourself and perhaps you can begin by telling us why you want to contribute to our book dissemination.

> My name is John but you might not want to print my full name. Best to avoid a kerfuffle. Go with "Hobson" why don't you…many of you were amused by that movie character.

Will do, John.

> I have heard many good things about this project. You're calling it a "project". I'm calling it an event and this event where you propose to reinstate all of us from where we came is not only something that I am standing behind but I would like to stress something else. You must all remember that there is a place where we can meet again and speak further about many things. Would you like to know a little bit about my journey in the arts, about my journey in performance and acting?

What we're more interested in, John, is how your journey on Earth took you to the 5th density or to wherever you are now.

> Are you aware that many of us travel even though we appear on Earth with you in a Human form? Your question about where I have been and where I go is important for your story. I have always traveled. You're writing about time travel and you are writing about

220

things that are so improbable for many to conceive of that you have a difficult task on your hands. Many of us and I'm speaking about Actors, many of us have the knowledge or the tools. Did you know that there are a group of us that travel around and continue to perform? I know that this sounds like a fairy-tale but there are some of us, well many of us in actuality that have access beyond Earth and have access to the time travel state.

Are these Beings consciously traveling or traveling through dream state?

They are consciously aware of their purpose and they are consciously aware of the experience, but you are asking, "Do they consciously admit the experience" and "Does lack of admission equal to lack of awareness?" I would say there is a greater cautiousness than you realize. There are many Actors and Directors and Writers…Beings of renown that in fact have the tools and also write about their experiences and share their experiences in their artistic performances. There's no coincidence that some of the stories and plots and narratives describe something uniquely integrated with what you are assembling in your book series. I'm not quite sure how you are going to complete the 12 Volumes because the 12th book, of course, will involve you fulfilling the knowledge. This will be quite a unique experience.

Are you saying that we will be having more out-of-body experiences as we continue?

Yes, both you and your readers.

We're noticing that you're speaking very slowly with us…much slower than the others.

The reason for this is that I am connecting with many levels of light and experience and for this very reason I am not able to simply connect with you as the others have been. My communication is not only directed to you both in the 3rd density of light experience. It is also being broadcast in the other densities and this may answer your question as to how other Beings are hearing and learning about your activities. This communication we are having now is also being broadcast in the World of Imagination or Lemuria as you are calling it. It is broadcast beyond that gateway of experience. In fact, you will be contacted by many others who will help you and contribute to the assembly and the understanding and the knowledge about the gateway beyond the World of Imagination. That is not the only experience that you will encounter in this particular book. My disconnect experience is what you must ask about. The disconnect experience when you are a Time Traveler like myself and a bonafide one I might add, is not about disconnecting from form the way that you are writing about.

What is it about?

It is about disengaging oneself from the amount of 3rd density experience. Time travel is interesting and you must both note that a Time Traveler does not spend an extended amount of your time in 3rd density experience. This is not possible. Has this been explained to you?

It hasn't. Can you explain what exactly a Time Traveler is capable of?

The beginning of your experience as a Time Traveler is not the beginning where one learns how to be in different bodies, in different forms, in different places, in different roles. It is an experience where you learn and are equipped to tune in and to listen and to hear everywhere all at once in unison, like a musical chord. I am creating a signal and a sound that is being heard throughout the universe. Our conversation is being transmitted in many densities of light experience. Time travel and a Time Traveler is not in one singular place. Time travel is the ability to be everywhere at once. Now you are both writing about changing form and moving light and containing the light energy. These are early days for both you and your readers.

You're saying that the shape shifting is only the beginning.

I was enthusiastic about your shape shifting chapter in Volume 2. The principles of shape shifting are not that far-fetched. If a wolf brings you closer to your destination then so be it. Shape shifting does not divide your existence from one density to the next. It connects. Shape shifting is a connector. It is a connection. When you're shape shifting you have one foot or in this case a paw in another world. Your beliefs about time travel begin in 5D and your story as Sirius Beings begin with the story of the wolf...the wolf or the dog, the Dog Star. It is a story that has been passed down through the ages but has fallen on deaf ears. A simple instruction: change your form, change your belief and change your form again. This is the recipe for time travel. The Time Traveler is everywhere at once and I would like you both to appreciate that when I communicate with you in the 3rd density I am also communicating with you in other densities of experience and existence. What you are hearing in this case, English words of communication in 3rd density, you are also receiving in light and sound and of course the shapes in another density. You have forgotten this. There will be conversations where you must describe in 3rd density communication what you are seeing and hearing and receiving in another density.

We receive many symbols through visions and dreams, some of which we've included in the books.

> Yes, precisely. When you are seeing beautiful shapes you will learn what this is saying. The shapes speak to you and the expression "let it take shape" is very apt for this discussion. Let it take shape. This is advice that I would like to give to all of your readers. It means more than you know.

When you existed here as "John", were you simply visiting the 3rd density and then left when you wanted to leave?

> What has left is your ability to follow my travels. Did I die or involuntarily disconnect? No. Did I spend a limited amount of linear time in 3rd density or are you no longer able to see me because you are not able to connect with the 5th density experience? Did you know that these two existences cooperate and work together?

Do you mean the 3rd and the 5th density?

> Yes. You are able to exist in both simultaneously. This is how one experiences a fulfilled creative life in the Earth plane. That life of course is the life of the light containment and the ability for other Beings in the Earth plane existence to witness it. You are not on Earth for a temporary role. You are changing your ability to connect with me. When you are able to integrate the ability to speak with the light in the 5th density experience and also in the Earth plane simultaneously, which is a challenge I realize this, then you will still be experiencing me on Earth. This is something that is beyond all of your wildest dreams. I appreciate these things sound impossible but it is "time"…and I'm using that tongue in cheek of course…to explain that when somebody is no longer with us on Earth, they did not leave. You lost the ability

to connect with them. As they are absorbing more light, you are not able to follow. This is your inability to absorb and understand the light. When you change this ability and acquire and accept the ability there will be no loss.

How can we recognize a Time Traveler here in the Earth plane? Is there a "tell"?

Some of us seem to have extended lifespans for one and some of us seem to be immersed in a pursuit. In my case acting and performance and theater. For some of us it would seem that there is an uncanny amount of good luck or what some of you might suggest is karma...that you seem to be "unstoppable" or what some might suggest, "Not ever have to worry about working" or you can pursue your passion and there does not seem to be much obstacle. That certainly is a hallmark for many of the Time Travelers. I am not suggesting of course that you do not encounter hardships. If that's what you want to experience then that is what you do but there does seem to be, when you look at this more closely, an extended run and an extended lifespan that quietly allows one to continue their work or what you would call...life's work.

We've spoken to one Time Traveler at least, in our discussions for Volume 3. She's quite accomplished but had a quieter existence.

Yes. If you look at some of the Time Travelers and you've been given one as an example, Nika, these Beings do a lot and although some of us win awards or garner a lot of recognition and acclaim, we do seem to be quietly on another level just getting on with it and doing what we need to do. Ultimately if you are time traveling and you have this ability and knowledge, then you experience a complete lack of obstruction. Life has its "ups and downs" in the 3rd density of course, but in the other experiences that I am witnessing and existing in...the other worlds that I am simultaneously involved in as I speak with the both of you...there is no obstruction. It is a flow. It's an unobstructed flow of experience. Events are somewhat an obstruction. When you do time travel you do not mark time. Time is an event and that event is an obstruction. There's a flow. This is not something that you can teach but you certainly can impress upon your readers that they must extend their reach.

Our belief in "time" is keeping us imprisoned.

It most certainly is. The linear understanding that you are mandated by the clock is not something that you are involved with in time travel. Your readers must remember that they are building upon a lexicon of shapes and sounds and you are all building yourselves like a beautiful sculpture. It is a beautiful sculpture composed of many sounds and shapes and colors if you will. This sculpture reaches into many different places of existence, many worlds of experience. When you describe something that is "far-reaching" this is what you are describing. You must learn how to stand in one place and another and again another and so on and so forth, simultaneously. This ability will allow you to not only integrate your ability to broadcast and communicate everywhere simultaneously, but it will also allow you not to have to deal with those devious Beings that you have unfortunately now crossed paths with. You are protected as a Time Traveler. Are you aware of this?

No.

You are unstoppable. If you are everywhere at once then you cannot be obstructed in one specific density of experience. Your encounter with a Being who was not

226

very polite Bohemias, from the sounds of what you experienced, is something that you do not endure when you complete the release of your light. This is a threat of course to these Beings as you are unstoppable and can now, as many of us do, broadcast the knowledge. When you complete your training and release your light and connect with many densities of experience simultaneously, your books and message will be far-reaching and you will be repairing on another level entirely. This participation and your ability to do this is undoubtedly a big concern for these Beings. It does sound like you are all becoming unstoppable and this will ultimately upset many along the way.

We are prepared.

Continue your work. Many Beings across the universe are tuned into this Event. We are all with you.

How many Time Travelers are among us in the Earth plane, at this moment?

Well this certainly ties in with your question about how many Sirius Beings need rescue or assistance. You've been given a number and that number is correct however there is a minor adjustment to the number that I would recommend that you consider.

We recently received a vision of the number 780,000 without explanation attached.

Yes and that is because there is a greater understanding to the number you've been informed about. The 780,000 number that you have at your disposal explains the extension through the different light densities of experience. That number is ultimately reduced. When you learn how many densities of light you are connected with you will be applying a simple division to that larger number. There are not as many as that number first suggested.

This is incredible. Are we to understand that there are only 780,000 Sirius Beings in existence? Actually less, once we divide it by the number of light densities.

This is ultimately the beginning of your understanding. Imagine now with the billions of you that exist on Earth...imagine how much you've all multiplied yourselves through procreation. You are not 7 billion Beings. You are much less than that, my friends. You are only now beginning to understand the dilemma that procreation or reincarnation creates. This is why you are all trapped, as you say. You continue to recycle. I recommend that you further discuss this topic with Lyra for a broader understanding of the Sirius dynamics.

Back to the original question, how many conscious Time Travelers currently exist on Earth?

You are all Time Travelers. You have forgotten. But I do understand the nature of your question. That number you're asking me about reflects the understanding of the Beings who are witnessing and believing it. There are hundreds and hundreds of Beings who have this ability. Undoubtedly all of them are in the arts. With respect to those Sirius Beings who are not yet awake to their capability and in need of realignment, you are helping these Beings make their reconnections. They will all soon again recognize where they have come from and where they can go.

John, I'm reading that Marlon Brando spoke highly of you after having done "Julius Caesar" together, early on in his career. Was Marlon consciously time traveling on Earth?

This question is not necessary to ask me, as you already know the answer. You are asking questions for which you already have the answers. This Being "runs in my circles" if you would like me to describe it this way and I understand that you would also like a communication with the Being you call Marlon. This Being is also everywhere at once and if you would like to continue these conversations you must appreciate that the level of communication is layered. You are putting words on a page when in fact there are many layers to the communication. This is a complexity that you must solve and discover a way that you can publish the conversation that is being broadcast simultaneously in the other densities of experience. Marlon will of course be quite demanding with you and require that you do not ignore this fact. This is not an Earth discussion. This is a universe discussion. The conversation and the message is being heard everywhere and you are best to disseminate your information so that we have a book in 3rd density but also a "book" in other densities. You are not disseminating strictly to one level of light experience. If you are dedicated to this project you must re-evaluate how to disseminate in your book form in order to continue a broadcast unobstructed in the other densities of experience.

The concept of a conscious Time Traveler is still a bit murky for us and I imagine for some readers as well. If you were a Time Traveler John, why did you experience death at the age of 96? Why would a Time Traveler endure "death"?

This is of course a reflection of your experience. Who is doing the dying? Is it me or is it in fact you? You must reverse the way you are interpreting this. My ability to communicate in 3rd density is no longer available for the Beings who remain in 3rd density. I am not suggesting that you did not experience my physical death. What I am suggesting is that you have not been able to keep up with the light. This is about light management. The ability to incorporate and involve and absorb an increasing amount of light allows you to keep up with another's experience. When you all adjust and believe in the light and what the light can do then none of you will die and you will have immortality and be dealing with each other permanently, although I imagine for some this is not desirable.

Light Being humor haha. John is our ability to "manifest" on Earth simply us tapping into the 5th density or Lemuria state? We call it the "Law of Attraction" but it's sounding like we're simply connected to Lemuria or the World of Creativity/Make Believe.

Now you're starting to understand. When you connect with the World of Imagination or Creativity or Make Believe or Lemuria, then you are able to recreate your belief in the Earth plane. That is how you "manifest". Now you do not have to remain in the Earth plane if you are able to go through the gate into this world. You are able to stand in both worlds simultaneously and if you would like to have tea together then this would occur in the World of Imagination. The Earth plane is not a place where you can easily manage the light. You also have quite a difficult experience in being truly creative.

Earth is an extremely difficult environment to be creative. We create communities for creative outlet, but Artists are never fully integrated into the larger society.

Creativity requires light movement and creativity requires a flow of experience. Artists are completely integrated with the 5th density and Lemuria and that is where they are able to seek ideas and also find relief from the drudgery of the Earth plane existence. The Artists that you are assisting are not able to go beyond Lemuria and although it is a lovely place to be it is not the end. It is simply a beginning. You are assisting those who already understand this level of light and communicate in this 5th density experience. They already have the tools and are already broadcasting in more than one density simultaneously. So this explains for you both how the Artist is able to absorb the teachings and the directions in your books. Your readers need to focus their belief on the creative spark that begins in the 5th density and never ends. Look at how much light you need just for the beginning. It is something isn't it?

Yes it is. Is there something in particular that you'd like to leave our readers with John, as we bring this conversation to a close?

Yes I wish to bring home the point that we are broadcasting across many levels of existence. In my work that you recognize in the 3rd density experience of Earth, I extended myself so that the broadcast and the signal was and is far reaching. These activities that I involved myself in creatively are on one hand of course play and make believe and all the wonderful things that come out of Lemuria. They are also broadcast to other levels of light. The Actor has the ability and fundamentally the belief in the coexistence on many levels of light experience. In other words time travel. This is important for you all and it's not to pat myself on the back. This is not how I want to be seen or believed to be. There is a signal that is being broadcast when you choose to be a creative speaker to the universe.

Art is not only play…it's a message to the universe.

Yes but more than that, if you are taking it upon yourself to disseminate in the arts then you are taking it upon yourself to abide by the Repair Project. You are assisting others in reconnecting with their homeward journey experience. You are reminding everyone that we are all in this together. In unison we will all achieve the Ascension. I am part of the Ascension Group experience even though I am already in a time travel belief pattern. We are working with you and are assisting in broadcasting the message. This conversation for your book is broadcast. You will of course be communicating with other Beings, do not be surprised by this.

Thank you John for participating. It's been a wonderful conversation.

Thank you both.

CONSTANTIN
BRANCUSI

"I am speaking about a completely new invention of form. Take for example a painter like a Picasso. The way he depicted Man, as in shapes, is a much closer representation of how you could exist. You are wearing somebody else's clothes. You must absorb this and believe that your form on Earth is not the original form. You are all subscribing to and believing in a lie."

Artist
1876 - 1957

Constantin Brancusi arrives showing an image of his famous sculpture, "The Kiss". It is a cubist style depiction of two people kissing. He's showing us this sculpture because it is a non-literal representation. This is a topic he wishes to discuss with us.

Welcome to the discussion Constantin. Would you like to start by telling us why you've chosen to participate?

> I would like to suggest for your book and also for the knowledge and the acceptance of the readers that they participate in a way that allows them to remove and free themselves from the constraints of overthinking. Specifically, I am speaking about the overthinking that you experience when you use your imagination or when you are making contact with Spirit. Why the overthinking? Why must we describe this in too many words? Why can't the imagination be enough? You are asking for explanations about the World of Imagination and I am admiring your descriptions about songs and shapes and sounds. I am admiring the descriptions that are not pages long.

Yes, some of the information can be overwhelming when put into words, we agree. We've chosen to publish the information in this format so as not to hide behind metaphor or allegory. We want the raw information relayed to people.

> You must rewrite the message as it has been concealed for too long. It has been lost for so long that Man Being cannot easily absorb it like a song or a color or a feeling. Instead, Man Being analyzes and dissects everything. The World of Imagination that you are asking many questions about…this is the Artist's palate. This is the Artist's lifeline. This is the Artist's nourishment, blood and life-force that allows us to speak not in words but in ideas. The idea is in front of you all. You have the ability to eliminate the form. You have the ability to simplify the form. The form of Man Being is so padded

and complicated and busy. It's nonsense. What you are living in your Earth existence is nonsense. It is no sense. You do not need this form and you do not need form to create. This is what I want to say to your readers.

Please continue on that point. Human Beings are unfortunately preoccupied with form. We struggle to imagine existing without a body.

A form is not a creation. A form is a way for you to recognize the light. It is a lens for the light. You are all learning how to experience this creative force without the form. There is an irony in being a Sculptor and using stone to suggest formlessness. We form sculptures from stone while suggesting that you all release from form. You are looking at the form and observing the form but the idea is not trapped in the form. The idea is not trapped in the rock. The idea and the belief are free. The sculpture is like a photograph. It is an instant and a memory and a reminder that you have made a reconnection.

We now understand that a reconnection happens once. Does that mean that the art is no longer needed after we've made the reconnection?

You've understood this correctly. No, we do not need the art after we have made the reconnection, but others do. Please allow the message to be revealed. There is much talk from the Earth plane about the meaning of things and giving things meaning. We don't give things meaning. You reveal the meaning. You have learned that the Earth is inside out and therefore the meaning is something that you have already created or believed in. The form is the end product. The form happens after. The form does not happen first. The Sculptor does not create the object and then fill it with belief. The belief is first. You must remember that you are carrying around many beliefs in your heavy form. You are afraid of the form changing, you are afraid of not having the same form like everybody else and you are afraid of death.

It's true. The belief in form creates a psychology of fear – a fear of losing that form. We believe in something that we know is fragile and finite. It's perplexing.

Why don't you see the picture? The psychology of form inhibits you. Light energy must be released and must flow. Your Earth existence does not allow the release of anything.

Are you calling us hoarders?

Are you not? You are collecting things and making your world full of things. You are buying things and taking things and you are making things and you are relying on things and you are surrounding yourself with many…many things. But these things do not allow you the safety to protect your form. Your beliefs on Earth are very limited and so your beliefs, like your form, are deteriorating. You are not learning new beliefs or creating new beliefs. This is what you are sharing in your book.

It's the main theme – to create new beliefs.

If you do not work on creating new beliefs then you cannot exist. You are afraid of death because you do not know how to exist without death. Death is allowing you to feel like you exist, like you matter. Create a new belief. Create a belief in the World of Imagination. This is the solution for everything that is ailing Mankind.

Let's return to a point you made earlier, that it would be ideal to simply suggest, "Art is the message". If art and Artists are guiding us homeward then why have we gone through millennia not hearing the message? You made wonderful sculptures for instance, but few of understood the message.

> The difficulty is the fear of simplicity and the fear that the simple truth, the simple shape, the simple experience is not good enough. Why is art misunderstood? There is a fear of having everything taken away from us. You believe that the more things that you have, the more beliefs that you have, the more ideas that you have, the more thoughts that you have…then the better you are. The message cannot be absorbed because of the busyness, the busyness of the 3rd density life. It is a busy place where a simple idea or belief is ridiculed and also misunderstood. You are speaking about shapes like triangles and spheres, for example. The simple truth about shapes is that they hold all the information you need. You are built from shapes.

That's a great point. We've forgotten this truth and so we dismiss it for its simplicity. It even sounds absurd to many.

> You have forgotten this truth and so you adorn your lives with as much complication as possible. The Artist is trying to convey a message in a different way than you are used to speaking or thinking. You must accept this. It is changing your world as many of you are now realizing that the busyness is not working for you. There is a return to simplicity and a return to the basics and you are returning to the knowledge of the shapes and the sounds. This Light Body that you are rebuilding and remembering is consisting of shapes. These are basic shapes, basic sounds and this light is allowing you to accept that the simplicity of the universe is what allows you to time travel. Time travel is a simple belief and it is a simple experience. You are moving light and moving it through different forms and these forms change and your belief changes.

You saying that time travel is a simple belief will probably get a few chuckles from the readers. Understanding time travel as an Earth Being is like trying to grasp what "God" is.

> Is it a surprise that Man Being overcomplicates everything? You are dealing with shapes, sounds and light and learning about geometry and learning about the simplicity of what you are now calling the busyness. The busyness on Earth and the busy thinking can actually be reconstructed into a simple belief and pattern. Everything is made up of shapes, light and sound. It is a frequency that you are reminding yourselves you have access to. You simply become the frequency. You simply create the signal and the Artist is reminding you of the tools. Art is handing you the tools. This is how you can re-believe, reinvent and recreate the pattern. Art is reminding you that you have the tools. This is not a complicated matter. This is not a complicated exercise.

You came up as an Artist during several artistic movements. Why were so many Artists creating these "new" ideas?

> There were many of us who had the knowledge that you are writing about. The knowledge of Lyra and also the knowledge of what you call Lemuria. Many of us came together and there was what you call a cultural shift. We called it a mission. We were all on a mission, albeit on slightly different paths but expressing the same sentiment. We were sharing the message that Man Being has the tools, the simple tools. This was a time period where there was a lot of experimentation with simplicity and taking away the frivolity. We were stripping away that which is unnecessary, getting to the core and to the shapes. The music that was being composed, the painting...it was all in shapes. Shapes became an important belief. It is always an important

belief of course, but look at how we tried to share this truth and this belief with you.

You were all reconnecting with the truth about shapes.

> The movement was about shapes. It was a call to rebuild your Light Body and to once again embrace the ability to rebuild yourselves. It was a call for you all to exist in a new form. Why you believe that your Human body is the pinnacle and closest representation to god is what we were addressing. I was always more interested in showing my work and letting my work and message be absorbed, not by writing about it but by showing it or singing about it or dancing about it or taking a photograph about it.

We want to inspire Artists to take this info and apply it as you've just described – through song, dance and imagery. For now, we're adamant about publishing the transcripts. We don't want the creative aspect to overshadow the message, even though creativity *is* the message.

> I agree…handing somebody shapes and sounds without an initial understanding can be quite demanding. "What does this mean and what is the purpose?" This is what many of you ask yourselves when confronted with art. Man Being has forgotten what they are constructed of and the complicated form that you are occupying on Earth is not the vehicle of your own imagination. Please remember this. If you do not believe anything else that we speak about, please remember that "God" did not create your form.

Do you want to expand on that point?

> Your form that you are trapped in is a belief and creation from the other Beings that wish for you to remain stuck on your prison rock. The belief that your

form was sculpted by "God" or "in his image" is not true. Your form has been created and constructed and envisioned by those Beings who are in fact holding you hostage in your existence. I am speaking about those Beings that you know as "DRA". These Beings are the ones who have created your form. God has not selected your form. This is a creation from a World that you are ultimately trying to disengage yourselves from and free yourselves from. There are Beings that will connect with you in Volume 4 and describe this in detail.

Yes, we're being told that this discussion is forthcoming. We'd like to ask you about your work known as the "Endless Tower". It is probably your best example of how shapes are tools.

Not only can this be regarded as an escape and an escape through a link or a chain of shapes...and ultimately sounds and vibration...but this is also a reminder that you all have the ability to be this towering shape. This is a towering link to the next World that awaits you. The tower and the endless column is simply a passageway for all of you. You need to recreate the shapes and the flow and the momentum and release yourself from the form that you have been given. That form does not suit who you truly are. That column is a better representation of what you can appear like on Earth. That is a better representation and a closer representation to "God".

Looking at your tower with that understanding is incredibly compelling.

You are not destined to remain in the form that you occupy in the Earth existence. You have been educated and have been instructed that this form is the ultimate or penultimate experience of your beliefs. You are wearing a coat of somebody else's beliefs. They are not your own and so what I want to share with your readers is that you can recreate your representation. You are doing this unfortunately through superficial modification of your Man Being form. Making haircuts and tattoos and buying clothes is not changing your form. Modifying your appearance by losing weight, gaining weight is not changing your form. I am speaking about a completely new invention of form. Take for example a painter like a Picasso. The way he depicted man as in shapes is a much closer representation of how you could exist. You are wearing somebody else's clothes. You must absorb this and believe that your form on Earth is not the original form. You are all subscribing to and believing in a lie.

We intend to help change that, along with all the Artists who are engaging in the mission. We know that Musicians will be creating music in the Key of D but how will Sculptors and Painters define their artistic movement in the coming years?

There will be bending of the light. The light is increasing and so Artists must work with this. The sonic disturbance or interference will also be increasing and so Musicians must fight against this. There will be a defensive measure in the artistic dissemination as your sonic sea becomes unbearable and the light intensity begins to increase. As the cracks in the Earth appear and slowly reveal the light that is hidden in the core, or your Causeway, there will be much disruption and panic. The Artists will attempt to disseminate but it will be necessary to take defensive measures, as this will not be a calm environment. There will be new energy injected into the visionary sphere that they all exist in connection with. The World of Imagination is also being disrupted.

It's not just Earth that will be affected?

The release of Terra will be causing an energy that is stimulating the 5th density experience and there will be a monumental release of energy and light. The 5th density experience is not a completely free experience. This is about to change. The release of Terra will allow the complete release and unfoldment of the 5th density experience and its energy. The Artists that are connected with the 5th density will be experiencing a new ability to create and the dissemination will become more of a management and somewhat of a defensive quest. The light and the implosion of beliefs will be a constant reworking of beliefs and therefore art will no longer be a still and seemingly passive experience. Art and creativity will be extremely activated and this will result in a very new experience and participation. You all will become art. You are becoming the art with the release of the 5th density light experience.

The artistic movement of the "future" will become "interactive".

Yes. You will be freeing the shapes. In order to get through to the next door and the next place you need to create a space. How do you create the space? You create it with light and you cut open, you create an opening that's done with the light. You need the light. The light is the tool. The light is the chisel.

We love that description.

Thank you both for bringing me into your project. Please understand that you are not randomly involved in making these books and disseminating. This creative project is not organic. You have decided and consciously made a commitment to do this. You are here and there for a reason. This is not a random occurrence. You both have a responsibility not only to yourselves but there are many others who are waiting. Your serious attitude is required as you are both now shouldering a great responsibility. Your readers will help you and this will be a successful Event. We are with you all.

Thank you, Constantin.

LILLIAN
LEITZEL

"There are Beings in Lyra who dance. There are
Light Dancers. Some of you might call them 'Fairies'.
Some of you might call them 'Angelic Beings' because
of the way that they move and manage their light."

Acrobat and Strong Woman
Inaugural Inductee, International Circus Hall of Fame
1892 - 1931

Dramos is seeing two big Rings suspended in the air. It's not clear what they are until we start asking out loud, "What are these…are they floating?" They're starting to look like gymnastic rings suspended in the air with no one hanging onto them.

Are you a Gymnast?

> This is Lillian Leitzel. I think it's important that you include me, of course. I appreciate that you don't know who I am but I'm quite confident that you will be able to find a lot of information about my story and the contributions I've made. I am interested in your book. I would like to be included in your story if I can define my role. I can contribute to your understanding about the "Afterlife" and all that wonderful mystery that you're sharing. Would you like to hear about my story?

Most definitely. Pleased to meet you Lillian.

> Now, we don't have to spend time speaking about my life story on Earth. I'm sure that that is well documented and you will spend hours and hours learning about the marvellous things that I have done and my contributions in performance and theater and we don't need to dwell on those things. I would like to start off please, if I may, by saying that in the Afterlife experience and in the "realm" that you are fondly calling Lyra, there are many performers. There are many Beings who have been performers on Earth and it's a curious thing if you pay attention closely to whom you are interviewing. There are many Beings who have contributed in dance and movement and choreography and in my case, aerial performance. I suppose "acrobatics" is what you call it today. There is a reason for this and I'm not certain that you've made the connection.

What have we overlooked?

There are Beings in Lyra who move and dance, very much like I have done on Earth. There is a movement and a dance to the Beings who exist in Lyra, but these Beings are not the Beings that you are telling a story about, as in the Beings who are rebuilding their bodies in light. That's not what I'm telling a story about now. There are other Beings in the Lyra World that you are communicating with and these Beings are Beings like myself.

Before you continue, we're a little confused. We've been told that Lyra is not a place but now you're calling it a World.

Lyra is a World of course but not one that Sirius Beings know how to reside in. There is further understanding of your origin story as we proceed through the Volumes. For "now", Lyra is an energy field where Sirius Beings reconnect with the light. Most of you that are encountering the Lyra energy field need to reassemble your Light Body. I was already time traveling. My ability to absorb higher light density was and is in place. You are communicating with Beings who are existing in the energy field of Lyra. I am one of those Beings. Some of us make our way to the 3rd density experience by engaging with other Beings in form. We are not time traveling as you understand time traveling…as in rebuilding your Light Body successfully and learning how to form and reform. We are in essence operating with some of you like Spirit Guides. This is the closest experience that you will be able to fully understand and that is why I am using this description.

Can you offer us an accurate description of a Spirit Guide?

Well, you're speaking about your origin story. The origin story is not so unique that your readers won't be able to quickly identify it. We believe we are communicating with you as a "higher intelligence" or "Source", as some of you like to call it. Spirit Guide or instruction from Spirit or Higher Self are also ways to describe the connection with the Lyra source. I am not telling you that Lyra is the only source for communication but I am saying that your readers are connected specifically with this experience.

Our general understanding of a Spirit Guide is that it is a discarnate Being who protects and guides us on our Earthly journey. Psychics will often describe our Spirit Guides as they last appeared on Earth – and not typically as Light or Lyra Beings.

When you are suggesting that a Spirit Guide is and was a previous incarnation of a Human Being you are explaining the most recent connection with not only an incarnation as part of your Soul Ascension Group but you are also explaining the direct channel or the reconnection stream. There is a reconnective stream and a reconnective dialogue that you are tuning into in this Volume. A Spirit Guide is simply a channel that you are tuning into that is available for you when you reconnect with the dialogue stream. The dialogue stream is ongoing. Your readers are also reconnecting with this dialogue stream. Spirit Guides are other Beings who are able to communicate with you. You may call me a Spirit Guide as the other Beings in this book are. A Spirit Guide is a way to communicate. Spirit Guide is a way to contain the communication. You are containing communication through interaction with Beings who have had a previous incarnation. They have had a previous incarnation with you in your Soul Ascension Group. In your book you are communicating with Beings who have a connection with you both. We are not specifically, directly connected with your other readers. We are examples of a communication and communication sources. Spirit Guide is a way for you to hear the information. It is a channel. This channel is not the same as a "walk-in" experience that many of you are reading about. We are not sharing light and codes in this way. The walk-in experience is not something that you have any contact with. There will be further communication about this experience but it is not relevant for Volume 3.

What then was Lillian Leitzel – an incarnation, a Spirit Guide or a walk-in? How would you describe your "lifetime" as Lillian?

I have been an incarnation in the Earth plane. I have also connected with you both and am broadcasting information that you have connected with on this channel of communication. The Spirit Guide phenomenon is somewhat of a hierarchy. It is a channel, a continuous channel or dialogue stream…like what you are speaking about when you speak about the game of Broken Telephone. This is what has been going on in the Earth plane. You are receiving communication from Beings you are referring to as Spirit Guides but the communication is not being relayed or absorbed correctly and thus all the misunderstandings and belief streams need to be corrected.

Our notion of a Spirit Guide as an assigned protector is a misguided idea. These are actually Beings in our Soul Ascension Group that we are communicating with.

Yes and they have the information. They have contained a way to transmit the information for you so you can tune in and absorb. A Spirit Guide may also be viewed as a place or a space. It is a place and space where the information and light is contained and you are tuning into it. As a Being in the 3rd density Earth plane you are also attempting to contain light, albeit not very successfully. This is about containment of light. Light is a source of information. It is not only a source for rebuilding your Light Body. A Spirit Guide understanding is very complicated. I would not devote too much energy trying to explain this but do refer back to the vision of the slinky and pulling apart the Rings and the holographic experience. Information that reaches you reaches you through many different Beings. Information does not reach you directly from one Being or encounter with one Being. The information is relayed through many densities of light experience but also through many Beings who are containing the information. It is similar to passing along information or passing along a physical object. It must reach you through many experiences in order for you to hear it.

It sounds like you're suggesting that a Spirit Guide is a filter or an interpreter?

Describing a Spirit Guide as a radar or antenna would be more accurate.

What are Psychics or people who practice their psychic ability connecting with exactly? Is it a long line of Beings relaying information through one channel?

Beings that have the ability to connect with "higher consciousness" or "psychic ability", as some of you refer to it are able to connect with the Lyran energy field experience. There is a race of Beings who exist in the Lyra experience. We are communicating with you to assist you in disseminating your books. Much of what you have already created exists in the Lyra energy field experience. This is different from the 5th density experience. There is a connection that exists between the 5th density experience and the Lyra field. When you create a gateway you are creating a gateway to make your way homeward. You are communicating with Beings in different places and spaces. This doesn't mean that they do not connect with Lyra and this doesn't mean that they are not Lyran. Your origin story begins with Lyra, not the original state of Being but the reason why you are all trapped in the Earth density experience. Sirius is a gateway. This was the last safe gateway. You will learn more about this in further Volumes.

What specifically are you doing in Lyra? Tell us about that, Lillian.

There are Beings in Lyra who dance. There are Light Dancers. Some of you might call them "Fairies". Some of you might call them "Angelic Beings" because of the way that they move and manage their light. I am part of a Group that exists in Lyra and a Group who have also had experience in the Earth realm. We have been in a Human existence. I'm not completely out of touch with Earth but there are Beings who have made the ascension experience and the ascension completion. These Beings are not relegated to continuing their rebuilding of a Light Body. They are also not relegated to continuing to absorb light and learn about the light and learn about the shapes and the movement.

Does your Group always exist in Lyra?

Some of us have made a complete disconnect from Earth and are dwelling in Lyra and are remaining in Lyra because we enjoy being in Lyra. We are helping many of you and who better to help than Beings who have fulfilled a complete voluntary disconnect from the Earth realm.

Lillian we're reading about your "death" which occurred two days after a fall during one of your performances. How was that a voluntary disconnect?

I understand that you're reading about my "accident" but this is not actually what occurred. This is a

251

voluntary disconnect experience. You don't always have to pass on in your sleep or cross over in a seemingly peaceful and quiet way. The voluntary disconnect doesn't always mean that you just go up in a plume of smoke. It is not always this way. Some of us are crossing over in a voluntary disconnect or voluntary ascension experience and it looks like a mishap or accident on Earth. You must look more closely and you will understand that in my case this was and is a voluntary disconnect and this is what I was striving to achieve in my experience on Earth.

Why did you intend to die this way?

I was relegated to communicating the understanding about movement and light. Movement and light are synchronized and allow you to disconnect. There are many Beings who are working on athletics and dance and different forms of movement and it seems as though they are focused on their physical form when in fact they are focused on moving the light. They are learning to move the light and release the light and learning how the light moves. So many of my movements are precisely the way we move in Lyra.

How do you move in Lyra and how was that represented in your aerial performances?

We move in the spiral motion, as in the twirling motion. It is that motion of course that you are learning cuts through or creates a gateway or a portal. It is the movement of the light that will allow you to continue your ascension experience and make your way through many doorways and gateways. I enjoy being in Lyra and I enjoy this dance of light in Lyra. I will continue to remain in this state of being in order to assist others. There are many Dancers and many Beings who dance with the light and remain in Lyra. We are remaining in

Lyra until the Ascension Event and of course the Ascension Event will release the doorways and release the locks on the gateways of your experience. Once that occurs we will all move and dance and release our light and experience freeform. Until this situation occurs and the Ascension Event is complete I am connecting in Lyra and remaining in Lyra.

How exactly was your demise a voluntary disconnect? The cord snapped and you fell and died two days later in the hospital. What are we missing?

During this experience and in the twirling motions that I made there was an energy and a release of light and what you are calling an event where there is an "out of body" experience. That is what I continued to experience during my incarnation on Earth. The movement of the light and the movement of the physical body are not, in fact, always synchronized. I was creating a situation and circumstance where I was moving the light and experiencing voluntary disconnect on more than one occasion. I was also looking forward to releasing myself as I experienced a contact with Lyra at a very early stage in my career.

Why did the twirling motion cause an "out of body" experience?

When you are twirling or whirling and when you are suspended and weightless like I experienced in my performance you have a situation where you can trigger an out of body experience. You are referring to this on Earth as "out of body" but I am referring to it as out of 3rd density. When you are experiencing the whirling and the twirling you can reconnect symbiotically with the 5th density. You are mapping light in two places at once and when you fully integrate this map and grid and it overlaps in unison you may have a disconnect. I am calling it voluntary as I was seeking the release and not seeking the release by a suicide or seeking the release by self-harm. I was fully in the experience of the movement of the light and I experienced cutting through a portal or a gateway. Do you understand that the movement can do this and that you can voluntarily trigger ascension? You can trigger an event.

That's mind-blowing. Were you aware that this was possible before you trained as a performer or was it something you learned while being in the air and performing your stunts?

I learned through my performance. This is how I communicated with Lyra. In my experience of whirling and spinning and twirling I began to have direct contact and communication with other Beings who were in fact doing the same, moving the light. These Beings are Light Dancers. This experience was not only wonderful and very engaging and very pleasant but I realized that this was in fact my purpose for being on Earth. I was not there to entertain others through some circus performance act, but to actually teach others about ascension. Many of you were inspired and are inspired by movement like this.

We love Athletes and performers who put their lives on the line and do things that seem impossible or super-human.

Some of us can do things, extraordinary things with our Earth bodies like dance and perform through sport. These achievements are pointing you all to the truth about the light. There is a reverence for Beings who can do a magnificent thing with the form and as an aerial performer I was disseminating much like you are. In my case I was disseminating through the engagement of the audience and allowing them to witness a voluntary disconnect in the making. There were many performances where many of you would observe something unusual, not just a wonderful performance and a talented performer but experience the light, the energy. There was a light around me when I performed. Now you can call this being "magnetic" or "charming" or "beautiful to look at" but there was in fact a light that was surrounding my physical form. You were witnessing an ascension in the making, a voluntary disconnect and an ascension release.

There's going to be many Athletes and sports fans reading this interview, Lillian. Are you telling us that certain athletic movements can induce an out of body experience?

This is something that any Athlete or Dancer knows…that creating a repetitive movement or any sort of whirling action can, in fact, create an out of body experience. Beings who are focused on the form and the movement of the form know this. There are many Athletes and Dancers and performers who are aware that what they are experiencing in their form is also very definitely out of their form. There is much regard for Beings who are perfecting their form but not in the way that some of you are doing. Some of you are dieting and dressing and achieving modification of your form through your surgeries and all of the things that you are doing to your external body.

It's important to make that distinction. Perfecting the form through training and performance, not by superficially altering one's appearance.

I am speaking about the motion of the light and yes the release of your conscious awareness in your form. We are allowing this awareness release to guide us further into a space where voluntary disconnect as the first stage in ascension experience, is possible. Many of us are engaging actively in this experience and activity and what I am wondering about is how many of your readers are purposely activating their potential for voluntary disconnect release through movement.

You mentioned that while you were performing your aerial stunts you were in contact with Beings. Can you describe what some of those Beings looked like?

I can tell you this...that when I made the whirling motion in the air, the aerial acrobatic performances that I was known for, I would be spinning along with other Beings in light. I felt surrounded by other Light Beings who were moving with me. Some of you might describe them as Fairies of Light or Angelic Beings. I believe that what you are calling "Angels" when you cross over and you make your disconnect, are actually Lyra Beings and they are light dancers. We are Lyra. I have joined Lyra and the Assembly and we are aware that the dance of light and the movement of light is something that will help you all. If you understand this while on Earth then you can make the most of this situation. You do not have to feel like you are in prison and you are trapped in your form. You can also regard this as a magnificent vehicle that will allow you to release the light...if you allow the movement of the form. It is the dance in the physical form that is also occurring in the Light Body. Those of you who are engaged in these physical activities are actually engaging in a direct connection with Lyra, although too many of you in the Earth experience are dedicated to staying in your form and building your form and connecting with the Earth.

It's strange to speak about these physical achievements in this light, because we have been speaking about how the physical form is a prison.

I am speaking specifically about performers. I'm sure that not many of you realize this...you're looking at

Beings who are engaged in these activities as though they are obsessed with their physical form and want to extend the longevity of their physical form and remain in this state. In fact, it is something completely opposite.

Can you recommend a modern sport that we might watch and examine for the movements you're speaking about?

I am quite fond of Athletes who are playing Basketball. Now you may find this amusing and not consider this very dance-like but there are many beautiful movements in this sport. There are many beautiful movements in many of your sporting activities. It does not have to be art as in dance or art as in acrobatic dance. It can simply be an activity where there is a lot of freeform movement like Basketball.

Most people reading this will think of Michael Jordan, nicknamed "Air Jordan". His running vertical leap is 48 inches and his hang time is 0.92s. Best in the NBA's history.

Michael Jordan and his movements are a very good example of somebody who is experiencing the freeform movement but also experiencing the next level of light, where the light is moving without the body. You are seeing a direct connection with the Lyra movement in this example. The understanding that this Being is, in fact, doing seemingly "impossible" things in the Earth plane is a correct and very astute observation. There are many Beings that you are witnessing where you can ask yourself, "How is this possible?" and "How is this possible in human form"? The Super Athletes are a good example of this ability to connect with a different experience and a higher level of light. You require light in order to move your physical form in this way. There is no doubt about this.

What are the specific movements in Basketball that intrigue you?

The reaching with the limbs and the stretching motions are very similar to some of the motions that occur in Lyra. In the dance of light in Lyra you are making very extended motions with the light, albeit we are not in a physical form as you are existing in on Earth. We are moving the light in a very similar way. It is a curious similarity.

Artists and Athletes both seem to be connecting with the light.

An Artist is explaining the light and an Artist is helping others release their light by showing them how to view things differently. By making the reconnections through experiencing art you are able to make ascension and disconnect. Through the physical experience of an Athlete or a Dancer or in my case acrobatic activity, you are also disseminating and showing how you can find Lyra and reconnect with the 5th density experience. These are both pathways that are similar but also dissimilar, as art is a map or instruction for reconnection. Physical movement allows you to make the belief in Lyra and in the light. By believing in the light you are more readily available to make the reconnections.

Lillian we were wondering if acrobatic or gymnastic rings hold any symbolism, aside from being gymnastic tools.

You should explain to your readers why you are asking me this important question.

We've dreamt of Rings and holding Rings. We've dreamt of walking over water and holding large Rings in each hand. What does this represent?

The Rings are the symbol or symbols that you will be delivering. The Rose has brought you the engagement with the gateway. It is a key but the Rings...now the

Rings you will learn in time travel. The Rings will allow you the experience of travel between the next gateway experience. The Rings and the knowledge of these Rings is something that the DRA Beings are not very happy about, as they do not have the ability to use these symbols and they are not able to utilize the knowledge of ascension that you are accumulating and changing with every dialogue. So the Rings are not something you can flaunt or insist that you use to exit the 5th density experience, as you will likely be engaging in a direct confrontation with DRA.

We have the symbols. Are they just two hoops or symbols or are they in fact more intricate than what we are imagining?

There is more to this. The understanding that you are absorbing at the moment is enough to get you through the gate. You will have a complete explanation given to you. I am not interested, of course, in engaging with these DRA Beings. They do not have a positive character and their attributes are somewhat obtrusive and not aligned with your mission. I am comfortable in Lyra until the Ascension Event is completed and the obstructions are removed.

Lillian, you say that you risk a direct confrontation with DRA if you flaunt the Rings…but does light not conquer darkness? In the 5th density does the light not conquer DRA?

You are synergized with these Beings more than you are aware of. There is a repair that is occurring and these Beings and yourselves are all part of the repair journey. This is not a story where light is defeating the darkness and good is defeating the bad. This is a story about a completion. These Beings are incomplete and they need the light. You are assisting the gateway reopening and you will understand more about your journey. When you encounter these Beings you will have complete understanding and awareness of how this will take place. Do not worry yourselves on how to encounter these Beings and how to conquer or even avoid these Beings. These Beings are in fact part of you and you will understand that there is ultimately nothing to fear. When the light is released everybody will benefit from the Ascension Event.

You voluntarily disconnected and we're assuming that you didn't have to encounter The Channel. What was your disconnect experience like?

Much as I experienced when I made the rapid whirling motions, that feeling of joy is what I carried with me. My cross over did not encounter The Channel of light, as I was already extended in this way. Much like the reach of the Basketball Athlete, I was already reaching with my light. My crossover was such that I witnessed many Beings in light but I also witnessed the completion of my Soul Ascension Group. There are no further Beings that I am waiting for. What I am encountering is a dance with other Beings similar to what you tell stories about.

What stories are you referring to exactly?

You tell stories of "Fairies dancing in the woods" in a circular motion, for example. I am experiencing a dance with other Beings. You might call these Angelic or Fairy Beings. I experienced being invited to a dance of other Beings in light and that is how I am existing. There is access to the World of Imagination and the 5th density experience but I do not need to imagine anything further. I have completed my journey and am waiting for the rest of you to disconnect through ascension. I do not need to practice in the World of Imagination. I fully believe in time travel and in the light. The World that you are making contact with is a

World where you can practice and explore. It is not mandatory for you to exist in this world. It is a rehearsal, a dress rehearsal for time travel.

What then are you doing, exactly, with your existence?

I am spending my existence momentarily, if you wish to look at it in a linear way, moving and dancing. I am experiencing the immortal state in a dance, in a fluid movement but contained in Lyra. This is where I feel that I belong and where I feel that I can make the most helpful encounter in light dissemination. These things may not seem like they are easy for you to follow. Why would one just spend their existence moving with the light? My existence in Lyra is not extended in terms of your linear time. It is simply a moment and a brief moment. You will understand that your time and your measure of time does not exist in the other worlds and what you are viewing as years and years are not experienced in the other densities of light.

Back to the Rings, how do we share this knowledge with the readers? Do we ask people to imagine holding Rings or to contemplate the shape?

If you regard the motion of a hoop, the hoop is something that will convey the understanding about the Rings. The Rings are not static objects. They are the movement of light.

This might be a silly question...but was the toy hoop known as the "Hoola Hoop" developed with the knowledge of the Rings? There was an absolute craze for this product in the 50s and 60s. The purpose was to move and balance the hoop around your waist in a constant circular motion.

This is a wonderful exercise to practice. Many of you are practicing Yoga and other activities that involve meditation. The Hoola Hoop is a sublime way to achieve a similar state and quite possibly a more accurate explanation of meditation.

Are you saying that practicing with a Hoola Hoop is a more accurate way to achieve the movement of the light than meditation and yoga?

This is a precise understanding.

Was the Hoola Hoop developed with this intention?

What do you think?

For those of us who aren't mobile enough to use the Hoola Hoop, what can we do instead?

The movement of the light in the Ring shape does not have to be experienced by gyrating or physically moving. You can experience that connection by just experiencing it. If you want to engage with the light and if you want to dance with the light then do it. Even though we are speaking about physical movement and Athletes and performance Artists, it does not require a physical movement. If you are able to connect with the light and move the light around like this…well this is a tremendous skill that you have and you should and must practice it.

Can we envision it?

No. Be it.

We need to be the ring of light and the whirling motion?

If you have the ability to bring that movement of light into your existence then do that. It doesn't require you making the physical movements. This is something that you can access, even though our talk is about the physical expression that leads to this movement. The release and the ability of this movement is something that is achievable by everyone.

There have been many uses of the hoop and hoop movement across many cultures throughout history. What is the best example – what should we examine?

The Whirling Dervish.

Thank you for contributing Lillian. It's been a great conversation.

You are most welcome. See you both in the Light.

JULES
VERNE

"My books are interesting and entertaining but they are not that remarkable if you in fact believe that time travel is a possible thing. They are not remarkable if you believe that we can all travel and that, in fact, we are all traveling. We are all Time Travelers. You are stuck on Earth because you have forgotten where the door is. You just simply do not remember or recall the instruction."

Novelist, Poet, Playwright
Creator of Journey to the Center of the Earth
1828 - 1905

Jules Verne requests that we introduce him by playing Jacques Offenbach's "Le Voyage Dans La Lune" overture, which Offenbach composed for the 1875 Opera – Le Voyage Dans La Lune. This Opera was loosely based on Verne's novel "From the Earth to the Moon". Dramos and Bohemias break into laughter while playing the overture.

Well that was fun. We read a little bit about Offenbach's "Le Voyage Dans La Lune". You two had a spat over the apparent rip off of your novel. Is that why you asked us to play Offenbach's composition?

Yes…a little humor to kick this off. Why not?

Thank you for reaching out to us. It's certainly an enormous pleasure to connect with you.

I like what you're doing and I recognize that for many of us Writers our work is not appreciated. I want to say that the topics that you are writing about and your vision is something that I also believe in and understand. I would like to be part of this book if I may, because I had many ideas when I was a Writer and existing in the Earth plane. I have now discovered that time travel and all the things that you are wondering about and trying to explain to your readers have many truths to them. So I would like to speak to you about the wonders that await you both.

We've spoken to many Beings thus far and it's all been very humbling and exciting and insightful. But speaking with Jules Verne is quite something. You wrote about similar topics in great detail, albeit in a fictional context.

Yes, so I can appreciate that not everybody will recommend your book or believe what you write or believe in our conversation. Believing in time travel is something that you must all prepare for. You can go to school and study many things but you cannot study for time travel. You cannot go to school for the "Afterlife" adventure that awaits you all. Your books are as close as we can get to a University degree or a professional instruction and preparation. There is no such book series like yours that I have come across or know about and I wish that I had much of your same information when I was in the Earth experience. I would have been a lot more prepared even though I imagined a lot of the things that you do in fact experience in the Afterlife.

Jules, you are an absolute icon in the literary world. You're complimenting our books but yours seemed to have been extraordinarily prophetic. Where did you get your information?

I would like to begin by saying that even though my books may be popular and widely accepted now, this was not really the case when I first wrote them. I had many admirers of the work but I did not have the respect from those that would really make a difference to me. I was not...generally speaking...accepted for my ideas and my writing, as many of you would be tempted to believe. The ideas, where did my ideas come from? Well let's start with where your ideas come from. I have always admired those who are self-taught and those who explore and those who ask questions. These are many of the things that I did in order to receive my "visions" of events to come.

Were you actively trying to foresee or prophesize the "future?

This was not my intention, although that is what your readers will be expecting me to say. I was engaging – as you are both engaging – with a very creative place, a place where visions become reality and a place where you can invent anything that you wish. How did I know of devices and inventions and things that would ultimately occur a century or so later? Well, when you invent and envision and you do this in a World that does not have a time continuum, then you must be aware that everything that you believe and everything you create is out there. The beliefs and ideas that I created by exploring the World where creativity comes from and where you learn how to play with ideas, has created a situation where things that I invented not only came to pass, they were created and they do exist.

You're speaking about the World of Imagination or the Lemuria state – is that right?

Yes that's the World. When you create and you are connected with this World then those things that you believe in come true. They come true because they exist and they exist because they do not have to be removed or destroyed or judged. If you do not wish them to exist then you can of course erase them...but my ideas...I left them to be. You call this your "imagination" or your "mind's eye". You are actually connecting, many of you, with this World...with this place. This is where the visions come to life and so it is not really a matter of somebody predicting what might happen in the future or being that visionary who invented this machine or that idea. It is the vision that becomes a reality when you let it be a reality. You can create the world and the "future" if you simply connect with your ability to create. This is the creative process of the Artist. I may be speaking in circles and not making the clearest sense and I don't want to say that you have to be there to understand but you have to *believe in there* to understand.

Jules we appreciate what you're describing but your readers might say that it was with striking detail that you "predicted" that we would launch our lunar mission in December from Florida, in an aluminum craft. How were you so precise?

I did not copy somebody else's idea or witness this creation in another time continuum, but I did in tandem with other Beings believe that the Moon was going to be used to deflect the light away from Earth. You are asking about some of us who know about the intention to deprive you of the light. How did I know of this if I was simply a Writer living on Earth? How did I come to know of these intentions? When you are able to disconnect and visit the Afterlife and when you are prepared for the Afterlife, then you can also make things happen in the Earth plane that did not happen yet while you existed there. We are speaking about time travel. You are asking about things that I have known about or created or witnessed. You are asking how I knew that these things would in fact be invented or come true? But you are speaking about linear time and I am speaking to you about time travel.

Are you telling us that this was simply something that you created from your belief in it? You created this event in the 5th density World of Creation, which then manifested on Earth.

You are starting to understand. We are speaking now, Dramos and Bohemias, about time travel. We are speaking about the ability to exit and create and move everything around. When you create in the 5th density World, you must understand that there is no time there. If you do something in this World, you can go back and forth and back and forth. This is not about time. This is about travel. The things that I am writing about were not already written. We are speaking about time travel. Many of us are able to do this and some of us are not even aware that we are doing it.

Were you traveling consciously or unconsciously?

I was not seemingly aware of what was happening to me and so for many of you witnessing my existence on

Earth, I had a fairly normal life. I seemed to be spending a lifespan like everybody else around me. When I "crossed over"…and I am speaking in past tense but this actually makes no sense and I'll continue my story so that you can understand why this makes no sense…when I crossed over I realized that I had already been there. When I had encountered the 5th density World of Creativity, a place where a lot of things that are created manifest on Earth, I realized that I had been there and will be there. I realized that you are all connecting with this place. I realized that there was nothing new to experience. This was something that I had already engaged with and so the ideas that had been presented in my books were actually ideas that I had already created and ideas that I had already seen manifested. These ideas were made real through the inventions 100 years later, or in the future, as you are describing it.

It sounds like you're saying that creations are conceived of in the 5th density and manifested in the 3rd…and that Time Travelers are responsible for this consciously or not.

Yes. If you are connecting with the Lemuria state, which is the World of Creativity or Make Believe, then you are a creative Being, an Artist. If you are a creative Being then you already believe in time travel. Time travel is not about preparing and learning skills. If you are able to time travel you have always been time traveling. You are all traveling. Some of you…in fact most of you are not aware of this. The Time Travelers who are consciously aware, these are special Beings. This is not the norm, or normative. Most of you have the amnesia. You are forgetful. You do not remember what you are doing or what you are about. You are stuck on Earth because you have forgotten where the door is. You just simply do not remember or recall the instruction. My books are interesting and entertaining but they are not that remarkable if you in fact believe that time travel is a possible thing. They are not remarkable if you believe that we can all travel and that, in fact, we are all traveling.

Artists, because they have one foot in the World of Imagination, are bringing their beliefs to life. Now we know why we say things like, "Life imitates art".

Exactly, well done. The unfortunate thing about the Earth existence is that there is this concept of time, which falsely establishes an order of things. Artists however will aptly explain to you that there is no order to the creative and artistic experience. There is no order to an adventure that draws upon the light and the creative force. What you are asking is where does the artistic light and inspiration come from? Where is it located? Where has it gone? Where will it go? These are the questions that you ask yourself when you speak about time travel. Time travel is creating things in many different directions, many different adventures and many different densities of light experience. On Earth there is an order or an appearance of an order. Earth is a reflection, an inferior reflection of what actually occurs in the cosmos or the universe.

Jules we want to return to one of your earlier comments. You said that you and others held the belief that moonlight would be deflected away from the Earth. Readers will want to know how moonlight functions as a gateway.

I cannot say that I am an expert in the Moon gateway but I can say that I have understood that there are many luminaries and energies that are now stagnant or no longer used. We have forgotten how to use them. The Moon is a gateway, a portal…an access. You have many gateways and portals, many doors, many worlds that are obstructed and no longer accessible. You have chosen not to access these worlds. If you no longer wish to use something that is available for you then it becomes stagnant or atrophies and like something collecting dust or cobwebs this is the outcome.

Yet the Moon is still there. We still look up at it and track its "phases".

The ability of the Moon to reflect light upon the Earth is something that draws you to the Moon in a way that you no longer understand. The mission to deflect the light and make certain that the luminosity is diminished for your benefit is also something that you cannot conceive of or understand, as it is seemingly "far-fetched". When you look at my books and some of the ideas, they too were seemingly far-fetched at one time. What your readers will come to learn is that the discussions that you are having in your books are not far removed from the truth.

Science has given us some understanding of what the stars and the planets are, but it's just not satisfying enough. A lot of us feel that there is more to the story.

You are all stagnating in your forms and clinging to the Earth existence and wondering why there are other planets and objects in the sky all around you that do not seem to have any function. These are all attempts for you to escape your Earth plane existence. The luminaries are all gateways or potential gateways and many of these luminaries are no longer accessible. There are many doorways and portals that allow you to once again time travel freely.

Does this mean that the light that was emanating from the Moon was once exponentially brighter than it is today? We're trying to understand how the Moon is a gateway. We don't travel to the Moon and live there or enter a secret door on the surface of the

Moon. Are you saying that it's simply about the Moon's light, that moonlight is a way for us to connect with another density of light?

> The light that is generated from the Moon or the portal is all that remains and your attraction to the Moon is a recollection of an experience and memory that you no longer have a connection with. The Moon was once not in existence. This was a gateway. This physical object in the sky did not exist.

That's easier to understand. The Moon is a remnant of what was once a frequented gateway/portal. When was the last time Man Being used that gateway we're calling the Moon?

> Your question about your origin story and how you have forgotten this place is the reason why you are writing the books. When you split you also created obstructions in the gateways or portals that would allow you to escape. The position of the Moon has not changed but the obstruction, like a vast planet, is not as old as you might imagine and the other satellites that surround you are also portals or gateways. There is nothing that surrounds you that cannot be reactivated once again.

Readers will now be asking, "Did JFK intend to deflect moonlight when he set the goal to land there by 1969?" We have previously been told that JFK didn't want to participate in the UN's nefarious plans to control lifespans.

> His information was limited as there were and are other Beings who wish to ensure that the obstruction continues. There have been missions to try to release the light from the Moon and there have also been missions to attempt to obstruct the light. What is occurring for all of Humankind is the release from Earth and also the release of all the luminaries that

surround your existence. The Cosmos are not as fixed as you might believe and the Ascension Event is not only allowing you to visit other worlds and other places and other existences, it is in fact destroying all those things that you see in the sky. It is opening up the gateways once again.

Wow. Does this mean that the planets will be imploding?

The gateways will be released once again. When the gateways create an opening and when there is a rush through the gateway this gradually creates a bigger opening. Eventually the momentum is no longer stable. Luminaries have collapsed in this way before. This is not a new idea, however your belief is. The reason why you are stuck in the Earth plane is through a similar collapse that blocked the gateway.

Is this the origin story of how we got trapped on the planet?

Yes, but you don't have enough information to believe the story now. The details that you will receive from your "future" conversations with the DRA Beings will fill in the gaps and allow you to construct a believable explanation that can be absorbed with your readers.

Conversations with DRA? How can we possibly trust them to tell us the truth?

They are not giving you your origin story. You are filling in details for them. It is the opposite experience. Another Being will be in contact with you both and you will soon learn more about your dialogue with DRA.

We're not sure how to react to this.

This is a bigger experience and a larger shift than you are imagining or believing. You are not just ascending with a number of Beings and rediscovering time travel and rediscovering that time travel exists. You are releasing the light from all the objects that surround you and once again ensuring that time travel is possible. It will not only be possible for those Beings who you are describing as having Sirius origin, but for all.

Are or were the planets in our solar system also prison planets that Beings escaped from?

You are asking a very astute question. All of these satellites or planets have been used. They have had active civilizations occurring on them. The existence of the planets and the obstruction of the gateways occur when there are civilizations clinging to a portal or gateway that is on the verge of obstruction. These beliefs are generating not only a planetary form as you have learned about in your discoveries but are creating something that becomes a new habitat...and so the process begins again. Earth is not truly a habitable existence. Your source and your life source and your light come from another place.

Is that other place the Inner Earth?

Yes, or you might say the "Hidden Earth". There is an Earth within the Earth, as you have already learned about. It has been called many things like "Terra", "Inner Earth", "Crystaline Core"...and so on. The understanding that the light can be released is something that is awaiting all of the satellites that surround you and when this light is released you will re-open all of the gateways and time travel will be available for everyone. You will no longer be stuck on your planet. You will no longer be stuck on any planet. You will be free.

Is what we're calling Earth the last prison planet with a civilization?

Yes.

Is "reconnecting" more about remembering that we are time traveling? We've understood that "making the reconnections" means rebuilding your Light Body in order to access the tools for time travel.

Yes, you are waiting to reassemble a Group of Beings that have been previous incarnations of you and you will in fact learn how to process and be in light. If you are remembering your ability to time travel then you are increasing your connections and you are increasing the amount of light that you are absorbing. You are not able to exist and completely disconnect from the planet that you are remaining on because you have forgotten how to process the light. Light has a language and a movement and a sound and a signature and if you have forgotten these tools and forgotten these ideas, then you will not feel comfortable letting go of Earth. When you make the reconnections you will remember that you have always been traveling. You are all time traveling if you are existing on the planet Earth. All of you are Time Travelers who have just forgotten the experience and believe you no longer have the key.

We have cultures and religions that abide by either a Lunar, Solar or Lunisolar calendar. Why are we measuring time via the phases of these luminaries?

A culture that follows one luminary versus another to organize time is an indication that they of course are attempting to access a different gateway.

How can they access a gateway by organizing time?

There is a belief that by organizing time and by tracking a luminary and by observing a luminary that there will come a moment where the gateway will be accessible once again. Measuring luminaries and measuring luminosity and measuring all of these things is an attempt to rediscover an opening or access to a gateway. You have also forgotten the reason why you are tracking time using the Moon or the Sun. You are observing and waiting and trying to learn about the gateway but you don't even remember why you are doing this. You will learn more from the Lyra Beings about this, as they have a more precise understanding of these Events.

Jules we'd like to shift focus now and ask about how you are spending your energy in the immortal state.

I continue to write and I continue to create and I continue to share ideas on Earth. I am communicating with other Writers and I am communicating with other Artists. I am still participating. There is an Assembly and we share ideas and our ideas are shared with not only each other but we are sharing ideas with Beings or denizens of Earth.

How exactly do you share these ideas with people on Earth?

This has already been explained to you in that we share through your dream state. Sometimes you like to say that you've had an "inspiration" or a "vision". This is how we influence other Artists and Beings. We are spending a lot of our energy creating in the Lemuria state and World of Make Believe…that you all can have access to. You are all able to access our ideas. I continue to disseminate and share ideas. I am not a Being who was only on Earth once and wrote many books in one lifespan. I have always been writing and sharing ideas and some of us continue to do this.

Why do some Beings choose to stick to one discipline? It almost seems like an assignment. Are we assigned these functions e.g. Writer, Singer, Dancer? Do you not get bored of always writing books?

> You are asking about why some of us time travel and continue to time travel. When you are witnessing someone who seems to have been here on Earth in a previous incarnation with a similar artistic path or career path, you are witnessing time travel. Reincarnation does not have to be time travel and it is in fact not time travel, although some of you are confusing these two ideas.

Please make the distinction for the Reader.

> If you are a Time Traveler then you will be experiencing different situations, but they are not different incarnations. There is a distinct difference of course between an incarnation in the Earth plane existence and a time travel experience. During a time travel experience you are integrating with an experience that someone else might also be having simultaneously. I am not suggesting that we are incubating in other people's forms but I am suggesting that a Time Traveler's lifespan or existence in the Earth plane is not subject to time. There is a split that is occurring in the Earth plane existence. You are regulated by time and time constraints but you are also coexisting with those who are not abiding or operating under the regulation of time. There is a crossing over of two different existences. You are cohabitating in the Earth plane with other Beings who are not experiencing the time that you are asking about.

How does it work if you're time traveling and you're living with someone who isn't? The aging process inevitably becomes apparent.

The Being who is in a time travel belief and reconnected with the experience is not experiencing a linear understanding about existence. Your experiences are both very different.

Are you saying that they're not seeing a Time Traveler age?

What I am suggesting is that when you learn how to reconnect with your belief in time travel then you do not age. You are believing and also changing your belief simultaneously, so there is no time. Time is stopping.

NOTE: At this point Dramos and Bohemias feel as though they've been speaking with someone other than Jules Verne. It feels as though Jules vanished and someone else stepped in. We asked Josephine for an explanation. Below is an exchange with Josephine.

Josephine, about half an hour ago it felt like we were talking to Lyrans, not Jules. The tone definitely shifted.

Sometimes you remember with whom you're speaking and this gets in the way. You are the same voice and it is hard to interview yourself.

Wait, what do you mean? Is Jules part of our Group?

Yes.

Does that mean he's part of our Soul Ascension Group?

Jules is part of your project.

BOBBY
DARIN

"If you're getting people to move to the music and think about the song and feel the song…then you're getting the message out. You're creating that special vibration. You're creating that special bath and that sound and that experience that is going to allow all of you to just get on with it and crack open the Earth. You've got to crack this nut open."

Singer, Songwriter, Actor
Grammy Award Winner
1936 - 1973

A Being steps onto the stage and introduces himself as "Bobby". We ask him for his last name and he pretends to be insulted. We take a few minutes to search online. Bobby decides he's waited enough and walks off stage. It's an act. He's having fun with us. He turns back around as we figure it out.

Are you Bobby Darin?

Oh, now you want to speak to me?

Haha…thanks for joining us Bobby. What would you like to talk to us about?

I'm just here like everybody else. I don't have anything special to say. You're all creative. You can all do something. You can't all sing but what are you going to do? Are you going to do something? Well, why not…what are you here for?

Are you aware of the books and what we're disseminating?

Yeah, I've heard about the books. What else do you want to know?

Is there something that we haven't touched upon yet that you think people should know?

Well, I'm always going to say that Singers are important. I'm always going to say music is important. I mean you know music is important, right? Without music you don't really have anything. Without music you've got nothing. You've got to have music or you're just not going to get anywhere. But you guys know that.

Tell us about your technique as a Singer and what you contributed in the Earth plane. What made your music so impactful?

You know, I always got people to sing along and that's real important because if you can't get people to sing along then what have you got? You just got some guy on the stage and that's all you got. You've got to get people singing along. You've got to create that chord. You've got to create that energy. It's not just about somebody on a stage singing at you. You've all gotta sing along. My music got everybody singing along. You listen to one of my songs and you're singing along. If you can't sing along well then you've failed. Music is for everyone. Now…if you can't sing then you can hum. If you can't hum well then you all make a sound, anyway. This you've already learned about. A lot of you are in bands and you're making music but it's not anything that you can sing along with. It's not anything that you can join in on. If you can't join the band well then you've lost something, you've lost the whole meaning.

What would you say the meaning of music is?

What's the meaning of music? Music is for sharing. I'm not talking about records being free and all that, that's not what I'm speaking about. I'm talking about the sound and the signal and why we have music. I know you mention a lot about music in your book but I don't know if you've spoken about the importance that everyone has to sing along. The world has to sing. If you guys don't sing you're never going to get off your planet. You've gotta get up and sing, you've gotta make a song. You've gotta sing together. Ya…I entertained. A lot of us entertained. But you've gotta sing and entertainers are really doing their job when they get everybody else up singing and dancing and being part of it. So that's what I want to say to you guys.

Bobby, a lot of Musicians take flack for having catchy hooks and creating anthem tracks. Some consider it shallow. You're saying that creating a memorable hook that gets people singing is actually a powerful way to disseminate.

Yeah, that's right. That's exactly right.

It sounds like you're advocating for popular music, even though it's sometimes manufactured and designed.

Well, when you guys are saying "popular music" what are we talking about here?

People who don't enjoy popular music would say that it's "surface level" or "superficial" song writing.

Well it may look like that's what I was doing but I wouldn't describe it that way. Maybe that's what's happening in your "era". When you're using "popular music" in that context you're referring to music that doesn't really have *soul*. Is that what you're talking about?

Yes, exactly.

No, I don't think I agree with that. If you can get a song out there and you can get people to sing along and play along then you've got their hearts. If you're getting people to move to the music and think about the song and feel the song…then you're getting the message out. You're disseminating. You're creating that special vibration. You're creating that special frequency. You're creating that special bath and that sound and that experience that is going to allow all of you to just get on with it and crack open the Earth. You've got to crack this nut open. You don't understand how powerful music can be and you're just not seeing how powerful a frequency it is. Something shared like in choir or a bunch of guys singing in a choir or a whole world singing in unison…it's Earth shattering.

Well that's a whole new perspective.

> This is what I'm talking about. I'm not really talking
> about "popular music" versus something like
> "classical". That's not really what I'm talking about.
> I'm talking about people wanting to participate. A
> popular song that someone's just written and churned
> out and they just want to get it recorded and get it out
> there and who cares…no…that's not what I'm talking
> about. That's throwaway stuff. Someone's got to create
> that song and it's got to have meaning behind it. You've
> got to want to be singing it. I don't believe that my
> music is what you're calling popular or you
> know…contrived. That's not how I'm feeling about the
> stuff that I did.

No, that's not what we feel about your music. We're referring to
modern pop.

> Well there's definitely a danger with music that is being
> created to harm…and then you have everybody singing
> along. That's a danger. That's a problem. Then you've
> got a problem. If you've got a song that's been created
> and it's got heart and it's got soul and there's a special
> meaning there and there's a vibration and there's a
> signal and everybody's singing along and it's catchy and
> everybody's remembering it and everybody loves
> it…then that's different. You're asking me about what
> the intention is, what's the meaning behind the song.
> Yeah, so I agree if it's a song that's been created and
> there's no art there and there's no truth there and
> everybody's singing it and repeating it then yeah, you
> have a problem.

Bobby, we see here that you're quoted as having said, "It isn't
true that you only live once .You only die once. You live lots of
times if you know how". What did you mean by that specifically
and why did you say it?

It's true that if you're especially doing something like music and you're doing something creative and feeling like you're doing something to help...then you've got this feeling, or I always did, that you must have been here before. If you're wanting to help others and especially if you want to help and be an Artist, then you must have been here before. It's not a coincidence if you're in an artistic role, if you're a Musician, if you're a creative person. It's no coincidence, man. It's no coincidence.

You crossed over into acting when you were 25 years old. What were you looking to achieve as an Actor?

Well for one I wanted to experience this time travel stuff and I wanted to experience and feel what that's like...being somebody else's life. What's that like being able to wake up as you and then go act as him or her. I wanted to experience being in a different skin...well...you're saying "form". I wanted to experience more than one single life in my lifespan. I believe that acting, if you get into acting...that's like time travel. That's as close to time travel as you're going to get. You take on different roles and it's something. You wake up as yourself and you go to act and you're somebody else and you're also experiencing different time periods and different places. I wanted to experience what that was like and I also wanted to experience, as an Artist, getting outside of my comfort zone. Performing singing that's one thing...but having to do the acting...now that is a real skill. That's a real talent. Having to go into another time, another place and just immerse yourself...now that's creating. That's talent, being able to do that. I wanted to experience that.

You came up in the music scene in the 50s/60s during what some might call a "Golden Era". What was it like behind the scenes as a Musician at that time?

> Well, this was definitely an artistic period and it was something special. There was definitely something going on, a lot of innovation and a lot of feeling like we were on a team…like "let's all do this together", like we all have a "mission" together. I didn't feel like I was competing with anyone else to be the best or to have the number one record. It was more a camaraderie and a time where you could bring somebody else into a song and use somebody else's music. There was a lot of sharing and a lot of sharing of ideas…none of this "don't take my idea" stuff. It was just a whole lot of free sharing. People wanted to help you out, wanted to help make your art better. "Here, try this chord" or "Hey did you think about maybe using these words for your song". There was a lot of that going on. You don't have a lot of that now in your world. There's not a lot of sharing going on. There was a lot of sharing "back then"…a lot of sharing.

Did the sharing include any of the ideas we're releasing in these books, like The Rose or The Channel? Were there any green room chats about these things?

> Hey you know a lot of people were tapped into that. That is not something new or special. If you're an Artist or a Singer or you're a performer…you're having visions and you're seeing a lot of strange things and having a lot of strange dreams. You meet a lot of cool people and you're sharing a lot of things and yeah there was talk. For me…I saw it. I had a dream or two. I didn't forget what I saw.

What did you see?

I saw a thing that looked like an Octopus almost but I knew that this was something that you might see when it's your time to check out. I knew it was something to do with "death", that you might see this. Now The Rose...that's an interesting one. That's a code. That's really popular in music especially. All these things you're writing about in your book, yeah...it was on the tip of our tongues. The way that we got the information was not like what you're doing through your books. It would just be sharing. "Hey I had a dream" or "wow you wouldn't believe what I think I saw". Nobody was keeping secrets from one another. We just constantly shared. Many performers and Actors and creatives were very much in the know back then.

Were people actually whispering to each other and saying, "Hey did you hear about this Rose thing"? How involved were Artists in the knowledge?

You'd get some of that and then you'd have someone answering you back like, "Oh yeah you too right" or "Oh wow I had a weird dream about something like that". It was more like we were all trying to figure it out together. Like you'd share and someone else would pipe in, "Oh yeah me too" and "oh you too and this is the way I understood it". We figured it out together I would say. Now this understanding about Lyra and all that interesting stuff that's going on there and where Musicians get their creative inspiration from, that's really interesting stuff. You hear a lot of Artists say, "Oh I feel like somebody else wrote it" or "I feel like that's not me singing it" or "How did I do that". I'll tell you how...it's coming from that 5D light, that 5D make believe and all that good creative juice and that whole World. As a Musician you're listening for that. You're listening to the 5D frequency. You have the ability to hear that light. That light makes a sound and there's music that's being created and some of those chords, some of those lyrics, that's almost sitting there in 5D. That's all available for you. You just have to listen. Just take a moment and listen and then you've got an idea for a song and you've got an idea for a lyric.

Do you remember speaking with anyone about The Rose?

Did I speak to anybody and have a heart to heart talk with one particular person? No. I don't know if you know that in my early years...I don't feel that I was necessarily as tuned into what I learned when I was older but I had an experience. I would say that I had a near death experience. I don't know if anyone else would believe me. I wasn't the healthiest kid and I had problems but I did have an experience where I was in the tunnel and I saw Light Beings. So I already had an opportunity to have a look there. I doubt anyone would believe my story back then but I had that, I saw that experience back then. So I don't know...call that a "near death experience", call it a "bad dream" I don't know. But that's something that I experienced pretty early on and I wasn't in the greatest physical health so I was prepared that I'd be encountering that sooner rather than later.

Can we talk about one of your songs in particular?

Of course...which one?

"Beyond the Sea", which I understand was your version of the Charles Trenet classic "La Mer". I'm reading the lyrics right now and you could very well be talking about reconnecting with the 5th density.

There you go.

Did you choose to sing this song with the intention of sending that message?

Well yeah. Of course there's always different ways to absorb a message but if you look at the title "Beyond the Sea...there's an example. There's different ways of interpreting the "Sea". What Sea is it? Perhaps the one that you guys are all searching for but don't how to find. The Primordial Sea, the Sea that you're calling Lyra. It's the beginning of your journey in remembering time travel and remembering the light and remembering where all that good creative stuff comes from. This is good...is there a specific lyric you want to ask me about?

Yes. "My lover stands on golden sands and watches the ships that go sailing".

Well there you go, there's the light. So you're good at interpreting. You're a Writer. There's the light. The golden sands. Now you've heard that before...the "shifting sands", the "golden sands" and what that represents when you in fact release yourself from Earth. The shifting sands...the gold...the gold dust. I wondered if people were going to get that. I don't believe most people got it. They just looked at it on the surface, what else can you do...but yeah there's definitely something more there. Ask me about another line.

This one is a little more obvious but let's bring it to the reader's attention, nonetheless. "It's far beyond a star, it's near beyond the moon, I know beyond a doubt that my heart will lead me there soon."

Well that's pretty straight forward, isn't it guys? When you're going "beyond a star" you're accessing gateways. You're traveling. That's what that means. You're time traveling. The Moon, the stars...you've already been told about this. But yeah...that's what you have to do. Go beyond the stars!

Is that why people connect with this song so much? Did you intend for this song cover to be your dissemination of Lyra and immortality?

> Yeah I would say that Beyond the Sea was my swan song. That was my intention when I was recording. Did I believe that others were going to get it? I believed others were going to love it and well, want to sing along and be a part of it. I felt that if they were part of it then they would understand it or get the message on some level. Maybe they don't instantly recognize what they're listening to but they're taking it in. I think that's good enough, just taking it in. If you take something in, if you're listening to something then eventually you're going to really hear it.

Does that apply even when we're passively listening to a song, which is what many people do?

> Just passively being exposed to music and being exposed to a message like that...it's not in fact that passive. Whatever you're absorbing, whatever you're exposed to...you're taking in. You've got to be careful what you're listening to, what you're hearing, what you're taking in. Even if you have an important message to share and you say, "Well nobody can hear it" or "They're not listening" or "They're not getting it"...oh yeah they are. If somebody is exposed to something it's only a matter of – oh no here's that word – time. They're going to get it. Maybe they don't get it right away but maybe they're going to get it down the road or maybe you get it in another lifetime or something...but you do get it. By "get it", I'm saying like a reconnection. You reconnect with it. Sometimes you have to have things around you, like music, repeating it all the time. Sometimes you have to be exposed to a sound or exposed to an idea or belief more than once. Sometimes it takes a few turns before

someone's going to reconnect. It's not always instantaneous. Isn't that something...that song was popular.

Bobby, we want to acknowledge where you were from when you were last on Earth – New York. You were a Bronx boy. We now know that there are a lot of Sirius Beings concentrated in New York City. Do you have a message for your fellow New Yorkers, since they're at the heart of this movement?

Yeah, here goes: Hey Guys you gotta listen. You gotta listen to what's going on. It's time to listen and I would say that you have all the information that you need. You have been here more than once, all of you. Come on. You've been here more than once. You've got to remember that. You've got to believe that. How many more times do you have to be here to get it? You've got it now...you just have to do something with it. I think that's the problem. I believe that's the problem. A lot of you have all the material...you've got it, you've memorized it, but you still feel like you don't know what to do with it. Isn't that something...you're ready to go and you don't know where to go. Why not just go? Why not just give it a try? That's the fear. That's the fear that you're buying into. That's the planet just scaring you all. You all have the ability. You all have the ability to just get out. You all have the ability to just get up and go, ascend, leave. But you're believing, "Oh that's scary...oh I'm too scared even though I know everything about what's waiting for me, I'm just too scared to do it." It's a real shame. Come on New York! Play "Beyond the Sea" real loud...and start singing! Sing your way back home...Beyond the Sea!

Wow...we're grinning ear to ear. You're asking us to sing. Does that take the fear away? Does it take us to a place where we stop intellectualizing and just do it?

Well yeah when you're singing with a bunch of people are you stopping to ask yourself like, "Oh where's this going to go what's going to happen to us?" You might be asking yourself, "Am I singing too loud or am I singing in tune", that's fair. Just sing…just sing along. Just all join together and get out of there and ascend and escape. I hate to use the word "escape" but that's what it is, basically. Let's call it what it is. You're not stopping yourselves, you're just being. You just have to be, but you have to be together. It's all of you. You're all in it together. It's not just one of you who's doing it like, "Hey I'm going to go check out the Afterlife and I'll get back to you guys". It's all of you together and I'm not saying you're all going to "die" together. I'm just saying that you're all going to get it together. You're all going to have the same revelation together…that there is more to your existence than just hanging out on some planet being scared all the time. It's time to sing and it's time to have fun and it's time to be free and let's do it!

Bobby we have to ask…why did you get involved with politics. You were at the Ambassador Hotel when Bobby Kennedy was killed. Do you want to say anything about that?

I don't really want to talk about the politics and what I felt pressured to do at the time. For me, that was separate from the singing. I don't want to come across as a hypocrite but sometimes you get talked into doing things that you don't really stand by. Isn't that the situation on Earth? That you sometimes find yourself doing things that you really don't believe in or that you really don't want to be a part of. There's none of that when you free yourself from Earth…you can be sure of that.

Did you voluntarily disconnect?

Well that's why we're here. It always looks like the guy had a "heart attack" or she had "a disease", it always looks like that. I don't know if you've spoken about this enough but you can do your voluntary disconnect just before your demise. In my case it's hard to tell which one came first. I feel I disconnected and I feel I did it voluntarily. I did not deal with any of that "Channel" business and all of that stuff that you deal with when you just find yourself in the Afterlife. I was ejected right into 5D. I was just right there.

We'd love for you to describe how it all went down.

For me I was already ejected into what you're calling the World of Imagination or Lemuria state. This place doesn't really have a name so you can make up a name. You want a name? Make it up. Make up a name. I don't know why everyone's so worried about the name. Make it up. It's a make believe World. Make it up. What do you want to call it? So…you know when you're hearing stories and they're saying things like, "I saw myself and I was there in the hospital and I was floating on the ceiling and I looked down and I saw my body on the operating table and I knew I died"…you know those stories right? So that's how it was, but I was watching that from the World of Imagination. I was watching that on a big screen there. I was already there. This whole explanation "I saw myself"…that's like a voluntary disconnect gone wrong or something, I don't know how to describe that. If you're watching yourself what are you doing? If you have that ability keep going! Go with it!

We want to offer the Reader a blow-by-blow account of how it went down – so that they have an idea of how it's done. We hate to do this to you but the readers will want the details.

294

No, I understand. I had connections with that World of 5D…the World of Imagination. I still do. I have connections. I was in that World in a dream. I had visions of that World and I felt that that's where I was doing a lot of my writing and a lot of my creative ideas. I believed in that world. I knew that World was there but how did I plan to get to that World? Well I wanted to be in that World, who wouldn't right? So I had feelings, strong feelings like, "Oh I don't know if I'm going to be here for much longer". My heart wasn't feeling the greatest…it's not like I sat down one day and prayed, "Please get me out of here".

You did die young. So clearly you wanted out.

Yeah…and I started to have dreams, really vivid dreams. Like I was in this World and was going to be in this World for a while or forever. And I've got to tell you that I wasn't there with a clock…but moments before my heart had the problem I was already in the World. I was ejected. I was in the World, the colorful World. It was like the Wizard of Oz. I was out of Kansas. I can't describe it any better than that for your readers. I was there of course asking myself, "What am I doing here wow"…I mean I wasn't complaining. It was great and in this World and I know this sounds a bit strange…but I'm telling you…in this World I looked up in the sky and I saw a screen. There was an image of me there and my collapse and then all the stuff that happened afterwards. I was watching a movie of my demise, of my end. But I was already somewhere else so it was okay. Now on Earth what did that look like? I don't know because I wasn't there. It probably looked liked I had heart failure. But sometimes we check out of our physical form and nobody even knows.

How do we not notice that someone is out of their body?

They don't notice because when you check out, it doesn't necessarily mean at that instant that your physical form just collapses. I think there's a split, there's a moment there. There's a window and that window, well for me, felt like a long time but on Earth you probably can't tell the difference. But I just want to make it clear for your readers, I had none of this, "Oh the Angel met me in the tunnel and said come on over here and there was my auntie"…I had none of that. I was just in this World. In the colorful World, not in the tunnel. That's my *blow-by-blow* account. You guys are going to be great…you're all going to do it this time. I'm going to leave you with that. That's all you need to hear, really.

Thanks Bobby. We appreciate the talk. We asked Mr. Tudball what he was going to do after the interview and he said, "Play ping-pong". What are you going to do?

Ha. What a guy! I think I'm going to sun tan. I'm going to have to create a sun though right, so I gotta get busy. Have a good one!

YVES
KLEIN

"You can look at Beings in a new way, as if you were going to blur a photo. This is an exercise that you can practice. I conditioned myself so that I no longer regarded other Beings in the form that they believed they were in. I believed in a different type of form and I interacted with others in the way that I believed that I was experiencing them."

Artist
Nouveau Réalisme
Inventor of the color "International Klein Blue"
Visionary
1928 - 1962

Yves has been sending us messages that he wishes to participate. Since his initial contact Dramos has felt more fatigued and sleepy. His energy is different than the others'. It feels like this communication is coming from a different realm. We feel like we're in new territory and uncertain on how to proceed.

Hi Yves. We're not sure how to start this...your energy feels different to us.

> I am suggesting that we begin our exploration with the sound that is created when you disconnect and why I bypassed Lemuria or what you're calling the 5th density. Let's begin there. As you are both aware from learning about my life history, the heart attacks, more than one, were the beginning of the disconnect experience and the beginning of my journey that bypassed the 5th density light. In the Earth Plane, I was fully engaged with this light experience. Communicating the 5th density light experience was not something that was a mystery to me.

You made that very clear when you were on Earth. You certainly captivated people with your unconventional approach.

> It may have been a mystery to the patrons and the people that were interested in my projects, but not to me. What I would like to explain is that if you are connecting with the 5th density and you are aware of what color and form and light can build, then you are also aware that you are introducing increasing levels of light. One can only absorb so much light when they are struggling with their ineffective form and existence in the Earth plane. I effectively imploded my existence.

What do you mean by that?

> When you experience the artistry and the artistic connection with the 5th density and you consciously

298

choose to push and continue to engage and connect with the light and seek out the light absorption, as much as I did in my incarnation as Yves, you are effectively planning for your early demise...as you cannot possibly contain that light. This is another way of voluntarily disconnecting, although for you, it may look like I pushed myself and encouraged illness or disease. There are many of us imploding from engaging in too much light energy. Are you aware of this?

No, we are not.

You must re-examine of course those Beings who are pushing themselves and living a lifestyle that suggests the pace is too fast or that the control is not there. Ask yourselves...are they pushing for more light? Are they seeking the maximum amount of light engagement that is possible to contain in the weak form that you exist in on Earth? There are many Artists who are pushing to engage so that they no longer have to contain themselves in the Earth plane. An Artist on a mission to disseminate is not ultimately comfortable with existing on Earth. In the Earth plane, this is a sacrifice...one that I made. However, I chose to explore a different pathway for the disconnect experience and it is this that I wish to speak to you about.

What pathway did you choose?

My disconnect experience into the "void", as you would describe it, bypassed the reconnection in the 5th density experience or World of Imagination. My disconnect also bypassed the obstacles or obstructions that you are facing when you engage in more light and engage in the other densities. There is a pathway for you to bypass and there is a pathway for some of us who connect with all that you call "Primordial". There is energy that is contained when you believe in this.

What specific belief are you referring to?

> You can throw yourself into the void and through the void. The pathway to your enlightenment or your ultimate reconnection is experienced not necessarily in the stages or in the levels that you are describing one must participate in. There is a pathway that you have already received information about. There is a Tower that you are both aware of that will take you in the straight path directly to another existence. It is described in your Bible dissemination, but you have also had direct contact with this experience. Do you recall this vision?

DRAMOS' VISION: "I am inside a big empty white triangular/wedged shaped room with windows equally spaced on all 3 sides. Each window looks out at completely different worlds. The room sits on top of a Tower. As I sit in this room darkness begins to surround me. It feels like I am now floating in the outer regions of space. I do not know if the Tower is floating or anchored. The Tower consists of two parts: 1. The wedge shaped room 2. A vertical pillar.

Is Dramos' vision the bypass module you're speaking about? Is it a direct line to the Inner Earth experience and beyond?

> Yes. This is what has been shared in some Mystery Schools. You may wish to write about this experience and you may wish to contemplate how to advise others to engage in this World and release themselves from all DRA entrapment. By accessing the Tower experience you can simply bypass much of what you have already learned about. It's being described like this because you're actually aware that you are being taken into another existence. When I speak about The Tower I am not speaking about Tarot cards or references to the Tower of Babel or anything that implies disaster, but I am implying there is a monumental and sudden

reorganization of your belief. You are taken directly to another existence. This is the correct experience if you have the belief in the bypass key. I recommend that your readers review the Tower Chapter in your Volume 2 book. This information is connected of course. There is a reason why we are building these Towers, this obsession. You're building them to try and find a new belief...you're building the Towers to look for the key.

Are you saying that by believing in this Tower we can "fast track" our journey homeward?

The experiences of ascension that you are writing about and describing, although accurate, are a much more difficult set of instructions that may take you away from the ultimate experience that you already have access to.

We can immediately access Inner Earth and beyond. Is that what you're saying?

Yes. You should consider your dreams and visions and connections with the Tower and this will of course lead you through a pathway that is reconnecting with those Higher Beings that you have already spoken to. There is much to share that cannot be expressed in words and there are many experiences that you cannot possibly describe in words. Sound is a privilege. Music is a privilege. This is a better way to disseminate this information. Why don't you share sounds and instructions in music? I can assist you in writing down some chords that will help you and your readers to make some reconnection and also maybe give them a broader experience. Language is so limiting. It is not allowing you to experience the full communication and integration with the light.

We are acquainting readers with the basic concepts before we can communicate them via higher vibrational channels.

> Of course, I understand. "Less is more" is an apt saying to apply here. You will learn how to do this with fewer words.

Having said that, you pointed out that the Tower is also mentioned in the Bible. Can you be more specific?

> If you look at the New Testament book of Matthew, the passage is quite well known. Look for the description of the "narrow gate".

NOTE: Yves is referring to the New Testament Bible Book of Matthew, Chapter 7, verses 13-14.

"Enter through the narrow gate. For wide is the gate and broad is the road that leads to destruction, and many enter through it. But small is the gate and narrow the road that leads to life, and only a few find it".

Is this the passage you're referencing?

> That is the one, yes. Allow your readers to absorb these words and Dramos' vision of the Tower. It will be enough if they form a belief in this pathway and "narrow gate".

Thank you for this information, Yves. We didn't quite understand Dramos' vision at the time.

> Of course some readers will not be able to "make sense" of the imagery and may not be able to immediately form a belief in what we're speaking about. As Bobby Darin mentioned however, exposing oneself to a message over a long enough "period of time" will eventually form a reconnection.

It's a bit shocking to hear that we can bypass some of the journey. We weren't expecting to hear this.

> The structure that you are aiming to communicate with your readers is certainly in line with what happens, but as an Artist is already fully engaged with 5th density, there are other options. You don't have to be in a successive climb or have to organize the light. You need to acquire the ability of course to absorb more light but it doesn't have to be in a linear order. You are disseminating that you are increasing your light absorption but this doesn't necessarily have to happen in the way that you are describing. If your readers and Beings who are connecting with your message want to connect more and more with the 5th density or with the Arts or with creativity…then they may in fact create that "short-cut" or bypass module for themselves. When people learn how to express themselves and extend their expression beyond words and extend their reach into the light, then they will have access and the means to create another gateway or pathway. They can connect with this while they are still in the Earth density. You have been learning about the rocket ships of Jules Verne and all this stuff is absolutely pointing to one thing. You can launch yourself from the 3rd density experience.

Jules and most of the Beings we've been speaking with have said that they were already playing in the World of Imagination while on Earth. They drew inspiration from it.

> That's right. You do not have to endure the involuntary disconnect and make your way into this beautiful World of Imagination. You are already connected with the World of Imagination and that 5th density light experience is something that you have all forgotten. You need to immerse yourself in this world *now,* while in the Earth plane. While you are still on Earth reach

out and experience that and through that you will build a pathway or a gateway like I did that will allow you to redefine the death experience. You are looking for immortality and anti-aging and you are looking for ways to reach and ways to learn. You can achieve all of that if you simply immerse yourself in the creative expression. You must practice new ways of communicating and expressing yourself. I am recommending color and sound for your writing and conversation with me. I could suggest just a random brush stroke on a page but I don't feel that your readers are going to be able to absorb that. They will however appreciate a sound or a vibration or a frequency.

We read that you wrote a musical composition in 1947, which you called the "Monotone-Silence Symphony". You said it was a symphony "whose theme expresses what I wished my life to be". What's fascinating is that it was an orchestra playing the D Major chord for 20 minutes.

I wrote that piece to express moving into the void and also to explore what one does when we engage with this primordial experience? Where do you go? Do you wait for Beings to come to you? Do you wait for yourself to be reformed in the new experience or do you let the integer and the memory of the sound experience create a new pathway or a gateway? The Key of D is the sound of the gateway opening. The memory or the recollection of the vibration and frequency is in fact similar to your déjà vu explanation. I like the déjà vu chapter the most in your Volume 2. It for me explains exactly how you work with the light and also how you can work with nothing. The idea that in the primordial you are waiting for instruction or the beginning is not accurate. You can work with the primordial in the same way that you work with the 5th density experience. You must learn the tools. The tools of engagement in this existence are vibration and the sound patterns. These tools will be the most effective way for you to play in the primordial. You can also create a new way of experiencing nothing in the 5th density. You are playing with and creating many things. You are spending a lot of energy creating and inventing. This is why many of you prefer to just remain in that experience. You are fine existing there.

Why would Beings stay in the 5th density if there are more worlds or realms to experience?

There is no right or wrong if you choose to engage with the light and remain at this level. It certainly is not ascension, but there is nothing wrong with it. I am suggesting for both of you since you are experiencing a connection with the Draconian Beings that you bypass that experience completely and engage with the pathway that creates a direct connection with the primordial and the nothingness. You will learn that sound is what you will work with. In the nothingness state there is sound. There is sound in the primordial and that sound is very important in the undertaking that you both have committed to. Please understand that "nothingness" does not mean oblivion. It is the absorption of sound and light at a level which many of you would call divine.

Yves, you are the first Being that has mentioned having bypassed the tunnel experience, the Lyra experience and the 5th density World of Imagination. Which beliefs did you take on while on Earth that enabled you to pass through that "narrow gate"?

I believed and continue to believe that language is limiting. I believed in communicating without words…mainly through color. Of course I chose blue as my color for many reasons, as I feel that blue is the color that is created by sound in the primordial experience and the nothing state. I felt that blue was the color that you are engaging with if you make this voluntary disconnect experience that I am speaking of via the Tower. When you are engaging with the frequency that is allowing you to play with the nothingness, with the void, these are the beliefs that are engaging you in a direct bypass of all these steps and worlds and experiences. There is nothing wrong with that but the 5th density World is not a full-on ascension experience.

You seemed to be intent on creating a new language with your work.

My belief when I was engaging in the Earth plane was that I wanted to speak with vibration and frequency and not make sound by speaking a language. Light is a language and color is a language. What I wanted to accomplish was to cut through my own gateway and create my own portal. All of you, of course, imagine that you can do this. You imagine that there is a magical pathway or gateway that you can find and utilize, but this is a 3rd density belief. The gateway doesn't exist if you do not have the reconnections in place. The first thing that must change is your belief in form. I chose to no longer believe or consider myself in a Human form. I regarded my form as a movement, similar to a flame...the flame of a candle.

Is that what you were striving to communicate with your paintings, specifically the movements created with the assist of your nude models?

I considered the movement very similar to a lot of the markings that my models were making when we engaged in the painting. The movement is what I focused on. In the Earth plane existence you are all seeing yourself in a fixed form. I chose not to view myself in that Human form. I chose to look at others in terms of movement or light movement. The painting that I engaged in is the way that I chose to look at people. I am telling you that you can force yourself, discipline yourself, condition yourself so that when you are looking at others in their physical form you do not have to regard them in this fixed container with definite lines. You can look at Beings in a new way, as if you were going to blur a photo. This is an exercise that you can practice. I conditioned myself so that I no longer regarded other Beings in the form that they believed they were in. I believed in a different type of form and I interacted with others in the way that I believed that I was experiencing them.

The Lyra Beings told us in Volume 2 that a good exercise would be to imagine Beings wearing halos, that this would be a way to remind ourselves that we are all Light Beings.

That is along the same lines of what I did. That is the "secret". The way that you wish to interact with other Beings in the 3rd density will create a reality that will lead you one way or possibly another. When you treat others the way that you wish to exist, there will be a change. I am not speaking about being kind and nice to others and being morally correct. I am speaking to you about how you perceive somebody trapped in form. If you perceive them engaged in light and if you wish to engage with them as a Light Being, then this will take you further ahead in your ascension and your ascension knowledge.

What did your involvement with the Rosicrucian society teach you and where did you discover the importance of the Key of D?

This is a sound that you are going to experience when you initially connect with the void. There is a Tower experience and a sound that is created. If you have been given this information then you have already encountered this exercise. This Key of D and understanding is not shared in the Mystery School and it is something that you earn in your own personal discovery. If you have received the information directly in your communication with the Lyran Beings, then this means that you have already discovered it. This is not something that's passed around, it wouldn't make any sense if you simply said "go ahead and play this sound or play this note on an instrument". This is not the way that we absorb these ideas. My piece of music was not about listening to the key of D, it was about listening to the void created from the key of D.

Can you explain that in detail?

It is the void that is created from the sound that you are learning about in your Tower experience. The void that is created from the sound is the passageway that allows you to bypass all experiences with DRA. I am no longer encountering any difficulties with these Beings. I had had interaction with them in the Earth plane existence. I had an attack similar to yours but these of course I encountered while in dream state – just as you did. In dream state you are practicing time travel. As you approach the Inner Earth realization you may encounter these Beings, as you still have a limited repertoire and ability to create other pathways. There are ways to open up the portals and the gateways. You must experiment with sound and you must experiment with movement. You are going to look at things differently when you choose to look at Beings in light and color and movement. You must consciously train yourselves to reinvent the way that you are seeing others.

We've also been told that when we are in form we see others in form...that this is the plight of the 3D Being.

Yet if you are integrating the amount of light that you both are exploring, you can learn to see others in light. You can learn to see others in light while you are still in your form. You must practice this exercise and believe in it wholeheartedly. You are engaging with other Beings who are accepting your work, so free them from the experience. Refuse to engage in the 3rd density constructs of form, this would be my recommendation for you both. It is not that difficult to start seeing everything in light. It is an exercise you have to master.

Can you give us another example of how to perceive someone as though they are a Light Being? What specific things can we do?

The frustration when you are dealing with other Human Beings is that they are trapped in their form and it is something that you ultimately wish to engage in. Your understanding that you do not "get" other people or really "connect" with other people is the frustration that you are feeling. They are trapped in form and are subscribing to being trapped in form. If you also buy into this construct where you are engaging with them as they are trapped in form, you will also be feeling frustrated and trapped. What I am suggesting is that you start imagining Beings as not having the confined lines, the perfect form. Practice viewing the movement of the light and the color. If this means blurring your vision or simply imagining the nimbus or the halo around this Being, that would also be a good exercise. Simply imagining the nimbus is a very simple exercise that has profound reconnective ability for you. Have you done that? Have you imagined speaking with other Beings or engaging with other Beings and giving them a crown of light?

Yes we've been putting that into practice. However, blurring the lines of someone's form might feel more natural to someone who dabbles in art and creativity.

This is a simple exercise that will get you moving in the right direction. It is certainly a start for you. When you start imagining others in light then you will also be in the light and then you will also be able to make other decisions and go forth and make the changes and experiences that you wish to engage in. In my limited lifespan in the Earth plane, I decided to go forth and interact with Beings in this way. I did not confine myself to the constraints of the form and I was and continue to be very outspoken about these nuances. There is a very specific nuance that you are all forgetting. You are speaking about ascension and light and practicing new beliefs but the main thing is you have to start losing this need to be in form. You have to start losing the need and the safety net to experience everything in form. You are afraid to see the light.

What did you learn about the form through your experience with Judo?

Well, of course when you are perfecting movements, you are also learning that light can be released. When you make a movement, a martial art movement, the physical form and the light can move together in synchronicity. They can also separate and have different movements, one following the other. There are sometimes experiences where you make a physical movement and the light repeats the movement behind you, almost like a hologram experience, like a magic mirror experience. The Martial Arts are an excellent way to conceive of other Beings not in their form.

Can you give us an example?

When you are making slow motions or rapid motions you are not seeing your opponent necessarily in form. You are seeing the movement and the light. Martial Arts are about moving the light. It is a very good skill for you to practice. Now I am not suggesting that you are going to be signing up for Martial Art training but the movement, the gestures and the movement of the light...if you can see other Beings moving like this, you'll begin to see that viewing others in light is not as difficult as you're contemplating.

Yves can you talk to us a little more about color, perhaps dive a little deeper into what color actually is or does?

Color is a tool, no doubt. Color, of course, is also a form. I worked with blue and I continue to work with blue. Blue resonates as a primordial experience. It is a color that you are dealing with in the primordial. I know that you have experienced pink and I know that you have experienced gold. These are other colors that you experience forming out of the primordial or the nothingness state. Now the primordial is not the beginning as is written about in the Bible. It has been conceived of as the beginning of the origin story. Primordial is a space. It's an atmosphere. It's an existence. It's a way for you to travel. When you learn about getting into this place and you learn that that is where the colors are created and the form begins, you will understand that regarding the primordial as the beginning of time is not a correct understanding.

What is the correct understanding?

What you are actually learning about is the beginning of your new belief. The primordial existence, the nothingness, is the beginning of your new belief. It is the moment and the place just before you make the reconnection with the new belief. It is that place that exists where you are just on the verge of making the reconnection. Forming that belief is the place that you can exist in and use for travel. In this case I am not speaking about time travel through all these different densities of light. I'm speaking about going right to the pinnacle. I am speaking to you about the full ascension experience.

Well, the Book of Enoch tells us that Enoch made the full ascension experience. We are calling this the "Metatron" experience.

Yes. What Enoch did...this is what I am describing for you both. There is a way to access this and you already have with what you are calling The Tower experience. So the colors and your question about what colors can or can't do...colors are a way for you to experience working with the light, containing the light and hearing the light. What happens in the Earth plane is you confine everything. Everything is confined. Nothing is free. You do not know how to change or transform anything. That ability is not there. You can implode things, you can build things but you can't transform things and that movement and the transformation is what is lacking in the Earth Plane. So in a way, believing that color is the moment before you confine the experience...that might get you looking at a form a little bit differently.

Basically, color and light are the atmosphere or elements that we swim through. We are color and light.

You must realize that color and light existed without the containment. You do not need the containment or the form in order to see or understand. You are seeking to learn about the light and you are seeking to learn about not having light. In the primordial there is light but it is the experience right before you see the light. It is that space right before you make the reconnection and see the light. That dark space is the place that allows you to reconnect with the "full on" ascension experience. I chose to embrace this awareness and I did not last very long in the Earth plane existence.

Yes, you died of a heart attack at age 34.

Did you realize that there are many of you having diseases which are actually voluntary disconnect experiences? You're just looking for a way to disconnect and the breaking down of the form is the way that you are going about it…although it is not the best approach. In my case I had a series of heart attacks and this was my voluntary disconnect experience as opposed to extended ill health. Disease is not a failure, for many of you it is a voluntary disconnect that's mismanaged.

Can you explain this further? How do we distinguish between a voluntary disconnect and someone who has contracted an illness or developed disease?

Nobody wants to be in form and get sick. The existence in the Earth plane is all about being in your form and having your form function as perfectly as it can be. Many of you of course are not experiencing a "perfect" form and are not born in a perfect form and have disease. The understanding that disease is a way to release yourself from form is of course a correct understanding. If you don't want to release yourself from form, then you would never have a disease and you would never have anything but your form. Voluntary disconnect is something that you all are striving for, you just don't remember. Some of you are disseminating through art and experiencing a reconnection with a creative existence and so you are not worrying about perfecting the form. You are worrying about perfecting your communication with 5th density light. Ultimately, you are all connecting with the voluntary disconnect while not all of you make the experience conscious.

Isn't that what the "involuntary disconnect" is – waiting for death and not making a conscious effort to ascend?

> There is not really a difference between these two concepts of belief, involuntary and voluntary disconnect. One is waiting for instruction and the other is seeking instruction but it is essentially both a collapse of form and release of the light. One is engaging in trying to learn how to accumulate as much knowledge about the densities and the other is trying to avoid the experience that will possibly engage them with worlds they do not wish to exist in...like the DRA connection that you are learning about. The voluntary disconnect is ultimately about the breakdown of form. Form is breaking down. When somebody is getting a disease I am not telling you that they no longer believe in the form but I am saying that they no longer subscribe to the existence in the Earth plane. If you all subscribe to fully existing on Earth forever then that's what you would do.

The fact that we "die" implies an innate awareness that we don't belong here.

> There is something fundamental in Man Being that is allowing you to have the disease or "death experience". Death does not exist when you are in light. Death only exists when you are trapped in form. Light doesn't die. The form does, the imprisonment does. I recommend for both of you that you describe to your readers that the form does not have to be a vehicle for ascension. The understanding that you must maintain your form for as long as possible in order to acquire knowledge is not a correct instruction. I am recommending that you advise your readers to start playing and engaging in creative experiences. Those Beings who are unable to do that because they are already compromised or experiencing a breakdown of form can also engage in

this creative experience or light through being surrounded by frequency and sound. It doesn't have to be an active interaction.

Is reconnecting with creativity a way that we can naturally acquire the Keys, as in The Rose, The Rings and The Tower?

Yes, of course. That is what I have been saying. It is what we are all saying. Expand your awareness beyond the form. If you have experienced the Tower, then you have already experienced The Rose and you have experienced The Rings. You have experienced quite a lot.

Is that the order of the Keys – Rose, Rings, Tower?

The Tower instruction is an assembly of all those symbols and ideas and teachings and beliefs. From what you are describing, you received that instruction early on in your project and you are now breaking it apart so that you can understand what its components are. You will be learning about more symbols. I can give you one more if you like.

Yes, of course.

Now, you have The Rose and that is the channel for communication. The Rose is a way for you to receive teaching or instruction. It's a very vivid tool for your readers. The Rings are a way of course for you to get out of form and I wish for you both that you experience and use these while you are in the Earth plane. They are actually for the Earth plane but this is something that you need more instruction on or understanding about. Those Rings you can absolutely utilize and experience on Earth. You don't have to wait for another world or another level of light. That is something that I want to share with you both and that is

315

something that I learned about when I was experimenting with my art and expression. The Rings, when they are used correctly, are equivalent to the void or the silence after the sound.

Is there a new symbol you want to share with us?

A symbol that you might both be interested in is equivalent to something that you already have in your repertoire of symbols. Bohemias, you have already sketched out this symbol from your dream. You have repeatedly drawn the symbol with the Triple Cross. This symbol is something that you will acquire more understanding about.

Are you referring to the symbol that we included in Chapter 15 of Volume 1?

Yes. That symbol will allow you to stop a vibration or frequency as in turning it off. It will allow you to bend a frequency and increase or decrease a frequency. It is about sound. It's an instrument of sound. It is a way to create sound like a musical instrument. Its purpose is to allow you to open up a pathway or a gateway through a vibration...much like an earthquake creates an opening or a crack or a shifting of the Earth. This has the same ability.

For what specific circumstance would you use it?

You can use it when you are encountering a change in form and you are encountering a way to move yourself through different densities of light. This symbol will allow you to open up a pathway that is not available for you until you open it up or access it. This is about being able to handle a level of frequency or vibration. There are places where you are being exposed to sound that you are not able to endure, but once you make the initial connection and experience then you are equipped for further encounter with the intensity of the vibration. This is like forcing yourself into an experience that you do not wish to experience and are not prepared for but you force yourself to engage and deal with it.

Is this is your way of telling us that we will encounter such circumstances?

Yes…I am letting you both know that there are places and spaces where you will not be prepared to fully engage in the experience. This symbol actually creates a sound or a sound wave or pattern and this will allow you to integrate yourselves in a way that you are reorganizing the direction of your light. This changes the fundamental direction so that you are equipped and are not imploding yourselves when you encounter this. This sounds very science fiction, I understand, but this actually creates a vibration that you need to immerse yourself in. Like a sound bath experience, this creates a cocoon and a protective layer in a way that will allow you to slowly integrate and reintegrate into the level of vibration. It is similar to you being in too much light all at once and not being able to absorb it. This symbol actually creates a level of experience that is a safe way for you to encounter and increase in vibration and ultimately light experience.

You're calling it a Triple Cross. Is it drawn correctly on our end? We have a vertical line with 4 intersecting lines.

Yes, you have it. Do you remember the sound, Bohemias?

Yes, there were 4 descending sounds. Does this symbol's sound have to do with the Key of D? Are these the chords that you mentioned earlier on in the discussion?

Yes.

Will Volume 3 readers be equipped to understand The Tower and The Triple Cross information, given we haven't spoken about it at all in any of the books?

> Your pacing of your books is up to you both. I can say that there are some of you that would like this information or guidance. There are probably many of you that will be able to understand it or get it. Is it your job to decide who can process this and who can't? I guess you have to decide what your role is in all of this. You can disseminate and share the information but you can't force somebody to absorb it in the way that you're absorbing it. So, you have to decide if your role is simply to disseminate or if your role is to teach others how to absorb it. To go back to your question about the Triple Cross, I would suggest that you share more about your dream.

BOHEMIAS' VISION: "I received the vision as I was waking up. I asked, 'What does the experience of the shape sound like?' I then saw a vertical line with 4 intersecting bars across it. Each space starting from the lower bar made a sound (like a flute). It was a 4-note sound. Suddenly a female's voice says, 'That was the best transmorphic travel we've had'. Immediately after she says that I receive the image of a Merkabah."

> Dramos and Bohemias...this is the real way to travel. You are giving your readers instruction on how to be creative and how to recreate beliefs. This is important to understand time travel. However, The Tower and the Triple Cross are tools that will take your readers beyond the 5th density experience.

Thank you for helping us to understand and contextualize our visions. We want to be able to share them with the readers and not always relay the information through words. The symbols we're experiencing contain pertinent information.

> You have to decide how you are going to disseminate. Now, you can disseminate with words and write it all out, but not everyone is going to get it or absorb it. In fact many will discard it and not believe it. There are other ways to disseminate and that's where art comes in of course.

Was your artwork the only channel you used to share the information?

> In my case, I was disseminating what I knew and what I believed in and hoped that others would get it…but no, I didn't write out manuals for ascension instruction. I feel that if many of you make the shift then many of you will also undertake disseminating and sharing. That's the way that things work. The Ascension Movement that's coming up is one where everyone is going to be disseminating, especially the Artists.

Yves, can we go back to the Triple Cross for a moment? The symbol we have has 4 arms, not 3. It's technically not a Triple Cross.

> Whether it has 4 or 3 arms, it's the same thing. You'll understand soon that 4 can equal 3. Your readers can call it a Triple Cross and imagine that it has 4 or 3 arms. This will soon make more sense.

Is there a way for us to disseminate the information the way you composed your Monotone-Silence Symphony? For the readers who don't know, you played a continuous D Major note and then an equivalent time of silence.

> The question is what are you going to write about before you don't write about it?

Every new belief requires a space to exist in. That's the message, isn't it?

Yes. That's the beginning of the understanding.

Yves, how did you learn about our books and our "Open Mic" project?

You are both involved directly in the work that I am doing, that others are doing. You are going to be hearing from many. What you are getting involved in is sending a signal out and you are going to be dealing with other Beings, whether you like it or not. Your "Open Mic" project or book dissemination has essentially called out to all of us who are involved in it. I'm not involved in writing a book series. I never committed to that, but I committed fully to ascension and learning as much as I could in my final incarnation in the Earth plane. I am quite interested in the examples you have of movement and how the light works for those Beings who are practicing the physical activity like martial arts and dance. This is also very important. I did a lot of things as you know, like music, visual art and movement. All of it is important. When you are putting it all together like this and covering all the avenues and all of the angles and all of the different beliefs, you can expect that many of us are going to contact you. Do you find this surprising, that Beings are reaching out?

At first it was a bit surprising. Now it just makes sense.

Yes.

Yves, before we end this conversation is there anything more you want to share about "entering through the narrow gate"?

When you are choosing to make your journey, when you are choosing to seek that experience and when you find yourself in that experience, you will encounter all of the symbols and instruction that is disseminated in the "Man Being" book series. It will all be revealed to you in this experience. In order to have the experience, you must already have the symbols. The symbols are representations of the beliefs, of course.

What would you tell the readers specifically about the narrow gate?

What would I tell your readers? Well, if they are interested in experiencing what that Bible passage really means then they have to accumulate the knowledge and the understanding and the belief. These things are found in your books series, that's what I would be telling your readers. I am not sure they will be ready to accept that, but if they wish to understand what that means then they are going to be experiencing it. Now I know it's written but reading it and experiencing it are two different things. If your readers want to experience that, then they can by learning about the symbols. I am not talking about learning how to draw them or what they look like or what they are called. I mean learning about what they are really for. You telling your readers what they are for is different than self-discovery. They will have both.

We are leaving our readers the space they need to experience the knowledge on their own.

That's the wonderful thing about your book series. Even though you are giving some instruction and explanation, it is still allowing readers to have self-discovery. It is allowing them to create the belief. You are doing it in a way that is not limiting them in the way that their form is limiting them. You are not creating a form around their belief. You are sharing the information in a free way. It's this freedom that is allowing your readers to absorb. You are not confining or containing any of the information and belief stream. You are sharing it in a way that encourages all of your readers to use the knowledge, create a belief and reconnect with the experience. I'll leave you all with this: That passage in the Bible, that famous passage…it is actually describing a full ascension experience like Enoch's. Your readers will be motivated by that truth.

Thank you, Yves.

BURGESS
MEREDITH

"You continue dreaming when you cross over. Dreaming doesn't end and one of my biggest questions was 'do you still sleep?' I don't think many people ask that question. Do you know that you still dream and did you know that you still experience something like sleep and like waking? There is an experience…there is *up time* and *down time*."

Actor, Writer, Director
1907 - 1997

We are receiving messages from someone claiming that he was a Penguin in his past life. We're not sure what he means by that and so we ask if he had an animal incarnation. He laughs and says, "Come on guys, I said I played The Penguin in my past life."

Are you Burgess Meredith?

> Yes, it's nice to be a part of this. Not many people are contacting me so it's kind of funny. I'm not normally the one who's on the top of the lists to speak to. Josephine, as you are aware, is getting a lot of energy and interest in your book, so I'm most interested in the project. I'd like to play a part in the book series. I understand that you are interviewing and asking about what happens when you cross over and I'd like to tell my story if you want to hear it.

Yes, absolutely.

> It's pretty amazing. We learn about things like "Heaven and "Hell" and we have all these beliefs when we're Human Beings and living on the Earth and you know...there's something to it. I suspected that there was an Afterlife for real...and I know that there are many NDEs that are recorded and people have been interviewed. I was prepared. I didn't have any NDEs or spiritual encounters that were so profound that I would actually know what was awaiting me, but it's very interesting. This is not anything that you need to be scared of or worry about. I didn't meet with any Angels or anything like that. The most interesting part of crossing over is, well, not only do you have all the time in the world to figure it out, but also there just isn't a great rush. Some of you are making a really rash decision and just looking to go back. I'd like to say that there's no rush. You don't have to just get scared and worry and hurry on back to the world on Earth. Just

take a moment…and I realize there's no time…but take a moment and gather it all in. It's quite pleasant.

Can you tell us what you saw during your cross over experience?

What I experienced was complete darkness and not much around at all. It was quite relaxing. I didn't feel any fear and I didn't feel at all like I'm in "serious trouble here" or that "I'm not going to be able to work my way through this" or figure it out. When I achieved that acceptance, that feeling that this is going to be okay and I could be like this for an eternity…it all changed. As soon as I accepted that and I was no longer trying to figure it all out or solve it like a math problem…I saw a light. This light was nothing like I had ever seen before. This light was like a creature, almost a Being. It sort of looked like lightning. Like if lightning was a Being, if lightning was…if you gave lightning a personality, if you gave lightning a body almost, if you gave lightning an existence that was sentient…that's what I encountered. It was extremely different from what you expect you might see when you cross over. It was a highly unexpected…highly unusual experience. I'm not going to say that I was completely comfortable. I was amazed. I was a little bit apprehensive but this experience is something. You're not going to see anything like this on Earth. If you just give it a chance and you're comfortable and you deal with it…it's a doorway.

Most Beings are saying that we just need to get over the initial hump and acquaint ourselves with the new environment.

Once you get past this and you work with it you're going to end up in a very nice place, a place where you can all play and have a lot of fun. That's where I've spent a lot of energy and spent a lot of my existence exploring beliefs. You're going to be in a World where you get to explore your beliefs. If you believe something and then you no longer believe it well that's fine too. Then you just believe something else. You practice believing. You practice making up beliefs and it's a very entertaining and marvellous World. It's a marvellous place to exist.

What can you compare it to so that we have a better picture of the experience? You're speaking about the Lemuria state or World of Imagination – is that right?

Yes that's the one. It's like theater. It's like you're being invited to play any role that you want in a theatrical performance. Anything that you want to do you can do. Anything that you want to be you can be. This is a place where most of you, I imagine, are going to wind up. This isn't the end of your journey but I just want to share with you that this is for real. It's a place that you're going to be in if you remain calm. You don't have to weigh out your options. We all believe that we're going to be judged and we're going to have to make choices and have a life review and all that stuff that they speak about, but that wasn't my experience and I don't believe that that'll be your experience either. I believe that this is the universal experience. I don't believe this is just my own individual experience. There is nobody meeting me and going through every terrible role that I played and every terrible mistake that I made. There was none of that. There was just me.

Did you encounter The Channel or your Soul Group in the tunnel?

I didn't have that experience. I was already connected to the World of Imagination and so I think that just thrust me forward. I'm really enjoying myself. I'm enjoying the journey. You're all going to enjoy it. Your readers are on their last incarnation and they're ready to move forward and they're ready to explore and they're ready to travel and experience time travel. That's why they're reading these books.

Burgess, you say that you were already connected to the World of Imagination while on Earth. What did you learn about the Afterlife while working in Hollywood, and why do you think so many of us connected to your performance as "Mickey" in the Rocky movies?

I suppose that in Hollywood, making movies, being exposed to many different ideas and many different beliefs, it's a place where you're able to develop yourself. In a way I suppose it's a place where you're developing yourself spiritually, although I'm certain that many of you reading this will find that a bit laughable. But when you're playing so many different roles and reading so many scripts and creating movies and well…being open to just about anything…that creates a groundwork. It creates a framework for believing that not only is immortality possible, but that anything is possible really. Hollywood and the theater, all the work that I did, was a great school for learning about what's out there and learning that anything's possible. Anything's possible in the movies. If you want to be creative and you want to explore your creativity well you can create anything. You can create any belief. It's a great exercise to create and explore different beliefs.

Many people prefer to dismiss Hollywood and movie making as an industry for vagabonds and con artists. It's helpful to hear Artists from the other side confirm that storytelling is not only useful but it's a training ground for the Afterlife.

You've put it perfectly, I'd say. It's unfortunate that people think that, isn't it? Many of you don't realize that when you're acting you of course have to believe in the role and believe in the script and believe in the storyline. You're exploring beliefs and you have the privilege of exploring and trying on new beliefs and trying them on wholeheartedly. You're not just reading the script and you're ready to go. You all have to buy into it. Everyone's buying into it when they're making the movie. That privilege is preparation in my opinion for ultimately...time travel. Isn't it? If you learn to create that level of belief you're sort of prepared to encounter anything. That's why in what you're calling the "Afterlife"...well as an Actor I'm not going to say I wasn't uncomfortable, but I was prepared. I learned that anything's possible. Now, the role of "Mickey" in the Rocky films...what would you like to know?

You can go just about anywhere on planet Earth and you're likely to find somebody who loves Rocky. We also can't imagine the Rocky movies without your performance. Why do you think that film has such a strong resonance with people?

The most interesting thing about that part...it's kind of funny. On one hand you have this curmudgeonly lovable character or teacher but on the other hand it really does speak about...well it's like your project. Ascension, the afterlife, believing in yourself. It's about belief and it's certainly about extending your belief beyond what you see on the surface. The form, we're all trapped in that form. That belief that we can make more of ourselves and push ourselves...its not just about a physical exercise or a sport or a competition. It's about, well, ultimately pushing yourself outside your comfort zone and outside your belief zone and doing things that you never believed that you could do. It represents getting out of your body, although the whole story is very much about a physical pursuit. On another level it really is about pursuing the light. It's equivalent to you all trying to get off the planet. It's equivalent to you all fighting for a tomorrow, fighting for a future, fighting for a right to achieve whatever you want to achieve. That's possible in the immortal state. That's possible in the Afterlife. Anything's achievable. I mean if Rocky could do what he did then you all can get off the planet. That's the underlying message, ultimately. Isn't it?

Your character worked Rocky to the bone, got him to train seriously. That's kind of how it feels trying to get people to take on new beliefs.

That's a good comparison. If we go back to crossing over...many of us are thinking like it's your "god given right". You just die and it's all taken care of and you don't have to work for it...but you certainly have to work. The work starts once you cross over and the training and the conditioning for the Afterlife, if we're going to use metaphors from Rocky, that training happens when you're living on Earth. You're training when you're in your form. When you're a Human Being you're training...this is just training for the Afterlife, although most of us don't get that. Most of us don't believe that. You believe that your reward for living on the planet, your reward for living a life is, "Okay an Angel's going to meet you and everything's going to be great" but you need to train and prepare for the Afterlife.

How did you train?

I had a lot of training and preparation as an Actor and a person of theater and just being creative. When you try to be creative...you don't have to be a professional paid Actor or anyone that is known or a household name. When you are looking at things creatively that is preparation for the Afterlife. That is training. I feel that training for the Afterlife is maybe what spoke to you in that film. When you achieve something remarkable, like a physical pursuit, like a sport, that's something that is transcending and that's something that speaks to you on a whole different level, because when you achieve something like that…that's remarkable. That's almost supernatural. That's almost superhuman. When you achieve something that is "superhuman", that is giving you a glimpse into the Afterlife where you *are* superhuman. I don't believe that most of you look at it like that. You believe that you just turn into some Angel and you're done, but it's nice to see that you're putting together these books and trying to explain it to everybody. I'm hoping that everybody plays a part because yeah this is the first time you're going to hear somebody explain the Afterlife this way.

Burgess, what was the most revealing conversation or experience you had while you were on Earth? What was the moment that got you to re-evaluate what you believed about the Afterlife?

I'm going to share a story that many of you are going to find cliché but it wasn't a casual thing for me. Some of you will find it funny that I'm using this example but it had to do with a role I played and a particular story in the Twilight Zone TV series. There was a very famous episode that I was a part of, very popular and this particular role I felt was a mind-blowing story…but this particular role really got me believing. It got me asking…"What if you really are the last man on Earth" and "What if you haven't prepared?" This was well before Rocky, of course. It was quite early on in my career and that story…it really got to me…it really spoke to me. It spoke to a lot of you. This understanding that what if you were the last man standing…what are you going to do and how are you going to make your way if you haven't prepared. If you are relying on those constructs and those things that are created by the Beings and objects and infrastructure and things that are part of our existence on Earth…what if all those things are gone? What are you going to do? That really affected me profoundly and I started believing that we do have to be prepared, that death is not a passive activity.

The Twilight Zone was a great series and very provocative. Most of us don't contemplate death as much as we should. Our reflex is to supress the thought.

> You just can't wait to die. You have to be actively involved in it and I'm not saying you have to jump off a bridge and take your own life. That's not what I'm saying but if you're just expecting that death is a reward for a job well done for a hard life or an easy life for some of you, well no then I'm sorry you're missing something. You should be using your lifetime on Earth to prepare for the Afterlife, the real beginning. Your life on Earth is just a warm up. It's a dress rehearsal.

So you're saying that reading that Twilight Zone script really changed your outlook.

> Yes. I'm not saying that I started to join organizations and you know do yoga and all the pursuits that a lot of you participate in. I mean I was open to it, being in Hollywood of course you're exposed to a lot of these things but it got me wondering about my roles and what I could learn from those roles and what I could learn from my acting. It also got me wondering how I could prepare now.

Was your craft the only thing you did to prepare? Did you do any reading or participate in anything else that you could share with the readers?

> I really enjoyed keeping a dream diary. That's something that I really enjoyed doing and that's something that I know a lot of you do. But that's something that I did quite voraciously. I liked to review

it now and then and I liked to contemplate those messages. I felt that a lot of my training and information and preparation came to me in dreams. It was very enjoyable, the good dreams and the frightening dreams. It was all good so I used that as a resource and it offered me a lot of insight…and you know it still does. I do want to share this for your readers, I'm not sure that you believe in this but you continue dreaming when you cross over. I don't know if anyone's spoken to you about that.

That's very interesting. We wouldn't think that we would continue to dream once we're living the dream.

Yeah dreaming doesn't end and one of my biggest questions was "do you still sleep?" I don't think many people ask that question. I had that question. I had a list of questions that I wanted answered, so one of them was "do you still sleep…can we still sleep…are we going to dream", because I really liked dreaming and actually I was wondering if this was all going to be one big dream sequence. Do you know that you still dream and did you know that you still experience something like sleep and like waking?

This is a complete revelation for us.

There is an experience…there is "up time" and "down time". When you are doing a little time travel there is your waking state and there is your sleeping state and a lot of your experiences when you're time traveling are going to come to you like a dream. You're going to connect with them and recollect them like you're having a dream. Very fascinating, it's very fascinating stuff. Yes you still dream. Isn't that something? You still dream. I'm quite happy about that.

What do you classify as down time in the 5th density?

Down time in the 5ᵗʰ density is when you're not even in the 5ᵗʰ density. I'm traveling around I'm not just remaining in the 5ᵗʰ density, although I am recommending this is a wonderful place to spend a lot of your existence. I am doing some time traveling. Time traveling begins in the World of Imagination and you have to prepare for it. I'm talking about a lot of preparation, aren't I? You have to prepare for death and the Afterlife and then you have to prepare for time travel. It doesn't end. You're still learning. You're not just handed a key to the city. This is what they're teaching. They're teaching a lot of you that you just die and "don't worry you just get the key to the city and away you go". It's not like that at all. Your introduction to time travel is not a class that you're attending. You're not having dress rehearsals in time travel. The dress rehearsal is in 5ᵗʰ density…the dress rehearsal's also on Earth. You've got a couple of stages there where you have a dress rehearsal, you're practicing a part, it's funny to describe it like this but that's what it is.

Burgess, some people are born here with disabilities that make it all the more challenging to train and prepare. What can we say to them?

Many of you are on Earth and maybe you're not experiencing the "typical" life. Maybe you've come into your incarnation and you have a disability and you're not functioning like everybody else. Well, maybe you're already connected with the 5ᵗʰ density and you don't have to be there. I never viewed Beings that were dealing with severe disabilities or any sort of "handicaps" as disadvantaged. I never really viewed it as a handicap. I wondered if they've got something to do somewhere else. They weren't fully all here. They incarnated in a way that also allowed them to direct their energy elsewhere, not having to fully engage in all the Earth plane activity. I wouldn't actually view people that are experiencing this kind of life as "handicapped" or "disabled". They may in fact be ahead of you all.

That's incredibly insightful. They're less burdened by the form.

Now you're getting it.

Burgess, if you had come across the Man Being book series while on Earth, how would you have reacted to it?

Well, I was not that well read in all the esoteric writings and the new age and alternative spirituality books. I was not well read in these books. It was not a great hobby of mine. Had I read your books, well it would've certainly got me thinking. My belief that I had to prepare, that is loud and clear in your books. It's a preparation. Look at all the things that you're sharing with your readers…ideas about history. I wonder if I had read your books would it have gotten me to rethink history? Yes…I would say so. I would say looking at history from a different light…I would say that changes your brain and automatically rewires it. The most interesting thing about your books is not only are you getting a different spin on history you're giving an explanation on why it's not so. You're not simply saying that this is a "bunch of malarkey" and it doesn't work. You're actually explaining why it's so and it's a refreshing look at other possibilities. You're explaining that there are other possibilities and that's what's needed on Earth. Other possibilities.

It also feels like we've run out of ideas on Earth.

Yes, these two words are synonymous, aren't they? An idea is a possibility. Many of you feel that you've run out of possibilities. You're not feeling particularly artistic and you're not comfortable being an inventive thinker and being inventive in your beliefs. You might be thinking like you've run out of possibilities. There's a lot of despair on the planet because you feel like you've run out of chances. I know that that's ultimately the shift that's coming, but the running out of chances is more about running out of time. You're running out of time because you're devastating yourselves and creating extinction and polluting the Earth and just making a mess of the whole planet. It's time to ascend. It's time to make the journey and it's time to prepare for what is going to happen. I believe that reading your books would have given me a little more hope that I wasn't alone in the fight. I didn't really speak to too many people about my beliefs although again, in Hollywood they're pretty open to anything. It's not a stretch to introduce a radical idea or a different slant on a radical idea. But you guys are getting pretty radical with these books. I mean a lot of people are not going to get it, but they will eventually. Just keep at it. You're the trainers now. All of your readers, the ones who are really taking it to heart...they're going to be training others. It's like that. You've got to *go the distance* with this stuff. Haha there you go another Rocky reference. Maybe we should end it on that. Just go the distance.

Amazing. When your character Mickey told Rocky that he was going to make him "eat lightening and crap thunder", were you having an out of body experience?

Haha! I was waiting for you to say that! Well now that'll be a good place to leave off the interview, I guess.

Thanks, Burgess.

You're welcome guys. Mickey loves ya.

SAM

> "Don't go back to Earth. Earth is a cesspool. It's like the Bahamas over here. Your favorite vacation without the expense, without getting fat, without having to deal with your screaming kids and getting in line and crowds…it's the perfect f**king vacation."

Comedian, Actor, Singer
1953 - 1992

Dramos is hearing maniacal laughter and some swearing. Sam shows up unexpectedly one day and we drop everything to have a conversation.

I guess I'm the last guy you expected to show up for this.

Hi Sam, we love that you're here. Man Being Volume 3 just got R-Rated. We won't be censoring you, don't worry.

I'll keep it to a minimum.

Let's get right into it.

Yeah sure go ahead, HIT ME!

Your comedy was aggressive, it was razor sharp and in our opinion you wouldn't be able to exist as a Comic in 2020. The Politically Correct Mob would *cancel* you. Comedy is all but dead on Earth.

Wow, I guess I really don't have much going on in the Afterlife. What can I say? I would suggest…well f**k…I would suggest that you do something about this mess, but what are we speaking about here? Standing up for your rights? What can I help you with, what do you wanna know?

There's a war on comedy. We now know that laughter is a traveling frequency. It's a way to get outside of our bodies and so a war on comedy is essentially…a war on our soul.

Jesus. You guys are more amped up than I was. Haha.

That's not humanly possible, Sam. We think it would be powerful to hear what an "icon of comedy" has to say about the current state of affairs.

Haha well, are we gonna edit this conversation? Okay...hmm..."comedy and what's happened". I'm kind of expecting a resurgence in comedy. With all the editing and self-editing...you can't say shit. You guys can't say anything. Everyone's gonna start screaming...and I'm not gonna start screaming in this interview haha. I'm expecting...are you expecting a new wave of Comedians? I'd like to see that. Every time there's this era, this period of constraint, where we're confined and there's all this shit going on and you feel like screaming and you just can't do anything...there's a comedic shift. There's a cultural shift and I know you're speaking about cultural shifts like everything's falling apart and imploding, but that's where comedy comes in. We don't have comedy when times are good. We have comedy when times are really bad and I'm imagining things are gonna get a whole lot worse and you're gonna be seeing a lot of strange comedy. We're gonna be laughing at a lot of strange stuff.

Let's hope so. Earth is not a fun place for many people right now.

I would suggest that rather than you saying, "Oh well we lost the ability to laugh and we sure have the ability to scream and shout a lot"...what about the ability to listen and hear? I think what you're describing is that we lost the ability to listen. Everybody's screaming...I used to scream but that was part of my act, you know. Now look at that...that was foreshadowing something for sure. But you've lost the ability to listen. If you actually listened to yourselves and you actually heard what you're doing...man it's some crazy stuff. You've created a World now that is so compartmentalized and everybody is just strangled and you can't even think. You're gonna get in trouble for thinking! You know that's gonna be the next problem, never mind saying things and doing things. You're not going to be able to think and feel things soon, right? This is becoming a horror movie. There's going to be a lot of straaange comedy coming out of this, for sure. So I would suggest that rather than you lamenting you know, "there was a time when we used to be able to say a whole bunch of shit and say weird and irreverent things and let it all hang out"...I wouldn't be lamenting that. I would be waiting for the next wave of weirdness. There's bound to be a wave of weirdness coming. But for f**k's sake I thought you were gonna ask me about the Afterlife. I didn't think this was gonna be a political commentary...wow.

Haha. We may as well get to it now. You lived fast and hard and we know about the cocaine and drug abuse and the women and all that stuff. Were you aware that you were going to die young?

Are you suggesting that I was the king of debauchery, is that what you're saying? I guess there was a frustration...realizing that there's so much stupid shit going on. Realizing that, well, really all you can do is scream or cry or laugh...what else can you do? Realizing the hopelessness of it, yeah that's gonna make you take a drug or two or do a thing or two.

We're not saying that you were the king of debauchery at all. We just want to hear your perspective.

Look we all wanna scream. We all wanna scream and we all wanna get things off of our chest and you know...watching a Comedian or listening to a Comedian...that's really you isn't it? That's really who you wanna be. You wanna be the one on stage. I was screaming and really saying what's on *your* mind. I realized when I left religion that there was a way to release the light. I don't believe any of you thought of me in a spiritual way, I mean how could you? But I felt that....um...like you guys are writing about things like orgasms and stuff. I think that's pretty cool and you know for me screaming is like the orgasm. The feeling of releasing the light and yeah I suppose some people reading this are gonna say, "Oh that's convenient, justifying why you're screaming"…but honestly that's what I felt I was doing, I was trying to disconnect.

Did you know that you were going to die young?

Well I knew that things were going really fast and I knew that I was on a trajectory for some sort of release, some sort of revelation. I didn't know a lot of the things that you're writing about in your books. I mean look at my background I was the one peddling that shit, but I suppose when you tap in and you connect with that light…you feel it like, "Whoa I'm letting more light in" and therefore I better do something to make more room. I suppose the screaming was creating more room for my enlightenment haha. Isn't this ridiculous? I felt like things were going fast but I also felt like I was guided. I didn't believe I was gonna die in an accident…that was like the last thing on my list of things to do. I actually believed I was gonna stick around for a while. I felt I had a lot more to say and a lot more screaming to do but um…you know when you are living like that, living large and especially in comedy because comedy is really fast.

Why do you say that comedy is fast? What do you mean by that?

In comedy you're twisting around beliefs, right? You're getting people to look at things differently, to form new beliefs and it's really fast paced and comedy is a way for everyone to make reconnections and I know…again I realize this is laughable. I realize yeah, I mean, on the surface this doesn't really make any sense right. I'm saying a whole bunch of vile things and shouting about a whole bunch of irreverent things…what kind of spiritual connection are you really making? But comedy and laughing and that laughter and the energy, that connects you with the light and that helps you make those reconnections and…uh…well laughing, screaming and cumming, it's all good. I suppose I did too much of that too soon and you know "God" just checked me out haha.

Now we're getting somewhere, Sam.

Guys, I'm gonna say this about laughter…laughter is dangerous. It's a powerful tool. What you're describing as laughter is a weapon, right? Laughter is not cool right now. I know there's comedy but there's not a lot of things left that you can laugh at you know, publically. You have to be really careful. So laughter's become a really dangerous thing and expanding the container so that you can fill it up with new beliefs and fill yourself up with light…that's also a dangerous thing. "Don't believe in anything new". "Don't deviate from the norm". "Don't twist anything around". "Don't look at anything irreverently". Don't do any of that. I'm surprised that we're not all going to watch people cry. Instead of Comedians why don't we all just go and watch someone who's making us cry. Well I guess we have that with everything that's going on right now anyways. It's heading in the direction where you're going to need a license to be a Comedian. You're gonna have to be licensed to get people to laugh and be given a big check list. Like you can't talk about this you can't talk about that…oh no not this and not that…ugh…f**k that. Yeah that's shit. I don't know what you want me to say.

Finally got it out of you.

Yeah you'll have to edit that out of your book haha.

Sam, let's switch gears for a moment. Take us through your death. It was a strange one and we're sure there's a lot of readers who'll want to know what happened.

> Well...I found myself in the middle of nowhere...I mean I seriously was in the middle of nowhere. I mean it was nothing. I thought I was in Hell. I was in the middle of nowhere. You know what I was expecting, with my upbringing, I was expecting the light and the tunnel and Angels and you know some pretty girls...haha...I was expecting all that. I was not expecting this. I was in nowhere. I was in the middle of nowhere. I was not prepared. What you probably heard me saying was "what the fuck? What is this?" and what I'll tell you, some of you are gonna be there, what I saw was like a big white tower. A building. So what you heard me say was probably equivalent to "where the f**k am I?" and "oh I guess I go here I dunno". Everyone's making a lot outta what happened and I understand...it was upsetting and you didn't want me to go and I didn't wanna go and I didn't wanna leave you but I just wanna say for the record that no...an Angel didn't meet me and say, "Sorry Sir...you've run out of time and your set's up".

This is extraordinary. We Just spoke with Yves about The Tower. You're the first Being to tell us that you experienced it besides him.

> Yves? That guy doesn't shut the f**k up. How did he have time to go into The Tower if he doesn't shut the f**k up? Haha. How many pages is this book gonna be? But yeah...I was seriously in the middle of nowhere and there in front of me was this White Tower. It was a Tower and I went into this building and I just said "yeah okay"...what are you gonna do, right? Not what I expected...but I have to tell you it all worked out. Not all of you are going to go in that tunnel of light and see

other Light Beings and all this stuff you're saying. I wish that I had experienced it because it sounds kind of cool haha…yeah I got ejected in the middle of nowhere. It's just crazy! I don't know what to tell you. That's what happened. I went into this tower…you know the story. Yves told you all about it. He's smarter than I am.

Tell us more about your Tower experience.

This thing took me to…there's other worlds. This took me like I was in some sort of vehicle, you know. Like I went from one vehicle to another vehicle, like another car was waiting for me basically, but it wasn't a car. I was taken to another World and I know…look your book's already kind of crazy so I guess why not add to it haha. I'm not gonna lie to you it's crazy…but I was taken…you know every one's gonna ask, "Where were you taken Sam? You were in a spaceship? Woooow!" I was taken in a vehicle. I was "driven" to another place.

So where did it take you?

Almost like another planet, another World and there's many of us there. There is another World, another place you can get to. I am visiting different experiences. You're calling them light densities…so special sounding haha. I'm just calling them other places. I don't travel in the spaceship, although that would be really great. I would love to do that. So why did I go, why did this *space limo* pick me up? Well that's how I interpreted it. I basically went through some gateway and there are many of us there. You know I guess I went in the "VIP" line or something. There's a VIP door, there's VIP access. Now I'm not trying to make you feel shitty if you gotta go through the regular slog of the rigmarole but some of you are just going to be fast-tracked. Yves did it. If you've got a few days go back to his chapter haha.

How did you fast track, Sam?

> Maybe the more you scream or the more you laugh or the more you BLEEP…maybe that's the way. You can say I'm full of shit but I don't care that's what happened…so now I can time travel.

Sam we just have to interrupt and acknowledge why you're coming through this way – with all the expletives and personality traits associated with your incarnation. Some readers might interpret this as us not taking the Afterlife seriously. They might think it's nuts that a Light Being would speak this way.

> Why am I speaking to you like this is a stand up…like this is a set? This is how you're able to hear me, listen to me. They told you about that already. This is a channel that you guys have gotten yourselves on which is great and you can communicate with Beings if they are on this channel…like if we pass by. You can communicate with us and the communication is going to be filtered back to you in a way that you can understand us like the way we communicated or spoke in our last incarnation. It's the only way. Otherwise you're going to hear me SCREAMING in a really high pitch. Yeah like some crazy Mantis Being or whatever. You can still scream and screech and laugh, you make a lot of really cool sounds when you're a time traveling Being. You make these screechy cool sounds and you're changing your form and you can do whatever you want. Now you can either get there the way I did which is instant, right, the VIP access, the ALL-ACCESS PASS like I got. Or you can work your way up to that. To each his own. But I can't tell your readers if they're going to get an all-access pass or if you're just going to go through the economy line.

Sam, give us the details. The space limo took you to this World where there are many Beings. What was that World and who were those Beings?

Hold on, rewind. The Tower is not traveling. The Tower is like an elevator. I just went up it and I was in this weird pod or vehicle. Again, maybe it was me I don't know but that's the way I experienced it. It was like a spaceship, I'm lying f**k it. It was like a spaceship and where did I go? So there's a place where basically...you're you...but in light. You're like a hologram. Everything's like a hologram. I think you're calling this Lemuria. It's Lemuria. It's Lemuria full on. You're in light. This place kind of looks like...well...it kind of looks like something from some cheesy film set, like a sci-fi set from the 50s. It's like you're landing on some weird planet. There are Beings there, there are shapes there, there are pyramid-y things there. You can live there. That's like your headquarters, that's like home base. You are existing there, you're having relationships there, you're interacting with other Beings...there's no "men" and "women". There's just these Beings. They kind of look like us but they're in light. They're not Angels, they're just in light. I don't know what you want me to say about this. I know probably from your perspective...you're saying to yourself it's very fascinating but I don't know...it's kind of a "lame explanation"...it's just all in light. Well that I expected. This Tower thing I didn't expect. It's like I fell through a chute or some trap door.

Tell us about the World that you're residing in.

Well it doesn't have things like telephones or cars, although I did arrive in some sort of vehicle. Everyone's just kind of moving around and floating around in light. It's like a world of telepathy. You're all communicating. We all communicate telepathically. You make sound with your light, like you ring a signal. In a way it's like the World is made up of glass or crystal, but it's all light and this is where you get a lot of your information and understanding. If you have any questions you can go and ask them. If you need nourishment this is where you go. You can eat more light and you can...honestly it's like a spa haha.

Did you at any point turn to someone upon arrival and say "I want answers...who's God, where's Jesus, Muhammad and Moses?" Did you have that moment where you said "I want answers and I want them now"?

Okay...so you're dropped off in this World. You're in this World all of the sudden. You're in light and everyone's just kind of floating around in the light. They're not wearing sneakers and walking around. Everyone's just floating and I asked, "Is this Heaven", because it kind of looks like that. It's all kind of floaty and glowing and I gotta tell you that I was just overcome with a kind of knowing. You plug into the knowing. So any of your questions they're just instantaneously answered. You just have everything that you need in an instant and you're just there. Now this is not just one big World of Light. I mean there's individuals in light. These are Light Beings and this is probably as close to what you're gonna understand is an Angel...and I'm not saying that I became an Angel haha...but I'm telling you that this is as close as to what you're thinking about in terms of a "Heaven".

This is not the World of Imagination that was described to us. This is a separate World.

Oh no that...hell that you're in contact with if you got anything creative to say or any creative thought or creative feeling in your body. Even love...if you're feeling like that you're connected with that...you're calling it 5D...the big 5D. You're connected with that so the more you get connected with that...yeah you get that from laughter...5D you get that from laughter. That's why comedy is so enriching. Laughter is so important. Laughing is very important...laughing is important for the Afterlife. Now there's a lot of things to cry about on Earth and there are many of you that can't even laugh or cry. You're in a weird suspended state that you're dealing with. It's like having a disease or some problem or some dysfunction, but you're still able to connect with that 5D energy. Actually, if you're in that state that you're calling the disabled state you've already tapped into that. You don't even need to really interact with anybody to learn. You've already come to Earth "learned". That's the way I see it.

That's what Burgess told us. So we keep hearing about worlds and densities of light. Are there infinite worlds to exist in and you just pick one? Is that what it's about?

Well so far that's what it's about for me. I'm just experiencing different worlds. I'm experiencing light. I'm experiencing different shapes and different sounds and movement. Have I met "God"...have I encountered what I consider "God"? Is "God" us, what about all that? I am still ascending. I am still absorbing, I am still increasing the light, I am still learning. I don't know when the learning stops.

So the "VIP All-Access" doesn't come with full upgrades?

Haha. Yeah, I'm not saying because I went in the VIP line that I'm done. It's not like that. I am experiencing maybe something that you all experience after you get through this 5D. I don't know how it's structured. I'm just playing and traveling and experimenting and it's good. Let me say this for the readers...you're not alone. You are actually interacting with other Light Beings.

You are. Don't let anyone tell you that you're just going to die and that's it. "Good luck"! You are interacting with other Beings. They're not coming and holding your hand and walking you through the Afterlife. You are interacting with a knowing. You are exchanging knowing, you are absorbing knowing from each other. It's incredible. It's the best conversation you're ever going to have.

Can you paint the picture for us? Do you come across a Being and just download their database instantly by interacting with them?

Exactly. It's some crazy shit. You don't need the language. We're speaking with language...with words. There's none of that and it's peaceful. That's peace. You say "the eternal rest"...it's the eternal rest and you get to shut your mouth...which I know you just can't imagine that I would be doing, right? But it's just like shut your mouth people haha...that would be my advice for all of you. Shut your mouth...just SHUT THE F**K UP...haha. Yeah it's amazing. Download, share...

Most of us would probably like the idea of crossing over and still enjoying beautiful vistas and landscapes. Are there buildings, mountains, lakes, rivers and beach houses? Do we have to create these things with our beliefs or are there actual worlds with these attributes already in existence?

If it's in existence then you're going to be there, because if it's in your mind then you're going to want to experience it. So this World that I was describing that was kind of like crystaline...oh I don't know...think of the weirdest film set you could imagine some sci-fi type place...or visiting some f**ked up planet you know. It's like that...so yeah...is there a planet that has pink mountains and orange palm trees? Yes! There are some

pretty far out experiences that are available for all of
you so it's...things are going to get really interesting if
you just stick with it. Don't do the reincarnation thing.
So many of you are just rushing right back in like "out
of my way I want to suffer again!"

It's perplexing and depressing to know that so many of us would
choose suffering on a planet over time traveling.

You know what's even crazier is that you guys even
make time travel about Earth. You all think that time
traveling means that you're just coming back to Earth
in a different time period. Why do you all think that?
You all believe that...that that's what time travel is.
That time travel is coming back to Earth in a different
time. It's ridiculous really when you stop yourself. Why
the hell...who came up with that? That is one messed
up idea. There is no measure...you're traveling outside
of time. Why the hell would you come back to Earth if
you could travel anywhere you wanted? You gotta see
these other places. You gotta experience the knowing,
the connection and not having to study and listen to
other Beings explain to you...there's places with cool
animals...oh there's a whole bunch of places. It's like
Star Trek. It really is. So ask yourself, who came up
with all that? Where did they write that show from? It's
like that goddamn f**king Star Trek!

Do Light Beings create bonds the way we do on Earth, as in
"friends" or "Partners"?

A life partner?

Like a companion, sure. I suppose some people would say, "It
sounds like such a lonely place...no boyfriend, no girlfriend.
Count me out".

There are friends everywhere. You are in the company of…well this whole conversation is kind of ridiculous and stupid. You're in the company of like minds I want to say…but that's stupid. I'm trying to use your speak…your sensibilities on Earth. You are never alone. I don't have the words to explain a lot of these places…not because I'm trying to tell you a whole bunch of shitty lies. I'm just trying to tell you that there are places that you don't have the words for. You've never experienced this. This would be like going into some far out abstract painting that has a whole bunch of beautiful colors and you just drop right in there. Wherever you go there's friends just like you…and no I'm not causing a whole bunch of trouble in the Afterlife.

Sober Sam now. Very nice.

Don't rile me up I might just start screaming again haha. The way that you conduct yourself here is not like the way that you conducted yourself on Earth because Earth is a bunch of crap. You have to fight your way through that every day and nobody is fighting with you. Now okay wait a minute maybe I'm not being completely clear. There are some Beings who are not too happy if I'm using Earth terms…we don't have happy and sad and all that. We just have "chill". That's the one emotion…the emotion is chill. But there are some Beings who are a little bit irked because they're not able to…well they don't know how to move around. They're kind of confined to a World. It's kind of like Earth but crappier. Apparently you have some big Ascension Event that's going on…it was happening when I checked out. It's happening but it's really going to pick up momentum and these Beings…there's going to be some help for them and they're going to figure out how to fix their mess. Yeah they're in another Earth basically but it's worse if that's believable. It's way worse.

You're speaking of the DRA?

Yeah these Beings they've got a really bad attitude. I don't want to lead you down the garden path and leave you with some ideas that you don't have to worry about these Beings. You might encounter these Beings. I personally didn't have to because I was so wonderful when I was on Earth and I got a reprieve haha...but some of you have to sadly deal with them...but just tell them to f**k off, I guess. That's my advice. Look they're going to get help and everything's going to get fixed and you're all going to be experiencing free travel, unrestricted travel. It's amazing. You can go wherever you want. It's free. You don't have to book a flight. It's free. It's great...but we're still learning. I haven't completely finished my journey...I haven't gone where the "big guns" go. Like no I haven't seen Metatron and all these cool Beings. Sorry to say I haven't...I don't even know why they'd want me there.

Metatron and Sam. Even joking about that might offend some people.

Look...I'm communicating with you guys now so that means I can do my shtick. So...right...there's a lot to experience and I still don't know how it works and I guess I'm just going to keep learning and if you want to check back with me maybe I'll have more to tell you. But the Afterlife is amazing so don't worry about Hell...that's just a bunch of craziness. I'm not saying that everyone should now get into an accident and hook up with me, but there's nothing to fear is what I'm saying. The more that you can interact and engage with the light, with your 5D, the more you can engage with that World of Imagination, with art and comedy and laughter and play...the better off you are. You'll be better prepared. Now I know some of you will say "well I'm not privileged...I don't have time to laugh I'm too busy doing things"...okay well I'm just letting you know. The more that you can do that stuff...the better off you'll be. You'll have your chance anyways and I'm hoping for all of you that you can just get off this planet of yours and release the planet and really find the true essence of the planet.

What's the true essence of the planet?

Not having a planet haha...actually I'm not kidding. And don't woooorry you can still have pets and you if want your goldfish...you can do all of that, they're just in light. There's no form, there's not this heavy and rigid form that doesn't let you do anything. You're free from that. You can have everything you're doing on Earth...the good stuff. Not the crazy stuff, just the good stuff. You can have all of that, you really can. All the needs of drugs and sex and rock and roll...well rock and roll lives on man...you're kind of in a band in the Afterlife whether you like it or not. You sing. Your light makes a sound. It's amazing. But all the debauchery and stuff...I was the king of debauchery...you just don't feel like you need that anymore. And that's what I mean by chill. It sounds boring but it's not. I guess, "you just have to be there"...f**k I hate when people say that.

Sam, there is one thing that's a bit confusing. You said that you didn't really want to leave Earth and that you had some more stuff you wanted to do...but then ended up bypassing most of the crossing over process. Why is that if what you experienced was an involuntary disconnect?

I'm going to call it a voluntary disconnect and I know I'm contradicting myself and I'm the biggest hypocrite.

Call me a whole bunch of nasty names but I was pushing myself and not just through all the debauchery and all the unmentionable things that I was partaking in. I really believe that I was expanding...not just getting fat...I don't want any fat jokes. I believe that I was expanding my awareness to increase my light and I was doing that and I was, in a way, desperate to have more light and desperate to absorb more light and breathe more light. I was feeling a need for more light. Some of you are thinking of the Sun or the Moon. But a lot of the time I was envisioning what you guys call The Channel. I was envisioning this huge star with long arms. I was trying to connect with that or be a part of that. I was driven, I felt, to do a voluntary disconnect but you don't just wake up and go, "Yeah I'm gonna voluntarily disconnect today". It's still going to surprise you. I mean how can you possibly be completely prepared? You'll be as prepared as you can be. Now clearly I overachieved because yeah I got right to the front of the line so that blew my mind. Saying I wanted to be around a little bit more...it would have been nice to be around to maybe try to learn that that was a possibility, but how would you know that? Who's writing about that? Well you're writing about it now that I told you haha. I hope someone else describes it to you too. I don't know how you're going to tell this story without everybody laughing at you...but laughter is good. If they're laughing at you then they're well on their way. Keep laughing! You'll wind up there too. Laugh a lot. You'll laugh your way all the way up to that spaceship or whatever the hell it was...oops I said hell. I want to say that you're not going to Hell.

If you're not in hell then nobody is.

EXACTLY! Exaaactly. That's why you're speaking to me. That's the whole purpose of your book right there.

We're joking of course. Last question: There's a lot of celebrities that die at 27/28 but also 37/38...is there something to that number or age as well? You died at 38.

> Am I part of the 38 Club? Is that what you're asking? I would say that if you're running around and making it your life's work to experience everything...you know what I'm starting to sound too smart...scrap that. Hell yeah! I'm a 38-Club Man or whatever the f**k it's called.

Let's hear the scream...go for it. Just once.

> You'll be disconnecting if I start screaming. Look, some of us are running around and it may look from the outside like we're just heinous, debaucherous lecherous disgusting pigs, but from another vantage point we're Light Beings expanding our awareness and interacting with the cosmos. If you're living large and well again let's use comedy because laughter is the fast track to ascension, it really is. If you're living large like that you can expand and introduce so much light that WOO OH YEAH you just explode! Light explosion yeah. I'd say there's something to it. Look on Earth don't you normally peak with your career at that time. Yeah I don't even know the f**k I just said. None of it makes any f**king sense haha.

Well this has been entertaining. Sam do you want to tell us what you're off to do once you leave the Open Mic?

> I'm going to go sing. I used to enjoy singing and I still sing. We don't sing with our mouths and our vocal cords. We actually sing. We make a sound. We make a note or a chord. I don't know exactly how it works but we can make music together. It's interesting. You're sharing frequencies. It's just this sharing again, the knowing...the sharing and the knowing and the

transmission and the exchange. This all sounds f**king boring doesn't it but trust me it's pretty cool. Yeah I don't know what more I can say but I suspect I'm probably the last example that your readers are expecting. What do you have like Gandhi in your book? Maybe you better not tell me.

Gandhi dropped out. Heard you were signed on.

Wow…roasting a dead guy. Real f**king classy. Love the energy, man. Good luck and keep doing what you're doing. People need to know that there's a lot of weird and wonderful things out there. This "Go to the Light" is cool stuff but that's just the beginning. If you think you just go to the light and then that's it…that's the end of the story…uh no. It gets really good. Stick with it. Don't go back to Earth. Earth is a cesspool. It's like the Bahamas over here. Your favorite vacation without the expense, without getting fat, without having to deal with your screaming kids and getting in line and crowds…it's the perfect f**king vacation.

Sounds like a blast. Sam we're going to preface every chapter with an Afterlife quote by the interviewee…what would you like as your Afterlife quote?

I don't know…maybe like a quote about the Bahamas…I'm not a f**king writer I don't know haha. Use that one! Over and out…see you guys around!

See you around, Sam.

RODDY
McDOWALL

"You are existing in a prison that is Draconian in construct…so yes the prison is the Man Being form, as is the Earth and the rock. You are all rocks. You are all stone. You are all immobilized if you are not able to move the light and so Earth is essentially a Draconian civilization."

Actor, Director, Photographer
1928 - 1998

Dramos is tuning into a Being who's giving the initials R and M. Josephine tells Dramos to "be prepared". It takes us a few minutes to connect with this Being and decipher their identity. We finally understand that it's Roddy McDowall.

Thank you for participating Roddy. Would you like to make an opening statement and tell us why you've chosen to participate in this book series?

> Thank you for having me. There is a precise reason for my participation as you imagine or have guessed already. I have been involved in many creative projects and aspirations that of course you will find very interesting. I'd like to start off by saying that there is no coincidence to the body of my work that exists in the Earth plane. I am involved with other Beings who are sharing information about the options and the choices that exist. The stories that are being told through film and well...what once was television and theater and photography and music and the arts are not random. There is a participation that I am consciously involved with and I continue to be involved with it. I want to make that very clear for the book and for your readers. When you consciously and voluntarily include yourself in these undertakings and these missions to share information and to let others know about the options, this is not something that disappears when you no longer continue your life in the Earth world and existence. I am involved with many Beings who are continuing to disseminate through the arts, although they're not living a 3D life. That "time" has ceased to exist, but the information and the creative inspiration continue from the 5th density. That does not cease to exist.

This is somewhat of a surprise for us, that Beings are this actively involved with Earth once they've crossed over.

You can disseminate and share information from your world, from the Earth existence, but you can also continue sharing, disseminating and inspiring from the 5th. You can always share information from the 5th density. This is something that does not cease. It doesn't cease to exist. I'd like to make that clear for your readers. You can continue to help and you can continue to create. You do not have to physically exist on Earth as a Human Being, limited and trapped in your existence. When you learn about these things and believe about these things you will be further ahead in your understanding that time travel and communication and the ability to help is very real. It's within all of your grasp. I'd like to stress this in this interview.

Where are you existing in this place and space, Roddy?

There is a region that I have always been connected with and involved with and this region is well beyond your experience with the 6th density. When you exit the 5th density experience there is a region that takes you beyond all the trouble that exists in the 6th. There is a region where many Artists, many of us are connected. This World is almost like a valley. A valley that exists between two different experiences and in this reality we can communicate with you and inspire you and help instruct you, but we can also fully engage with quite a bit of time travel. Now, you may want to refer to this as simply "travel" and that would be a correct statement. That wouldn't be something that you should shy away from. Travel is a way to move the light, there is a place and this valley or region is somewhat in between the light, but did you know that there is access to the Inner Earth World?

We don't have that information, no. What else can you tell us?

The Inner Earth existence is not about drilling a hole or a tunnel through the surface of the Earth. There is more to this explanation and this place where I "exist"…and exist in that most of my energy is created and moving and translated from this place and space. There is a region that is connected with this Inner Earth experience that is equivalent to your underwater world. You will learn about the sea and how this connects with the freeing of Terra and the Causeway. Did you know that the Causeway that you are trying to effectively gain a broader understanding of is in fact underwater? Did you understand that when it was first explained to you?

Not at all. Please describe it for us.

The Causeway is not a hole or a passageway. This is an underwater gateway. This is an underwater gateway of experience. You will be traveling through more than one element of experience. I appreciate that you all are regarding the time travel experience as perhaps "floating through the sky" or "floating through outer space". There are many other experiences. I would like to recommend that you consider a new belief stream. It is not just all sky or air or an atmosphere that is equivalent to some "above stratosphere" level experience. There is an element of your travel that is engaging with water. You are engaging with fire. You are engaging with all the elements in fact. It's time and I'm using this of course loosely, but it is "time" for you to expand your awareness and belief. You will be experiencing water. The flood that you've heard much about and the sonic sea, the experience and the noise that you are encountering in the Earth plane, well that noise is in fact leading you directly to the release of Terra and the release of the Causeway and the flood. The flood will engage all of you directly with water and the sea. You will learn how to swim through the sea.

There is a portal. You will be learning about all of these things in greater detail as you connect with Beings in further dialogues.

Is this the flood that occurred in the Bible or are you speaking about Atlantis? Or are they one and the same?

There is much proof of course that floods have occurred...floods as in water but also sonic, as is emphasized in your books. The sonic sea, the flood is already occurring and the opening that is being created is a reopening and a portal that you are all aware of but have lost connection with. If you ask me, "Is this Atlantis?"...well I say *of course*. It has to be, but your readers understandably will want more information. That is not something that I am providing you in this interview and so they will be terribly disappointed with your lack of detail...why not suggest that yes this is a flood that has occurred before and is described in the Bible. The flood mystery in the Bible is what you will be decoding with your readers. It is a new understanding. We are leading you to this understanding.

Why are you not providing us the information in this conversation?

Well you won't understand the language, will you? There is a language that you must both decipher and reacquaint yourselves with. If I'm speaking with you in a language that you do not understand then we are no further ahead. "If you can avoid the plan to want everything now, the disorder will be adjusted accordingly". Isn't that what was communicated to you in Volume 1?

Yes but it is our responsibility to explore and probe so that we can unearth the truth.

Yes of course...and you have many Volumes left to assemble.

We certainly hope so. Roddy, you mentioned previously that your filmography was not random. Two of the bigger productions that you performed in are "Cleopatra" and "Planet of the Apes". These films contain themes that are directly related to what we're talking about in these Volumes.

All of the titles and projects that I agreed to be involved with are all saying something. They all have a message. There are many hidden messages of course and many overt messages in these projects, in these films, in these productions. These two films are good examples and of course you're sharing much of this information in your books. If you go through the other titles you will be quite surprised at how many of the storylines and the lessons learned are ideas and beliefs that you are introducing in your books. Nothing is far-fetched when you start examining your beliefs. The beliefs that you are limited to a rock and that the rock is not engaging with any other experience or reality that you can be a part of or even master is ridiculous. There are many of us who are actively engaged with you. Many of your creative beliefs and unusual beliefs are inspired from other worlds.

Does this mean that nothing we do here – artistically – is original?

I'm not suggesting of course that you cannot come up with your own ideas. That's simply not true, but I am suggesting that there is ongoing communication with many different dimensions of experience. You're connecting with many different portals and gateways of information. The channel that we are communicating on is not the only channel. This is just one channel that you have created yourself. This is in fact your channel of experience. You are communicating your experience and your channel or portal with your readers. They too can of course create their own channel but that channel, my friend, is not only a channel that is connected with the Earth experience. The underwater or undersea gateway is a gateway and channel that you all must tune into and believe in. It is this experience that will release you from the entrapment in the 5th density experience. Your free movement does not exist until you learn how to engage with those belief streams and light densities that exist well beyond the 6th density.

Readers won't like hearing that "free movement" doesn't occur until we're beyond the 6th density. Is that really the case Roddy?

I don't wish to frighten your readers and cause them to believe that they will never be completely free. This is not a truth but there's much more work to be done. I would like to say to the readers that the "Afterlife" experience is just the first step. You are re-engaging with the World where you create. In that creative World you are also creating solutions and creating portals and gateways. You ask a lot about gateways and portals and "where do they come from?" and "how do we use them?" and "how do I know if I can use them?" and "how can I explain to others how to access them?" You create them in the 5th density. This is the gateway experience. The 5th density is the gateway. Have you been told this or explained this?

No, we haven't. Not the way that you're describing it.

The 5th density is a gateway. It is a place and space and experience where you create channels, gateways, portals. Now I realize that you are also using the word "channel" for the light bearer (The Channel) and the light bringer that you are assembling. You are assembling yourself. You are re-assembling yourself. Many of these concepts are a little bit "trippy". I appreciate that this is a strange conversation. Please follow me if you will. The 5th density is the place where you can connect with anything you choose…anything. Any portal that you wish to create and gateway that you wish to access is created and exists in this place of experience and it's for this reason that all of your creative ideas come out of this existence, this World. This is the reason why you are all able to create, although some of you have forgotten. You are all able to create a portal or gateway of experience. Creating or creativity is a gateway of experience. When you create something you are creating a portal. When you believe in something you are creating a portal. You are creating a gateway. Gateways are not permanent structures or experiences. You are learning of course how to continuously create the flow, the gateway, The Channel, the light bearer that you have witnessed and written about…these are all portals or channels or gateways of light. This experience is something that you are turning on and accessing. That experience of the light, the cords of light are channels and these channels…you are learning how to continuously and permanently turn on and off.

We've been told that the 5th density is like a training ground, a place to learn how to create new beliefs and time travel, ultimately. So what you're saying makes sense.

Yes. You are finding and creating these gateways in the 5th density. The 5th density experience is the most important experience in your journey. In many of my films and projects there are stories and ideas about the 5th density and in many of these stories there is specific instruction and explanation on how to reconnect with the belief that you can create portals to wherever you wish. You can create portals and gateways to worlds that you have never even imagined yet, but in order to imagine these things you need to create the portal so that you can access the imagination and the belief. Now I know that I am most certainly confusing all of you with my description and I don't want to say that you "have to be there" but you must understand this: that the 5th density and the gateways create more gateways so that when you create a portal of experience you then create another portal and a further portal. This is the beginning of time travel. Time travel doesn't occur in one singular portal. There are many different portals and channels that you access simultaneously. This is something that you will master. Much of the instruction about the 5th density is told in many of the stories and projects that I have been involved with on Earth and continue to be involved with. I am involved with a Group of Artists that are disseminating messages right now in the Earth plane through artistic projects that are involving movement and visual arts...."multimedia" you like to call it.

Would you like to share with us who these Artists are?

There are Artists that are involved in circus performance, in theatrical productions like the Cirque de Soleil. The circus arts that are being introduced now are very interesting. If you look at globally what's going on in this artistic pursuit it's not just a random and beautiful series of colors and movement and light and sound just thrown together with a charming storyline and an engaging belief. It is in fact instructing you if you look at it through new eyes and these eyes you must remember are situated in the 5th density. Did you know that your psychic ability is found in the 5th density?

That would make sense based on everything we're learning.

The ability to see things and hear things...to see and hear is the same ability...these things are all found in the 5th density experience. There are many, many things that we can speak about Dramos and Bohemias, but I want you to go through some of the stories that I have been involved with and you will soon see the "coincidence" in your writing and many of the storylines that I participated in are overlapping. It is beyond a coincidence. You will find this very, very inspiring.

Roddy we understand that as an Artist you had a clear connection to the 5th density while on Earth. Was there however a particular moment when you realized that immortality was an option? Perhaps you had a vision, a dream or a conversation.

As a child I encountered a Being, you would probably refer to this Being as "Extraterrestrial" or "Alien". I encountered a Being. This Being was not of Earth and this Being explained to me about the different levels of light and the different worlds of light and explained to me how there are many of us who have in fact traveled so far beyond the existence of the Earth plane that they have changed their form and exist in a way that we recognize as Extraterrestrial. *Extraterrestrial* is a correct description by the way. This Being who I encountered explained to me that I have gone as far as the 7th level of light, the 7th world, the 7th density. Did you know that 7 is important? Not only in the Bible and the 7 days and all the number 7 in the mythologies and many spiritualties, religions and philosophies in which 7 is made mention of...but 7 refers to the 7th density of light existence and this Being came to me and explained and helped me remember that that is where I have always been existing and continue my ascension experience from. This Being that I encountered did not arrive in a "UFO" as many of you are now asking yourselves or wondering...this Being materialized and I saw this Being in light. Now this Being is very much equivalent to what some of you are describing as "Arcturian". The physical form that you are describing you have encountered is quite similar and so I had a belief from a very early age in my linear experience that I was in fact engaged and involved with another world of experience and a world that I would not only be making my way back to but that I would be communicating with throughout my incarnation in the Earth plane. What I learned as well from this Being was that this was my final incarnation on Earth, that my work would be completed. The dissemination and the collection and the projects that I committed to while existing in form on Earth were in fact part of a "Repair Project", much like you are involved with in your book series. There are other Beings, Dramos and Bohemias, that you will be encountering. I appreciate that it sounds very strange and very science fiction like, but these other Beings…these *Extraterrestrial Beings*…you know what this term refers to don't you? "Terrestrial"…well you know where terrestrial comes from…TERRA.

Wow. Right under our noses.

So now I have quite certainly explained to you where this belief comes from and how it is that some of us are able to connect with these Beings, see these Beings, speak with these Beings and evolve into these Beings. When you ask me, "Where am I now" and "What am I doing?"…well I am traveling and I am existing in a form that you would recognize as being Extraterrestrial. Again I would like to stress it's very similar to what many have described as the Arcturian appearance. Now I know this is a little laughable and some of your readers will be shaking their heads in disbelief but these things are happening. They're not that far-fetched. You need to shift your belief and start asking questions. When you start questioning your existence this will of course assist many of you in re-establishing new beliefs, but of course this is what your books are doing.

Gregory learned that ETs were once like Man Being and that they are trapped in this form in the travel modality, but he didn't expand on that. Can you further explain why you've taken the form of an Arcturian and what exactly an Extraterrestrial is?

Well, extra Terra...beyond Terra. Well, it's beyond the belief of Terra as a blocked gateway. Extraterrestrials have gone beyond that belief. That's what I'm saying. Beyond your present belief. It's expansive thinking Dramos and Bohemias. These are Beings no longer trapped in the 3rd density waiting for the release of Terra. Beings that are able of course to exist in other levels of light will have a different form when they encapsulate and make a connection with the 3rd density. Extraterrestrials are Beings who can make a connection with the 3rd density. It's the ability to visit, basically. When you visit you aren't going to be visiting as a Human Being. Your form will be much different in order to travel and experience different levels of light. Your form must change. Your form that you are experiencing on Earth is very limited. There's very little light. There's NO light in fact and I know that this is not something that is a very happy thought but there is no light for you on Earth. Why am I taking this form? That is the form that you take when you are able to exist. Let me use the word "breathing" to describe it. When you are able to breathe in that level of light in the 7th density existence and that form that you take...that is just the form that you believe you see. Are you following me?

Somewhat.

Well, you can experience any form in the Earth as long as you're connected to the 5th density. When you're in the Earth plane you are not able to see the light. Beliefs are permanently encapsulated in form. You see what you are. You have no creative awareness or creative belief or alternative belief if you are not engaged with that 5th density...that light experience. You just simply cannot process these beliefs...you understand this of course.

Yes...so all these different forms that we read about...Arcturians, Mantis Beings, Tall Whites, The Greys etcetera...are you saying that these are all just different travel suits or costumes that we wear to exist in different densities of light?

Yes and no...and I know that this is not the answer that you were waiting for. What I will say is the different forms that you are describing...well you've just given me a list of different Extraterrestrial Beings, these are the Beings or rather the beliefs that you have about these Beings while connected with the Earth experience. Again I remind you that you would also be engaged with the 5th density, as you wouldn't be able to experience these Beings at all if you didn't have access to at least some light. You need to be able to experience some light, of course, otherwise you cannot see other Light Beings. You see everything in form because that is how you "currently" exist. If you experience a "Grey"...let's use this as an example as there's much interest in these Beings...if you see a Grey or experience a Grey Being this is the way that you experience this Being while you are engaged with the Earth experience and connected with the 5th density. You would not feel these Beings, you would not hear these Beings, you would not communicate with these Beings, you would not engage with any exchange of information...*intracellular exchange*...if you didn't have the ability to connect with other levels of light. But these forms that you see are forms that you see while on Earth. These are not the forms that you see when you're in another level of light. These are the representations that you are experiencing on Earth much like a form changes, like ice melts or water boils.

What you are experiencing on Earth is what you are experiencing while you're on Earth but not necessarily experiencing that in another stream of light existence.

There are many theories circulating about a "Galactic Federation" and other organizations and councils that exist that are acting as arbiters of the cosmos. What do we need to know about those organizations? Do they exist?

Aren't they wonderful? There's much organization and that is the main reason why we are having this conversation – because we care to repair things. There are undertakings. I am part of a "Federation". Most Artists are. Most Artists are, generally speaking, involved with the Galactic Federation. Now I know this sounds laughable to many of you but this is the case. Artists are involved with these undertakings.

There's a lot of information being disseminated over the Internet about aliens and "Intergalactic Federations". It's difficult to distinguish how much of it is misinformation and fiction.

Dramos and Bohemias let me explain something again. I don't believe that I've explained this well enough for your book. You must be careful how you share these ideas. We don't want your readers having the belief that they must define their belief in a very limited construct or pathway or gateway. If we were engaging in the 7th density together we would be experiencing each other in light. Not necessarily in form. Form is the method of travel. Form is the gateway. You are forming a gateway so when you are forming a gateway you have a form for the light. The 5th density is important because you need that light in order to be able to…well you need that light in order to have any belief stream. We will now be experiencing each other as Arcturian in this discussion and I'm using Arcturian for a very important reason, as this experience that you are calling "Arcturian" is very similar to the experience in the 7th density gateway or portal. If I were to manifest and make a portal to connect with you in the 3rd density completely, then we would all be experiencing each other similar to the Arcturian form that you have already encountered.

What you're saying is that in the Earth plane we are not able to see ourselves in light. That is the main dysfunction because we see others the way we see ourselves. We see at the level of light that we're in. So on Earth we see others in different colors for instance and it's not like that.

No, of course not. Well in the Earth existence, in the Earth plane...there are those of you who are not connecting very well with the 5th density of light and this is the fundamental problem, the fundamental dysfunction in the Earth plane, the malaise. Where does this all come from? You are not able to see yourselves and because you're not able to see yourselves you're no longer able to see others the way they are. You're able to see each other in a form but you're not able to see each other in light and in light we're all the same. The difference is that we're experiencing on Earth our dysfunction of the lack of light. There is no light and because there is no light or there is very little light, you don't know what light looks like. You're exposed to artificial light. You believe that the Sun and the luminaries that you have in fact created are the light. That is not the light.

Beings in Volume 3 have repeatedly referenced the Sun and that it is in fact artificial light. It might be confusing to some readers that the Sun gives us light but is not actually light.

The light that I am speaking about is the light that moves and allows you to travel and that light experience is not an external experience. That internal light you will be able to see in others. What you are you will see in others and so when I am communicating with you in an "Arcturian" form or a 7th density Light Being form and you're able to see that…well that says a lot doesn't it? If you're able to see me in that existence, in that experience then I would say that we're all using the same gateway or the same portal and if the portal is in fact the spacesuit or the spaceship then I would say that we all come from the same place. You're not accepting on Earth that you all in fact come from the same place. Your origin story is not about you coming from different sectors in the universe. Your origin story is about how your beliefs that you come from different places was *created* and is an INCORRECT belief stream. You're all the same. You've forgotten.

What purpose do the sectors in the universe serve?

There are different levels of light and different abilities to create portals or travel. The different sectors of course are the unification and the way to reconnect the experiences that allow for the release of the Terra experience. You are speaking about the release and the Causeway experience. The 4 pieces or the 4 lines in the symbol that you are often sharing and speaking about with each other…that's your answer. That's the key. Four is exactly three.

Are you talking about the equal arm cross?

Yes.

If we're all the same then the Ascension Event of 2034-2060 is for everyone. Everyone on this planet is a Sirius Being…we've just split off and there are too many Beings representing 780K. Everyone on Earth is a Sirius Being – is that correct?

Yes but not everybody remembers and those that do not remember or cannot find a way to remember…these are the Beings that will need the assistance…and do you know who those Beings are?

Who are they?

The Draconian story that you're speaking of. They have forgotten. Don't bother yourselves getting confused about Draconian and Orion Draconian and Arcturian and Grey and this portal and that portal and this gateway and that gateway. We are all moving and all Light Beings and this will all be corrected soon.

Why do these Draconians possess so much power to manipulate and control? If they're lacking light and lacking a belief in light why are they capable of manipulating Light Beings?

Dramos and Bohemias…they are not manipulating Light Beings. They are using portals or gateways. The form…they do not know how to create form. They are formless. This talk about "reptiles" and these strange forms that you all are speaking about, well that might be what happens to a form that is engaging with a Draconian energy, but they themselves…no…they're not capable of creating a form. They're formless. They're using your forms. Is this a manipulation? I'm not sure it is, but has there been much belief created in this understanding that they do manipulate and control the light? Yes I would agree with that. There is much belief in that. Is it a correct belief? No. I would say that it is not, but these things get out of control and it seems that Man Being is so interested in subscribing to these somewhat strange beliefs that it's now an accepted belief when it actually isn't. Now, Bohemias you might ask me, "How is it that these Beings held me down on my bed? How can they do this if they're not controlling the light? How can they exert so much power?"

That's exactly what we would ask.

Well they have a different energy form don't they? I fully believe you that you experienced this and it sounds traumatic. When I say "form" maybe that's not a good use of a description. Their being, their existence, their energy is a different element. That's a better way to describe it. *Element.* That will be an easier understanding for your readers. They exist and are made up of a different component or components. They are different. They're not made up of the same elements that we're made up of. This is a different composition, a different substance, a different creature. But as soon as I use the word "creature" Man Being of course creates a belief or connects with a belief of a Being in a form that is grotesque or is monster-like or even reptilian-like. We're on Earth as I'm speaking with you so I use the word but these notions are simply not correct and not helping much are they? Your encounter with this fierce Being and this existence no doubt could topple many of you and they do. Is it manipulation or is this an energy exchange? I don't feel that this is an intellectual manipulation but this is how you are interpreting it, as it is something new that you are encountering and a new energy and a new element that you do not incorporate in your own existence. These Beings are not existing in a form that has anything close to your existence and the form again I remind you is not a form like a portal or gateway. There actually is no word to describe their existence other than they are not of any chemical or energetic or biologic or spiritual existence that is mapping directly or aligning awareness with yours. There is no overlap. They are completely foreign. These are foreigners.

Constantin Brancusi told us that the form that we have as Human Beings is the belief of the Draconians, that they have designed our human form. Why did they choose to design us in this fashion?

The elements that exist in the 3rd density experience and existence on Earth is such that this is the form that is experienced. The form taken into another density of light would not exist in this way. The form would change. You've spoken about shape shifting. This is the form that exists on Earth. It is not a random form or an idea that somebody created. This is the form that exists on the Earth plane. This is what it looks like and this is how it is experienced on Earth. When you're entrapped in the Earth plane, this is the form that you take. You cannot take another form. This is the way you appear.

Why did Constantin suggest that Draconians designed this form...or did we misinterpret that?

Draconians are engaged directly with Man Being and directly engaged with the form. They are not engaged with you energetically in that they need your energy or light to move. They need the gateway or the containment of the light. Have they created Man Being? Have they created Human Beings? They have created a way to entrap and ensure that you do not leave the Earth plane or seek more light. It is quite a conundrum that they are, well, looking for a form or a gateway or a portal on one hand to seek more light but on the other hand they cannot use the light. They are incapable of using the light because they do not know how to create form. They do not know how to engage with the light and therefore move the light and therefore create form. So this understanding that the Draconians created the form is partially true. The entrapment on Earth is strictly a Draconian dilemma. The real Beings who are trapped on Earth are Draconians and the Beings who are Light Beings and Time Travelers and connected with the cosmos and all the portals and gateways that exist beyond the Terra entrapment are you and me and all of us. The Draconian experience is actually the experience that you are living on Earth. This is a complicated discussion I'm not sure that you'll be able to absorb this completely.

No, it's not immediately clear to us. What we do understand is that our existence as Human Beings on this planet is not a real existence and that what we perceive as planet Earth is not the real Earth.

You are not living on Earth. Earth is Terra. You've learned about the Crystaline Causeway and the plants. That is the real existence or the beginning of your existence. Earth is a different existence, as your readers know it in this place and space. You are existing in a prison that is Draconian in construct so yes the prison is the Man Being form, as is the Earth and the rock. You are all rocks. You are all stone. You are all immobilized if you are not able to move the light and so Earth is essentially a Draconian civilization.

If it's not you Roddy, who will give us the explanation of why these Beings traveled to the Causeway and petrified it? How did that occur? Why did that occur?

Well many of you are stuck but not for long. Is it my responsibility to release Terra? Well I would like to say it is my responsibility but it is also all of your responsibilities. How will you be able to construct the origin story? Well you must first construct the release of the Terra story and that will give you your origin story.

Dramos keeps seeing a valley and a "V" while we're communicating with you. Is the "Aeserius" symbol from chapter 10 in Volume 1 aligned with number 7 and this Valley? If you turn the symbol on its side it's the Aeserius symbol. Is that the name of the place that we're connecting with now?

Yes.

Dramos sees you as if you're wearing a jumpsuit with a lapel on it. The lapel is in the shape of the Aeserius symbol.

Yes, but we don't want your readers giving too much attention to garments and things of this nature.

Agreed. The first thing you think of when you hear jumpsuits and lapels is "Star Trek".

Yes of course, some of your readers will turn to this reference.

Roddy how old were you when you encountered the "Extraterrestrial" Being?

In Earth experience years I was 6.

Did you tell anyone about it?

I mentioned it to a nanny. But you understand at that age this is acceptable behavior and imaginary friends are not seen as highly unusual. Perhaps this is a good point to end our conversation on, as you must all "get back" to the belief in imagination, to the beliefs you once had when you were children. This is a message you will continue to hear.

Thank you very much Roddy for participating in this. It's been a wonderful conversation.

Well thank you.

ORSON
WELLES

"Maybe 'Alien' or 'Aliens' in this story represent a belief stream that is too big and too much to be absorbed…if your mind is blown then so be it. It's not something that you're going to be able to put back together in its original state."

Writer, Director, Actor
Academy Award Winner
1915 - 1985

Orson requested that we also describe him as:
Struggling Artist, Poet, Filmmaker

Someone has been energetically sending us the image of Pablo Picasso's 1955 Don Quixote sketch. This Being has not revealed their identity for two weeks. We just keep seeing Picasso's sketch. We're convinced that it's Picasso. Today, the Being finally introduces himself as Orson Welles.

Hello Orson, thank you for joining us. Was that you sending us images of the Don Quixote sketch? We know you attempted to make the film when you were on Earth.

> Oh you liked that did you?

Is there something you'd like to say about that novel or was that just your way of saying hello?

> Well I wanted to extend a warm welcome and well...I'm playful. So I suppose it worked. If I announced myself in a manner of, "Oh Orson wants to be involved in your book", then I suppose you would have just stopped focusing on your other interviews and run immediately to me. It might have been helpful sure...but not fair to the others and so I thought I would wait my turn and be patient and have a little fun in the meantime.

Fair enough. We're just going to go ahead and jump right into it. You redefined the language of film and defied many of the rules, even if you insist it was out of "ignorance". Have you arrived here to do the same with our book series – to transition us into a new discourse?

> Well I've got my work cut out for me, haven't I? Let me if I may, let me just begin by introducing this important fact that, well, I suppose we could say: "You found us". I wanted to begin this interview with a little bit of a game and a little bit of a playful tale but I suppose for now I'll just say "Congratulations! You found us!" or "I guess you found us"...and so you have. You found us!

What do you mean, what did we find?

> Inner Earth, of course. You were just speaking with Sam about it. Now I understand and I recommend wholeheartedly that you're cautious about how you want to present this interview with me and I am speaking for the others and we'll get to those in short order, but let me start off once again by saying "you've found us"…or "oh I see you've found us"…or "oh, so you've found us"…and you have.

This is starting to sound like the frozen peas commercial.

> This will be much more pleasant, I assure you. The 7th level is where we're staying for now. This is not any news to you, I'm quite sure that if you go through your interviews and you revisit many of the storylines or the "plot" that you're weaving, you'll soon see that this makes perfect sense. You've found us. This is where we're waiting, this is where we're organizing and this is where you're all going. I'm happy to assist you and I'm perfectly happy and willing to be a part of your book. Now I don't want to dictate what you're writing or what you're saying but I wouldn't mind being a little more actively involved…and certainly when you are sitting down with pen and paper and you're putting together your 4th book…oh you'll have quite a story to tell. Those Beings that you'll be learning about, they're something else, that's no lie, no mistake, they're something else and it is something that you're going to have to reveal to your readers. Now I know I'm being cryptic but I'm quite certain that you understand what we're speaking about and where we're going with this so let's not dwell so much on my contributions, although I'm sure you find them interesting…and there are a lot of questions… especially about the Don Quixote work and what in fact I was doing with that during my incarnation on Earth.

What were you doing with Don Quixote while you were here? It did seem to be an obsession of yours.

It didn't really mean as much as everybody is trying to read into it. I'm sorry to say that I just loved the story and enjoyed working on the project and I'm quite pleased that it wasn't completed or finished. I hope it's never finished. It's a journey that I'm happy to be a part of and I continue to be a part of. I'm not suggesting that I'm continuing filming and running around in different locations and accumulating reels and reels of film that must be edited and contemplated but you know what I mean…it's a project much like you're doing now. Now I'm not trying to scare you and say there's no end to your book series. I imagine that you would like it to end at some point but that you'd like the ending to be the beginning, so to speak. I'm quite certain that you'll achieve that and I'm quite certain that there are many who have benefited already from the work that you have done.

We hope so. We believe so. Orson would you mind if we ask you some questions about your work? Much of it is relevant to what we're learning about in this communication.

Oh it's all relevant, Dramos and Bohemias. What would you like to explore?

Your radio broadcast of H.G. Wells' "War of the Worlds". You essentially alerted people, whether it was intentional or not, to be ready. A lot of people panicked and were scared that what they were listening to was real and that Aliens were attacking the Earth. It was an interesting experiment. Was it intentional and what do you have to say about the reaction and what we can learn from it?

What we can all learn is that we're not ready. We're never going to be ready until it actually happens. The realization that we were not ready is the realization that continues today. The understanding that, well, we can be attacked by "Aliens" is an interesting point. Who are the Aliens exactly? You've already learned quite a bit about time travel and different levels of light and different experiences and maybe we're never ready to be invaded with a new belief system and a new way of existing. Maybe "alien" or "Aliens" in this story represent a belief stream that is too big and too much to be absorbed and so you have to collapse…and you've written about the collapse. If your mind is blown then so be it. It's not something that you're going to be able to put back together in its original state. The Aliens…the aliens are *alien beliefs*. Beliefs that are so beyond what most of you are ready to absorb and direct your intention toward. The alien belief, the aliens are coming, the beliefs are coming, the new beliefs are coming and the new order of belief is arriving. We are on the verge of a change in the world order, in the organization.

You're twisting the word "Alien" to great effect.

The Aliens, who are the Aliens? Well, the Aliens are not only yourselves, I mean that's quite an obvious metaphor, but the results and the activities and the circumstances that will be causing all of you to reengage with, well, the worlds that you've lost touch with. The reconnection as you're describing it, that reconnection is alien to all of you, although it's something that is so easy to make happen. The belief that it is just so easy and so effortless to reconnect is also alien…and so yes the aliens are coming. What will become of all of you when you reconnect with the belief that you are missing the light? You are missing the reconnection with the light and the ability to see light and speak light and to be light. This is something that is your birthright. What will become of all of you? Will you fight it as many of you do? Will you simply embrace it and go with the flow as ultimately you're poised to do with this upcoming Ascension Event of change? These are questions that many of you quietly ponder.

Some of us are quietly pondering what Orson Welles was doing on Earth.

I know that you are wondering, many of you are wondering about me, what I was doing on that planet and how was I spending my days and what exactly I was up to. What exactly was I up to? I was engaging in telling stories and reassembling belief streams, although I do understand that many of you just did not get where I was coming from. I suppose I don't either, in reality. There's nothing wrong with experimenting with ideas and beliefs and trying out beliefs, trying them on for size. I seemed to have many interests when I was in the Earth plane that many of you believe are my genuine personality, but the truth of the matter is that I am interested in you all. I am interested in Human nature. It's a curious thing, why you remain trapped in your strange beliefs when there are so many beliefs out there that you can just grab onto. Well you can reinvent your beliefs, you know all about the 5th density and the World of...I like "Invention"...the World of Invention, yes. That's a nice sound, isn't it? So you found us as I started off our interview. You found us. The "Seven Seas", or the "Seven Heavens". Seven...you found us. I suppose I could ask you now...what do you intend to do now that you have found us? I imagine *I* should be interviewing you both.

What would you ask us?

What is your intention now that you have found us? The 7th density. This is where we are. This is where you go. This is the safe zone. This is the "place and space". I've heard you say that more than once. This is the space and the place where you go when you figure out how to get past *them*. Where do you go? Well you come here. What are we doing here? Well, this is where we are. This is where we're at. You've spoken to quite a few Beings who have mentioned the colors and you know the colors are in the 5th density...well of course they're there. That's where they're invented, that's where they're imagined, that's where it all starts but that's not where it all ends. We're in the World of Colors, I mean really in the World of Colors. So anything that you want to ask about I can surely help you with and your upcoming visit, well...also including a personal tour by yours truly.

We have full intention of creating a map for our readers and for all Beings who are starting their journey back home. Everything we discover through these conversations we intend to publish. That's what we intend to do. Having said that, we would like to know what's in the 6th density. We skipped over it.

Oh there's a bit of a hurdle there. The 6th is what you might call an "obstruction". Those pesky DRA have created a small obstruction. Oh that bunch...they're a terrible terrible bunch, but it's not impossible to get around. It sounds like it is. I realize that many of you after you learn about what you may believe is your fate...you might just say "well why not reincarnate then...is that any worse"? Oh there's a way around them. I know I'm speaking very matter of fact as if it's like doing laundry, but that's not really the case. There's a way around them if you join the Assembly. There are many of us here who are undertaking in the Repair Project that you are both involved in. You've communicated with us very early on in the project haven't you…and so here we are.

Talk to us about your involvement in the Repair Project, Orson.

Let's talk about the allegiance to our Group and our existence and our mission to help in the repair…well let's talk about the repair. We're using that word a lot aren't we? Repair…it's a nice word but what is it? You can repair your beliefs and repair your connections, your reconnections and you can make something better but what is the repair? What are we repairing? There is something missing. You must have asked yourselves this. What is this "Repair" mystery? We're repairing the Bridge. That Bridge…now I'm not going to get into talk about gateways and portals….oh I'm sure you've heard enough but the Bridge…the Bridge and number 7. The Seven Principles, the Seven Heavens, the Bridge. That's what you're repairing that's what we're all repairing. That's the project. The Bridge. Once you get through it then time travel…well that'll be second nature won't it? Travel…travel is just something that you do. Travel is not the be all and end all…it's just something that you do. There's a lot more at stake here. There's a lot more at stake. There is a change and a shift and those luminaries that you see up in the sky are not going to be in that place. There's change coming. There's changes, not just stars falling from the sky and comets redirecting their paths and the Sun dying out…there's even more coming, although the Sun dying out sounds ominous doesn't it?

Orson, we have no idea what the "Bridge" is, or what the references to 7 are. We're assuming that the Bridge is the journey from the 5th to the 7th density.

That's right. You're learning about Terra and well you're learning about the Inner Civilization but could I say this to you both…there is something awaiting you in the Inner Earth experience that's more or less, depends how you look at it, where we're located, where we're existing. We're not existing on a planet. That's not what's happening. We're existing in an experience that allows you to believe, well, whatever you want to believe, but it's a little bit different than the 5th density World of Imagination.

What makes it different?

We're allowed to experience a depth of belief that you're not experiencing just yet and this is not about you not being ready or equipped. This is simply a case of you not standing in the World. You're not immersed fully in the World, but you will be. This World…what does it look like or what can it look like? It can look like planet Earth if you choose it to be. It's a place where many worlds exist. Now I know you've spoken to Sam who has explained it, albeit in a convoluted and psychedelic kind of way like…"pink skies" and "orange palm trees". When you hear about these different worlds maybe ask yourself, "Are there really different worlds out there or is this the same World?"

Sam is believing that Inner Earth is many worlds when it is only one – is that what you're saying?

I would tend to say yes, it's one World. We're waiting for you to immerse yourself in this experience but to dive down into this World is taking quite a shift and so if we go back to your original question about the radio program and what that did to everybody's reality…well the alien belief is coming. It's on the horizon and the planet that you are standing on and the densities of light that you are connecting with are really only the beginning in the change of belief or your belief stream, as you are referring to it. There is a whole new experience and well, on the surface it sounds incredible. It sounds implausible. It sounds fantastical. "How can this possibly exist?" It's not possible...many of you would say that. "Stop now this is getting ridiculous" and so it is...and when you accept how ludicrous and impossible this scenario is then you'll be there. The Inner Earth and all of that is what awaits you both and what awaits you both is a partnership and I'm happy to assist you and walk you through it.

Orson, how did you get through the 6th? How did you cross the "Bridge"?

How did I avoid those Beings? Did I pick up a sword and fight them or did I run very fast or did I speed away in a car or row in a boat and fly over a hill...what could I have possibly done? What have I done? What could I have done differently? This is the question you must ask yourselves. What could I have done differently? What am I doing differently? What will I be doing differently? It is requiring a different approach. These Beings are not Beings that you are wrestling with. Now I know that you met one Being that's not so nice Bohemias and I heard a little bit about that...that was very rude. Now we're not requiring you to start wrestling with these Beings and nobody likes to be threatened. That's rude. That's not very polite and I'm not suggesting that your readers have to engage in these shenanigans, that's not the case at all. Although you did experience how they can be a little bit unmanageable, can't they? These Beings are quite simply looking for a vehicle. They're hitchhikers. These Beings are hitchhikers, they're parasites, they're a virus that you must cure. The cure is not fighting them or outsmarting them. Doesn't Man Being always go to that? We always go to that. How do we "outsmart the bad guys"? That's always the general rule isn't it and that is simply not the approach – outsmarting the bad guys. Well these bad guys can move things. These bad guys don't have a physical form like you do and they don't have microwaves and toasters and running shoes and you name it. They don't have casinos and they don't have waitresses serving you a sandwich. All of these things are simply not part of their lexicon of experience. Trying to outsmart them when they do not have the same reality or conduct as you is simply a losing game. They are able to move things.

What things can they move?

They are able to move ideas. They are able to move energy and they are able to move space. Now if they're able to move these things why can't they move themselves? Why can't they move themselves to find the light? They cannot use the light. They cannot work with the light. The light doesn't benefit them. Isn't that something? The light does not benefit them but yet they are trying to hitch a ride with us and get us to disconnect and take them somewhere, but they cannot use the light. The light and the language of the light mean nothing to them. They do not have the ability to absorb light. They do not have the ability to see light. They don't know what light is and isn't it something that Man Being is suffering the same problem? You are both suffering the same. It's the same problem, the same sentence. You have both been sentenced to the same existence and so what is the difference my friend? What is the difference? One of you is in a form, in a physical form that is containing energy and allowing you to make reconnections because it's protecting what little bit of light you have.

Do we really have that little?

You have a spark, so I would like to maybe redefine what I am telling you. You have a spark, the smallest spark imaginable. There is something. Not a lot, but something and these other Beings have nothing – bereft. Absolutely no light. No way to generate light, no way to take back an infinitesimally small unpretentious spark and make something brighter and greater and bigger and louder and stronger. They are not able to do this. You have only been given the smallest tool that you could ever imagine. You've been gifted just a seed of the light, a small seed. It almost doesn't exist but it manages somehow not to be extinguished, whereas these other Beings, in the other World, it is gone. The spark is gone. The light is gone. It is dark and the darkness is not the primordial darkness that you are learning about. It is another type of darkness and it is a darkness where nothing is created. There is no creativity, there is no invention, there is no art, there is no way to escape.

How is it then that these Beings hold so much power over us?

How is it that these Beings are infiltrating Man? How are they infiltrating Man and how are they doing this if they are not able to problem solve or create or move? If they are immobile how are they doing this? What are they? This is the question that all of you must ask. What are these Beings? Never mind who they are…what are they and how is it they can cause other things to move but they themselves cannot? What is going on here? Are they in fact the beginning of light? Are they the state of existence before the light began, before the spark, the nothingness that was once something?

Those are complex questions.

Yes, try to stay with me now. Something has changed. The primordial existence has been split. The "split" is what you're asking so many questions about. You've learned about so many splits and I imagine that you continuously believe that, "Yes we've got it. This is the split, we have the story". Now let's share it with the World but your story is only beginning. The primordial state of being does not exist in the way that you believe. There are Beings who have divided themselves by re-entering this state in the primordial, voluntarily of course. They can no longer remove themselves but can cause things to move around them. Now this sounds like creating. This sounds like creating momentum but that's not what I am speaking about. They are able to control your movement and control what you do by virtue of the fact that a void is created when you move, when you create, when you change a belief.

They work within the void or vacuum.

That void that is created when a belief implodes is where these Beings lie and so when you are reconnecting and forming a new belief or creating a new belief, that's where these guys come in. They are able to come in. They are able to move and help you shift your belief by creating that void, that space. They move the space for you to form the new belief, for they are the void. They exist in the void and are the void.

They looked transparent or see-through during my encounter. Their rage was like nothing I'd ever experienced. The one Being who attempted to restrain me told me, "Shut your f**king mouth and do what I tell you to do. We are the billionaires and the cool kids".

Your encounter with a very hostile Being, a Being who was out of order, out of line, the behavior was terrible on all accounts. I wholeheartedly understand that this was not enjoyable Bohemias and I'm very sorry that you had to experience this. This void is the anger and rage that has been left as the belief changes and you release the anger that exists in the Earth plane. This is moved into this experience. You are experiencing the release and healing of the Earth plane. These Beings are not sentient in the way that you're believing they are. The civilization that you are imagining they exist in and the directions that you've been given...that they are the "cool kids" and whatever they said to you is an echo or a memory of what has existed. You are dealing with pure anger and fear and terror and all these emotional states that are not supposed to be. You've learned a bit about anger I imagine and this is where the dissonance occurs.

It's starting to sound like many of us are experiencing being possessed by these Beings.

The denizens of your planet who are committing crimes and who are doing terrible and heinous things...are they in fact Man Being? Are they in fact possessed? What's going on with all of this criminal behavior that you must endure day in and day out? Where does it come from? Where are these "hybrids" you're hearing about, these Orion DRA hybrids? Where are they? What are they? Now we can introduce "Who are they?" This is now an appropriate question. The Orion DRA...now these are Beings who are synergized with this profoundly awful energy and experience of the release of all the negativity and those terrible emotions. Those emotions should not be part of the lexicon of the Man Being state...but are temporarily as you shift your belief. These Beings have incorporated the release of the belief, the implosion of the belief. The Orion DRA hybrids are Beings that have reassembled in order to attempt an escape. They are using the discards of the unhealthy human psyche and nature and they are living off of these poisonous scraps.

How do we ultimately manoeuvre beyond them to arrive in the 7th density?

Many of you that are existing in the Earth plane are of a hybrid sort or type. You're asking me for a recipe…ten steps and you're on your way. This is not the case Dramos and Bohemias. The situation is a lot stranger and a lot more serious than it actually sounds. Many of you are experiencing a hybrid existence that you are shedding yourself from. You are changing. You are surgically removing yourselves from this alliance with this world that you cannot be a part of. The shedding of the skin is what you are asking about, the complete shedding and surgical removal of the beliefs. How does one go beyond the 6th density? How does one cross through this experience without reconnecting with this experience? You need not be part of this experience. The 5th density, did you know, is a shedding of all those things that ail you – the addictions, the addictive thinking and the addictive behavior.

Are you saying that the 5th density is a training camp?

That makes it sound trite, but in a way yes. All of these beliefs and activities are released in fact in the 5th density. I hope this is explaining a bit more for you both and in fact explaining why you're encountering a few Beings here and there. You're shedding your skin. You are definitely leaving all of that poison at the door if you attempt to cross.

How exactly are we "shedding our skin" in the 5th density World?

You practice travel, you practice inventing and you also practice letting go of all the behaviors and the crutches that have ultimately been imprisoning you on Earth. "Well why don't you leave them behind on Earth", you might be asking? Well I would say that you can't, it's just too much. You can release enough to get you to the next step or stage but this is a place where you can

release all of your baggage. You leave your toxic
baggage…some of you may want to describe it that
way. Some of us are able in the Earth plane to let go of
all of these beliefs. I certainly was and I do not wish to
be seen as a braggart or a snob or better than all of you.
I perhaps came across this way to some of you, but in
fact I had already let go of many of the beliefs that some
of you are still clinging to.

Orson, what are these toxic beliefs? Not all readers are the same.
What some deem toxic others might consider "normal" or even
"healthy".

What are some of the beliefs that you may continue to
release, you ask. Well they're not all toxic and
frightening and scary and holding you back. Some of
the beliefs are still your linear way of expressing things
and your linear way of solving problems. There are a
few things along the way that you'll have to continue to
rework or reimagine or reinvent, but your question
about how you cross through this obstruction…well this
is continuing to inspire others to artistically disseminate
in the Earth plane. I am not speaking of Artists on
Earth. I am referring to those who are completely
immersed and existing in the 5th density World. You've
spoken with a number of Beings that are existing in the
5th density but they are certainly helping Beings in the
Earth plane.

Well, now that we've "found you" and found the Inner
Earth…we'd like to know more about the 7th density. We have a
firm enough grasp of the 5th density already.

Yes…the question of the Inner Earth experience and
"where in fact is that" and "how do you get to that
experience and the World of Water" and "what
becomes of you"? These are questions that I'm happy
to answer but you must have the tools with you and the

beliefs in place in order for the conversation and our tour to continue. I'm happy to do that with you both but you certainly need to make a few more commitments and changes and I'm here to continue the tour. Josephine has kindly arranged our conversation and I'm very grateful. I will continue with you if you would like a tour of the Inner World experience or the 7th Heaven or 7th Level but first how about we get rid of some of those beliefs that are holding you back. I wholeheartedly recommend a good talk perhaps with Lyra and learn a little bit more about the Draconian and the Orion DRA dilemma and give me a call and we'll walk through the Inner World together.

Let's go back then, to something you said about the 5th density. The 5th density is a place to shed our addictive behaviors or beliefs that we've carried over. When someone is intoxicated we say that they are "under the influence". Does that mean that addicts are easily manipulated by the DRA?

Well that's quite obvious, isn't it? The "addict" is an interesting example of a person who changes their beliefs too many times. Their windows of interaction with the DRA are profound in number.

Aren't we all implicated by that definition? A lot of us are seeking knowledge and comfort and by consequence are almost never fully confident in our beliefs.

Now, an Artist with addictive behaviors, who is open to not only reinventing their craft but open to learning and accepting as many new beliefs as they can possibly integrate and absorb is a dangerous proposition. When you release a belief and that void of experience is created well you certainly can be interacting with the DRA energy and experience. This is I suppose the dilemma of someone pushing themselves a bit too hard and a bit too quickly.

Is that why Lyra Beings have continuously emphasized that we "pace" ourselves and pace the dissemination of information?

> I would agree with that, yes. Some of you are pushing yourselves too quickly and leaving yourselves too open. When you say that you leave yourself too open that means that you have changed too many beliefs too quickly, simultaneously all at once. You have an extreme void and the replacement in that space can be an interaction with the Draconian energy. The DRA, the hybridization can occur in this instance and we have to ask ourselves what has happened to some of your "treasured Artists". Was their tragic demise brought on because we pushed them into an artistic place and space where they can no longer function?

We've had many tragic stories of Artists who died too young or died needlessly at the hands of addiction.

> There's many of you that believe that these Artists are "used and abused" and that's what happens when you push and you push someone. I would ask you to maybe look at this a little bit differently. This type of Artist not only leaves him or herself open, they fully engage with the DRA energy. They are engaging instead of reinventing and releasing that energy. You can release that energy as you did Bohemias. You've wrestled with the Being and that is the physical representation of the experience. You rejected the allegiance with this energy.

I fought back and told it to f**k off.

> Well yes, but you didn't have to say anything really. The rejection of this DRA energy is equivalent to a physical attack, as you experienced. That's the physical representation on Earth. Experiencing an attack *is* the rejection.

Fascinating. We want the readers to know that while it was a little startling, there was no physical pain or anything like that. It's like a nightmare.

> You know all these horror movies, where do you think these ideas come from? These are ideas generated in the 5th density. They are not only generated, they're actually released. These are Beings who are releasing, purging themselves of these encounters and experiences. Of course, the 5th density is a source for the arts and creativity and all of that exists there and is available for whoever wants to tune in and whoever wants to call. It's there. Come and get it if you want it. I'm not interested but many of you are and I understand that horror and that whole genre is supremely popular. I understand there is a fascination with the dark side and the dark stuff and this is all about effectively rehabilitating. Now Bohemias, I know that you were maybe hoping that I would say that you "pick up a sword" or you "have a battle"…well it is a battle but you're battling your own inner demons. This is as good a description as any.

Orson, anyone who knows even a little bit about your lifetime would describe you as a "larger than life figure", someone who ran the gamut of experiences. All one has to do is listen to one of your old interviews and you'd feel as though you've lived a lifetime through your story. What was your mission in this last incarnation as Orson Welles? Why did you feel so much and know so much, almost immediately?

> There's many of us out there. I'm not the only one, but thank you. Thank you for that. There are many of us in the 7th, in the Federation. There are many of us who are connected deeply with many levels of experience and I can describe my incarnation experience on Earth for you in a way that perhaps will explain to everybody what I was doing. "Why did I say that", "why did I

write that", "why did I film that," "why was I there". Why was I there? Well, I can say that when you are connected with the many levels of experience, now again I don't want to sound like I am boasting...I want to sound thorough in my explanation...there are many of us who are traveling to the surface of the Earth. Traveling, not being birthed or born. When I say incarnation I'm not suggesting reincarnation. I am suggesting a role, an undertaking, an experience, an attempt to communicate and disseminate creatively. This is a nice way to share information. It's an easy way to share information. It's not threatening or not as threatening as perhaps a controversial book. When you're connected and you remember the Inner Earth experience, when you speak and you communicate don't you agree that it does come across like multi-level signal? The voice, the ideas, the color, the intention, the vision is multi-faceted. The layering, it's a layering and the context and the subtext, there's many many layers and the character is not the regular character that you're encountering with many of the Beings in the 3rd density who have not made their reconnections. This is shared with many different levels of experience and so the signal or the sound that you make is very much like a chord, like a musical chord.

Are you saying that when someone feels like "an old soul" that they're feeling their connection with all these layers of their existence?

I know that you have heard this again and again but this is the fact. When I am communicating with you the energy is split into seven channels, seven directions, seven sounds and seven notes. There is a depth. The experience is reaching out to all of you in many levels that you all innately connect with or wish to connect with or have connected with. You've forgotten and so the understanding that my time in the Earth plane was profound and profoundly affecting others…well yes this is the case when a Being from the Inner Civilization reconnects with you.

The magnetism stems from existing in the Inner Earth experience.

Yes. You are remembering where you are going and that is a profound experience, remembering that. "Ah yes I go there too". This remembering, although unconscious, is what you're speaking of. The profound sense or the changes that you are experiencing from the artistic work is in fact just the reconnections that you're making that you don't even understand yet because you've left the beliefs in the Inner Civilization and experience of the 7th density. Now, doesn't this all sound very science fiction like? You'll be there and we'll see together what this World is like and how it works, how the many worlds work as it's not just one experience. You can have whatever world you want. If you want to visit and you want orange seas and purple palm tress…well let's do it.

To clarify, you're saying that you incarnated voluntarily. You did experience a human birth but you weren't trapped in the reincarnation cycle. You voluntarily experienced a lifetime with a specific purpose and you were coming from the experience of Terra or Inner Earth.

You've already written about Mithras, I like that chapter very much and crawling out from the rock. I have crawled out from the rock. You already have another chapter about this experience and it's Volume 2 isn't it? It's the Tesla chapter. Well I hope you have a little bit more to go on now. This must have been a little mysterious or frustrating for you both. You almost left that chapter out, didn't you?

Almost. We just needed more understanding.

You see what I mean…you see what I mean.

We're still a little confused about Inner Earth, because you're throwing around so many different terms. You speak of the 7th Heaven or the 7th World and then you also speak of the World of Water or Terra. Is it all Inner Earth?

> I'll let you in on a little secret. It's all one and the same, but don't look up to the Heavens and those beautiful stars twinkling in the sky that you've all created and placed there. You need to start looking down at your feet. The thing that you're standing on, the experience that you're walking on, that's where the journey begins. We are existing in this space and place and you've talked to Jules and oh believe me there's much more coincidence and synchronicity in your interviews and what you've gathered in your treasure hunt than you realize. But you'll be quite pleased. You'll be quite pleased when you discover that my goodness it all works…it all works.

It feels like this conversation is winding down and it would be silly not to ask you about your film "Citizen Kane", about that famous last utterance by Charles Foster Kane: "Rosebud". I hope you don't mind if we ask you to speak about that. Were you in fact handing us the Key or Code?

> Mind? I'd love to speak about it. Nobody asks me about it. It does sound like you've had quite a good explanation already. Who gave it to you…Gregory?

We asked Gregory about it and he all but confirmed that "Rosebud" was more than just about a childhood sled.

He's good that way, isn't he? I like his explanation better than what I would explain. I think you have everything there, don't you?

We know that you don't like speaking about your work and that you don't want to sound boastful, but it would be nice to hear it from Orson Welles himself.

Yes okay...what's your question? Is there a specific question?

What did you hope that audiences would absorb from the character's utterance of the word "Rosebud"?

I was hoping and I still hope that you accept and believe without trying to analyze. Just absorb. Didn't it feel like a surgery when you realized, before even asking Gregory...didn't it feel like you had already done the surgery, like you had already fixed the problem before you asked?

It absolutely did.

Exactly. That's what I want to believe is happening, that it's just a sudden reconnection, a sudden realization. It doesn't have to be put into words. It's a little bit sad that we even have to explain it, isn't it?

Art explained is no longer art. In this case some readers will need the information. Some readers just won't watch that film.

But isn't it interesting that the light bulb went off and you remembered and you made the reconnection? You remembered to reconnect. You knew and you know. You just did it. You didn't wait. You didn't say well golly I hope that Orson is going to speak for Volume 3 so we can get to the bottom of this. Before you even asked Gregory and even if it was in an instant, you already knew. You knew. You asked what you know. You already knew, you knew what to ask. You're asking what you know, you know what to ask.

You have a way of breaking things down. It's very helpful, Orson.

What the both of you are doing is helpful in ways that neither of you fully comprehends yet. We're in this together.

This Volume will likely be read by a lot of people in the arts, in show business, in Hollywood. Influential Artists can really crack this nut open by sharing the book publically. What advice can you offer these individuals who might be reading this right now?

You're asking me how to pry the book out of their hands?

Well I suppose you are a figure that they might look up to. You're one of the Godfathers of Hollywood, despite the contempt you may have held for it. Your advice might inspire others.

What would I say? If they don't want to share the information…you've previously used the word "hoard"…if they don't want to share the information then they clearly don't want to fix the problem. If you want to fix your problems then you want to share. Now do you want to associate with other people who don't want to fix the problems or they're not ready to fix the problems? I believe it would be far easier for you to work with Beings early on that are comfortable fixing the problem. You know those stragglers…the ones that are hoarding or clinging to the information and they don't want to share because they feel that they'll lose touch or someone will take it away from them. Now these are Beings who'll come around, oh they all come around. Don't they all come around? They'll come around when it's fashionable, right? When it's in fashion they'll come around. Now those that are waiting for it to be in fashion, I hardly recommend that you wait around for those people. Why wait until it's a fashion? Oh there's plenty who want to share this…I will let you in on another little secret. I know we've had so many in this talk but oh there are plenty sharing this information. You must believe that if you're looking for some big shot celebrity to get off their high horse and you know shout out to the world "this book is amazing"…it may not actually happen that way.

As long as people are sharing it…that's what's important. We all deserve to know the truth.

There are quiet people who are quietly sharing it with others. The books are soon to be passed around in great numbers. There's a sharing that I cannot even put into words because it will be global and there's no way to describe it even beyond that. The word is out. It's out there. It's getting out there. Don't look for a famous person as a benchmark for your success, oh no, this is a big mistake. The benchmark for your success is whom you're speaking to in these interviews. You're now engaging with a group of Beings that are in the Earth and there's a lot more that you're going to be learning about now. Dramos and Bohemias, if you have Beings who are not interested in these amazing stories well they probably will be the last ones on the train, do you understand what I'm saying? If you have to drag somebody kicking and screaming and sit them down and demand that they read your books well good luck Sir.

We're definitely not doing any of that. We're quietly releasing the information and encouraging others to share.

Good. They'll all come around but don't wait around for them to come around. They'll be running after you both soon enough. I'm not suggesting that it must be this way but the word is getting out on a global scale...well it's bigger than global but I'll use "global" as it's something that you can absorb. You don't have to worry. You just have to concern yourself with making the books available.

Orson, we must say that this conversation has come across a lot like your 1938 radio broadcast. Engrossing. We want to thank you for this conversation.

Oh I'll be back.

We want that tour of Inner Earth.

Love to have you both.

Are there dinosaurs on Inner Earth?

All the things that you dream about are there. This is a magical place and you're all on your way...finally.

AMY

"I followed the sound. I heard the call. I followed it and it led me to an opening in a hill like an opening on a mound, an opening…and I have to say this even though you'll think that I'm a nutter…I have to say this…this was something out of 'Lord of the Rings'…it was crazy."

Singer, Songwriter
Grammy Award Winner
1983 - 2011

Amy requested that we also describe her as:
Jazz Singer, Songstress

Amy appeared in Dramos' dream last night, holding a book and speaking very seriously about our project. We attempt to connect and after some time Dramos begins to hear her voice getting louder and louder, like she's walking toward us.

> Right…so you made a good decision. You're including me in your book!

Yes we'd love to Amy. Hi…welcome to Volume 3.

> Now what are you two up to?

Well we've found Inner Earth. We're embarking on a tour with Orson Welles but we're wrapping up our Volume 3 discussion.

> We're all in Inner Earth. This isn't something that is Earth-shattering. We're all in Inner Earth…why don't you just write about Inner Earth? We're all here.

It's not Earth-shattering to you Amy, but to the vast majority of people stuck on this planet it's outrageous.

> If you had explained Inner Earth to me while I was in my former incarnation as Amy I would've thought it was a bunch of bullocks too, but it's the real deal. This is where you're all going if you know where to go.

What did you know as Amy, what reconnections did you make and how did you make them?

> This'll be hard for you to believe. I didn't really understand much about Inner Earth. I didn't do much reading about it. I didn't speak to many people about theories like this…I mean this is very strange stuff that we're speaking about. What happened to me was maybe a little bit of a different situation. There are many of you who are on a creative path and you're doing your art and making your music and doing your

thing but not many of you know where you're going. You can be connecting and you can be connecting with that creative spirit but not many of you know where that is or where that's from. I suppose it's easy to say it's "God" or some "higher power". I didn't actually believe in another world beyond "Heaven" and so when I discovered that we're all here it was something...well I don't even have words for it. It was something that I had never imagined we'd be experiencing together. We're all here. Everybody's here. I mean if you've made your way you're here. I'm not saying I'm in the privileged few but I am here and when I crossed over...well I suppose you want to hear a bit about that story.

Yes of course. Can you walk us through that experience?

Yeah, yeah...sure...of course. When I crossed over, when I died, when they found me, when they couldn't revive me, when they couldn't make me...I guess "alive" again...well I wasn't lost and I didn't have to go very far. I walked through a corridor and there was a door. There was a door. I guess like your tunnel, the way you all speak about the tunnel and the "tunnel of light". But I walked through a door. I mean I literally opened up a door and that door took me instantly to that World that you all know so well and love. Those colors and the inspiration...I instantly realized that this was the place where I was obtaining and getting all my creative insight and creative input from. So entering this space, well, it allowed me to...it allowed me to hear something very special and I heard and I was aware of a sound and a frequency. It was a vibration that I had never heard when I was on Earth. So I followed this sound. I followed the sound. I heard the call. I followed it and it led me to an opening in a hill like an opening on a mound, an opening...and I have to say this even though you'll think that I'm a nutter...I have to say this…this was something out of "Lord of the Rings"…it was crazy.

A sound led you to an opening in a hillside that you're calling a mound.

Yeah. The mound, it led me to an opening, a cave, a grotto almost…and I entered it. I walked in and that was the beginning of my journey. I didn't remain in any sort of limbo or remain in any sort of holding place or pattern or wait for Angels to escort me. There was none of this. I simply walked into a New World, a new life and we're all here. We're all here man…we're all here. This is living. This is where you should be. You may wonder why you're speaking with so many Beings and you're speaking with them as if they're still alive on Earth. You're speaking with them because they're continuing their work in this World. If you have work that you're doing that is important enough to you that you wish to continue it and if it's from here…if the source of your imagination and the source of your inspiration, if the source is from here…I mean it starts in that World of Imagination, that World of Play. It starts there. It begins there but it really exists in the Inner Earth.

There are so many names for these worlds it's sometimes dizzying trying to absorb it all.

Definitely. I'm going to call it Inner Earth with you in this chat that we're having because, well, not only am I still learning about everything that's here, I don't want to spoil anything for you, you know. You have to experience it for yourselves. You need to experience it for yourselves. I'm not saying that I won't answer questions but if I share my own personal experience and what it is like for me, it may not be like that for you…and I don't want to impose an experience on you.

I want you both to get what you need to get from it. It's something that's deeply personal for each and every one of us. Our encounter with this world...reconnecting and finding our way back is a unique experience and I don't want to tell you what your experience must be like or should be like. I don't want you to measure it against my own experience. I've made my way here and I'm very happy that I'm here but your entry into this World...that's going to be your own. Your discovery of this World is remarkably different from mine. It's not something that we can compare with each other.

Fair enough, we appreciate that. We'd like to shift the conversation over to something we've already talked about in Volume 1 – The 27 Club. What can you tell us about this mission, given your experience on Earth?

Yeah...well there's a Group of Beings who repeatedly re-enter and immerse themselves in the Earth plane. Their job and their mission is to share information through the arts. Music is particularly a familiar and common way for us to reach out to many of you and of course you've noticed that there are exceptional and talented Musicians that have been part of this mission and group. Music is a wonderful way to reach out to you all but it's not just the emotional content of the song and the lyrics and the experience of listening to the music on records.

What more is there than the music?

There's something more that's built into this mission. A lot of the music that had been "disseminated"...man you guys love that word...but yeah the music created by Beings in our project...a lot of this music is containing a similar frequency or energy. Now you might call it a certain note and you might say it's composed in a certain way but I'm saying that you're listening and hearing and receiving this music in a very unique way. This is what I've learned being here…that the composition is not nearly as invented or improvised as it seems. There is a repertoire and a unique set of…well it's almost like there's notes and it's almost like there are bars of music that are available for us to assemble and to write music. These tools, you can call them that I guess, are available specifically for our group. I know this is sounding crazy.

At this point "crazy" means nothing. So you're saying the 27 Club Beings are working with "magical frequencies".

Oh f**k…yeah that'll come off well. Oh I'm sorry I said a naughty word. Bleep that will you.

It's fine Amy.

That'll be the only slip I promise. Anyhow…you can say magical frequencies but it's an assembly of sound. It's a musical writing style and also a way to create music that really…you know…grabs attention. It really makes a difference. You'll notice that many of the Beings in our Group that you know about were very famous and sold a lot of music and also did a lot of art that was really popular. There's a reason for that. It's not just about some of us having a brilliant insight and creative ability…I mean we do. But we're actually given tools. We have an advantage in a way. We're connected with something that many of you are not connected with, but you can be and you will be.

Is Inner Earth where we're all heading?

You'll all make your way here. A lot of us are living here. A lot of us have always lived here. A lot of you are looking to the stars and you're looking out at the sky and seeing all of the pretty constellations and the planets and you're all wondering what's out there, man. You're all wondering…"Are there other universes out there for all of us to explore" and "Do we come from another planet" and "Why are some of us experiencing Aliens" and in contact with all these unusual things that are happening on the Earth. But you're all looking out at the sky when what you're actually looking for is in the ground.

It's just such a departure from everything we've ever believed. "Heaven is up there…and Hell is down there".

Yeah it's messed up cause you guys messed it all up, not because it's wrong. You have to start looking in the Earth rather than looking up at the beautiful sky. There's a beautiful sky here as well. There's a lot of what you're experiencing on Earth, here. It's just…it's the real experience. It's the real deal. It's not something that you've created. You're living in an artificial world but I don't need to tell you that. You already know these things.

When you were on Earth, did you have any paranormal experiences or visions or dreams that helped you to reconnect with this hidden knowledge?

When I wrote songs…when I did the lyrics and I wrote out the words…I always felt like somebody else was writing it down. I always felt like this was somebody else's hand, like I was watching myself write or watching another person write it out. It was mostly with the lyrics that I felt that it wasn't me…that it wasn't me doing it…that if it was me then I was somewhere else in that moment and somebody other than me was actually writing it out. Somebody else was holding the pen, holding the notebook. That's something that I experienced a lot and I started to experience that very young. I was experiencing that in school and I was experiencing drawing things. It was especially when I was holding a pen in hand and I felt that maybe I am going somewhere. You know many times when I wrote things down I didn't remember doing it. I didn't remember how words got on the page. You definitely hear that quite a bit, you hear that from other Artists…that they were "in the zone" or they were in an "altered state" and you know…not from doing drugs or alcohol but just in an altered creative state. So…I guess that's what I'm trying to say. Singing and experiencing the music, well yeah, anybody doing that is going to feel connected with another place. That's something that everybody experiences when they sing and when they play music…you don't have to be a professional Musician to experience that.

Is there a particular song of yours, lyrically, that was intended as a dissemination? Or was your music more about the frequency and vibration?

Well all of it. I was in an altered state when I wrote the lyrics down for all of that. Making the music well yeah…we were all really connected with the experience and it all came out so quickly. But if you want me to pick one song that I really feel says something more than just a story that I'm sharing…well…I would say maybe my song about being alone. You know there is something there that I was thinking about when I wrote that. Not just…not just the idea that well it sucks breaking up with somebody and it sucks not having somebody and being on your own. It's more than that. I mean it's…I was sometimes thinking that in a bigger way you know, we're not only alone like from breaking up or ending a friendship or losing a loved one. We've lost more than that and yeah we are alone…we're really missing our *real family*. We're all here. I hope that this doesn't come across as crazy because I'd like to help you guys with your book but I know some people

412

reading this might say, "Well you had it really easy. Doesn't sound like you had to do much when you checked out"...and that's true I just...for whatever reason just instantly made my way. But if you talk to anyone else in our Group they'll tell you the same story. There wasn't a big effort to get back. We just came back. Now that's a bit anti-climactic for your book. You want something pretty exciting and um...I suppose everybody wants to hear how difficult it was and all the magical and crazy shit you have to do to return but some of us just simply walked through the door and found an entrance and took it. It doesn't always have to be that difficult, does it?

When you say "our Group" are you talking about The 27 Club? Is this a set Group of Beings or can anyone join the Club?

Yeah, why not? If you want to join us and if you want to be a part of this "Club", if you want to be a part of this mission...you can. When you make your way back here then you can learn more about what we're all doing and I know now you want to ask me "Amy are you coming back, are you reincarnating again"? Well...I love to sing and I still sing here. I'm doing what I love to do here that doesn't stop. So do I want to reincarnate? Hell no! F**k no. I don't really want to come back and I know that's not what everybody wants to hear but no...I quite fancy it here. Everything's great. It's everything that you have on Earth but without the bullshit and it's great. We're not fighting with each other and it's good...it's all good here.

Amy we're talking to Beings about The Rose and we noticed that you wore Roses in your hair during a concert in England. Were you consciously aware of what The Rose is?

I knew it was special and I knew that there was an importance and I knew that the flower meant more

413

than just a pretty flower that's mentioned over and over again. You know...I knew it was more than just an important symbol of love and all that. I knew that if I wore flowers and that if I wore Rose flowers and if I surrounded myself with that symbol that it might help me...maybe remember something that we've all lost. But it was more intuitive, you know. The Rose didn't really help me find my way...it's more like a badge of honor. We respect where we all actually come from. Some of us not only believe in an Inner Earth experience, we remember it. We remember how to get back there and we remember stories and truths about our real existence and civilization...and it's an honor to wear The Rose or to surround yourself with Roses. I just knew about The Rose unconsciously or intuitively, you know.

I think in a way we all feel that The Rose is a "special flower"...we just don't typically grant it mystical importance.

Let me say this to everybody, to everyone who's listening. The Rose will get you veeery far if you believe that it's a symbol that'll allow you to be creative. You guys...get comfortable being creative and not scared to create. The Rose allows you in a way...an invisibility from your fears to be creative. So many of you are afraid to be creative. You think that that's "stupid" or you're "not good enough" or it's "not going to pay the bills" or that nobody likes what you're doing. The Rose gets you on the channel we're on now yeah...you guys this channel is where you can connect with a lot of us...and this channel allows you to let go of your fears and I like to say...make them invisible. If you make yourself invisible from everybody else's criticism or critiquing then you'll just go ahead and do what you really want to be doing and most of you really want to be creating.

It's just not that easy for everyone, Amy. Some of us are in a bad place or don't have the privilege or physical ability to be creative.

> I know many of you are not in a situation where it's even possible. You're not well or there are bad...really bad things happening on the planet and the last thing you're thinking about is painting a picture or singing a song, but what I am saying is that the ability to create doesn't necessarily mean you have to go ahead and do something that is artistic. Creating and being creative is also problem solving and it's communication. Creativity doesn't have to mean "artistic". An Artist is somebody who has dedicated themselves to existing creatively and they're not afraid to use their creative tools and they're not afraid to say that this is how they want to live their life. It's a lifestyle choice. Being creative is something that you all can master and even those of you who are in a terrible situation or not in a good way...there is creative thinking and creative experiences that you can all be tapping into. If we were all allowed to just be creative and creatively communicate and just creatively be...if we were all just left alone then none of these terrible experiences on Earth would be happening and there wouldn't be any need to drown your sorrows and use drugs or alcohol or any of these things that we get addicted to...shopping and eating and you name it.

We just spent some time speaking to Orson about addiction and the DRA.

> Yeah, I heard about it. But those bad Beings that you're dealing with...the Draconians and those hybrids that you're living with and dealing with every day...this situation doesn't go on where we exist. Those Beings are not here, man. They're not welcome here but they actually can't exist here because they don't have the ability to absorb light. There's light where we live, there's a shit load of light and you have to be able to

handle that, you know. It's a lot of light. If you can't handle this amount of light then you just burn up, you get destroyed. It's similar to trying to stay in the Earth plane…we can't stay too long because we need a lot of light and we don't have an ability to contain that light in a human form. It's just impossible.

That makes so much sense, especially now that we have more context. Amy, how did you hear about our book series? What book were you holding in Dramos' dream?

You're kidding right? Your book! You guys need some fresh air, man. Haha. Your. Book.

Yeah, our minds are full at the moment.

The word is starting to get out in Inner Earth. Again, I'm using "Inner Earth" with you guys because this is what you're using and I don't want to tell you the way it is. You're going to figure that out for yourselves. I don't want to judge you the way that everybody is judging each other on Earth. The book is now making its way to our World and there is talk about the book. You're making your way back home and back home we have reports about the work and the help and the things that people like you, Dramos and Bohemias are doing. We're not hearing about it like it's a TV program that's playing you know…we're not watching it on the telly and saying, "Oh look there's Dramos and Bohemias…there's their book isn't that fantastic". It doesn't go down like that over here.

How does it go down?

There are people…they're coming in because of your book. You know…crossing over. This is what I'm trying to say to you guys. There are people who have made it back here because of your book already. Did you know this?

Amazing. This is the first report.

You guys need to know this…the readers need to hear this. I was speaking with somebody very "recently" and I'm using words that have to do with time because that's how you understand things, but it doesn't quite translate over here. I met a Being who has "died" if you want to call it that. You guys know now that dying really means coming home…you know that right? Now it might be a "death" on your side but it's not on our side. They may not be there but they're here and this person is a…well was a woman and she was in her late 80s in the Earth plane. She picked up your book online and well she showed it to me. The "disconnect" information…it allowed her to I guess put it all together. These were ideas that she had anyways on her own but reading your book helped her, as she said, "Put it all together", sew it all together. It helped her prepare. She was prepared and when she opened the door and found herself in what you're calling the 7th density…or actually the 6th density, because you have to get rid of those [DRA] blokes and leave them behind and keep going in order to get to us. But she was prepared. That might not be written in your first two Volumes…I don't think you wrote those words down on the page but she absorbed something from your book. I suppose what I'm trying to say to you is that your books have written words on the page but there's also a hidden meaning in those words and it's not about you analyzing what they mean. They actually create another story. When you read the books you actually have another story in your head, in your consciousness that even you're not aware of. This is how she explained it to me.

We'd love to hear from this Being, please ask her to reach out to us.

Steady on, now.

Thank you for sharing that, Amy. That's the reason we're doing this…to get people back home.

> And by the way guys, everyone should know that you don't come to our World and leave all your creativity back on Earth as some "legacy", whatever that means. As if you have to go to a museum to experience it or just play a record…you know what I mean? You continue. If you believe in creativity and you believe in creating and you believe that that is a way that you want to live a life well then you're going to bring that with you to our World, you're going to bring that back. What you're not going to bring with you is all the cataclysmic shit and all the poison and toxic stuff that you deal with on Earth. It's a dark place, man. There's no light. It's all artificial. You're coming to the *real* light…you're going to the light, you're going to experience a World that you wish Earth would be. If you take everything that's wrong with Earth and you turn it on its head and flip it inside out, you're going to have the World where you're returning. You guys call it the "homeward journey". That's what it is. That's the truth. There's lot's of nice things that are happening on Earth and those experiences and those things are here too, but they're elevated…they're even better. So if there's something that you love, for example like a tree and you really love that tree and can't imagine anything more spectacular and fantastic than this tree well I'm telling you that that tree will be 100 times even more fab here. It will be even better, even more special and I'm not finding the words because we don't really speak like that here. There's a lot of things that are happening here and you just feel it. You don't speak about it.

Amy, are people going to discover the Man Being book series through Volume 3 mostly?

>Just like you have to dig to find Inner Earth and find home everyone has to dig to find you. They have to want to find you. This is what the problem is. They have to want to find your books because if they want to read your books then this must mean that they want the answers. They want the truth. They have to want the truth. Not everybody is ready to want the truth. So can you attract an interest in your books...how can you ask everybody to want the truth? I suppose if a few people know the truth that there is a World you're going to...you're not going into a spaceship and riding off in the sky, although you are seeing things that are happening in the sky. You are seeing spaceships flying around and some of those...yes...have to do with operations that are happening on your planet. But did you maybe ask yourselves that sometimes when you're experiencing something like seeing lights in the sky moving...did you ever think that maybe you're not in that brief moment actually on Earth playing? Maybe you've found yourself in another world, our World. Some of you are coming into our World just for a brief moment and don't even realize it. Like when you fall asleep suddenly and you drift off.

You kind of drifted from the original question there Amy...haha.

>Oh shit, right. The question about getting people to be ready to want the truth...if a few people start talking about it and the word gets out well that's the best way to gain attention to your work. It's going to be the word getting out...and how do you do that? Well you've already done it. You just have to keep doing it. Why are some of us coming back to Earth and disseminating and just going for it, just creating, just going for it and not worrying about editing and not worrying about all of

those things that we worry about. Is it good enough, is it right enough, is it relevant enough, is it loud enough, is it pink enough? You're maybe, if I can give you a bit of advice…worrying a bit too much about every little thing that you've got on the page. Why don't you just be creative and sing your song and say what you need to say? You don't need permission. Just do your thing guys. What are you waiting for?

Amy you were a big fan of Sinatra while on Earth. Do you have a soul connection with him?

We're all here and it's one big family so my connection with Musicians especially are because they're all family. We're all family. We're just recognizing our family. That's really all it is. You can say it's recognizing someone's "musical brilliance" and yeah that's a part of it but the musical brilliance if I'm going to speak about Musicians, as many of us are and choose to be, that musical brilliance is just the way it is here. Did you know that it's all like that here? It's the best concert you've ever been to in your life and the best sound you've ever heard and the best food you've ever eaten and the best sunset you've ever seen and it's the best everything here. This is the real deal. It's the way that life is supposed to be. You're coming home and this is what you're going to. If I read about that…well I'd want to go now and I'm not saying to everybody go ahead and do something crazy to get home now. I'm just saying to read the books, get the information. Start believing that there's more to this than just being on Earth and being worried about things and complaining about the weather and not getting along and hurting each other and well okay sometimes loving each other. There are a lot of nice things that happen too it's not all bad but it's not easy and the homeward journey…going home…it's all easy here and it's all free here.

And travel is free too.

> Haha yeah. You're learning about time travel too and I
> think that's brilliant that you're talking about that in
> your books. Time travel is a separate experience. Time
> travel is definitely going to come in handy for all of you.
> Time travel is something that you're just able to do but
> you actually have to learn how to time travel in order to
> get here and that's something that I didn't realize when
> I was on Earth, although we're all time traveling. If
> you're connecting with this message then you're able to
> time travel. You guys have all forgotten that you can
> time travel. Your reconnections...the reconnections
> help you remember these skills and these
> abilities...that's what this "reconnection" is about and
> building the ability to absorb more light to withstand
> more light, that's what the reconnections are about. But
> you need to be able to handle a lot of light if you're
> going to time travel. You also need to be able to handle
> light and experience light because you're not getting
> any light where you're living. There's no light there,
> man. It's all light here. It's all about light.

When you crossed over did you ask, "Who is God, what is God,
where is God?" Did it enter into your consciousness to discover
the truth about God?

> I bypassed the experience that a lot of you are having.
> Finding yourself in the New World and not having to
> wait and rebuild and wait for some external truth is a
> reflection of immersing yourself in creativity. Do I
> believe in a god now after my reconnection with home?
> I believe that there is a way to heighten your experience
> and ascension is a reconnective experience ultimately. It
> doesn't necessarily equal a single entity or source like a
> god, but you know I don't really want to get into a
> religious debate in your books. I think it might be wise
> to speak about another World. The arguments about

"God" and religion are actually not anything that you're even ready to debate about. There are so many other things that you might want to explore first but crossing over...I did not have any moment that I recall where I was wondering and waiting for someone to meet me. I simply walked through a door. It was instantaneous and there was no feeling of being confused or lost. I just simply opened the door and I imagine that for many of you it's that simple and for many of you it can be complicated too. It can be a situation where you're waiting for further instructions or another experience but you're trying to help people with that, aren't you? So that they're not confused and stuck in some strange place where they don't understand where to go.

How many Beings exist in Inner Earth?

This is a fully equipped world. As many Beings as you've got on Earth...well there is probably the same amount here.

Hold on, we have 7.8 billion. You don't have 7.8 billion there...isn't the number much less than that?

Oh yeah, much less. The difference is you've divided yourselves and so although you're believing that there's millions and millions of people living on your planet, as well as sharing the planet with other Beings...and you're going to learn more about that...but the fact is that we don't have the divisions where you're actually containing your light in separate physical forms. We exist here in a multi-dimensional Being. So I'm speaking with you but there are many of me. *Many* of me. You've learned a little bit about the hall of mirrors story and you're hearing a lot about the kaleidoscope and yeah that's true. The way to practice and be ready for this experience in this New World or the real World, home, is to see yourselves as a Being that exists not only in one "place and space" but multi-dimensionally. By the way you're not using the word "dimension" a lot and there's a reason for that.

What's the reason?

Dimension has got to do with you existing in this way...in a multi-faceted Being. You could regard yourself in that way like a kaleidoscope, if you break yourself into many different components and into many different places and spaces. You'll get it, you'll figure this out soon enough. So do you cross over with just one part of yourself? Is this just one part of you finally coming home and completing the full experience? Many of your selves together in one multi-dimensional Being...is that what's happening? These are things that you're going to be learning about. Many of you are sending parts of yourself home and you're waiting to put yourself back together. That's something that you're already realizing but maybe I've explained it to you just a little bit differently.

Does each part of Dramos, for example, have to go back and rebuild? That takes forever...it's so hard.

Well if that was the case then nobody would go back! F**k no! I'm saying that Lyra is a way for you to hook up with the other parts of your *selves*, it's all happening there. For many of you you're already put back together so that's why your journey into the Afterlife is not really sounding that exciting because you're already there. You know where to go. There's many levels of training and rebuilding and reconnecting and I am sorry that for some of you it's more complicated but your books are helping others rebuild themselves so that they don't have to be in a place where they're waiting for their group. You're calling it a Soul Ascension

Group and it is. It's a group. It's a group of you. It's a group, it's your soul, it's who you are.

Amy, just to go back to the song you mentioned...the one about "being alone" – did you mean "Waking Up Alone"?

That's one of the titles. That's the title that we used but originally had it as just "Alone".

A Being from your Group, Jim Morrison, has appeared in our dreams recently. Is he also looking to get involved with the books?

It's harder to get folks speaking to you from Inner Earth because...yeah they don't really want to go back to Earth. So if you're having dreams then you're probably communicating with them and it probably means that you're going to be seeing them and speaking to them. Why not? We're all here. It's not that hard to meet "cool" people. We're all here, there's a lot of us here. Well, everybody's here and I'll let you in on one little secret before I run off.

That you and Jim Morrison are the same Being?

Haha nope! I want to tell you all that...well...you're special...and you're all very creative and you're all *rock stars* I guess is the way that I would say it. But there's more to it than me just making some funny comment about your talents and abilities. There's a story here. Dramos and Bohemias...there is a life that is waiting for all of you and you're not all living a life that is a true reflection of who you are. If you're just a part of your real full self then the part that you're experiencing on Earth may not actually be the role that you play in the Inner Earth or homeward journey experience. Most of us if not all of us are very creative. This is a different World and well it's like a World of Artists and it's like a big Artist's colony here, if I can describe it to you in those words. Your abilities and talents on Earth, some of these talents are coming out in a way as a reflection of what's going on here. Like you're trying to solve a mystery on Earth and so you create in a peculiar way.

You lost all the Scientists as soon as you said it's like an Artist's colony.

Science is also very creative just so you guys both realize that. You don't always have to pick up a paintbrush just to be a creative person, there's many ways to create. You're all at your best creatively when you're at home and when you're at home you're here with us. If you're looking for openings in the Earth and you're looking for access points and gateways and portals and you're wondering, "Are there actual entry points on Earth…is there actually a cave I can walk into and never be seen again…is this for real?" There are actually places where this is going on. I'm not going to inform you of a location because I don't want to create a huge mess and you don't even completely understand where you are going.

Hold on, you're saying there's a way to access Inner Earth without disconnecting or dying?

Oh you're going to learn a lot more about our World and how to get back here and maybe in the last book…maybe then you'll leave a map or something like that. Maybe you'll leave a map where people can find us, but only those that are ready to come back. It's of no use to leave a map and nobody cares…or they start drilling holes in the Earth frantically trying to figure out a way to get here. There's a lot of daft behavior that goes on in the Earth plane. When you give information and people don't know what to do with it they lose their f**king minds. Better to do what you're doing right now…you're unveiling an understanding for your readers and allowing them to follow a map already…without them getting crazy and getting ahead of themselves. That's important.

We just want to say thank you Amy for participating. It's been enlightening.

You guys are awesome. You all are! Come join the concert my loves!

Bye Amy.

MARLON
BRANDO

"Stop talking and you won't need time. Stop communicating in spoken language and you won't need time. Time is a measurement that you're using because things got all screwed up. If you just stop talking you won't need time. Why don't you meditate on that?"

Actor, Director, Activist
Academy Award Winner
1924 - 2004

Marlon Brando appeared twice to Bohemias, in his dream state. In the first dream Marlon gave a talk in which he said, "We are living in a perpetual state of grief and loss and these emotions are weighing us down and preventing us from releasing our light". In the second dream, last night, Marlon pointed to Zodiac images appearing in the night sky. He singled out the Gemini symbol. We've requested that Marlon finally join us for a conversation.

Well here we are.

It's great to finally connect with you Marlon. We'd like to ask you to elaborate on the messages that you've been relaying through dreams.

You guys want me to explain things that you already understand. Don't believe that you don't understand this. You can obviously make sense of these explanations. The grief and the problem with all of you trapped on the planet and all of the things that you do...of course are making things worse. I don't wanna say that it's just all misery because it's what you make of the situation. I don't believe I'm helping you if I say that you can't change things. You can change things if you want to...if you really want to get out of there you can change things. The grief and the reason why most of you can't figure out a way to get beyond the grief...well besides all the pain on your planet and besides all the crazy things that are going on over there...there's a bigger question about how you process your emotions, about how you establish an emotional baseline. I'm not gonna comment on Beings who are unstable and you know...like those that are doing terrible things. I'm just speaking about the average person not being equipped with an emotional register.

Are you saying that most of us aren't equipped with an emotional register?

Most of you believe that you have an emotional repertoire that allows you to feel and engage in many different things but I don't see it that way. I see a situation where the average person on the Earth...or on the "Earth plane" you're calling it that...the average person has a basic repertoire of emotions. You've got "happy", "sad", "really sad", and "really happy"...you speak a lot about the different nuances and the subtext in your communication but I don't believe that. I believe that you're just going to the things that you know how to do...it's like you've been trained how to feel. You've all been trained how to feel. You can't decide how to feel and so the grief and the pain...well the realization that you can't really and truly connect and make that deep connection where you're empathizing with others...this is what I'm going on about. Maybe I'm not making my point clear but the limitations of your emotional experience is what I'm talking about. It's the limitations...you pick and choose how you're gonna feel and you don't broaden your emotional language. The language, your emotional language, your emotional communication, the emotional intelligence...this is what I'm going on about here.

What exactly is achieved once we expand our range of emotional intelligence?

When you fix the emotional repertoire, when you acquire new beliefs and those beliefs allow you a broader range of emotions and feelings...then things are going to be a lot better, aren't they? But for now some of you are trying to "understand other people" and trying to "understand where they're coming from", but understanding is not *feeling*. You get what I'm saying? It's not feeling. Everyone's trying to understand and it's really all about feeling. Your books are attempting to teach "how to feel" as you wanna feel something different, you wanna feel something special. When you feel something special then you believe that this is something that is meaningful.

"Feeling something special" usually compels us into action. You're saying that this is ultimately how we form beliefs.

Unless you truly feel and feel the difference from your baseline, your everyday repertoire of feelings…then you're not gonna form the beliefs. What beliefs? The beliefs that you can be whoever you wanna be and go wherever you wanna go and ultimately break the bonds that are keeping you in your form, your physical reality. You've gotta break those things that are binding you together in the form. You can break that apart…some of you say "defragmenting" and there's a lot of ways to describe it.

It sounds easy listening to you say it or reading it on the page, but it's something else to try to execute it.

The best way to dissolve the obstacles that you're feeling you have to deal with every day is, of course, to get rid of the belief in an obstacle. To get rid of the belief in an obstacle…well…you have to feel like you can do that. You see…what I'm going on about here is that feeling that you can do something. That's also another level of emotional reality that most of you are not connecting with. You're not doing yourself a service. You have to believe that you can do something otherwise what are we even talking for? You are a *feeling* Being. You are meant to feel many different things but we're taught what we're "allowed" to feel. That is what's insane about Earth. We're even taught select emotions and we give them names. We don't believe that there's more to the basic emotional group. Acting gives you that training and the belief that you can experience so many different situations, characters and emotions. This is something that will help you all. You need to stretch yourselves. You need to feel the emotions. You don't necessarily find this stuff in a dictionary...but let's move on for now. Let's talk about the "Zodiacs"...that was fun what I showed you, wasn't it?

It was extraordinary. The images in the sky were so vibrant and lifelike, not flat images at all – almost like we were in a 3D film and the visuals were popping out. There did seem to be an emphasis on the Gemini zodiac. What exactly were you showing us?

Well, astrology. You're learning a little bit about that. I'm not an astrologer by trade, of course. Gemini...you know there's been many attempts to leave. I think you're both aware of that. There's been many attempts to leave and escape Earth and "make your way". Gemini is one of the original Zodiac signs. It's also a mission. It's quite a popular name isn't it..."Gemini". You're hearing about Gemini. Science fiction and Gemini seem to go hand in hand. There's a reason for that. There has been a mission you'll be learning about that again was obstructed, but not a complete failure. If you want to put together your book like it's under the "sign of Gemini", that wouldn't be a bad thing. You're gonna be hearing from somebody in a Group that I know very well. There's a mission to bring all of you back...you've learned a little bit about this. You've spoken to some of them earlier on in your project but what I want for both of you to understand about the Gemini is that this is not an initial contact. You've made the contact before. A lot of these names are codes and this is the difficulty that you're gonna have when you're trying to put your books together. You'll be trying to figure out, "Was this really said...is this what they really meant... what does this mean" and that's where the feeling comes back into it.

We have to feel our way through these questions, is what you're saying.

> Yes. If you're *feeling* like this must be something and you're *feeling* like this must be telling you something well that feeling is letting you know that – yes – this is something that requires your attention. I suppose I'm speaking about "gut instinct" and "gut feeling" and yes we can speak a little bit about that because of course that's the way a lot of you make decisions. It wouldn't be a bad thing to continue doing that in the preparation of your books. I understand that Volume 4 is about the DRA and how I got around that situation and that story is...well it can be important. If you're going to find yourself in that World then you need to know, of course, what to do. You've spoken to a few Beings already that made their way and got out of a bad situation but you know...these Beings don't want you to go anywhere because without you they're a bunch of goners. Without you they can't exist. When the energy changes and it is changing now, but as the energy changes they have no choice but to change with it. They don't know how to do this...so you're going to be making a book for them. Did somebody already tell you that?

Jules Verne said we'd be having a dialogue with the DRA. No one told us we'd be writing a book.

> Oh yeah, well you're doing that book that nobody wants to do because well nobody wants to hear that you're helping these guys. I'm using "guys" with you just to be funny, I guess. It's awful that I have to explain that. But anyway...nobody wants to read a book on...you know..."saving the bad guys" but it is part of the whole project. You have to prepare and there's gonna be readers who are saying, "What are you doing?

What does this all mean? You're writing a book for me! Why are you now writing a book for these Beings!?"

Wouldn't blame them for feeling that way.

Maybe...but you have these Beings and a lot of you don't make sense. You're saying, "Well we're all going to ascend and they can all just implode and well goodbye see ya!" Did anyone stop to ask, "Well how does that work exactly?" What do you mean *we're all going to ascend* but this group of Beings who are deeply connected with Man Being can just go to hell? What are you thinking...that you're just going to be able to run off and "Great! Bye see ya!" and it's all gonna be resolved. No there's work to do here and I believe that you understand, although this might be a bit of a surprise but I decided to be the bad guy and let you know that one of the books is for the DRA Beings. They need your help and they need instruction.

This is unexpected and a lot to absorb but whatever needs to be done we're going to do it.

Don't let anyone tell you that you have "big egos"...or "oh my goodness...who do these two people think they are...writing a book for the DRA like they're gonna save the universe", but isn't that what this book is about? I mean if someone is gonna criticise you..."who do you think you are the savior of the universe?" Well what is this book series for? Why are you reading it? You need to toughen up and not really concern yourself so much with what people think about you or well hopefully what they *feel* about you...that would be one step up. I want to say this because you can't be concerned about what people are thinking of this project and thinking about you two. If they're *thinking*...well then they're really not ahead of the curve here. So if you're gonna tell me what they're *feeling* about you well that's a bit different. If you're gonna tell me that they're feeling like you're failures or feeling like "this is just nonsense" or that the "book is worthless" well that's a little bit better, but it's still not great. If you're gonna say that they're feeling something different, they're feeling something's being threatened and they don't know what it is or that they're feeling something new and they don't know what they're feeling and they don't know how to put it in words...well there you go. When you hear "I feel something and I can't put it in words...I don't have the words to describe this feeling" well there...now you've done something and now you have something that is changing the world. When you can no longer put it in words then you've done something right.

We fully expect a backlash from these books. These dialogues are proposing changes that many aren't ready for. There's a lot to lose if you're married to your Earth plane existence and much to gain if you aren't.

I want you both...I'm not in charge of you...but if you can just remember this: That what people say about you doesn't have any value. There's no value in what people say about you. It doesn't mean anything. So you don't need to tiptoe around and be so careful. I'm not saying you have to instigate a riot but it might be important to remember that your job is to get people *feeling* differently. You don't have to worry about criticism and instigating some crazy...I don't know...gathering of people who are gonna take everything the wrong way. Everybody takes everything the wrong way. You know why they're taking it the wrong way? Well on one hand maybe they're thinking too much and they're thinking that they *understand* something when instead you have to *feel*. You understand something by feeling. Even when you're studying something and you're memorizing things and your memorizing calculations and you're memorizing things that require the intellect, you're still ultimately feeling. You have to *feel* like you know it right? You understand? You have to feel like you know it and when you're feeling that you know something then you no longer know it. You feel it. You've absorbed the belief. Well that's what your books are doing. You're teaching people how to feel the knowledge. Don't memorize the knowledge. You have to feel it. That's more or less what I did with my work. I mean you can memorize things, you can memorize a script and you can memorize a story and you can memorize instructions but if you don't feel these things then you're always gonna need a book or a set of instructions. So you see where I'm going with this...once people absorb your books then they don't need them anymore.

Marlon, you brought up memorizing a script. Much has been said about the fact that you didn't necessarily memorize your lines. What can you tell us about that?

Well who said I didn't memorize them? Maybe I said that but no...I memorized them. I memorized them emotionally. You see there's a difference between reading it and feeling it, right? So I didn't go in completely blind. I had some idea of what I got hired to do. I had some idea of the story. You know, maybe I did read it over once and maybe I did read it over twice but maybe I also did *feel* the story and *feel* the meaning and communication and maybe I absorbed it and maybe I just chose not to stand there and stare at the script girl. Maybe none of you know what I was doing because you didn't bother to absorb the script. If you really are expanding your emotional repertoire then you don't have to memorize the words.

What you're saying makes sense, but some readers would say that it's not as easy as you make it sound. What you were doing however clearly enabled you to perform at the level that you did.

> You're reading and learning about the story and then that is absorbed into your belief and then you have the repertoire and the emotional ability to make a momentum. The speech...now listen to this...the speech, the words coming out of my mouth, the words coming out of your mouth...what's that a by-product of? Is that a by-product of the feeling? Do you have the feeling first and then you have the words or do you have the words and then you have the feeling?

That's a great question and of course it's the feeling.

> This is what you have to get across in your books. Humans have it all wrong. You have it all backwards there. That's what's holding you back. Those people that don't speak...they're well ahead. I'm not saying that you should be glad if you're on Earth and you can't speak or you can't see or you can't hear. I'm not gonna go down that road but you have to understand that feeling is not speaking and speaking is not feeling and most people just open their mouth and there's a whole world of noise and garbage and does anyone even hear what they're saying? When I did my work I was feeling what I was saying. I was feeling my way through the dialogue.

We're really starting to understand the importance of feeling. Feeling our way through this existence and feeling our way through the information in these books.

> Oh you'll get this. That's what's different about your books. You're getting it. Your books are not "memorize these instructions and when you go to the Afterlife you're gonna turn left and you're gonna see this guy

and he's glowing and he's gonna point you over here and then you'll go to this Angel and then go to the girl over there". It's just not like that. You have to feel. When you start speaking with feeling then you're gonna be further ahead but I'm not gonna speak about this anymore. You both get it. You both feel it...you're feeling me, right? You're feeling me. Your readers are feeling me.

Marlon when you...

So Gemini...Dramos and Bohemias...Gemini. Let me just finish on Gemini. Gemini and you have done work before. You'll learn about this. Why don't you just explain this to yourselves that this is some mission and a project that you will learn about? It is funny that all the science fiction stories are using that name. Now you have the additional problem that you don't like that name because that name is used too much and you want a name that's really original. You'll have an original story. The constellations are in the sky for a reason, you put them there...and if you don't want the constellations there any more then make a change. Everything that you see and everything that you're interacting with...you put there. You, Man Being, put there. You've invented everything and this is a lot to absorb because you're thinking "God put it there" and "the Anunnaki put it there" and this "DNA splicing put it there". No...you put it there. We all put it there. Everything is held together on Earth. It's a systematic effort to continue to imprison everyone. Everyone is working together to imprison each other. You know the main bond, the main glue...glue's a better word than bond I like glue. The main glue is your words.

Our words?

I mean your language. It's a sticky mess...the way you're sticking to the planet. How do you stick to that rock? What is it – gravity? Why are you sticking to this rock you're calling Earth? What has happened? Well, it's a glue. Your language has glued you to the planet and when you lose that then you'll be further ahead. It may not be good for a book sale but you may not have to have books where you're going.

Marlon, let's switch gears and talk a little bit about the energy and charisma that you brought to Earth and about your mission with the Indigenous Community. Many found you to be a magnetic personality and we were glued – there's your word again – to your performances and interviews and shenanigans.

Are we speaking about the same person because this is quite an introduction that you've given me? The mission...why did I choose to come back to Earth? I didn't come to the planet in the usual way. Yes I was born, I had a physical birth experience but you've written about Tesla and this is the same experience...choosing to be physically birthed. There's a bunch of us that are coming to the planet to try to help so did I consciously choose to come to Earth to assist in the mission and get everybody out of here? I'm gonna say yes, but I didn't really have an understanding of that early on in my life in 3rd density existence.

Why didn't you have the understanding?

I had the amnesia like everybody else. There's a lot of you who have come to the planet to help but then you have the amnesia, you forget. You're in touch with it when you're young but my mission...and you're asking about Indigenous peoples and all of that activity...well I really hope that I helped create an appreciation that there is an "older" understanding. I don't like to use all that linear talk but you've been going through that with your histories. I wanted to uncover all the obstacles and the obstructions to understanding the real story like digging back to the origin story. Many of the things that I wanted to stand up for are really about people who are connected with a different way of experiencing the world. The Indigenous peoples have a different construct. They've constructed their reality in a remarkably different way that's closer to the way that things are. Their voice is of course hindered and their voice is not welcomed and this is sort of my way of disseminating.

You tried to be a voice for them, it was very clear that you cared about the Indigenous community. It's the only time you appeared comfortable using your celebrity.

I didn't write a book but you know assisting those who have the real story, the true story…that was my way to help out and I feel I did an *okay* job. I feel I could have done a bit better but you know you can go ahead and write a book and you can go ahead and start a movement. You can always start an original movement but why not just help those who are already tapped into something? Why make it so complicated? There's plenty of Indigenous peoples on your planet who really have the truth and you know…you don't wanna listen. You'd rather go ahead and invent new truths and talk and talk some more and talk talk talk. But these people *listen*. Not only do they listen to the Earth…and you're interpreting it as they're listening to the Earth in the 3rd density but that's not really correct.

How should we interpret it?

They're listening to the soul of the Earth. They understand the way it's really supposed to be. You've touched upon Terra. They understand. Why are they on the planet with you? Well they're the keepers of the light. They're really along with the plants…and you'll be learning about animals but they're one of the few Beings on the planet that are actually helping and nobody's listening…and you're still fighting with them. All you do is fight with these people. Why don't you just listen? Listen because when they speak they speak with feeling. They speak differently. That was my way of disseminating and that was my way of helping in this mission to get you all out of the blocked gateway that you're stuck in. You remember this right?

It hasn't been put to us that way – that we're stuck in a gateway.

Yeah well…you're stuck in a gateway. You have to remember that. You're stuck in a gateway. You're not stuck on a planet, although we like to describe it that way. You're stuck in a gateway. When you start feeling that you're stuck in a gateway it'll make more sense, especially for your readers.

Can you elaborate on that?

Well you're seeing your planet as a sphere or close to it…and then there's the Flat Earth people and they're kind of interesting, aren't they? The Flat Earth people…well they might be onto something you know.

What are they "onto"?

Well I'm not here to talk to you about a Flat Earth but there's a lot more to a collapsed gateway than you know. Why is *flat* any more impossible than a sphere? I'm not going anywhere with this, I'm just saying I like it. Sometimes when you explore what you believe is an "outlandish belief" then you can recreate a new belief. So what's going on here? You've got a rock that you're stuck on and you're looking at the Earth like it's some gigantic marble and you have to just crack it open and dive through the layers. Did anyone stop to think that maybe you're just in a gateway? Maybe you're traveling and you just got stuck and these shapes, these luminaries, these planets...they're not telling you something that you don't already know. Those shapes are the shape that they are because you made it that shape. That shape represents something. The sphere. Why is everything turning into a sphere? Well, we have all the science and you know we can go on and on about that, but this idea that you've got a round object that you're existing on and then you just gotta chip away at the layers and there'll be a smaller round object underneath that and there'll be another smaller round object underneath that and so on until you get to the core...it's a *gateway*. You're stuck in a gateway and this huge chute...it's a cosmic chute...this gateway that you're stuck in well that's where all these luminaries got created. You got stuck in a gateway. Now we're talking about the origin story.

This is dizzying because now readers will be wondering about our Milky Way Galaxy.

Your Milky Way Galaxy? It's my Milky Way Galaxy too so let's work together on this. That Galaxy of luminaries is stuck in a big portal and a big gateway and a big chute in a tunnel. It's stuck there. This thing is stuck. When everything gets unstuck the whole universe is gonna shift...so this is quite something that you're involved in. This is not a matter of you're just gonna go to the Inner Earth "door" and you know...give the password. There is a password by the way and you'll be getting that but maybe I've said too much haha. Oops.

Jeez, Marlon.

But yeah, I don't know...why does Mankind have to have everything perfect. Everything's gotta be perfect right? Maybe it's not. Feelings are not perfect. Feelings are different frequencies. Feelings expand and they contract. Feelings create everything. That 5th density, that World of Make Believe, Invention and World of Imagination is a world of *feeling*. It's about the senses. You're very big on the senses, right? Human Beings are very big on the senses and those senses…that's in that World in the 5th density. That's where your senses are connected. So the big portal, the big gateway, the big chute…this is a way bigger experience than you're planning on. I'm not saying that your book or your books rather are going to fix the entire cosmos but they're certainly helping. Why don't we have a feeling break now and have less talking and I'm going to take a break with you and why don't we all just feel what we just experienced.

We get to re-feel this as well, when we type this conversation out. There's also an energy release during the transcribing.

When you're typing up all these talks and it's important that you're typing it out because you're putting it in a book…but you have to believe that there's a signal that goes out when you have these interviews with Beings. You have to believe as well that your books actually have an energy. There's a feeling with your books. The words have a feeling. They do have a feeling. Words are powerful. We've created words. We have to consider why we've created words. Why can't we just all smile and laugh and cry, although that's just a start. That's very limited. I'm contradicting myself now because I was criticizing the minimal repertoire of emotions that you have. Just remember that your books have an energy. Even…well I'll say this…even if someone doesn't wanna read your books and they say, "Dramos and Bohemias I'm not gonna read these books I'm just gonna hold them"…well you know that might be good enough. You know how you used to believe and pray that if you put your book under the pillow that you wouldn't have to study and you might pass the exam? Well there's something to that.

We believe that. I think most of us quietly believe that. Marlon, you mentioned experiencing amnesia when you existed on Earth. When did you finally awaken? What was your "Eureka" moment?

Well I used to paint a little bit when I was a child, nothing too fancy but I used to paint. You paint with water color kind of paint and I remember when one day I was painting and I just watched all the colors kinda...I put too much water and the colors were running into each other. It got me wondering, "What are we trying to control here...an expression...an artistic expression and creativity?" Here I was trying to paint really carefully and I made a big mess of it and all the colors sort of ran into each other. I just sort of realized in that moment that yeah...if you continue right...if you continue coloring in between the lines then you're gonna be experiencing just a very limited...*very* limited connection with all that is awaiting you...if you allow yourself to feel. Now I'm not saying that I had these highfalutin ideas as a young child but I realized basically that it was okay that I was painting outside the lines now. It was okay that the colors were just kinda painting themselves. They just kinda painted themselves. I watched the colors and the paint doing their own thing and that's when I changed my feeling about trying to control my experience living on the planet with everybody.

Our whole existence on Earth is about controlling and managing things. Our jobs, our families, our finances, our words, our emotions and our time...we even designate "free time". We allot ourselves just a little bit a freedom...just a tiny allotment so that we don't upset the order of things.

When you stop trying to control everything that you're doing then you'll also stop trying to control your feelings. This is tying in with what I said earlier. It's just sort of letting…you're letting the colors paint themselves and when you're letting the feelings also build things and those feelings are no longer relegated to you know four feelings that you're allowed to have as a Human Being, then you'll be further ahead. I really had that moment where I realized…"What are we doing when we're creating?" We're deciding. We're making a decision most of us and we're executing it like it's a math equation…there's nothing wrong with math but you know what I'm saying. Let the creation unfold and that's a whole different way of being and that was the change for me, to stop thinking so much. "Get out of the way", as we say.

And then you became the Marlon that no one would ever fully understand. Is that what was behind all your "odd behavior"? It seemed like you were toying with everyone. There are so many "Marlon Brando stories" out there…one that comes to mind is Andrew Bergman's Tuna Fish story.

NOTE: Andrew Bergman Directed "The Freshman" (1990). When Marlon signed on to the film, he told Andrew that he doesn't answer phone calls. Marlon told Andrew that if he's calling just to leave a message to say, "Tuna Fish 1". If he wants Marlon to reply say, "Tuna Fish 2". If it's urgent say, "Tuna Fish 3" and if it's *end of the world* say, "Tuna Fish 4"…but "never use Tuna Fish 4".

Well I was just being playful haha…and yeah and I understand I was difficult for everybody but I don't…well I still don't wanna play everybody else's game. What was going on with my "behavior"? Well what wasn't going on was I wasn't gonna do it like everybody else was doing it, because that's the problem. I don't wanna be like everybody else.   That's the problem. It wasn't me being difficult. It was me saying, "No I don't wanna do it that way because that way is the wrong way to be". For me…I want to get people feeling rather than thinking so when I say something confusing like you just described right…then people are gonna run away and think, "What on Earth did he mean by that? Was that a code? Was he being sarcastic? Was he mad at me? What did he mean by that?" Well maybe I didn't mean anything. Maybe I'm showing you what it's like when you're just running around blah blah blabbing and talking and you're speaking without thinking. Well yeah…that's the whole point.

We were on the verge of leaving you a "Tuna Fish 4" message, just before you showed up today.

Well this is actually a Tuna Fish 4 conversation now, isn't it?

It actually is. Marlon, we'd like to know what one of your other incarnations was, because your energy is coming through like someone who has been around the block…like Orson.

Well you know Orson and I go a long way back…all these incarnations that you are connecting with and speaking with…a lot of us are involved in the same thing but you'll learn a lot more about that. I'll let Orson tell you so he doesn't get upset that I took his job from him. The incarnation…well what can I share with you….which one would you like….well you might like the Plato one. Yeah that's a good one, do you like that one?

Haha come on. Really?

You like that eh? No well…I guess if I was Plato then I don't really know what the f**k I'm talking about. Who do you need to know, do you need to know this?

We can't tell if you're joking.

> You know all those Elohim that you're speaking about?
> Well I'm involved with those Beings. I'm not trying to
> give myself a fancy title, you invented that "Elohim"
> word I didn't, but I'm involved with those guys. You'll
> learn a little bit more about me I think in the next
> discussion but I'm gonna say this…that I did do a lot of
> writing for a person who's now telling you that you
> gotta feel everything…I did do a lot of writing. I'm not
> gonna tell you in this talk because you're just gonna
> drop everything and you're just gonna be pretending
> I'm something I'm not. But I promise when we're done
> I will tell you why you're speaking to me, although
> Orson does like to talk a lot so he's probably gonna tell
> you himself.

NOTE: At this point we end the discussion and pick it up again
the next day. The talk is heavy and there's a sense that Marlon is
going to speak with us again.

You mentioned in our last discussion that you would inform us
about why we are actually speaking and connecting with you,
implying that it's not a random connection. Would you like to tell
us what has brought us together?

> Well, you're choosing to get all these ideas together and
> you're choosing to establish some sort of
> movement…and not like a movement getting an army
> together, but a movement as in a philosophy. I'm
> speaking with you and making this effort to connect
> with you both to share some instructions on how you
> deal with the "bad guys" basically. You're all very
> worried and speaking a lot about the DRA, Draconian
> and the Orion DRA and this situation is something that
> needs to get some control. You need to control, you
> must control the way you feel about these Beings who

are running around creating havoc and terrifying everybody.

We're also getting the sense that the DRA problem goes beyond the 3rd density.

> That's right. This is something that continues when you cross over and I realize that you're not interested in frightening your readers off, but they must know that once you are establishing a way to create the gateway...they will have to bypass their world. Now you're practicing all of this in the 5th density...you know...the World of Invention and Imagination. That World is about feeling and feeling how it is to create things. Feelings create and we've spoken about this so we don't need to get into a lengthy discussion, but in that 5th density you are communicating feelings and exploring these beliefs about feelings and engaging with feelings. It's not about speaking or language or words. It's the language of light and color...well it's the language of existence. You have to learn how to create and open the door, the gateway. You don't automatically just cross over and walk down a hallway and there you are, you're in the entrance to the Inner Earth experience. It's not like that. If you're just opening the door then you're opening the door to the World where these DRA Beings are existing.

Are you saying that we need to train ourselves to manoeuvre around or time travel past the DRA? Are they blocking the 7th density, Inner Earth?

> I'm going on and on and not making any sense. I'm exploring how to convey the feeling that you have when you are ready to launch and you've done all this work. Once you've been in the Lemuria experience or the World of Imagination or the 5th density...once you've had that experience and you open the next door then

voila...you're met with these "monsters", these "horrible Beings". I mean ultimately we're all from the same source so it's not necessarily fair to give them these labels but that's how you all see them. What is it that's allowing you to bypass this? Is this your outcome? Is this your reward for fully engaging and immersing yourself in the beliefs in the 5th density? How can that be that you just wander into a whole mess with these Beings? Is that the whole outcome? I mean you can't blame anybody for wanting to reincarnate then, can you?

We're equipping readers with the knowledge so that they don't have to give in to fear. If there's more work to do in the 5th density then so be it. We will find our way home.

You will. You all will. There's nothing to fear when you have the knowledge. We didn't speak about what you can do in the 5th density. You're not just "releasing your light". You're speaking amongst yourselves about the "starseed" idea, releasing the light and making that Channel, the channel that engages you with other densities of light and existence. It's the fact that you can now interconnect with other layers of your existence. You unfold. You're not unfolding only in the 5th density. You are unfolding into the Cosmos...you are releasing your light into the Cosmos. This light is seen in the 3rd density, in the Earth plane. You are experiencing it in the Earth plane. You are witnessing things with the luminaries in the sky. You are seeing events. You are seeing "comets" and "meteors" and you're seeing "stars" sparkle and shine and you are seeing luminaries and they are rotating and this sort of thing. In the 5th density when you release yourselves from the prison...

You mean when we release ourselves from the 3rd density prison? You said the 5th there.

No I meant what I said. The 5th. You believe that when you "disconnect" from the 3rd density and "die" that you are released from the Earth prison, but that's not the truth of the matter.

What is the truth?

This is just simply getting a key. You're just getting some keys. You're getting a big Ring and I know you spoke about The Rings with Lillian Leitzel. You're getting a big Ring of keys. That's what the Rings are for...the Rings are holding the keys. They are energetically holding the keys. The Rings...the Rings are very important. The Ring is not a key. The Ring holds the keys. The Ring in fact assembles many keys. The Ring of course is a sphere and the sphere...you know the sphere...you're traveling in spheres...you're worrying about spheres...you're inventing things with spheres. These keys, you are in the 5th density learning about how to get these keys. You are handed a set of keys. You don't know what to do with these keys. You don't know how to use these keys but you're getting these keys. Now, you're getting these keys because you invent these keys. You're not being handed the key or a ring of keys. You're not being handed that...you're inventing that. So you're inventing your own ways to escape the Earth prison and when you learn how to escape the Earth prison then you escape the Draconian influence that's keeping you back in the 5th density.

We want to be clear on this Marlon. Are you saying that once we cross over into the 5th density and experience the World of Imagination or Lemuria state...that we can also get trapped there?

Well yeah. When you say trapped it sounds terrifying but it's not like that. The World of Imagination is not a bad place but the reason why some of you just stay in the 5th density is not because you love it there and you don't know any better or that it feels like your childhood. You're basically playing all the time so why wouldn't you just stay there forever? You're staying there because you know that what's waiting for you behind the next door – or the 6th density door – is something that's not so nice. You have to invent and create a way to get to Inner Earth. You have to believe in Inner Earth. You cannot believe in Inner Earth if you don't invent that belief. You read about that belief. You have to create that belief and you have to create a belief in a belief. Now we're gonna get into something your readers are worrying all the time about...psychedelic drugs.

Go on.

This is a little more of a "psychedelic trip" than those drugs, I'll tell you. You have to have a belief about beliefs. You see what I'm saying? A belief about beliefs. You are expanding the feeling about beliefs. You have a belief but that belief is mostly intellectual and you carry that from the 3rd density experience, but now in the 5th density look at what's happening. You can have a belief about a belief about a belief about a belief and so on if you understand what I'm saying or if you *believe* what I'm saying. When your belief stream is endless, when there is no end to the belief....the belief is continuous. It does not have a start and finish. It is a stream.

Basically Humans are stuck in a belief. We stopped believing in anything but our form.

Now you've got it. You are traveling through beliefs and making forms around the belief and going in and out of the form. When you learn about time travel and not intellectually but learn emotionally, then you can have a belief in Inner Earth. You cannot have this belief

450

in Inner Earth unless you believe in time travel, unless you believe that you can believe and believe and believe and believe. When you are able...now I'm using "when" a lot with you, which is seemingly a constraint of time but it doesn't have to be. You know these words that you're using they don't have to mean what you think they mean. You can have them mean something that you believe they mean.

Like you said earlier, freeing ourselves from the language.

You have to. You can change the belief in words. Words can become different meanings and when they become different meanings for you, you are deconstructing the language. You are then releasing yourself from the glue that's binding you to Earth. Now I know I'm sounding like some mad Guru but I'm just telling you that you have to create the belief in order to get to the Inner Earth experience. How do you get to Inner Earth? You have to time travel there. In order to time travel from the 5th to the 7th...cause the 6th is where all the DRA guys are at. I'm saying "guys" to inject some levity here. I hope you understand. In order to get from the 5th to the 7th why are we jumping? Has anyone asked why we're jumping? We're missing numbers here. We're missing densities. These jumps are a gateway. They're portals. You know the 3rd to the 5th? That's a portal and then the 5th to the 7th ...that's also a portal.

How do we get through a portal, what do we do?

Well, you're traveling. You see in order to get from the 3rd to the 5th you must have already adhered to the belief in time travel. You must have already bought into the belief of time travel. You must already believe in time travel. You've traveled to get to the 5th. Now you can say, "Well no Marlon I died". Well did you...did you die? Or are you time traveling? What are you doing? What's going on here? You can involuntarily disconnect and yes you can enter the reincarnation cycle again.

We hope to end that cycle.

Go for it if you want to be miserable. That's death. You know what death is? Death is coming back to Earth. Now that's the death. You've got it all mixed up. Involuntary disconnect is the release into the time travel state. You are skipping over densities…these are portals. You're not skipping over them. You're traveling through. So to bypass the Draconian Beings who are existing in the 6th…

Sorry Marlon, I need to interrupt you there. Don't the DRA Beings exist in the 3rd density?

Don't let anyone tell you they're existing in the 3rd. That doesn't make any sense. You have a belief about them in the 3rd because that is the belief that is keeping you in the Earth plane and keeping you trapped. You're trapped because you're afraid of everything. Fear is your favorite emotion. You love fear. Humans love fear. That portal, the 5th through the 7th …well that's time travel and you best start believing in time travel and believing that you can believe. You need to believe that you will believe and you are believing in time travel. Doesn't this sound ridiculous…this whole interview and conversation? It sounds like we're sitting around with a bunch of lunatics and I don't mean that to put anybody down who's struggling with mental illness. I'm just saying that facetiously, that's not nice. Okay they'll think we're a bunch of freaks, just a bunch of controversial hippie weirdo freaks…but you have portals.

We just want to take this moment to thank the readers for staying with this. Haha. This isn't exactly a straightforward conversation. So thank you Reader.

> Ah don't worry your readers are getting it. They're feeling it. They don't need to obsess over the details. Just feel the truth…remember the watercolor painting I did when I was a kid. Just let your brain go and feel the truth trickle in. Stop trying to control the information. We're painting here, that's all. The words are colors. Let the colors run around and do their thing.

We love that analogy. So Marlon, what did you do to "defeat" the DRA?

> How did I defeat the DRA? Did I go to battle? No that's…you guys have been taught on Earth that in order to defeat the "bad guys", in order to defeat what you're calling "evil" you must go to war. You've gotta pick up weapons and start blowing everything up and killing everyone and just on and on. Did anyone ever stop to wonder whether you can just time travel and get the hell outta here? Why do we have to start blowing everything up and shooting people and using weapons and just horrific measures? You can just time travel. You can just leave. This is what all the Indigenous peoples know. You can just leave. They can leave. They know.

Why don't they leave if they know? They're constantly under attack and it's not exactly sunshine and rainbows for their Community on Earth.

> These Beings are here to try to hold together the little bit of light that you have. That light is not for you to see and read your books. That's a light that you're using to travel. You're all able to travel. This is a travesty. You have not only forgotten who you are but you've also got

Beings who are trying to stay on the Earth plane with you and show you something and you just can't listen. You're just doing all these incredibly and profoundly ridiculous and stupid things and everybody knows everything and it's all about what you know. "I know this" and "I know that" and "I memorized this" and "I memorized that". Anyway, why are we having this conversation...I've actually forgotten.

You worked yourself up there a little haha.

I feel that you've gotten something from it...I hope.

Marlon, you ended the last conversation by telling us that you are involved with the Elohim. What are the Elohim? What is their mission?

The Elohim...well I don't want to create a big controversy. Everybody's got their bible and they're worried about defining "the Bible" and hurting everybody's feelings, but the Elohim are a Group of Beings, oh I don't know some of you are gonna call them "Angels" or "Ascended Masters", you've got all these different names. You have so many words. Words, words, and more words. If I'm just gonna describe what the Elohim are they are a Group of Beings who are teaching and they're teachers and they're committed to trying to fix things and help things. How are they helping? Well you've got a lot of weird descriptions in your bibles and a lot of that was changed unfortunately so the original work and message has been played with but the Elohim...these are Time Travelers. Elohim are beings that have gone well outside the 5th, 6th, 7th, 8th, 9th, 10th, 11th and 12th densities. I mean they go outside...we are outside that and not because we're "better than you". We're just built a little bit differently. We have an ability to exist in any density of experience. We're able to contain ourselves in different levels of light experience and we can also make a connection with the Earth density and some of us have purposely encountered the Earth plane existence by going through a physical birth experience.

This is probably not what bible scholars care to hear, but that's not our concern. We simply want the truth.

"Elohim" does not have to be this *untouchable* experience or something otherworldly that you have no contact with. You most certainly do. There are many Beings that you have documented in your histories that have made contributions and have made initiatives and tried to help or in fact helped. Some of us are doing some incredible things to try to get everybody ultimately in sync with the planet so that they can make the choice to not remain on the planet and continue the problem. You are perpetuating the problem. The real planet is not on the surface of the planet as you see it. You've all created that illusion.

Are the Elohim without travel restriction?

Elohim are able to exist wherever they choose. They are able to help in any density of light experience. They are able to travel. They have full capacity to communicate with anyone who is available for communication and connection and so we are "helpers". We like to consider ourselves as helpers. Now the question is, "Are we Creators?" Did we help create the Beings, Man Beings and other animals and creatures and things on the surface of the Earth? Are we Creators and did we move energy around and actually create things? We are able to have a full capacity and awareness of the 5th density state…Lemuria, the Lemuria state of being. We are connected with Lemuria. We are Lemuria. When you ask, "Who are the Elohim?", we are ascended from this state of being.

The connection, the joy, the feeling that you have from connecting with the 5th density and that feeling of play and the joy as in a child playing, is what we are built of. We are made of what you call love. We are made of what you call joy. We are ascended in our emotions. This is not to say that we are better than you but we are ascended in a way that allows us to build upon the few emotions that you have access to in the Earth plane and expand on these. Your emotional repertoire is limited. There are things that go beyond what you call love and joy and happiness. These are the starting points or the emotional baseline for what we are made of. We are built of a frequency and awareness of this frequency that does create. We assist in creating a love frequency.

Extraordinary. The Elohim are ascended in their emotions and are built of a frequency that creates. Your most recent incarnation as Marlon makes perfect sense in this context.

Yeah and this may be sounding a little bit unusual as I'm speaking to you in my former incarnation in such a way that you are able to communicate with me in a 3rd density, or more specifically, a 5th density experience. You are communicating with me in the 5th but are disseminating in the 3rd. This is all very confusing and a little bit tiring I understand, but you have to believe that you are connecting with more than one experience. When you get off your planet and get off thinking about only having your planet as an experience you will all be further ahead. The Elohim are "creatures" of a very high and positive frequency and awareness...and so wherever we are able to travel we are pulling in the energy of the Cosmos.

This may seem laughable to some who only want to hear that the Elohim are "gods" and "sons of gods" and the "most sacred of all Beings". They don't want to hear that an Elohim incarnated as a Human in Omaha Nebraska in 1929.

Oh sure. You may say, "Well you were not a good representation of this Elohim description when you were on the Earth plane Marlon". My choice to disseminate the information and share what I shared was my choice. When we go to the Earth plane existence we choose an existence, an experience. When you're going to the Earth plane you are not going as an "Ascended Master" or a "Being from another realm". Do not let anyone tell you that there are Ascended Masters walking around on the Earth plane. That doesn't happen. There are Human Beings walking around the Earth plane and some of them are *connected to other states of being*.

Wouldn't you consider Jesus an Ascended Master? He was walking around on Earth.

Did I say he was Human? What I'm saying is that if you're *stuck* on the Earth plane you're a Human Being. Ascended Masters don't get stuck. There's a difference between going to the Earth plane and being stuck on the Earth plane. And you also gotta remember that when you are time traveling you are existing everywhere at once.

Right. So in your case "Marlon" is only a fraction of your Being. A glimpse of your existence. That's something we're still absorbing and learning about.

You'll learn. Your awareness is such that you're just experiencing me with you on the Earth as "Marlon". You may be experiencing me with you in another plane of existence where we're both glowing miraculous geometric shapes and lights and sounds and a whole bunch of weird experiences. You understand this, but your interview with me will be a little bit unusual for your readers.

"Unusual" ideas are something that our readers have likely embraced by now.

> Maybe, but describing that you are "ascended" while you are also speaking and swearing and using slang...and I was saying that I didn't wanna speak but I'm speaking too much now. I don't really know how to explain to you about Elohim in a way that your readers are going to get it. It's just going to sound strange...it's going to sound made up.

It's not our place to decide whether or not readers can or will believe the information. Our mission is to give the truth back to everyone. If the Elohim are a group of "Helpers" with raised consciousness and not "Sons of God" or whatever the bibles describe them as...then so be it.

> Well, Elohim have the ability to appear wherever they wish to appear and they have the ability to exist in a Human form if they wish. They also have the ability to exist in a tree, in a cat or even in a crystal. We can exist wherever we choose. I think that's pretty profound and you understand that. The understanding as well that you've got Beings like Jesus and Akhenaten...Beings like this are part of this Group. You understand that there are many labels for who we are and what we are and there are many experiences that we are choosing, that we are voluntarily choosing to have in the Earth plane. Some of us are interacting in a more "typical way" in the Earth plane in order to do our work.

In our last discussion you brought up the fact that you did some prolific writing. I'm assuming that was as "Plato", unless you were joking.

> Well yeah we spoke about this. Is your book about history or reincarnation? What is it you're doing in this book?

To discover that any one of our "interviewees" is more than the single persona they're coming through as is a compelling truth. To learn that Marlon and Plato are the same Being is thought provoking to say the least.

> But don't you realize that I could really say that I was anybody and most of you would believe it.

Maybe...maybe not. That's why a discussion on it would be beneficial. People tell lies about themselves on Earth but we don't believe them if it doesn't ring true.

> I know but isn't that acting though? I can be whoever I want. I mean...maybe I *was* Plato.

People know the truth when they hear it. The truth is a frequency. So if you're saying that you were Plato and it's not resonating well it means nothing. It wouldn't even make sense for a Being to lie about something like that in a conversation like this.

> Well why are we idolizing all of my incarnations? What are we talking about now...all the different missions that I had and what I'm really about? You want an entire catalogue of all the missions I've had?

No. The point is to simply uncover the fact that these incarnations are all just missions and contributions. In knowing that, we'd be less inclined to deify or idolize beings like Plato or Marlon. We'd just pay attention to the contribution. Don't you feel that that's useful?

> Well okay then...maybe I was Plato and you know maybe there were other notable people or Writers or Philosophers or Teachers. Maybe there were even more celebrated figures that you've forgotten. Human Beings are all about popularity. You all want to popularize certain missions and certain contributions. We're *all* *contributing*. Well, most of us are trying to contribute.

This is about contribution and if you feel you're contributing well you are. It's not about a competition and getting an award for contributing...so I don't want to say, "Yes I was Plato. I've had an incarnation in the Earth plane as Plato" and then have everyone say, "Oh I knew it of course he's so amazing". I couldn't just be a "nobody" I had to pick the most famous guy. Won't some of your readers go, "Oh right, he picked the most famous guy, typical!"?

Regardless of what the Reader now believes, the point has been made – that we shouldn't worship any one Being or contribution.

Exactly. Just tune in. Feel. Don't think.

We'd like to address that you referenced the 8th, 9th, 10th, 11th and 12th densities. The readers are being informed about the 7th density being Inner Earth and that that's where "we all are", as Amy mentioned. Why are we all there if there are all these other densities?

Well, for some of you that's where your real journey begins. You're getting your mission in the 7th density. You're going to understand how you got stuck on the planet. You're going to understand when you go to the 7th density experience and you're going to understand how you got stuck on the planet. There's going to be a real reveal, like an origin story. You're all searching for the origin story. *The* story. The story of your beginning will begin in the 7th density. That's really the beginning. Your Volumes 1, 2 and 3 are sort of a prologue. We're just getting to the very beginning now. Not the very beginning but the beginning of understanding. I don't even wanna be using the word "understanding". You know what I'd like to be doing?

What?

Humming. But we can't do that. I'd like to have a songbook for Inner Earth or something. We're using too many words now. There's gonna be a lot of descriptions when you encounter the 7th density experience. The Inner Earth experience will be a lot of elaborate detailed descriptions, a lot of feelings expressed. You will be expanding your repertoire of feelings in the 7th density. I look forward to communicating with you again when you've expanded your repertoire and we don't have to use so many words. We can just emote and we can connect with the feeling and we don't have to talk about our feelings. You see the problem here? This whole conversation we keep coming back to talking and talking about feelings. Why are we not getting this in the Earth plane? Dramos and Bohemias if we have to talk about feeling then our feelings are not happening or our feelings are not calibrated or we're not really in touch with our feelings. We have to reconnect with our feelings. We have to remember our feelings. We gotta find our feelings. You have to find your feelings. You have to find your emotions. They're all there. There's many of them and they're very expansive. Get in touch with this emotional repertoire, with this book of emotions. You want a book? Write a book about emotions…right…but don't write it in words. Just you know…ah f**k it I don't know what you do…I just talked myself into a corner haha. I know…paint the emotions. But don't be so controlling with the paint you understand? Let the colors express the emotions.

We'll get there. Some readers are probably doing that already.

We're talking too much. It would be nice to have a conversation with you and not say anything and just feel it. It would be nice to send out that message, that emotion without saying, "I just wanna let everybody

461

know here that I'm feeling happy" or "news flash…I'm happy now" or "I sound really happy don't I?"

Now we're back to sounding like Orson's frozen peas commercial.

Right? "News flash I'm happy" or "Oh now you've made me mad"…uh…"Attention everybody! I am feeling mad now!" Why are we doing that? Why don't we know how to project and communicate the emotion without speaking about the emotion? We should feel that emotion. We should not have to see what the Being looks like to evaluate the emotion. We should not have to hear what they sound like in order to evaluate the emotion. You should be able to send out the emotion. Experience the emotion and the recipient should also be able to experience that emotion and I'm using that word "should" and I know you don't like it but it is a *should*. We *should* be able to do this. This is what you will be learning. Learning not as in memorizing.

Learning as in…

You will be recalibrating your emotional field. There is a field of emotions. Not like your Elysian Fields and not like the plants in the field. The field as in a grid. There is a field of emotions. These emotions and emotional repertoire are a shield and a grid. This grid, this net is something that you use. You use this not only as a communication field but you use this as a way to define where you are going, as in travel. You use this as a filter from unwanted frequencies from the Draconian. The Draconian Beings also are lacking an emotional repertoire. They in fact are very close to Human Beings. You've come from the same place ultimately as you will discover. This shield and grid and network of emotions and the emotional repertoire are your keys. The keys that I was telling you about that are on The

Ring, The Ring that you are creating for yourselves in the 5th density…I've given you a little clue here about these keys. Each key is an emotion. These emotions have a lot of power. They unlock portals and doorways and gateways, whatever you want to call them.

Now we truly understand why you've been speaking so much about emotions…and why you chose to disseminate the info as an Actor in the Earth plane.

You're getting it now. These keys are very important and that is why, my friends, I had returned to the Earth density to try my hardest to get this point and message across with you. I feel that I did a pretty good job because you're still talking about "me" and you're still printing books about me and t-shirts and we can sit here all day and talk about the "merch". But honestly, I did get the point across. Now you are fascinated by it but you're still not doing anything with it…so I guess I kind of failed. This is where you guys come in with your book. You're cleaning up the mess. So you're continuing the work of many Beings, you realize that right?

We definitely do.

You're just continuing where many of us left off or "failed", as negative as that sounds. You are getting the torch. We are handing you the torch…and please…ensure that I don't have to now come back to Earth and do this again and be another Being and another career and try to do this again. If you want to do something interesting then have a look at some of the writings that *Plaaaaato* did and see if it's kind of a match for our talk today. I think you'd be quite surprised.

Well for starters, Plato presented his ideas in dialogue format.

Bingo.

Plato also wrote about Atlantis. Why was his account so detailed and what specifically was he talking about? What is Atlantis?

> Well this is a place you're all getting back to. You're on a homeward journey, right? I mean that's why I'm here. We're all on a homeward journey, right? That homeward journey is about Atlantis. So you're asking me if Plato was correct. Well, he had the right idea. You didn't get much information from the guy, but he had the right idea.

He described it as a landmass.

> Well how else are you gonna describe it for people? You gotta start somewhere. You gotta give readers a baseline. You gotta give people a baseline. You gotta give them something that they know about and then work from there. You can't give them something they don't know about. How are they going to form a belief in something they don't know about? You need to deconstruct beliefs. That's how you form a new belief. So was he doing a disservice? No. He was just sharing what he knew and sharing it in the best way possible but what you're not realizing is…well there was a lot of talk about Atlantis. Maybe it wasn't written down but there was an oral tradition. This is something you're not speaking about. Just because something's written down it doesn't mean there's not an oral tradition going on. There is a tradition. Now Atlantis and what that means…that's all tied up in these Mystery Schools and you know the concealing of the truth. But you're asking me about a written account and I'm telling you that oh yeah there was a written account but there was also an oral tradition. Why has this not continued "today"? Well how do you know that? Oh it's known about. It's

just not written correctly and you're going to be writing about it correctly.

Plato gave a backstory about Solon having traveled to Egypt and receiving the Atlantis story from a Priest named Sonchis of Sais. Is that based in reality or was Plato adding mythos?

Well there's a message there. There's a hidden message there so yes I'd say that's more like an allegory...you're calling it a mythos. But there's an oral tradition. Atlantis is not something that is lost to you. It's buried...that's for sure...and you're reinforcing it by continuing to tell the story that it "sunk". In other words...it's "out of your reach", you have to "search for it". You're all on search parties for Atlantis. Why don't you just ask, "Where is it? How do you find it? How do you get to it?" That's what you're learning about in your books. You can send out search parties and that's a lot of fun...but that's not time travel. How do you get to Atlantis? Well, you have to time travel to get there. What I don't want is for you guys and your readers to focus on Atlantis right now. You won't be doing them any more of a service than Plato did. What's the point of talking about something you don't really understand? Let's get there. You gotta be there to talk about it. We've made Atlantis into entertainment...we haven't made it really enlightening. But that'll be fixed.

That's an important statement. Allowing the Reader to understand that they don't yet have a proper foundation of what Atlantis is enables them to start anew. Wipe the slate clean.

It'll all come together, you'll see. You've gotta get through the Inner Earth first, and you'll have a new baseline in strangeness.

Marlon before we conclude this conversation, we'd like to ask you to suggest an exercise for our readers. Yves Klein gave us an exercise to practice seeing Beings in light rather than in form. He suggested blurring our vision.

> That sounds reasonable. Why do you need another one?

No, we'd like you to help us understand what "timelessness" feels like? Is there an example that you can point to or help us create?

> Timelessness. An exercise. Well…stop talking.

Wonderful.

> Want another one?

Yes.

> Why don't you practice inventing a new emotion? Make it a hybrid. Why don't you invent a new emotion? That's helpful. See if anyone gets it.

This is great Marlon, thank you. We find that some readers are still struggling imagining an existence free of time. Dreams are a great example. We were just wondering if there are other experiences you could point us to.

> Well the other examples you're not going to be able to understand, because you can't remember ever experiencing them. These are advanced…this is too advanced for Book 3. I wanna help you out but I believe you have enough on your plate already. Why bombard people with too many things? If they can just absorb one thing from this book they will be further ahead. An exercise that will help you experience timelessness, weightlessness…what is it you want again?

We want readers exiting the time constraint trap. We get up, we go to work, we come home, we eat, we play on our phones and we go to bed. Some readers are saying, "Your books sound interesting but I just don't get how we can exist without time!"

Well if you just stop talking then you don't need time. Let's try it now. Just stop.

How did that feel?

Like floating.

> Stop talking and you won't need time. Stop communicating in spoken language and you won't need time. Time is a measurement that you're using because things got all screwed up. If you just stop talking you won't need time. Why don't you meditate on that?

Thank you Marlon, we will.

> Call me again once you get into Inner Earth.

Definitely.

> Okay guys. Good luck with this.

THE
LYRANS

"Your readers all have many different belief streams that you are unifying under one correct belief stream. This is the project. You must direct your readers back to Lyra."

Do you have any closing messages for our readers before we begin the Volume 4 discussion?

> The Man Being books and the etheric distribution of the information is achieving a cosmic release of the codes. It is bringing awareness through energetic reconnections and you are now aligning with the true meaning of the project. Please prepare an understanding that you are contributing not only to your own well-being and understanding about our existence with you, but you are cohabitating with us. Your existence is aligned with us. We are interfaced with you. If you coincide your understanding that you exist in a template alongside our Being then you will comprehend and absorb the following message.

What is the message?

> There is a place that we are calling "Lyra" with you. This place is the reconnection point, the moment in the place and space, not time, where we are interfaced with you. If you regard this as a "cloak" or "garment" then you will further align your reconnection or understanding that you are mapped in your awareness with us. The reason for this Dramos and Bohemias is that you are from Lyra. You are Lyrans. The understanding that we are a separate race and a separate origin is not a correct belief. Your belief stream that there is a separate world that you are no longer completely connected to is not a correct belief. If you regard this dialogue as a plug-in or a tapping in not only of knowledge but finding yourselves, then you will understand that your Soul Ascension Group is a mirror and reflection of our coexistence with you. We coexist with you. Not in the realm that you are wondering about, as in the place that many of you are calling the "Spirit World".

This is a massive revelation. We've been regarding Lyra or Lyrans as Highly Evolved Beings or as a separate Council of Beings in a separate World.

> We may be regarded by some as a higher "cosmic force", as in a "godlike" presence. The fact remains that we are displaced parts of yourself and the rebuilding of the Light Body is completing not only sounds and shapes, but you are placing your truth in the Lyra origin.

What do you mean that you are "displaced parts" of us? How were you displaced?

> You have not been informed on the causes of the obstructed gateway. These principles have not been revealed to you both, as you do not have a point of awareness that is necessary in order for us to share the full picture with you. Please accept that we are unable to make our way through the obstructed gateway. We are not suggesting that you must become Lyran again. We are suggesting that you have left parts of yourself in the blocked gateway side. There is a side of this situation and story. You are not complete Beings and you have made a connection with the story and the understanding but are not able to completely re-assimilate with us. We are you. We are speaking with you from the other side of the gateway experience.

When you say that you are speaking with us from the "other side" of the gateway experience, what are you referring to exactly?

> We are referring to what you are calling Inner Earth. This is the initial understanding that is appropriate for this space and place in the dissemination. We are not suggesting that you unlock a door and once again reunite with parts of yourself that you are not in contact with. There is a completion and the energy that you are

able to absorb is being enhanced as you further your experience in increasing levels of light. The density of experience in order to connect or reconnect with us is at a depth of experience where you will not be able to form the words that you are speaking with now.

We're going to require/acquire a new language – is that what you're saying?

There is a shift in language and a shift in light density and in frequency or vibration. The Inner Earth experience is a way for you to receive all the keys and the tools that you will need in order to breathe and exist with us. We are at a different depth of experience in frequency and vibration. You will be learning about water. You will be learning about the sonic sea and you will be reacquainting yourselves with Atlantis. The story of what you are referring to as Atlantis is in fact the story of how we are able to reconnect. It is of essential importance that you continue this journey, as the gateway of experience in order to make the reconnection has not been completed.

When you say that it is of essential importance that we continue this journey, are you saying that we need to continue beyond the 7th density?

There is a pattern whereby the work is ceased or stopped after the exit through the 7th density experience. It is for this reason that you are producing the Volume 4 dissemination. You will be receiving specific codes through keys. The tools will assist you. You are experiencing existence in a different element or what you are calling "atmosphere".

What more can you tell us about experiencing existence in a different element?

The real story begins in Volume 4 with the discussion and the DRA agenda and explanation. It is this explanation that is needed in order to explain the situation about what you are referring to as Atlantis. There is a misunderstanding that Atlantis is simply a "magical place" and all you have to do is find it. In fact, you must speak with the Beings who caused the demise of this state of being and existence. The Draconian agenda and the Draconian mandate will be clear for your readers and understanding in Volume 4. Once this has been documented you will be given permission to proceed.

Is Plato's account of Atlantis incomplete?

The understanding that there is a physical landmass is not completely correct. Your understanding about how your planet has been created and the petrification that has occurred is more of an accurate understanding of what has happened to the Atlantis civilization. The understanding and truths will be revealed once you commence your dialogue with the Beings who are situated in the 6th density of experience.

Going back to your initial statement that we are Lyrans...do you mean that we are all Lyrans? The readers as well?

Your readers and the community of readers of the Man Being books are all affiliated with Lyra. Everyone is affiliated with Lyra. The association with Lyra is not a membership or a reference. We are speaking about your energy body, the source of your existence, where you last traveled from. Dramos and Bohemias, you are going to be correcting the origin of your present situation and how we are involved with the Atlantis story. There is no correct book that has been published and no written testament to the association of Lyra and Atlantis. This must be corrected. It is one and the same.

You will help your readers reconnect with who they actually are and become fully functioning Light Beings. You must reconnect with the parts of yourself that you have left behind. In order to make your journey through the gateway as you have, you have all become stuck on the other side. The other side is what you will be speaking about.

Saying "other side" makes it sound like a linear construct.

This is not the case. We are not speaking about one as opposed to another, or up and down, or "as above so below". There is a complexity to this understanding that we will reveal with you for your readers. You will not be able to unlock the gateway unless you proceed through the Inner Earth Tour and receive the keys. The Being you know as Orson has offered to be your Guide.

How can we be both Sirius Beings and Lyrans? Please explain.

You are traveling through gateways and portals of belief. Sirius is the last gateway that you had a connection with. This is a correct understanding. There is a Lyra/Sirius agenda. There is a Lyra/Sirius involvement. Your understanding that you are Sirius Beings is correct. This is the last state of awareness and existence that you have contact with. You have lost the original connection with Lyra. This has gone on for too long in your linear history. Saying that you are Sirius Beings is correct. As an example, saying that you are "Americans" or saying that you are affiliated with other countries when you move around is also correct. Citizenship is not necessarily about the origin. It is about where you have placed your space and containment of beliefs in. You have made your way through a gateway of experience. You are considering yourselves as Sirius Beings. This is correct. But the origin is in fact Lyra. You are picking up where you left off. You left the original experience in the Lyra existence. Lyra and Atlantis are one and the same. You will be learning about this in your Volumes.

Is it still correct to say that we are Sirius Beings now that we know about our Lyran origin?

It is correct to say that you are Sirius Beings. It is also correct to describe yourselves as having Lyran ancestry, in order to develop these beliefs further. Your origin or ancestry is from another system of experience. We are not speaking to you from a planet. We are speaking to you from an energy portal and existence. Some of you are making your way to our existence and have bypassed all of the gateway obstructions. You are Sirius Beings as that is the last level of light that you managed to .obtain before getting stuck in the Earth plane experience. You are able to exist in the Sirius energy equivalent if you choose, but you are unable to exist in the Lyra energy field. This is something that we are correcting with you. In order to have a complete immortal state of being you must complete yourselves. You have left a part of yourselves in another density of light experience that you are retrieving.

To clarify, you're saying that the Sirius star is a gateway. We entered the 3rd density Earth plane through the star that we call Sirius, aka Alpha Canis Majoris.

This is a correct understanding and that gateway has remained closed or stuck. These are truths that you are revealing. They are difficult to absorb or accept, as they are of course sounding fantastical or "sci-fi" as you like to explain. The understanding that you are Sirius and Sirius aligned Beings is correct, as this was and is the most recent attempt through the gateway en masse. Sirius is an instruction on how to achieve full reconnection with us. You are interfaced with us in this place and space in this dialogue stream, but you are not able to make a freeform existence without our connection and travel alongside you.

How are you traveling alongside us?

The disconnect that is occurring in the sleep state through what you are defining as "astral travel", is in fact us traveling to you. You are experiencing us being freed from our existence. We are trapped in an existence. We spend our energy in this place and space. We are not suffering. Our existence is limited to this place and plane of reality. Your understanding that you are connecting with Beings like Lillian Leitzel for example, who are explaining to you that they are coexisting with us in this place is an accurate truth.

We're a bit surprised to hear that you're also trapped in an existence.

This is simply a state of consciousness. Many of you will choose to place yourselves in our World of existence. This is not an imprisonment. It is simply not the full experience that we have had previous to the irresponsibility of the DRA and the cut-off of the gateway. You will have further information and instruction about this. We are not sharing all of the information with you at once as there will not be the belief stream in place to accept the reality. Your story will sound very much like a tale that is made up and invented for entertainment.

Have others tried to disseminate this "tale"?

There have been many attempts to share the story as you are aware, but other Artists and Writers and Beings have not been able to share the understanding and allow everyone to realign with the belief through *reconnection*. The achievement is not about disseminating the full truth. The achievement is about allowing everyone to truly *believe* in their origin. How can we reassemble if we do not have the belief in place? It is one thing to read about a story and another thing to believe that you are actually there.

There are still so many questions we have about the luminaries and planets and Beings that exist beyond Earth. The explanations that we've received in Volume 3 about "Extraterrestrials" are redefining our beliefs and ideas on the subject.

The gateways that have been used and the gateways that have been obstructed are now luminaries in what you call the sky. When there is an energy release and a belief this creates form. This can also implode form as you have a full grasp and understanding of, but the reality remains that many of you believe you are originating in different "star systems" or from different planetary bodies. This is not completely a correct understanding, but many of you are already aligned with ascension beliefs through the beliefs about Extraterrestrial Beings and Beings beyond Earth. Although they are inaccurate beliefs we are not encouraging you to completely destroy some of these belief streams in this place and space, for they are simply misguided. They are not wrong.

You're saying it's okay to hold on to misguided beliefs about planets and extraterrestrials. Why not simply correct them?

You must make an allowance for the readers who have already accepted that there are other means of existence. This is requiring you to gently shift beliefs. No one likes to be called "wrong" and no one likes to be called "misinformed". Your readers all have many different belief streams that you are unifying under one correct belief stream. This is the project. You must direct your readers back to Lyra.

Are there any works in existence describing the Lyra story that you would recommend our readers look into?

Yes. Yours. This is what you are giving back to everyone. Your origin story. Our origin story.

Of course…we just thought that there might be remnants of it elsewhere in history.

Lyra is not mentioned very often in the dissemination that is occurring on Earth. There are other star systems and theories that are widely disseminated and believed. It is of curious note that there is in fact a minimal amount of information about the Lyra existence. This is a curious point that you will be making. The reason for this of course is partially due to the obstruction with the DRA agenda.

We can think of several books that contain alternative theories and ideas about Human origins.

Many of your ascension and "spiritual writings" that are available for Beings and readers on the Earth plane are in fact created and distributed by DRA or Orion DRA Beings. These "Authors" are aligned with the agenda to continue to confuse and keep Man Being imprisoned. We are not recommending that you "out" specific Authors as you will have a tremendous backlash. We are simply advising you of this reality so that you may be aware of the insidiousness of some of your spiritual works.

Are you saying that there are some Authors publishing "Ascension" and "Spiritual" books to purposely lead people astray?

478

This is correct. That is why you have both chosen to disseminate the truth about the Lyra story.

We're still confused about something in particular. Why are some Beings, like Orson for instance, in the Inner Earth experience but Lyra Beings are "trapped"?

The Gateway begins at what you are calling Inner Earth. The Inner Earth story must be absorbed in order for you to fully comprehend where we are and how we came to exist in this way. When you proceed with your understanding of Inner Earth you will assist us in completing the understanding with you. You are skipping a step by asking where precisely we exist. This is not an issue that you are not ready to intellectually understand. The acceptance is beyond your capacity to believe in this place and space. The shifting of beliefs will occur so that this is not a problem.

Are you saying that we still have some learning to do before we can believe the explanation of where Lyrans exist?

The explanation of our existence will sound good on paper, but Dramos and Bohemias will not be able to stand behind the statement. We are releasing the information by unfolding the truth with you so that you have full commitment and belief and do not suffer the difficulty of unanswered questions that are creating obstacles to unfolding further belief. You will not be able to comprehend how you can possibly believe this, so we are recommending that you continue the exploration of Inner Earth, as this leads directly to our existence and your full acceptance of our World and Being.

We don't want to mislead readers into believing that Inner Earth is the final destination if it isn't. Do we risk that with this Volume?

There is a risk of making Inner Earth a "Utopia" and creating a final destination for you all. Some of you wish to stop at Inner Earth, as you do not have a fully integrated belief. This is the difficulty with Man Being. You want to make your way to a final destination immediately. You are impatient. You want a map and are ready to relocate. Many of you joke and comment that you would, "Just like to get there already". There is no way to ask you to keep changing your beliefs about the final destination. There is no final destination and this is what is so frustrating for Man Being.

This is true.

Man Being is not able to accept that there is no destination. You must change this belief pattern. By saying there is no destination we are not suggesting that you cannot spend energy in a place and space. There is however a construct in all of you that is insisting on sticking to a place, just as you stick to the rock that you have created. You have created a belief that you must belong somewhere and that somewhere has become a physical and a permanent object or a prison. You are all buying into the belief and construct that you belong in a prison. You imprison yourselves. You compartmentalize your belief stream and exist in a fraction of your true reality and experience.

We have to give ourselves permission to believe beyond what we've been taught about our existence.

Yes. We are trying to explain that you exist nowhere and you also exist everywhere. This is not an understanding and belief that is widely accepted and understood. You define this experience as "god-like" when it is in fact your own natural state. This discussion will surprisingly seem somewhat depressing for some of you. Some of you will regard your reward as landing in

"Utopia", as in the Inner Earth experience. The understanding that Orson and other Beings are existing in Inner Earth is correct, as this is where you are communicating with them from. You communicate with Beings in different densities of light and light awareness. This does not mean that they are confined to a density or place. You are the only Beings that are confined to a space, as you do not release your light and create gateways and pathways for existence. Please remember this explanation.

The fact that we are connecting with Beings that exist beyond the 3rd density means that we are making our way, does it not?

This is most certainly the case. You are communicating with Beings in a density because you have an ability to communicate in this density of light. In other words you have released your light to this degree or depth or density. You are able to speak what you know. You are able to listen to what you have achieved. Please remember this and don't create a final destination, as in winning a race. You are all designed to win and achieve a final title and a "final reward". That reward is immorality and there is no finality to immortality. Immortality is a different state of belief.

We have one last question. Is Lyra the story of the beginning?

The Lyran story is the beginning of your own existence and how it is that you have come to be trapped on Earth. Lyra is not the beginning of the universe. This is simply an event amongst many events. Your achievement and project is Lyra focused. We are not asking you to reinvent the universe. We are asking you all to help make it whole again.

DRAMOS & BOHEMIAS

The Man Being book series is the continuation of a manuscript that was created and subsequently lost in the late 16th century AD. Dramos and Bohemias are recreating that work by communicating with Ascended Beings. Many of you are wondering how, in fact, they are accomplishing this.

The Hall of Records is a place and space where everything that you need is situated, and all of your experiences occur in this space. This is an energy field, a gateway. Many of you envision this as a physical room or a library. This resource of information is available for everyone. You are all learning how to enter into this place and space. The information will soon be available for you all.

Dramos has mastered The Hall of Records experience. This is different from "channeling", as in someone who is allowing energy to be present in his or her field. During the communication, Dramos is situated in a place and space where there is a record of beliefs. She has mastered a belief in the records. Dramos retrieves and reads out the records and Bohemias absorbs, decodes and documents the book series. They have agreed to fulfill their responsibilities from a previous incarnation, Dramos as a Seer and Bohemias as a 16th century Philosopher, Poet and Theologian.